ABOUT THE AUTHOR

Christine Hammacott is a prize-winning short story writer who has now moved on to writing crime novels. She is fascinated by the psychology of crime and, in her first novel, explores how in just a few days a happy, confident person can become a frightened lonely victim.

Christine is a graphic designer who runs her own design consultancy. She lives in Hampshire, UK, with her partner Rob, daughter Amelia, and dog-shaped shadow called Patch.

The Taste of Ash

pentangle
press

Copyright © 2015 Christine Hammacott

Christine Hammacott has asserted her right under the Copyright, Designs and Patents Act, 1988 to be identified as the author of this work.

This book is sold subject to the condition that it shall not, by way of trade or otherwise, be lent, resold, hired out, or otherwise circulated without the publisher's prior consent in any form of binding, cover other than that in which it is published and without similar condition including this condition being imposed on the subject purchaser.

All the characters in this publication are fictional and any resemblance to real persons, living or dead is purely coincidental.

ISBN 978-1499590838

Book design by The Art of Communication www.artofcomms.co.uk
First published in the UK 2015 by Pentangle Press www.pentanglepress.com

To my family for their love and support

To my partner Rob and daughter Amelia.
And to Mum & Dad for giving me the life belief
that I could achieve anything I set out to do.

Note from the author: Lee-on-the-Solent is a small seaside district on the coast of the Solent about five miles west of Portsmouth, UK. Lee-on-the-Solent is usually referred to as Lee on Solent by local people and appears both ways in the book.

Acknowledgements

A huge thank you to my fellow writers:
Richard and Helen Salsbury, and Eileen Robertson for their
encouragement and input over the years in helping hone
my writing skills.

To my fellow Pentangle Press colleagues:
Wendy Metcalfe for her friendship, encouragement
and meticulous editorial input.

Carol Westron who has been beside me through thick and thin
as friend, mentor, encourager, writing buddy and editor.
A massive heartfelt thanks. You have so much to answer for!

And finally, special thanks go to my family
especially my partner, Rob who understands, without complaint,
that I need space to write.

Thank you all for helping make this book
the best that it could be.

CHAPTER 1

The shrill blare of an alarm wrenched me from sleep. I pulled the duvet up over my head. Just five more minutes. Blindly I reached an arm out and groped for the alarm clock, bashing wildly. I was sure I'd hit the snooze button, but the wailing didn't stop. I rolled over to do it properly and saw that it was 2:16 - the middle of the night. That couldn't be right. And the noise wasn't coming from the bedside.

Now that I was more awake I recognised the wailing as the smoke alarm. My flatmate, Claire, had been stumbling about as if drunk when she came in a couple of hours ago. Had she got up to make some toast? It wouldn't be the first time. And she was always burning something. I thought I could smell smoke.

I slid my slippers on and stumbled, yawning, towards the bedroom door. The noise was unbearable. And the smell of burning was strong - too strong. Fingers of smoke clawed under the front door of the flat from the stairwell beyond and hung like a thin ghost in our small hall. Suddenly I realised the building was on fire.

Panic seized me. What should I do? Should I phone the fire brigade? Where was my mobile? There was no time to find it. I had to get out.

I threw open the door of Claire's room. 'Fire!' I screamed. 'Wake up.' She was comatose and snoring loudly. I shook her. Claire snuffled. She gave a small cough but showed no sign of waking. I threw back the covers. 'Fire!' My voice was a screech. It choked into coughing as I hauled her from the bed.

'Go away,' she murmured irritably.

I slapped her. That woke her. Her hand flew to her face.

'We've got to get out. There's a fire.'

I grabbed her arm and led her back to the hall. The smoke was getting thicker by the minute. I pulled my pyjama top up across my face and reached for the handle of the front door.

'Zoë, don't!' But I already had the door open. Heat and smoke rushed in. I sank to all fours, struggling for air. The stairs were ablaze, a greedy wall of crackling fire advanced towards us. I couldn't even see the entrance of the building on the floor below.

I let the door go. It shut with a thud and the noise subsided. Now what? Through the thin cloth of my pyjama mask, the noxious stench of the blistering paint was ripping the back of my throat. I reached out for Claire but she was gone. I thought I heard faint coughing and crawled desperately towards it. Claire was yanking at the handle of her bedroom window. 'It won't open.'

'Let me have a go.' It was locked. 'Where's the key?'

Frantically, Claire fumbled back and forth along the windowsill. 'I can't find it.'

I bent, groped along the carpet. Wisps of smoke were seeping through the floor. I found an earring - but no key. Claire hammered pointlessly on the windowpane.

I glanced around for something to break the glass with.

There was nothing except the bedside lamp. 'Out the way.' I rammed it into the double glazing. The lamp broke. The glass didn't. I pushed at the glass, then kicked it. But it wasn't going to budge. Coughing with the effort, I gave up.

'We've got to find another way out. Come on. My window's unlocked.' Talking was an effort between gasps for air.

Back in the hall the smoke was so dense I couldn't see anything. My eyes stung. I grabbed Claire's hand, pulled her after me.

'Shut the door,' I croaked as we reached my bedroom. I rushed to the window and pushed it open then we leaned out, sucking in air. My throat was like a crushed straw. All I could think of was breathing and then, as breathing got slightly easier, of getting out.

The old converted house had high ceilings and the frosty concrete below looked hard and unforgiving. Even though we were only one floor up, the ground seemed a long way down. 'We've got to jump,' I said.

Claire gave a small jerk of a nod.

'Go,' I urged. I glanced around the room. Was there anything to help break our fall? Not much would fit through the window. I grabbed the duvet, bundled it out.

Claire stood transfixed, staring at the ground. 'I can't.'

'You've got to.'

Soon there would be nothing left. Was there anything I could save: my Apple Mac, my clothes, my books, my paintings? My eyes fell onto my portfolio of graphic design work. I couldn't afford to lose the print samples, getting replacements would be virtually impossible.

Claire slid back along the wall. 'The fire brigade'll be here soon.'

'You don't know that. We haven't called them.' Grabbing my portfolio, I dropped it cautiously out of the window. It landed with a slap on the concrete.

'It'll be okay,' said Claire.

'No it won't. You'll die if you stay here.' Smoke was pouring in under the bedroom door now and the floor felt warm. Beside the window there was a pair of trainers, still coated in mud from a run. I threw them into the garden too. There was a loud crash from the stairwell.

'We've got to get out! Now!'

I didn't want to leave her, but I had to go. Climbing onto the windowsill, I shuffled forward. As I eased out over the sill I realised my mistake. I wriggled back in, turned around to face the building so that I could drop. I glanced down, lowered myself, toes tracing the wall. Suddenly I was aware of flames licking the window of the flat below. Just then an explosion shook the building. I lost my balance and fell. The duvet did little to soften the landing. My slipper slid on the fabric and my foot twisted over. I was face down, winded. Beneath me the ground was icy and the thin fabric of my pyjamas little protection. Then, like a tsunami, pain gripped my foot.

Biting back pain, I scrambled away. When I looked back, Claire was silhouetted in the upstairs window. The room was bright, as if a light had been switched on. I watched with a gut-wrenching feeling. This could be the last time I ever saw Claire alive. A wave of guilt overwhelmed me, and I turned away unable to watch. What else could I have done to get her out?

Jump. Please jump. You can do it. It looks worse than it is. Silently I pleaded but the words wouldn't come out. A noise made me turn back. Claire was dangling from the windowsill as I had done. Her nightdress snagged on something and pulled up to reveal her nakedness. She tugged at it to release it, then gripped the window frame. Her movements had the jerkiness of an old film.

'You can do it.' My voice was hoarse, little more than a whisper.

She stared at me for a moment, then her gaze slid along the ground. I thought she wasn't going to jump - but she did. She landed better than I had. Reaching down to grab the duvet, she bent nervously as if she expected the windows in the ground floor to blow out, but they were already gone. The ground was littered with shards of glass. Relief washed over me and I started shaking. Claire scrambled over to me.

'You stupid cow. What the hell were you playing at?' I caught her arm to shake her, but found myself hugging her instead. The thought that I had abandoned her, and she could have died, made me sick.

She was shaking. I was shaking. By the dustbins at the very end of the back garden we clung together like children, wrapped in the reassurance of each other's embrace as we watched the house burn. The fire was now in my bedroom.

I remembered my portfolio. Cautiously I crawled to retrieve it and the trainers I'd thrown out, before retreating once more. My foot hurt so much I didn't even try to put the trainers on, simply handed them to Claire, whose bare feet were bleeding from the broken glass.

Time stopped and numbness descended. In the flat I'd felt confused, dazed, frantic, but adrenalin had moved me forward, made me aware. Now I didn't know what to do. My brain had switched off. I was conscious of my body; the rippling shivers and twitches, the searing pain in my foot, the constant noise of the fire like a tune that wouldn't finish. Claire couldn't stop coughing.

It was a clear night. The stark white moon didn't look real and seemed to form no part of the black sky. Instead, it looked like a toy that someone had tossed into the fir trees at the edge of the garden.

A dusting of frost coated the grass and path. I gazed at the pattern of stones, protruding through the worn concrete. There was a crack by my feet, a sharp crevice where the ground had sunk and split. At some time, someone had tried to mend it but the light smudge of filler was powdery and crumbling. To my left there were paving slabs, uneven and darkened with age and splashed with paint. Weeds grew in the gaps between.

Then someone was hurrying towards us, a man I recognised as one of the neighbours from across the road. 'Are you okay? Are you hurt?' He crouched beside Claire and tried to persuade her to breathe slower. 'The fire brigade are on the way.' He kept glancing wide-eyed at the building. 'I think we should get away from here.'

The man carried my portfolio and I leaned on him as he led us down the path of the neighbouring house, and out towards the road. Dimly, I was aware of a siren that was getting louder, but it meant nothing. A dark void had opened up and I could feel the heavy pull of it sucking me in.

Finally it registered that there was blue light glancing off the surrounding buildings, flicking on and off eerily. At the road there seemed to be people everywhere. Firemen rushed all over the place. Neighbours, in nightclothes and coats, stood motionless in their front gardens, or pressed against the windows of the surrounding houses watching. I felt conspicuous and, despite the blanket they'd wrapped around me, I couldn't get warm.

A fire officer joined us. 'Is there anyone else inside?'

It was the man from across the road that answered. 'There's a chap lives downstairs. I haven't seen him but his car's there.'

I gazed at the house in horror. I hadn't given our neighbour a thought. What if he was still in there? I searched the crowd, expecting to see him but he wasn't there.

The paramedics arrived. Inside the ambulance I leaned back, breathing deeply from an oxygen mask, pulling it away as bouts of coughing overtook me. I could taste smoke and ash. My nose was dry. The back of my mouth felt lumpy.

The hiss of flames and water filled the air. Another ambulance arrived. I closed my eyes, wishing I was asleep and that this was nothing more than a nightmare. Nausea overwhelmed me as it occurred to me what would have happened if I hadn't woken.

There was a commotion at the house. Suddenly the paramedic grabbed some stuff and rushed to join his colleague. They were bending over something on the ground. The faint smell of fried bacon came to me. Yanking the oxygen mask from my head, I stumbled from the ambulance and threw up. The shape was unmistakable. Even in the semi darkness, I could tell it was a body.

CHAPTER 2

Hospitals freak me out. The events at the flat were squeezed to the very back of my mind as the horror of being in A&E occupied that space. Most people think hospitals make you well. It isn't always true.

The last time I was in one was when Mum died. Although this wasn't the same place, it still raised ghosts. Everything stirred up memories: the bleach-clogged heat; the way the lino squeaked whenever anyone walked past; the rattle of trolleys; swish of curtains. In the adjacent cubicle Claire was still feasting on oxygen, a ragged pattern of breathing and coughing.

As I waited in my cubicle, memories of the endless sessions of chemotherapy Mum had endured filled my thoughts. I couldn't blot out the memory, the sickness, the way Mum shrank before our eyes, the sink plunger that was permanently in the bathroom because the bath kept clogging with clumps of her hair.

My heart was running at a furious pace and my head was banging as if a heavy-metal drummer had somehow got inside. Logic told me I should stay and get my foot sorted but I couldn't. I had to go.

Hopping precariously, I headed for the exit, hugging the wall in case I lost my balance. Although unable to put my foot to the floor, it wasn't going to hamper my escape. The weight of my portfolio wrenched the joints of my fingers and bashed against my leg, threatening to trip me up. I blanked out the discomfort, continued my erratic, slow, painful progress.

'Where are you off to?' The nurse who had been keeping an eye on me stopped me half way down the corridor.

'I need some air.' My guilty excuse sounded feeble and started me coughing again. From the lift of her thin eyebrows and the glance she shot at my portfolio, I could tell she knew I was trying to escape.

'You need to wait for the doctor.'

'I just want to pop out for a minute...'

The nurse cut me off. She wasn't about to listen to an argument even if I could have thought of one. 'You need to keep your foot elevated. It may well be broken,' she said sternly, taking my arm to steer me back towards the cubicle. She abandoned me momentarily to duck into a side room, re-emerging with a wheelchair. 'This should be easier.'

She pushed me back to where I'd started.

The cubicle where Claire had been was now empty. 'Where's my flatmate?'

'Don't look so worried. We've taken her up to a ward. She inhaled a lot of smoke so we want to keep an eye on her a bit longer. And she'll be more comfortable up there.'

The nurse took my portfolio from me and helped me back onto the bed. Once she had plumped the pillow at the bottom end, I laid my foot onto it as I had done before. 'As soon as the doctor's seen your x-rays, he'll be along. Now stay there.'

I wasn't about to admit that I was going through hell but something in my expression must have alerted her. 'I take it you don't like hospitals much?' she said.

'You could say that.'

She laid a hand on my arm and spoke conspiratorially: 'I'll see what we can do to get you out as soon as possible. But - you'll have to promise to stay here where I can find you.'

I was alone in my cubicle prison again. The curtain walls might as well have been made of stone. Rather than creating privacy they made me feel isolated. I pleaded silently that the doctor would come soon so that I could go. But go where? I hadn't thought of that and my spaghetti brain couldn't find an answer. I curled onto my side, tucking into myself and wishing Mum was here.

My photos! I should have saved my photos. In the heat of the moment, it hadn't occurred to me. I'd grabbed what I'd seen. Now I cursed my stupidity. The photos of Mum were irreplaceable. I couldn't hold it together any longer and began to cry.

The movement of hospital staff across the narrow gap between the two lengths of curtain fabric was like catching glimpses of traffic on the motorway when you're trapped in a jam on an A road. Someone with particularly squeaky shoes hurried past the cubicles and I shuddered.

'I'm looking for Zoë Graham?' The voice behind the fabric wall was male but high pitched. I brushed away the tears and rolled onto my back, expecting to see a young doctor but it was a police officer who approached. 'Zoë?' I'm Police Constable Travis. I need to ask you a few questions.'

'What about?'

He was probably in his mid twenties with fair hair and penetrating brown eyes. It struck me that the combination of colouring made him look slightly satanic. He was tall. He seemed to tower over me and it was intimidating. I moved upright, shifted higher up the bed, and tried to compose myself. Even though there were other people around in nightwear or hospital gowns, the knowledge did little to curb my feelings of vulnerability. I pulled the blanket across my legs like an invalid.

The policeman took out a notepad and pen. 'We're trying to get some idea of what happened this evening.'

'Do we have to do it now?'

'It won't take long. Is there anything I can do?' The offer was an empty one.

'Can you get me out of this place?'

He gave a small laugh. 'Sorry, you'll need a doctor for that. Can you tell me what happened?'

With the back of my hand I wiped away the trail of tears that lingered. I couldn't understand why he wanted to talk to me. 'There was a fire,' I said, sniffing. 'What more is there to know?'

'Have you any idea how it started?'

'No.' A sudden thought occurred to me and I became hot and defensive: 'You don't think it's my fault, do you?'

'Is there any reason why I should?'

'No.' My brain conjured an image of the iron I'd been using earlier in the evening. Had I left it on? I'd been drying clothes on the radiator too. Had something caught alight? Guilty heat flushed my skin. No, the fire had started downstairs. I was sure of that. And I remembered putting the iron in the kitchen to cool. 'It didn't start in our flat,' I said. 'It started downstairs. The man downstairs smokes. All summer we've had to put up with the stink of his bloody weird smelling cigarettes. Maybe he fell asleep with one in his hand?'

The policeman made a note. He flipped back a page on his notebook. 'Three of you live in the house. Is that correct?'

'Not together. It's two flats. Claire and I live upstairs. Neil Wyatt lives downstairs.'

He wrote it down in large rounded movements. 'And you and Claire, how long have you lived in the flat?'

My mind couldn't deal with anything except being stuck in hospital and the horror of memories. I had to think hard, which was ridiculous for such a straightforward question.

'We moved in in June.'

'June this year?' I found the policeman's gaze unnerving. It felt as if I should feel guilty about something, though I had no idea what. I shifted, fidgety, irritable.

'No. Last.'

'So that's nearly a year and a half then?'

'I guess.' My confusion made me sound like an idiot. Or as if I had something to hide. I was feeling so choked up, sooner or later it was going to erupt in hysteria. 'Why are you asking me all this?'

'We have a duty to investigate all serious fires,' the policeman said. 'How well do you know Neil Wyatt?'

I answered with a question of my own. 'Is he dead?' I'd hardly given him a second thought. It could easily have been me, or Claire, that the firemen had found in that state.

'He's in intensive care. He's in a bad way.'

'God.'

The policeman repeated his question. 'So how well do you know Neil Wyatt?'

I shrugged. 'I don't...' Talking had made my throat hurt and I couldn't swallow properly. There was a glass of water on the trolley beside the bed. I tried to stretch for it but it was just out of reach. The policeman handed it to me.

'You don't get on with him?'

I shook my head and took a long drink. 'I don't know him. He's just someone who lives downstairs.' In fact, there was something strange about Neil Wyatt that I couldn't pinpoint, but it didn't seem appropriate to mention it when he was struggling to stay alive. 'I hardly ever see him. And when I do, he never says much. Not even good morning sometimes.'

I watched the water swirling around in the glass. Arcs of reflected light danced wildly on the surface. My hands were shaking. It felt as if I was outside of my body looking in on the scene. 'Look, it's been a really long night. My foot hurts like hell. And this place is really creeping me out. I hate hospitals. I'm not trying to be awkward but I can't think.'

He gave me a reassuring smile. 'Okay. We'll leave it there for now but we'll need to talk to you again. Where are you going to stay?'

I wrung the blanket between my hands and stared at my aching foot. 'I have absolutely no idea.'

'She can stay with me.'

For a moment I thought I was hallucinating and closed my eyes, but, when I opened them again, my stepfather was still in the gap between the cubicle curtains. The feeble strength I had left dwindled at the sight of him. Anger surfaced, as it did every time we met. I swallowed hard and bit down on bitter words until the policeman had taken my stepfather's details and gone.

Then I turned to my stepfather: 'What the hell are you doing here?'

CHAPTER 3

'Are you okay?' My stepfather moved a chair towards the bed. From the constant dragging of furniture, grey scuff marks scarred the floor. But he didn't drag the chair. He picked it up, carefully positioned it, and sat down. As he did so, the scent of Palmolive soap wafted to me; evoking another mix of memories.

'It's very hot in here.' He unzipped his beige coat. Underneath his shirt was crumpled, as if worn before, and unusually it wasn't lashed like pallet wrap into his trousers but tucked in carelessly. When he was always so fastidious about his appearance, it was odd to see him look even remotely dishevelled. It was hard to believe he was the same man who'd been screwing around while mum was in hospital dying.

'What are you doing here?' The dismay at seeing him was there in my voice. I couldn't do anything to hide it and there was no point anyway; my stepfather knew exactly what I thought of him.

'They rang me. They said you'd been brought in from a fire,' he said. 'I got here as quickly as I could.'

'Who rang you?'

'The hospital.' He leaned forward and took my hand. I snatched it away. His skin was corpse cold, but it wasn't the temperature that revolted me. Why was I still allowing him to make me feel this way?

'They rang you?' I asked stupidly, trying to make sense of it. 'Why would they ring you?'

His reply was a gentle murmur: 'Apparently you gave them your mum's name and telephone number.'

'Why would I do that? Mum's been dead years.' I stared at him in confusion.

My stepfather reached for my hand a second time, so I folded my arms across my chest to prevent him touching me again. Rejected, he sat back in the chair. 'You were probably in shock.'

I didn't respond. I was racking my brain for the memory of recounting mum's details. Scarily, it didn't seem to be there. The events of the night had become a blur. Certain images persisted; I could see the wall of fire on the stairs, the hard concrete below the window, and Claire silhouetted against the light. I could still smell the fire, still hear that awful shrill alarm. But the sequence of events after had merged. Maybe he was right. Maybe I was in shock.

'You didn't have to come.' I sounded like a belligerent child and hated myself for it. Even after all this time, his betrayal felt raw.

My stepfather gave a small lift of the shoulders. 'I had to be sure you were all right.'

He'd kept away from hospitals when mum was ill. He hadn't wanted to know then. So why had he come tonight? If only I had more family, a brother or sister. I realised suddenly that I should have said my boyfriend. Ollie was the closest I had to next of kin.

'I don't know why they rang anyone,' I said. 'It's not as if I'm badly hurt.'

'Maybe it's policy when they bring you in by

ambulance. Besides, presumably they needed someone to come and fetch you.'

'I don't need anyone to fetch me. What do you think I am, a bloody newspaper? I'm a grown woman. I've managed perfectly well without you until now.'

'I expect you have. For your mum's sake then.' His words were a knife slicing through me, shaming me. I glared at the sanctimonious hypocrite. Seeing him in a hospital environment evoked all my hatred. With him here I was a teenager again, and I just wanted to run away. Ironic! I couldn't run anywhere.

He glanced at his watch. 'How long have you been here?'

'You don't have to stay.'

'That wasn't what I meant.' He shook his head and his gaze did a circuit of the small cubicle then shifted to the corridor beyond the open curtain. 'I just wondered how long you'd been waiting.'

'I don't know.' Time had become fluid. It seemed as if I'd always been at the hospital but it also seemed only a moment ago that I was in the smoky flat.

'So, what are you waiting for? What's the prognosis?' he asked.

I examined my hands. Most of the fingernails were filled with dirt. I began to pick it out. 'They think I've broken a bone in my foot. I'm waiting for the doctor.'

'That's not so bad then.'

It depends whether it's your foot or not, I thought, but remained silent.

'Do they know how the fire started?'

It was as if someone had shot an accusatory blast of cold air across my skin. The hairs on the back of my neck rose. 'Before you ask, I didn't leave anything on the cooker.' I pushed thoughts of the iron away. 'I still don't smoke and I didn't leave anything hanging in front of the fire either.'

'I don't suppose you did. You're far too sensible for that.'

Was he being sarcastic? 'Actually, it started downstairs,' I said. My arms were locked across my chest now and my voice had got harder as the memory replayed. 'The hall was on fire. It was really going some, popping and roaring. We couldn't get to the front door and had to jump from a window.'

He frowned. 'The hall? Strange place for a fire to take hold. There's not usually anything to burn in a hall. It's not a rough area is it?'

'Far from it. I didn't say it started there.'

My stepfather's brow was creased the way it always did when he was trying to work something out. He ran a hand across his stubbled cheek. 'With the police involved, I wonder if they think the fire was started deliberately.'

'The policeman said they always investigate serious fires.'

'Really? I'd have thought it was the fire brigade, unless there was anything suspicious about it. In a hall I'd assume the most obvious thing is that an accelerant was used.'

Typical that my stepfather should claim to know all about police procedure. He always thought he knew about everything. But what if he had a point? The idea that someone had started the fire deliberately was appalling. The room began to go weird, colours fading, shapes distorting.

'Are you okay? Zoë? You're as white as a sheet. Zoë?'

'I thought I was going to faint.'

'Sorry. I didn't mean to frighten you. I was thinking aloud.'

Someone nearby was retching. The overwhelming, stomach-churning horror of memories welled inside me again, bearing down on me, trying to crush me into a blubbering wreck. My stepfather looked equally uncomfortable. He had aged since I'd last seen him. It must have been at least five years since that meeting; a brief chance encounter in Southampton. In the interval since, his hair had thinned and greyed, the lines around his eyes had deepened, and there were more broken veins in his face. With the heels of his hands he rubbed hard at his eyes.

'I think I'll see if I can get a coffee. Do you want one?' He took a small money pouch from his pocket then poked around with the contents. 'White no sugar?'

He'd remembered.

'I've already had something to drink, thanks.'

I closed my eyes as he wandered off. He'd told the police I was going to stay with him but there was no chance of that. What if that bitch he was screwing had moved into our house? What was I going to do though? I began to think about the flat again. Just how badly damaged was it? Could I still live there?

The back of the bed dug into my shoulder blades. Thumping the pillow into shape, I dragged it higher, settled back against it and tried, unsuccessfully, to get comfortable.

The nurse returned, this time accompanied by a doctor.

'I've had a look at your x-rays,' the doctor said. 'As we suspected, you've fractured a couple of bones here.' He held up the computer pad to show me the break to the side of my foot. 'A cast isn't really going to help but we'll strap it up and we'll give you some crutches. You'll need to keep off it for a few weeks. Now I'd like you to stay in overnight to make sure there are no after effects of the smoke but I'm told you're afraid of hospitals, is that correct?'

I glared at the nurse and nodded. The doctor conferred with the nurse for a moment and checked my notes. 'Is there someone that can keep an eye on you over the next twenty four hours?'

I wasn't going to stay a moment longer than I had to and I didn't want to give him any excuse to doubt me. 'My dad,' I said, nearly choking on the word.

'Okay. Then I'll discharge you. You'll probably cough up a blackish mucus for a few days. But if you have any breathing problems I want you to go straight to your GP.'

My stepfather reappeared as the doctor left. He must have been lurking the other side of the curtains.

'They're just going to strap my foot. Then I can go.'

The nurse pulled a trolley into the cubicle. She carefully put a fabric dressing on me, then a huge plastic boot over the top, securing it with Velcro ties. 'Have a practice with the crutches and I'll see if I can find you something to wear,' she said.

'I'm not going home with you,' I said once the nurse had gone.

'Where else are you going to go?'

'I'll call my boyfriend.'

'It's five o'clock in the morning. It makes more sense, seeing as I'm already here, to call your boyfriend later.'

'He'll be up soon anyway.'

My stepfather shrugged. 'It's your choice. I'm too tired for an argument, Zoë. But the doctor said someone should keep an eye on you and the police are expecting to find you at home.'

But it's not my home. He was right about being tired though. 'Will there be anyone else there?' I said.

'Like who?'

'Your fancy woman.'

'I live alone.' So she hadn't moved in then. It was only for one night, not even that, and I wouldn't get much sleep at Ollie's if his flatmates were getting ready for work. I conceded with a nod and put on the clothes the nurse supplied, trying not to think about where they had come from.

My stepfather picked up my portfolio and I let him lead the way out. 'Stay in the entrance. I'll fetch the car.'

I waited outside. After the stuffy heat of the hospital, the cold air caught in the back of my throat, stirring another bout of coughing. The idea of hobbling around for weeks made me despondent. A fractured foot would have been a hindrance under normal circumstances but with the uncertainty of everything, it felt like a disaster. I thought grimly of my neighbour. He wouldn't be leaving hospital this morning. Would his injuries keep him hospitalised for months? Would he leave at all? I might be on crutches but I'd been lucky, I told myself.

When my stepfather pulled up across the road, I noted that his car was yet another new Renault. He opened the passenger door and took the crutches from me as I collapsed gratefully into the showroom-clean seat.

It felt as if I'd just completed a marathon without training. Every ounce of remaining energy had seeped out of me. My arms and shoulders were like jelly. My legs seemed to be made of lead. My stepfather waited while I settled, then shut the door. I sat with my eyes closed, breathing in the smell of polish and air freshener. Then I heard the click of the boot opening, felt the draught of air, and the vibrating thump as the boot was shut again.

'Wrap this around you.' A plastic bag was thrust into my lap. Obediently I slipped out the neatly folded checked rug and pulled it over me.

'You look washed out,' he said. 'Let's go and get some sleep.'

But I couldn't, not yet. In the last few hours I had been forced to move from one endurance test to another. Each phase took so much effort. And there was one more that I needed to make. 'I know we're both tired but... will you take me back to see my flat first?'

CHAPTER 4

My stepfather looked dismayed, though I don't know why he found the request to see the flat so strange.

'Can't it wait? It's been a long night. You're shattered. We both are.' Fog had formed on the inside of the windscreen so he began to fiddle with the heating controls to clear it.

'I need to see it,' I insisted quietly. I wouldn't settle until I knew one way or the other exactly what I was facing. 'I'm sorry if I'm being a nuisance.'

'I don't mind running you around.' He seemed to be studying me. 'I just think it would be better to see it once you've had some sleep. If it's really awful you'll cope better when you're not exhausted.'

He wasn't going to help then. I glared at the creeping gap where the windscreen had cleared. It felt as if it was pulling me in. I could get out of the car with a 'don't bother I'll find my own way there' but I didn't have the energy.

I tried again: 'I doubt this'll seem any different later today. And it would involve coming back over. I know it's not going to be pleasant but I need to know what I'm facing.'

My stepfather sighed. A deep frown cut crevices in his forehead. The shift of skin made the lines around his eyes more prominent but the alteration didn't last long, and his usual composure flattened his features again. 'Where are we going then? You'd better give me some directions.'

The journey back to Lee-on-the-Solent was snail slow. I'd forgotten how cautious a driver my stepfather was. On the motorway the speedometer dawdled reluctantly towards sixty but refused to nudge past. I struggled to keep my irritation battened down. Folding the car rug in half to form a shawl, I wrapped it tightly around me, crossing the corners to secure it in a loose half knot.

My pulse was the only thing that had any inclination towards speed. It raced so furiously that my breathing had become erratic. What would I find once we arrived? Maybe it wasn't as bad as I imagined. Perhaps I should have listened and come later. I couldn't acknowledge that I'd been wrong. I stared blindly out of the side window.

When we arrived at the flat, fire engines were still blocking the road but the actions of the fire crew were less urgent. The fire must have been out because the hoses were being reeled in, ladders and breathing apparatus put away. A couple of police cars had appeared.

My stepfather parked and I saw that the white van we had stopped behind was sign written with the name of a local television company. Nearby a cameraman and reporter were filming.

'Good God!' my stepfather exclaimed, staring up at the house. In the dawn light, the full horror of the damage was apparent. The building was unrecognisable.

'I'd better talk to someone,' I said.

'I can imagine what they'll say. I doubt you'll be living there any time soon. It looks completely burnt out.'

I opened the car door.

'Hang on, I'll get your crutches.'

A thin layer of cracked ice had formed in the gutter. A large slippery patch extended across the road. The smell of damp ash was so strong I could taste it. It clung to the back of my throat as if I'd swallowed a mouthful.

A fireman prevented me from getting too close. 'Keep back, please?'

Sat in the ambulance earlier, I hadn't taken much notice of the front of the house. Now I saw that on both floors, where windows had once been, there were just dark gaps. Fragments of curtain snagged at the shards of the upper windowpane. A trail of soot led up the once white wall of the bay and what was left of the front door hung limply from its top hinge. Items of destroyed furniture stood desolately in the front garden. The smell of smoke was still really strong.

'How bad is it?' It was a stupid question. 'Is it like this upstairs?'

The fire officer gazed at me but I couldn't tell if he recognised me. 'I live here.' I shrugged down into the rug feeling cold.

'Not any more.'

'Isn't there anything left?'

'Sorry love. The place is completely gutted.' Someone called out to him and the fire officer turned away.

'What the fire hasn't got is probably damaged by water,' my stepfather murmured. His hand rested on my shoulder then gave it a squeeze. I moved out of his reach. Why did he always have to say things like that?

While the fireman was distracted, I sneaked closer to the flat. I don't know what I expected but the devastation inside made me catch my breath.

From a light bulb, hanging in the centre of what was left of the ceiling, water dripped rhythmically. The lampshade that had surrounded it had been reduced to a warped skeleton. Lumps of unidentifiable material, that might once have been part of the ceiling, walls or furniture, formed a thick layer of black rubble everywhere. Protruding from it, close to the window, were the remains of what I assumed was once a glass-topped coffee table. A bowl of fruit balancing on the edge was virtually intact and, remarkably, some of the apples were even still vaguely green.

I thought about what I had lost. All of my things: all of my photographs, clothes, computer. Was it really all gone? And a few of Neil Wyatt's apples had survived. Where was the justice in that?

'Let's go,' I said, turning away. 'I've seen enough.'

The house where I grew up appeared to have changed little since I had seen it last. The front garden was tidy and winter pansies edged the drive in a neat row just as they had done when mum was alive and we were a family.

I followed my stepfather inside. The hall was warm. A couple of his coats hung on the row of hooks just inside the door. It looked barren compared to the array of clothes that had been bundled on there when I was a child.

'Are you hungry?' My stepfather propped my portfolio against the wall and closed the front door, throwing the catch.

'Are the windows locked?'

'Yes, but there's a key on every windowsill.'

That didn't reassure me. There should have been a key on Claire's windowsill. My stepfather took his coat off and hung it up. Still tightly encased in my rug, I followed him into the kitchen. The keys to the back door and window still hung on a hook by the fridge.

'Is toast okay?'

'Fine.' I leaned against the worktop while my stepfather washed his hands, then filled the kettle and cut bread for toast. He must have noticed my scan of the room.

'The odds of this place going up in flames as well must be a billion to one.'

'That doesn't mean it won't happen.'

'No. But it's highly unlikely.' He took margarine from the fridge and reached up to the cupboard for plates. 'Zoë, please sit down before you fall down.'

Obediently I sank onto a bar stool. Coming back hurt, a dreadful dull ache for the past. Somehow, it felt as if, in returning, all the intervening years had been in vain. After all, there was nothing to show for them. I had less now than when I'd moved out. And I was being taken in by the man I despised.

The kettle began to boil. 'What do you want, tea or coffee? Or would you prefer cocoa?'

'Tea,' I said, smiling, 'I remember how bad your cocoa is.' The sudden memory of the way he had made it, mixing the powder with sugar and cold milk to form a dark paste before adding the hot milk, came flooding back. There were always stringy globules of skin floating on the surface because he never scraped it off.

I ate the toast and drank the strong tea. Yacht varnish, mum used to call it. Being in the house felt strange. I was a guest in a place that was familiar and I used to call home. The echo of my childhood evoked a feeling of unease and I wasn't sure how to react or feel. The place had such vivid memories, all good up until the point when Mum got ill.

'I'll make up the bed in your old room,' my stepfather said. 'You know where the towels are. Are you going to need a hand getting up the stairs?'

'I'll sleep on the couch,' I blurted, appalled at how pathetic it sounded.

He regarded me for a moment. 'Are you afraid to sleep upstairs?'

I didn't answer.

'It's perfectly understandable in the circumstances. I can bring a duvet down, but you'll rest better in a proper bed if you can face it.'

'I can't.'

He nodded and started clearing away the plates and

mugs, depositing them in the sink.

'Why don't you make yourself comfortable then. I'll get some bedding.'

As quietly as possible, I unlocked and tried both of the windows to make sure they opened. I dropped onto the sofa, loosening the rug but unwilling to shed it completely. The sofa was different, a cream leather one that looked newish and was slippery and uncomfortable.

'Is one pillow enough?' My stepfather dropped a duvet and pillow down beside me.

'Fine,' I said wearily.

'Do you need anything else?'

'No. Thanks.'

I sat there for a while after he had gone. A toilet flushed and floorboards creaked overhead. I didn't have the energy or mental capacity to work out how to climb the stairs to go to the bathroom myself. If I got desperate I'd wee in the garden. Once the movement above had ceased, I sneaked out to the hall and slid open the catch on the front door. I couldn't bear the thought of being locked in.

CHAPTER 5

The distant hum of a motorbike and the incessant mewing of a cat outside of the window were the only sounds I could hear. The room was dark. Thick lined curtains blocked out most of the daylight, yet from the clock on the mantelpiece I saw that it was late morning.

With the distance of sleep, the events of the previous night seemed surreal; like a drama watched on television rather than real life. But the fact that I was in this house rammed home how dreadfully life had changed.

I listened hard for the sound a radio, the rustle of newspaper or some noise that would indicate my stepfather's location. He must have gone to work. Typical that he hadn't hung around when someone needed care.

Being in this house made me feel vulnerable. There were too many ghosts; a history of emotions I had no intention of reliving. If I allowed it, they would swallow me up. My focus had to be on getting my life back on track. I had to get my thoughts in order, start working out what to do – except that my brain was still mush. I felt weepy, numb and exhausted. I couldn't really believe it had happened. Why? I lay there, the carousel of muddled thoughts spinning round and round, an unceasing blur.

Eventually, in the hope that being upright would make a difference, I sat up. My whole body ached, as if I was going down with the flu, and there was a nagging throb in my foot. Cautious flexing made me wince so I strapped the boot on. It made it feel as if my foot was protected and stabilised. Moving around wasn't going to be fun. At least I hadn't been badly hurt like poor Neil Wyatt. Was he still alive? I'd been lucky. I shouldn't lose sight of that.

Easing back the covers, I found the duvet cover and pillow slip were covered in grey smuts. If my stepfather had said anything about washing or changing when we got here, I didn't remember. I'd better take a shower and remove the evidence of my misdemeanour before he appeared. I should get the duvet cover into the wash. Slowly, I swung my legs to the floor and bent for the crutches.

In the hall, I called out but there was no answer and my stepfather wasn't in the kitchen. However, the crockery we had used was gone so he had been up. Where was he now?

In daylight, I noticed that the hall and kitchen had been repainted. Both were different to how I remembered. Although the changes were subtle, they were enough to make me feel that it wasn't quite like returning home after all. I noticed another change; my stepfather now had an answer phone, which surprised me as he didn't usually embrace technology. He had also bought a microwave - but that was probably from necessity as he couldn't cook.

I suddenly realised I ought to ring work. I perched on the low unit that housed the telephone and directories. Guy would be going berserk that I hadn't called, especially as we were in the middle of some big projects. He had probably been round the entire office, badgering everyone for information on my whereabouts. I could imagine how the conversation with Guy would go and couldn't face it, so I asked to speak to Nick instead.

He took a long time to answer. 'Christ. Whatever excuse you're going to use, it had better be good. Guy's on the war path, especially as it was your design that was chosen for the branding job.' There was bitterness in Nick's tone. He didn't like losing but then neither did I and I'd been determined to win this corporate identity - it was just the kind of project I needed for my portfolio. Having a prestigious name like Stanton, Summers and Cox Design Agency on my C.V. was all very well but I needed good, recent work to go with it if I was going to get anywhere. It was typical that this should happen during the best job of the year. Yesterday I'd have been elated at the prospect of producing the entire branding package. Now there was no pleasure in my success.

'Oh, it's a good excuse all right,' I snapped. 'There was a fire at my flat. I spent half the damned night in casualty.'

'Blimey! You serious?'

'I'm okay. Thanks for asking,' my response was sarcastic. Nick was a good designer but his people skills were appalling. I reached for my portfolio, still propped against the hall wall where my stepfather had left it.

'You must be okay or you wouldn't be talking to me,' Nick said.

'You figure?' I couldn't stop the sarcasm. 'I might be ringing from the hospital.'

'Are you?'

'No. That's not the point.' Why was I even getting in to this? 'The point is, I've broken my foot. And I'm homeless. I'm not going to be in for a while.'

The portfolio had taken a battering. One side was badly scratched and the edges were dented but, considering what it had been through, it wasn't too bad. I unzipped it and began flicking through to check the contents. Although some of the plastic sleeves were damaged the samples inside were okay.

'Hang on, you live at Lee on Solent, don't you? That

was on the radio this morning. Some bloke's in hospital in a real bad way. They said the place was gutted.'

'Yeah. So, can you let Guy know?'

'You can tell him yourself. He's in his office and I don't think he's on the phone.'

'Rather not. Just let him know, yeah.'

'He's bound to ask when you'll be back. What shall I tell him?'

'Tell him what you like. Everything's gone. And I mean everything. I've got nowhere to live. I haven't even got any clothes or any bank cards to buy some new ones.' Or much money in my account to fund them anyway. 'Tell Guy I'll ring him when I know something,' I said and hung up.

Stating my situation out loud was like a slap in the face. I sank back against the wall as the enormity of the task ahead overwhelmed me. There were so many elements to think about. I didn't have a clue where to start. Somewhere to live, even if it was only temporarily. I couldn't stay here. Perhaps Ollie would put me up. Although we'd been going out for years, I'd always evaded the question of us living together. It felt hypocritical asking him, but I didn't see that I had much choice.

There wasn't a Portsmouth directory in the unit on which I sat, so I had to ring directory enquiries for Ollie's office's number. Losing my mobile was another problem. When I finally got through, Ollie was out and the temp on reception wouldn't give me his mobile number. She grudgingly took my message but I wasn't convinced she would actually bother to pass it on. If she didn't, I had no other way of getting hold of him.

Zipping the portfolio up again, I headed for the kitchen and coffee, hoping the caffeine would perk me up and I could begin to think more clearly about what needed to be done.

It was a juggling act to fill the kettle, switch it on,

then collect together the items required for a drink. It had never occurred to me how awkward simple tasks were when mobility was impaired. Every movement had to be thoroughly pre-planned. It was long-winded and frustrating.

I abandoned the coffee as too much effort. I needed the loo, and while I was upstairs I should have a shower too. But what was I going to change into? I remembered the bed linen and went to get it, pushing the bundled duvet cover along the hall floor with one of the crutches.

The idea of going upstairs worried me, but it was something I had to overcome. I couldn't remain on the ground floor for the rest of my life. I stood looking up the stairs. I would do this. I abandoned my crutches. It would mean hopping once I was up there, but that was easier than trying to deal with them as well.

The simplest solution for ascending proved to be shuffling up backwards on my bottom. At the top, hanging on to the bannister, I pulled myself to my feet. I had done it. Going down would be easier.

I decided to run a bath instead of balance in the shower and hoped there was enough hot water. I let the water run and went in search of clothes. My old bedroom had been redecorated. It must have taken a lot of coats to cover the heavy purple that I'd painted it. My bright geometric curtains had been replaced with a more conservative stripy blue pair.

The wardrobe proved bare of clothes, which was hardly surprising as I'd taken all of my possessions when I moved out. I'd given the stuff I didn't want to a charity shop. Now I wished I'd left some of it here. The wardrobe contained only a stack of novels and some jigsaws. I picked one up. '3 pieces missing' was written in red biro in one corner of the lid. Most of the puzzles had bits missing. They used to be kept in the back of the wardrobe in my parents' room with the Scrabble and Monopoly sets.

I ran my hand over the box. The edge had been

repaired a long time ago. The tape was brown and crisp, and had started lifting away from the surface. The time I had flu came flooding back to me. For a whole week I had been wrapped in a blanket on the sofa, watching terrible B-movies and doing jigsaws, while Mum made chicken soup and hot lemon drinks. I put the memory and the jigsaw back.

The airing cupboard on the landing contained only sheets, towels and my stepfather's clothes: Y-fronts, socks and nylon tee shirts. I eased a bath towel from the pile and went to check on the level and temperature of the bath water. I still hadn't found anything to wear.

Cautiously, I tapped on the door of my parents' room. Only it wasn't any more. My step father had repainted it, but the same curtains hung at the window and a large silver frame of photographs of Mum and I hung on the wall. I studied it. It was a collage of images, from our early days as a family to later ones of me parachuting in aid of cancer research while at university. Why did he have all these pictures here? I turned away and went back to the task of finding some clothes.

Going through my stepfather's wardrobe made me feel like an intruder. The shirts hung limply on wooden hangers, as if wearily queuing to get out. There were several of the same design in different colours, or rather shades, ranging from brown to beige and navy to pale blue - unimaginative, boring. Brighter than anything else, a lumberjack shirt caught my eye. It looked as if it had hardly been worn and I had a vague memory that I had given it to my stepfather one year for Christmas. I took it off the hanger, feeling that I therefore had some justification in taking it back. I would just have to manage with the trousers I'd been given at the hospital.

I shut the bathroom door and undressed, being ultra careful with the strapping on my foot. I should have anticipated how difficult getting into the bath would be, but I didn't. Getting in was an exercise in genius. If I hadn't been fit, I'm sure I would never have managed. As it was, by the time I lay down, I was shaking with the effort.

The water was hot, my legs and belly flushed crimson. With my eyes closed, I tried to blank out everything except my breathing, but the enormity of my situation overwhelmed me and I began to cry. I lay down to wash my hair and the water turned soapy grey. Eventually it grew cold and a sound downstairs got my attention. I listened hard.

'Hello?' My shout echoed around the room.

The stairs creaked. 'Are you in the bath?' asked my stepfather.

'Yes. Was that okay?' He was just outside of the door, which I'd been afraid to lock. I covered myself with my hands. 'I thought you were at work.'

'I was made redundant last year. I thought you'd probably want a bath so I left the hot water on. I'll switch it off now. I got you some clothes. I hope they're the right size. You look about the same size as your Mum. I'll leave them just outside of the door and make us something to eat.'

'Thanks.'

I struggled out. A grey tidemark ringed the bath. I found a cloth and wiped it away, then wrapped myself in a towel and opened the door to find out what he'd left for me.

A plastic bag lay on the carpet. Inside were a pair of tracksuit bottoms, a tee shirt, sweatshirt and packs of knickers and socks. I couldn't forgive him for his unfaithfulness to Mum but, I had to admit, he was doing his best to help me on a practical level.

CHAPTER 6

'How are you getting on?' My stepfather's voice cut into the blankness where my thoughts should have been. He was peering intently at me over the rim of his reading glasses, waiting for an answer, but I couldn't think how to respond. I was getting nowhere.

Despite sitting there for over an hour, the sheet of notepaper was still virtually blank. What did I need to do to get my life back on track?

'Do you want a hand? Two heads and all that.' My stepfather gave the newspaper he was reading a harsh flick and began folding it up. The actions were slow and purposeful and when he had finished, and it lay on the arm of his chair, the paper looked unread. 'What have you got then?'

'Not much,' I mumbled. It was an embarrassed understatement. All I had written was: One, Let work know, which I had ticked. Two, contact bank. Three. I could not think what three could possibly be. 'I'm not in the right frame of mind for this,' I admitted.

'It's got to be done.'

I let the notepad drop to the carpet and tossed the pen down after it. 'Not right now it doesn't. I'm too tired. I need a clear head.'

Part of the problem was that, until I'd spoken to Ollie, I was in a state of limbo. He still hadn't rung back. What if I couldn't stay there? What then? How could I think of stuff that needed doing tomorrow when I didn't even know where I was going to sleep tonight?

'Was it a rented flat?' My stepfather, clearly undaunted by what I'd said, continued. 'You ought to think about ringing your landlord.'

'It's through a letting agency. They're just round the corner from the flat so they probably already know.'

'You should still call them. If only out of courtesy.'

Sod courtesy. 'I don't know the number.'

'And then there's your bank.'

'Look, I know you're trying to help,' I snapped, 'but can't we just put the TV on instead.' My thumb traced the coloured band at the seam of my new tracksuit bottoms. The need to flee was building to a crescendo. How much longer could I hold it together?

'I'm not trying to bully you, Zoë. I just want to get you thinking. You won't be able to do much tomorrow, being a weekend. But the bank should be open...'

The sound of the doorbell cut him off and he went to answer it. I breathed a sigh of relief but it was short lived.

'Zoë, the police want to talk to you again.' Two plain clothes police officers followed him into the room.

'Hello Zoë. I'm Detective Inspector Green. This is Detective Constable Banstead.' DI Green was a hard-faced woman with a severe haircut and a sharp grey suit. She noticed my crutches. 'How are you managing?'

'It's early days.'

'Of course.' DI Green nodded, as if she understood, but it was obvious she was simply making conversation before getting on to whatever they had really come for.

She sat down in the armchair across from me, adjusted her jacket so that it wasn't pulled tight under her. 'We'd like to ask you a few questions.'

The policeman glanced around, looking for somewhere to sit. As I was occupying the entire sofa and the DI the armchair, there was nowhere for him so he perched on the windowsill.

'I don't know anything. I told the policeman that at the hospital last night,' I said.

'There are a few things we need to check.' DI Green consulted a notebook.

'Has something happened?' asked my stepfather, hovering by the door. 'I didn't think the police investigated fires unless there was something suspicious about them.'

DI Green glanced at him then back to me. 'We have reason to believe the fire may have been started deliberately,' she said softly.

'Arson?' said my stepfather.

'I'm afraid it looks that way.'

'What! Why? Why would someone set fire to my house?' Who would do that? Who were they targeting? My head span. Were they after Neil Wyatt? It couldn't be me or Claire. The coughing started again. I grabbed a tissue and blew my nose. I'd been coughing and bringing up bits of black all day.

'Are you okay, Zoë?' my stepfather asked.

'Sorry. I was... Do you know how Neil Wyatt is?'

'Not good I'm afraid. Considering the intensity of the fire, it's a miracle that he's alive. If he doesn't pull through we could be looking at a murder enquiry.'

'God, that's awful.'

'How did it start?' my stepfather said.

'We're still investigating.'

As if they wanted him out of the way, DC Banstead suggested my stepfather make some tea. My stepfather hesitated, then obediently went to make it. While he was gone, DI Green began running through the same questions I'd been asked before. I confirmed the answers.

'Has anything out of the ordinary happened lately? Anything unusual?' she said, changing tack.

'Like what?' Nothing came to mind. Was there something I was supposed to remember? I stared at the policeman who was scrawling in his notebook.

'People around that you haven't seen before? Anyone hanging around outside?'

'I'm not really there much.'

In contrast to her sharp appearance, the DI's manner was surprisingly gentle. Perhaps the attire was her way of competing with the men. She crossed her ankles, which were small and bony.

'Have you, or Claire, had any arguments with anyone?'

'You don't think this has got anything to do with us? I'm not in the habit of falling out with people.'

'I wasn't inferring...'

'Wait. There is someone,' I blurted, suddenly recalling. 'Someone hanging around, I mean. A man came to the house looking for Neil Wyatt. It was a few weeks ago. He was really angry, shouting and hammering on the door.'

'Had you seen him before?'

I rubbed my head to try and clear it. 'I don't think so.'

'What did he look like?'

I tried to recall. 'It was dark. Um...'

'What age do you think he was?'

'About Neil Wyatt's age. Fortyish.'

'White?'

My stepfather returned, carrying a tray of mugs, which he passed around. I took the one he offered, irritated by the interruption, and answered the DI's question.

'Yes. He was white but quite brown, you know tanned.'

The detective helped herself from the sugar bowl my stepfather had left on the table. 'As if he'd been on holiday?'

'No. As if he spent a lot of time outdoors. He had that sort of weathered look. I wondered what he could possibly want with Neil Wyatt. They were so different. Neil's like a left over from the Eighties with his floppy hair and bad music. That's all he plays, Blondie, Madness and that awful pop stuff. It's all we've heard in the summer when the windows were open.'

The policewoman didn't comment. 'Can you tell me what happened when you saw this man? Start from the beginning.'

I sighed. 'I'd been running. I've been training for a half marathon that's coming up in January. It's probably out of the question now. I'll never get my fitness levels back in time.' I shook the thought away and tried to concentrate on remembering. 'It was threatening to rain so I cut my run short. It was about eightish when I got back to the flat. I began to work through my warm down routine. Claire was in the lounge, by the front window, looking out and waving. At least, I thought at the time she was waving. She told me afterwards that she was motioning me to get inside.'

'Do you know what day it was?'

I shook my head. 'It would have been a weekday, probably a Monday or Tuesday because those are the days I do the longest runs.'

I looked at DI Green, wondering if she was going to ask me anything else and when she didn't I carried on. 'I was just going in when this man barged past and started hammering on Neil Wyatt's door. But there was no answer. I told him what I thought of him for knocking into me. I was switching the light on when he came at me. He said something like, "Where is he?" And I asked him who he meant. He said, "That bastard that lives here." And I said, "how the hell would I know".'

In my mind's eye, I could see him standing in front of me, threateningly close. His bullying should have intimidated me, but I was angry rather than afraid.

'He reeked of aftershave,' I said, suddenly remembering the heavy cloying scent.

'So what happened then?'

'I told him to leave. And he said, "I'm not going nowhere". I told him that if he didn't go I'd call the police. He was right in my face but I slipped past, ran upstairs and slammed the door. I thought he was going to smash Neil's door down. But after a minute it all went quiet and I saw him stomping away down the road.'

'And he was definitely after Neil Wyatt?' DI Green clarified. 'You said he referred to him as "that bastard". Did he use his name?'

'I don't know. But he was hammering on Neil Wyatt's door.'

'You didn't call the police?'

'I didn't think it warranted it. But I told Neil when I heard him come in an hour or so later. I was angry.'

'How did he react?'

'He swore. Said that was all he needed. Do you think that man started the fire?'

'I don't know. There's no evidence to suggest it. But we'd like to eliminate him from our enquiries.' The detective was silent for a moment. 'I'd like you to come into the station to do a photofit. We need to find out who the man is. I'll make arrangements and give you a call. Can I have a contact phone number?'

My stepfather reeled off his number and she wrote it down.

'I won't be here,' I said.

The detective passed me a business card. 'Well, there's my number. Please let me know if you do go somewhere else.' She rose. 'And if you think of anything else, please give me a call.'

My stepfather showed them out, then came back and leaned on the top of the sofa.

'Don't say I told you so,' I said.

'I wasn't going to. Thank God you're all right. I can't believe it, can you? You hear about these things on TV. You don't expect them to happen in your own back yard.'

I swung my legs down. 'What kind of person does something like this?'

'Hmm.'

'I wonder if Neil Wyatt did something to provoke it.'

My stepfather took the policewoman's chair. 'From what I've read in the paper, these things are often caused by money or drugs. What kind of place were you living in?'

'Just a normal flat,' I snapped. I got up and made the long journey up to the loo, thinking over what he had said about Neil Wyatt and drugs. What kind of person was Neil Wyatt? What had he been up to? His cigarettes had certainly smelt like cannabis. Was he a dealer? I knew nothing about him.

When I returned to the lounge the television was on. 'Ollie rang,' my stepfather said. 'He's coming over.'

CHAPTER 7

At seven Ollie still hadn't arrived, and I began to worry that he wasn't going to. Waiting had made me irritable. What was taking him so long? I studied every vehicle that passed. Being propped against the edge of the windowsill wasn't comfortable and I had to keep changing position. The curtain secluded me from the room and I was reminded of the hospital cubicle. On the other side, my stepfather mumbled comments to the television. Did he usually talk to himself? Was he lonely? Perhaps taking redundancy hadn't been a good idea.

Finally, I spotted Ollie's Golf cruising up the road. 'He's here.' I hurried to open the front door. As soon as he saw me, Ollie wrapped me in his arms. 'Your dad told me what happened. Are you sure you're okay?'

I breathed in the familiar scent of him as he pinioned me. His breath was warm in my hair and, although the zip of his coat scratched my cheek just below my left eye, I didn't move. I never wanted him to let me go.

When we finally parted, I said: 'Is it all right for me to stay at your place?'

'Of course.' He didn't hesitate and I was grateful.

'You must be Ollie.' My stepfather appeared in the hall and held out his hand.

'We're going,' I said.

'Don't you want a cup of tea or something first. Ollie's only just got here.'

I glared at Ollie, daring him to agree to any kind of delay.

'Thanks. But the traffic's bad. It'll take us a while to get back to Portsmouth.'

Well done Ollie, full marks for reading my mind.

Cautiously I stepped over the threshold and turned towards my stepfather. 'Thanks for coming to get me and for the clothes. I'll pay you back as soon as I get sorted.'

'Don't be daft. There's no need for that.'

There was; I didn't want to owe him anything. I made my way towards Ollie's car, my stepfather following.

'You should take it easy for a few days.'

I stared at him in disbelief.

'I know that sounds like a contradiction, and you think I'm an interfering old sod, but the quicker you get things sorted, the quicker things will feel more normal. You also need to rest. If you need any help don't be afraid to ask. Oh, and what about an address and phone number? In case the police call.'

'I've got her card,' I said, coughing.

'I still ought to have a number.'

Ollie reached into his jacket. 'I'll give you one of my business cards.' He rummaged in his pockets, drew out a card and pen. 'This is the number and address of the flat,' he said, writing it down.

I stood there stiffly, unsure how to say goodbye.

'I wish I'd seen you again under happier circumstances,' my stepfather said. 'You know Zoë, you're welcome to stay.' He must have known it wasn't an option. I opened the car door and he took my crutches from me as I got in.

'Look after her,' he said to Ollie, passing him the crutches to put on the back seat.

'The sheets are in the washing machine.' I said, by way of conclusion. I didn't admit that they were grimy. 'I haven't switched it on. I wasn't sure how to use it.'

My stepfather nodded. 'Let me know if you need anything. Anything.'

'Sure.' I reached out to pull the door closed. 'Thanks.'

My stepfather stood there, hugging himself against the cold, but he didn't hurry inside. I felt guilty for being so abrupt but I couldn't stop myself. Despite his help, it didn't change what he had done or how I felt about him.

Driving along the motorway, I was relieved to be away from my stepfather, but also worried that Ollie hadn't understood what I actually meant about staying. My shoulders ached with tension. I was emotionally and physically exhausted.

'You know I said can I stay at yours, I didn't just mean tonight.'

'You want to move in, right?'

'Only until I can find somewhere else.'

'Charming.'

'You know what I mean.'

'I'd be offended if you didn't want to. Anyway, where else are you going to go?' He laughed. 'Unless you want to go back and live with your dad.'

'That's not even remotely funny. Do you think the others will be okay about it?' As a friend of both of us, I knew one of his flatmates, Mike, wouldn't mind. It was Darren's reaction that worried me. Darren would mind. It was just a matter of how much. I didn't blame him. After all, having girlfriends stay over for the odd night was one thing, having them move in quite another.

'They'll understand.'

'I hope so.' I glanced out at the junction and realised where we were. 'Can we stop at ASDA? I desperately need some clothes, although I'll have to borrow some money.'

'It'll be really busy.'

'I know. But it'll be even worse tomorrow...Oh damn! I've left my portfolio behind. And the rest of the clothes Keith bought.'

'Do you want to go back?'

As the one thing I still owned, I wanted the portfolio with me, but I couldn't face my stepfather again. 'It's probably as safe there as anywhere else.'

'Sure?'

'I'll go back for them in a few days.' Frustrated, I dropped my head back against the headrest. 'How was your day?'

'Trying, but rather easier than yours.' He proceeded to tell me about the building problems they were facing, and the tedious site meeting he'd been stuck in since mid morning, but I was only half listening. We pulled into the supermarket car park and Ollie stopped near the entrance so that I could get out. 'I'll find somewhere to park. Are you sure you're up to this? You look knackered.'

'I am, but I desperately need some clothes.' A gust of wind took the car door as I opened it, slamming it back on its hinges with a groan. I need a coat, I thought. I need a lot of things. But today, it would have to be the basics. I reached in to get my crutches. 'I'll meet you in the clothes section.'

With Christmas less than six weeks away, the rails just inside the entrance were crammed with party outfits, but I needed practical clothes that I could wear virtually anywhere. It was a daunting task, but positive to be doing something, no matter how small.

'Oh God. Where did you get that?'

Up to his usual tricks, Ollie strode towards me with a wheelchair and attached trolley. 'Your carriage, madam.'

'I'm not riding around the store in that.'

'You ungrateful woman. I had to fight an old biddy with one leg for this.' He rubbed his elbow. 'She put up a hell of a fight. And now you say you don't want it?' He circled me like a solitary war party Indian. 'Come on get in. And think yourself lucky, I nearly got you a mobility scooter.'

I slid in. 'I suppose I should be grateful,' I said, feeling emotionally lifted by his mischief.

'Exactly.' He grinned. 'It's for your own good. Besides it'll get it done quicker.'

I pulled a face at him. 'Bully.'

He ignored me. 'Where to first?'

'Underwear?'

He cocked an eyebrow at me. 'You mean you haven't got any on. You don't know what that's done to me.'

'Sorry to disappoint your fantasy,' I said, 'but I have, and they're probably the kind of big pants your mum wears.'

He laughed. 'Give us a look.'

'Bog off.'

Slowly we made our way along the aisles. Looking up at everything gave the store a strange perspective, and I soon found that most things were out of reach. I wondered if people who use wheelchairs permanently ever got accustomed to the frustration of it. I hooked a bra from the rack and another fell off with it. Ollie bent to retrieve it.

'Boring.' Putting both back, he reached for a loose black and turquoise set further down the aisle. 'This is more like it.'

'I can't afford to get too much,' I warned. 'I need practical stuff.'

'This is for me.'

'I'm sure you'll look lovely in it. Are you sure it's your size?'

He held it against his chest. 'What do you think?'

'I think the day you start wearing women's underwear you'll be single again.'

'You never heard about Andrew Hopkin's stag do?' he

said, grinning.

I put my hands to my ears. 'Please don't tell me. I don't want to know. I'll end up with a picture in my head I can't get rid of.'

Ollie's laugh is a great infectious bellow. 'Let's just say we were very drunk and someone had confused stag with drag do. What size?' He waved the bra at me.

'I imagine you'll need a 42 something,' I told him. 'And a couple of chicken fillets.'

'I'd rather see it on you.'

'In that case a 34c.'

He swapped it for another and dropped it into the trolley. 'They should put footplates on the back of these things. You could use them like toboggans then.' He spun me back towards the rack, then changed his mind and rushed us over to the socks. 'We could have a wheelchair trolley dash.'

He held up three packs of socks in different designs. 'The middle one,' I said, but he threw them all into the trolley.

'Where to next, madam?' Doffing an imaginary cap like a footman, he made a noise like a ticking clock and hurtled me down the aisle.

It felt good to laugh.

Ollie hooked a glittery top from the rack. 'What do you think of this?'

'It's nice. It's like my blue one.' Like the blue one I used to have, I thought sadly.

'We'd better take it then. And what about this?'

'Ollie. Be sensible.'

'Right. Sensible. You need a sensible coat.' He steered me to the kind of coats a granny would wear. 'How about this? It'll go with your old lady knickers.'

I poked my tongue out at him and wheeled myself over to a row of warm looking black woollen coats.

'Boring!'

'Practical.'

Ollie threw a bright red glove and scarf set into the trolley.

'You're getting carried away. Remember you're paying for all this. This is going to cost a fortune.'

'Oh no. I forgot.' He picked up a couple of small items from the trolley. 'Better put a few of these things back then.'

For a moment I wasn't totally sure that he was joking. 'I will pay you back,' I said. 'I'm just not sure when.'

He nodded. 'Will two weeks give you enough time? 59.1% interest or sex every night.'

The pop music playing across the store was interrupted by a female voice talking about the latest offers. I caught Ollie slipping a bottle of my favourite perfume in amongst the clothes.

'We should get a take away meal. If there's any left,' I suggested.

'We'd better go and get it then.'

'You go? I'll have a look around, see if there's anything else I need.'

As he walked away, I wondered if he really was as agreeable about everything as he said. Or whether he felt he didn't have a choice. I tried to wheel myself along, and found that it was harder than I'd imagined so I got out. I located the smoke alarms and batteries. There must have been an alarm somewhere in Ollie's flat but, if there was, I'd never noticed. Anyway, one was not enough. I picked up three and hid them in the trolley among the clothes.

CHAPTER 8

'Looks like everyone's out.'

I followed Ollie's gaze to the darkened flat on the second floor. The large Victorian villa must have been an imposing building in its day. Now, like all the surrounding properties, it looked neglected. In places the white paint was peeling away in thick slices, and the original windows had been replaced with plastic half bar that made it look ridiculous.

Ollie bounded up the eight stone steps to the entrance and dumped the shopping bags under the portico. I leaned wearily on the crutches. With the exception of the top floor, all the rooms have high ceilings and that means a lot of steps. Perhaps this wasn't such a good idea. I'd been so eager to leave my stepfather's I hadn't considered the stairs. What if there was a fire here? How would I get out? Where else could I live?

'Are you coming?'

Slowly, I went to join him. I couldn't think like this.

Getting to the front door wasn't too bad, but inside the steep, carpeted stairs proved more difficult. I'd almost perfected a way of doing it using one crutch and hanging onto the bannister, which worked okay but was rather slow.

'You should be behind me in case I fall,' I said, pausing to give my arms a rest and catch my breath.

'What, and have you land on me. No fear. I'm quite happy with my bones intact.'

'Thanks a lot.' Just then the lights went off as the automatic timer ran out. Thrown into sudden disorientating darkness, I groped for the handrail.

'Stay there. I'll get it.' A moment later the lights came on again as Ollie hit the switch on the landing wall above.

'Are you okay?'

'Not really. I can't go any faster. I haven't got used to these damned things yet.' I breathed deeply. 'It's exhausting.'

'Hang on.' Ollie ran up the rest of the stairs to the flat. His feet pounded on the creaky staircase above, slowing as he neared the top of the flight. When he came back the shopping bags were gone and he'd removed his jacket. The light extinguished again and he hit the switch.

'Here. Take your arms out of the crutches.'

'Why?'

'Because I said so.' He held his hand out in expectation but I didn't relinquish my hold. The carpet was dirty, where no one took responsibility for cleaning it, and the thought of going up on my bum was disgusting. There were even cigarette butts on a couple of the stairs.

Ollie curled his fingers as a prompt. I pulled my arms free, leaning against the wall for support.

'Right,' he said, laying the crutches down. He squeezed past then grabbed me, hoisting me into a fireman's lift. I wasn't expecting it and thought we were going to fall.

'Put me down.'

'No chance. We'll be here all night.'

'This isn't a good idea. Am I supposed to be upside down?' The position felt precarious. Looking down the length of his back, the stairs seemed steeper than ever and his shoulder cut into my hip. Ollie let out occasional grunts as we climbed the stairs. The light went off for the third time. Ollie faltered and I felt him reach out for the banister.

'Put me down,' I said. 'This is dangerous.'

'We're nearly there.' As my eyes adjusted to the gloom, I saw he was right. Weak streetlight picked out the edge of each stair. Ollie staggered on a couple more steps then released me. He sank against the wall moaning and pretending he couldn't straighten.

'Are you okay?' I said, trying not to laugh.

'You're going to have to go on a diet.' He groped for the light switch.

'That's pure muscle.' I held onto the banister for support while he leaned backwards, massaging his lumber region.

'We're going to have to look at getting a stair lift then. I can't do that too often.'

'You don't have to,' I said indignantly. 'Once I've got used to the crutches, I'll be able to manage on my own.'

Ollie straightened and went down to fetch my crutches. My limited attempt at mounting the stairs emphasised how vulnerable I was. I hopped over to check that the fire escape was accessible. Apart from a couple of plastic chairs, stacked tight into the corner of the landing, the black metal staircase was clear. At least this building had two ways out.

Ollie let us into the flat and while he collapsed onto the sofa recovering, I dug around in the shopping bags for the smoke alarms.

'Bloody hell, how many of those have you got?' he said.

'Only three.'

'Three! Don't you think that's a bit O.T.T?'

'I don't care. Where's the best place for them?'

'ASDA!'

I ignored him. 'How about, one in here, and one in the kitchen?' I suggested and passed him two.

'What, now?' He shook his head but gave in gracefully, and went in search of a screwdriver. He probably knew I wasn't about to back down. I watched him insert the battery into the alarm and climb onto the chair to reach the ceiling. But, even though he stood on tiptoe and over-stretched dangerously, he couldn't reach.

'It's no good. We'll just have to leave it on the side somewhere. On top the bookcase maybe.'

'No. Smoke rises.'

'Well, I can't reach the ceiling to screw it up. We need a step ladder.'

'Maybe one of the other flats has got one.'

'Hang on. I've got an idea.'

He disappeared into Mike's bedroom then re-emerged hauling a chest of drawers, minus the drawers. He clambered onto it and screwed the alarm to the ceiling.

'There.' He prodded the red test button. Shrill beeping blasted the room. The terror of the previous night slammed back into my mind with startling clarity. 'Shit. Sorry.'

'It needed testing,' I said, releasing my ears as the noise stopped.

He gave me an apologetic smile and went off to fit another alarm in the kitchen, calling out to warn me when he was about to set it off.

'Where do you want this last one?' he said.

'In the bedroom?' I collapsed onto the bed, watching him, too tired to move. Now that precautions were in place, I could begin to relax. 'I know you think I'm being neurotic,' I said. 'But I can't help it.'

He gave me a peck on the cheek.

'Stop stressing. You've had a shock. If you were paranoid normally I'd be worried. But you're not.'

Ollie eased down on top of me. He seemed to see the position I was laid in as an invitation because he bent and nuzzled my neck.

'Actually, it makes a nice change being able to look

after you,' he said. 'You're so level headed and in control usually.' The rasp of six o'clock stubble scraped my cheek. When he nibbled my ear lobe, tortuous tingles rippled down my spine towards my groin. A hand across my hips secured me, preventing attempts I might make to escape, though I had no intention of doing so. He kissed me and I caught the faded scent of day old aftershave. 'I know I tease you, but I do understand,' he said.

Exhaustion, frustration, and anger, made me needy and I clung to him.

'I love you,' I said.

'I love you too.'

I kissed him hard, ran a hand up inside of his shirt, playing with the fine hairs of his chest.

He whispered in my ear: 'Are you going to show me those big pants now? I'm dying to see them.'

While Ollie slept soundly, I lay in bed fidgeting. The weight of the duvet pressed down against my foot and every time Ollie turned over he seemed to kick me. I tried to empty my mind, but the thoughts in my head were a wriggling mass that wouldn't let me settle.

The flat was silent. As usual on a Friday night, everyone was at a bar or club. Normally we would have been out until the early hours too, but tonight we had eaten our ready meal and gone back to bed.

I put some clothes on and sat on the deep windowsill, hanging the curtains around my shoulders to prevent the streetlight disturbing Ollie. A pigeon, huddling against the other side of the glass, regarded me with a beady eye every time I moved. Perhaps, because I was usually here on a Friday evening, it felt like a normal start to the weekend. Already I'd got used to the idea of being in the flat, and the panic I'd first felt about being trapped had subsided. It was significant progress.

The wind snaked between the buildings, making the

telephone wires whip and vibrate and the thin trees in the buffer garden opposite bend as if they would snap. The lights of the shop on the corner blinked out. A taxi pulled up and the occupants of a building down the road spilled out, shouting their goodbyes. A group of youths staggered down the middle of the street singing tunelessly. After they were gone the road was empty for a long time and I turned my attention to Ollie. He looked younger without his glasses on. In the dim streetlight that bled into the room his eyes were shadows. The monochrome contrast of pale skin and pillows to his shaggy dark hair made it seem as if he had partially merged with the bed. It would have made a good art study.

I shifted, stiff from balancing in the same position for so long. I longed to lie down in the warm and rest. Motionless beside the window, I was absorbing the cold, which permeated from the glass and a draught at the base of the ill-fitting plastic windows. I put on Ollie's dressing gown and the plastic boot, grabbed my crutches, and went in search of alcohol to help me sleep.

There was beer in the kitchen, but I needed something stronger. I turned my attention to the lounge where, after a bit of searching, I found a bottle of vodka. Pouring myself a large glass, and wishing there was something to go with it, I flicked the TV on, but I wasn't really watching it.

About an hour later, the door crashed open and Mike and his latest girlfriend, Sarah, fell into the flat giggling. All the way up the stairs they were laughing, and although I considered making my escape, I wasn't sure I could move fast enough.

'Oh. This is where you've got to,' Mike said when he saw me. 'Where have you two been? You were supposed to be meeting up with the rest of us for a drink.'

'Didn't Ollie ring you?' I was surprised that he hadn't.
'No, he didn't.'
'How do you know,' said Sarah. 'Your mobile's flat.'

Mike laughed sheepishly. 'Oh. Yeah.' He staggered across to the sofa, leered towards me, and planted a wet kiss on my cheek. 'How the devil are you? You look like shit.'

'Thanks,' I said. 'You don't look so good yourself.'

In contrast, Sarah looked immaculate. Her glossy black hair was still tidy, despite the wind outside. How did she manage it? At the end of a night out with the gang I looked as if I'd slept in a bush. Even if I had straightened my hair before going out, by the time I got home it was back to its usual mop of curls; especially if there was the slightest hint of dampness in the air.

'So, where's Ollie?'

'In bed.'

'And you're not with him. God, you've been together too long.' Mike perched on the arm of the sofa and gave me a hard stare. 'You okay?'

Sarah bent to whisper in his ear: 'I thought you were going to take me to bed.'

'Why don't you start without me? I'll be in in a minute.'

Sarah straightened and, blushing, stalked off.

'You shouldn't tease her. She obviously can't take it.' I took a large swig of vodka, emptying the glass. What did Mike see in her? Clearly she didn't trust him. In our early college days Mike and I had gone out, but that was a long time ago, before I'd met Ollie. Now we were just good friends.

'I only say stuff because she gets embarrassed so easily. So what's happened? Are these yours?' He picked up one of the crutches, which I'd laid on the floor. 'What's happened? You haven't broken your leg, have you?'

'Fractured a couple of bones in my foot. But it's a long story that involves jumping from a building.'

'Christ. Sounds serious.'

'I'll tell you about it tomorrow. You're needed

elsewhere.'

He shrugged. 'I'll wake her up if she's fallen asleep. Give her a prod in the back with my...'

I put up my hand to cut him off. 'I get the picture.'

'You okay, apart from that?' He motioned towards my foot.

Just then the door to Ollie's room opened and he staggered out, yawning. 'How long have you been up?'

'I don't know. I couldn't sleep.'

'Why didn't you wake me? I could have stayed up with you.'

'Why? You were obviously knackered.'

He looked to Mike for back up. 'Did she tell you?'

'Tell me what?'

'I've said she can stay here for a while. There was a fire at her flat.'

'Bloody hell! Lee on Solent. That was on the news. Is Claire all right?' He gave a nervous laugh. 'The two of you haven't been cooking again, have you? I'm kidding. Sorry. It's not funny. But you have to admit it's the obvious assumption.' Typical that Mike would make a joke when he didn't know how to react.

He grinned, then looked more serious. 'No, I am sorry. But at least you're not hurt.' He nodded towards my foot. 'Not badly anyway. Think I'll go before I put my foot in it again. Oh sorry, pardon the pun.'

'Said he'd be all right about it,' said Ollie, as Mike closed his bedroom door.

I sighed. 'It wasn't Mike I was worried about.'

CHAPTER 9

Despite endless repetitions, the player of the electric guitar couldn't get the sequence right. Even with one ear muffled by my pillow, it sounded as if the instrument was being tortured. I rolled onto my back and saw Ollie glaring at the ceiling.

'What time is it?'

'Too early for that shit.' He moved and wrapped me in his arms.

'Mind my foot! Is that Darren?'

'Who else!' Ollie was tense with anger. Reaching out, I ran butterfly fingers across his chest and snuggled closer. The wiry scrape of Darren's hands along guitar strings, and the slap of a plectrum with each strum, continued with irritating regularity. Then abruptly, half way through the sequence, the playing stopped.

'Thank God for that. It wouldn't be so bad if he could actually play. Though I suppose it could be worse. He could play drums.'

Ollie yawned. 'Actually, he's pretty good on drums.'

'Then why does he play, and I use the term loosely, the guitar?'

'Because, and I quote, "no one pays any attention to the drummer".'

'That figures. Arrogant git!'

The guitar strumming resumed. As if the sudden noise had sent a jolt through him, Ollie threw back the duvet and marched naked out to the lounge.

'Do you know what the fucking time is?' Darren didn't get a chance to answer. 'You're a selfish prick sometimes.'

'Who you calling a prick? Anyway... I've got to practice.'

I could just see them through the open doorway.

'Not at this time of the morning you don't,' said Ollie.

'I've got a gig tonight.'

'You should have thought about that before. Anyway, who you playing to, the deaf society?'

'Fuck off.'

'I'd love to. But with that shit going on I'd struggle to concentrate. Now pack it in or I'll shove that guitar where the sun doesn't shine. And then the only way you'll play it is by farting.'

I sank back into the pillows giggling. Ollie and Darren's fights always involve huge amounts of testosterone. I wondered where this one was headed, then began to worry that it might affect Darren's attitude to me moving in.

'What's going on?' The new voice was Mike's.

'I was just telling this prick to shut up.'

'I've got a gig,' whined Darren.

Mike spoke through what sounded like a yawn. 'At the Pig and Poke, isn't it? You coming?'

Ollie didn't sound keen. 'It depends whether I have to listen to any more of this shit right now.'

'There's a crowd of us going,' said Mike persuasively.

'I don't know. I'll see what Zoë wants to do.'

My brain did tortuous acrobatics, trying to devise a viable excuse to avoid going. But I need not have worried, Darren clearly didn't want me there.

'It's not a birds' pub,' I heard him mutter.

'That's true,' said Mike. 'The place's got a bit of a reputation.'

There was an element of pleading to Darren's voice: 'It should be a good night.'

If they all went out I would have the flat to myself, a few hours of welcome solitude.

'How is Zoë?' asked Mike.

'Remarkably okay.'

'Why? What's the matter with her?'

Ollie explained briefly to Darren what had happened and that I was moving in. He stopped mid-sentence: 'Bollocks!'

The sound of Sarah's voice came to me. Ollie made a hasty retreat back into the bedroom to avoid her.

'I thought it was Darren that wanted the audience,' I said laughing. 'Looks as if you put on a show of your own.'

Ollie stroked his penis. 'I can play my instrument a damned sight better than he can play that guitar. If you give me a minute I'll show you.' Ollie climbed back into bed. 'He's got a gig tonight. He wants some support.'

'I heard. I have no desire - whatsoever - to hear any more of his playing. But I don't mind you going.'

'Thanks! But I was hoping to use you as an excuse.'

'Please don't. He'll never forgive me. Anyway, think of it as retribution for making him stop this morning.' I stretched my foot. It had become stiff in the night. 'With a bit of luck the rest of the band will drown him out. And, it might be a laugh.'

'It might turn into a brawl.'

'Maybe that's why he's so keen to have your support.'

'Safety in numbers you mean? Just what I need.'

'Well, on a purely selfish note, you helping him might make him a bit more amenable to me staying.'

'He'll be all right.'

I wasn't convinced.

In fact, all morning Darren seemed to avoid me. I couldn't work out whether he didn't know what to say - or if he was so irritated that I was staying he didn't feel inclined to talk to me. Either way, it made me uncomfortable. I wanted to curl up somewhere quiet with a good book but even that was denied me; neither literature nor peace was accessible in this flat. The only consolation was that Sarah had gone.

Sat at the kitchen table with a pad and pen, I pursued the task I'd failed to do at my stepfather's. It was still difficult, especially when it came to remembering the names of insurance companies. Claire had dealt with most of that. I would need to find Claire so that we could make a claim. I wanted to see how she was doing anyway, but I didn't have a clue where she was.

In the lounge, the angle of a table seemed to be the subject of an argument between Mike and Darren. Although so far it was reasonably amiable, I could see that if they didn't resolve it soon it was headed for a full-blown row.

'It's NOT flat.'

'It's all right,' said Mike.

'Like hell it is.' Through the doorway I could see Darren standing with his arms folded. The makeshift snooker table they were arguing about was set up in the middle of the room, occupying most of the space. The legs were missing, so the two sofas had been pulled together to form a base, making it higher than it should have been and somewhat unstable.

'This isn't going to work. It was a stupid idea.'

'No it wasn't.'

'Yeah, it was. We can't play on it like this.' Unwittingly, I caught Darren's gaze. 'Look at this, will you.'

Surprised by the inclusion and despite the way that I was summoned, I got up and went to join them; there was no point antagonising Darren.

'Tell him. It's not flat,' he said.

'You're not cheating are you, Mike?' I said.

'How can you cheat at Snooker?'

'I don't know. But if there's a way I'm sure you'll have found it.'

Mike grinned and clutched his chest in an overdramatic way. 'That is so hurtful.' He racked up the balls. As he eased the frame away one began a slow roll. It slid across the felt, gathering momentum. I expected it to bounce off the end but, before it was half way down the table, Darren snatched it up. As other balls started to move, he slammed the one he was holding back onto the table. It struck the cushion and ricocheted back and forth.

'Well?' Darren motioned impatiently towards the table.

I followed his gaze, and considered squatting down to check it, but with nothing stable to hold on to it would probably be a struggle to get up again. Even without crouching, I could see that one sofa was fractionally taller than the other, which was why Darren was adamant that the table sloped.

'What make is your watch, Darren?' Noticing it, I suddenly remembered a similar one on the man who had come looking for Neil Wyatt. It had a dark strap and several dials within the face and had looked expensive.

'Why d'you want to know that?'

'I thought it looked...pretty special.' I didn't feel inclined to explain and flattery always worked on Darren.

'It's a Tag,' he said, then added as if I was an idiot, 'that's a Tag Heuer. One of the most expensive watches you can buy.'

If you're stupid enough! I leaned against the wall, wondering if I should phone the police. It was probably insignificant but they had told me to ring them if I remembered anything.

'The table?' snapped Darren.

Mike glared at him. 'What the hell's up with you? You've been in a bad mood all day.'

'Oh fuck off. I don't have to put up with this shit.' Darren stomped into his bedroom, then out again carrying a sports bag, and left.

Mike began racking up the balls again. 'God knows what's up with him. He can be so bloody anal sometimes. If he's worried about this evening's gig he should have practised.'

I wondered if it was something else that was annoying him.

'Do you want a game?' said Mike.

'No thanks.'

'Who's upset Daz?' said Ollie, as he came in, carrying a bucket and sponge, which he stowed under the kitchen sink. The oily smell of car wax hung about him like cologne, as he gave me a peck on the cheek.

'That'll be me,' Mike said, laughing. 'Want a game?'

Ollie swung his coat over the back of a chair and glanced at the snooker table. His hands were red and he rubbed them together vigorously.

'It's not flat. Grab a couple of those books and prop it up this end. I need to get some feeling back in my fingers.'

I left them to it and went to find the business card the policewoman had given me. Back in the kitchen, where I had more privacy, I rang the number. The DI was unavailable and I was put through to another officer. I told him about the watch.

'That's it,' I concluded apologetically.

'Thanks for calling. Any information can help. You never know where things are going to lead. While you're on, I've just been told we've been trying to fix up a photofit. Can you come into the station on Monday? Say at two o'clock?'

I thought about the logistics of it. It would involve taxis or buses - and money I didn't have. 'I haven't got any way of getting there,' I said.

'I can arrange for someone to collect you.'

'OK then. Oh, one other thing,' I said, as it occurred to me. 'Can you give me some contact details for my flatmate, Claire Randall? I need to discuss some things with her, insurance claims, that sort of thing. But I've no idea where she is.'

'Er, hang on. I'll check.' In the background there came the tapping of a keyboard and a phone ringing. After a few moments the policeman reeled off a Winchester phone number and address. I wrote it down and rang off, feeling pleased with myself for thinking of a way to get in touch with Claire. However, there was no answer when I called the number.

The door opened and Ollie came in. He took two cans of beer from the fridge.

'I've just spoken to the police,' I said, following him back into the lounge. 'They want me to go in for a photofit on Monday.'

Ollie opened a can. 'Do you want me to take the day off? I'm not on site. It's a bit short notice but it is kind of an emergency.'

'No need. The police are going to pick me up.'

'There'll still be some running around to do though, won't there?'

'Maybe. I expect a lot of it can be done by phone. It might be useful to have a chauffeur later in the week though.'

'What's the photofit about? Who are the police trying to find?' He handed Mike the other can.

'Just someone who came to the flat once. The police want to eliminate him.'

Mike laughed. 'That's pretty brutal policing, isn't it?'

Ollie turned towards him. 'Eliminate him, very good.'

Mike pocketed the last ball and gave a whoop. 'Want a game?'

'No, you carry on. I don't think I can.' I indicated my stork-like stance.

'You've managed when you were pissed and a damn

sight less stable.'

'That's as maybe. But it didn't hurt if I fell over then,' I said, taking the opportunity while Ollie was distracted, lining up a shot, to have a swig of his lager. 'I've got things to sort out. And anyway the table's still not level.'

CHAPTER 10

I went back to my list making but my limited concentration was diminished and I was restless and fidgety. Like an itch I couldn't scratch, Claire was on my mind and I couldn't shake her off. The overwhelming need to see her was consuming; to talk over the details of what had happened with someone who had actually been there and understood the implications. I had rung the number the policeman had given me several times, but if Claire's parents had an answer phone, it wasn't switched on. So it wasn't even possible to leave a message for her. Perhaps if I went to her house she'd be back by the time I arrived. If not I could at least drop a note through the door. Anything was better than doing nothing.

Mike and Ollie were still playing their haphazard game of snooker. I got Ollie's laptop out and looked up Claire's parents' address on Google maps.

'Can I borrow your car?' I asked.

'You're joking, right?' There was panic etched on Ollie's face as he looked away from lining up a shot. It was like seeing someone from a horror movie freeze framed.

Mike laughed loudly. 'Funny, Zoë.'

'I'm not talking to you.' I turned to Ollie. 'I need to see Claire.'

'Do you honestly think you can drive?'

'The doctor didn't say I couldn't.'

'He probably didn't think you'd be that stupid,' said Mike.

'Butt out. Driving's different to walking. You don't have to put the weight on your feet in the same way.' My foot didn't ache as much today, or maybe I'd got used to the dull pain. Even though it wasn't actually giving much to support, I'd put the strapping back on, which kept it warmer and somehow made it feel a little more comfortable. I'd swapped the plastic boot for a trainer and for a while had been flexing and pushing my foot against the kitchen chair leg; practising operating a pedal. It hurt like hell.

'What about if you have to do an emergency stop?' Like a deep gash a frown bridged the gap between Ollie's eyes.

I wasn't convinced that I could do it either, but the compulsion to see Claire was so overwhelming that I had to try. 'I know it might be a bit painful but I need to do this.'

'Keep selling it, babe,' said Mike.

'Shut up.' Ollie and I spoke in unison.

Ollie chalked his cue and bent to line up the shot again. 'Do you know where Claire is then?'

'At her parents' house. In Winchester.'

Ollie looked up at me. 'You don't honestly expect to drive all that way?'

'It's only about half an hour.'

'Half an hour there. And half an hour back. Minimum. More like forty-five minutes.' Ollie took the shot and the balls cracked together. They rolled across the felt but not one was pocketed. 'Why don't you call her?' he said, straightening. Mike walked around the table, studying it intently.

'I tried.' I knew this was the weak point of my argument. 'There was no answer. I'm not sure it's the right number. But if it is, I thought maybe Claire would either be back by the time I got there, or at the very least I could leave a note for her to call me.'

'Maybe. Actually, we ought to arrange to collect your car somewhere,' said Ollie, as if it had suddenly occurred to him.

'I haven't got any keys.'

'Oh. No, of course. You'll probably have to contact the dealer for another set. Nothing's simple, is it?'

'Tell me about it.' I steered him back to my question. 'That's why I want to see Claire. I just want to talk to someone who's going through it too.'

He nodded. 'Okay. All right. You've ground me down. I'll take you. Just give me five minutes to slaughter this muppet.' He checked his watch and looked smugly at Mike. 'With a bit of luck we'll get delayed and miss Darren's gig.'

'Don't you dare. I'm not going be the only one to suffer. He's in a right mood as it is.'

The traffic on the motorway was heavy and it was a relief to come off on the Winchester turning. Through the amber avenue of trees at St Cross we sat in traffic, nudging slowly towards the road works. The hold up was frustrating. I breathed deeply, glad I wasn't driving. Was Claire going to be there? Was I finally going to see her?

'Take the next left,' I said.

'Are you sure this is right? It's a bit posh round here.'

I examined the street map I'd downloaded. 'Claire's family have got money. We need to take the third turning on the left, then first right.'

'What made her leave all this and slum it with you?' he asked.

'Oi! I think she found living at home restricting. She never really said that much about her family, but her parents sounded pretty controlling. This is the road.'

Ollie gave a whistle. All of the houses were large, with sweeping drives bisecting their manicured gardens. The majority of cars parked in front of each property were BMWs, 4x4s or Mercedes.

'This can't be right surely,' he said. 'Claire comes from this? You'd never have guessed.'

'I got the impression Claire was a disappointment to her parents.'

He blew out his cheeks. 'I can see why, considering she's got such a lack of ambition. Crikey. There's a Bentley in that driveway. I'm glad I cleaned the car this morning.'

Ollie stopped. 'I can't see any house numbers. I'll have to knock on a few doors. What number are we looking for?'

'I don't know. It's called Willow House.'

'Do you think there's a willow in the garden?'

'Maybe. But this one's called Chiltern Cottage and I doubt you can see The Chilterns, and it certainly isn't a cottage. So I wouldn't count on it.'

Ollie wandered up the path of a grand mock Tudor building. He knocked on the front door and waited. When the door opened an immaculately dressed elderly woman appeared, flanked by two small, yapping dogs. Ollie retreated. I saw the woman shake her head then point further up the road. Ollie nodded and turned, waving his thanks.

'God knows how anyone delivers anything round here, none of them are numbered. She says to try further up the road and on the opposite side. She doesn't know the name Randall. I'm assuming Claire's parents are still together and their name is the same.'

'I guess so.'

We drove on twenty houses or so. I felt anxious. We were so close. To fail would be unbearable, but, I reminded myself, there had been no response when I had rung her. It was likely they were still out. Disappointment was beginning to set in.

Ollie clambered out of the car and went to speak to a teenager sucking up leaves with a noisy orange machine. 'He's just hired help. But he did see a girl with ginger hair coming out of the house opposite. Could be Claire. I'll try it. There's a car in the drive, so maybe someone's home. This investigative stuff is kind of fun. Who do you reckon I should be, Sherlock Holmes, Hercule Piorot or Morse?'

'Inspector Clouseau more like. You're pretty clueless.'

There was no answer from the house opposite but he pointed at the border between two properties where there was a tree with draping branches, which could have been a willow.

'I think this could be it,' said Ollie, leaning on the sill of the car window. 'I'm sure that's a willow.'

'She's not in then.' It had been a wild goose chase and we'd failed. I felt despair clawing at my insides. I tore a piece of paper from my notepad. It was a bit scrappy and seemed totally inadequate but it was all I had. I composed a note; writing that I hoped Claire was okay, giving her Ollie's mobile and the number for the flat, and asking her to get in touch urgently. Folding the paper, I wrote her name on the front. Ollie posted it through the door and I prayed that she would get it and respond.

I dropped my head back against the headrest. Now what? I was frustrated that my plan hadn't worked, and worried that we still might have the wrong house. I was no closer to talking to her.

'There's nothing else we can do, is there?' I asked, as Ollie got back into the car. 'Please don't say I told you so.'

'I wasn't going to. Unfortunately, all you can do is wait. If this is the right place, it's down to Claire now.'

'I could have a long wait,' I said, despondently.

Ollie sighed as he started the car. 'What about me? I'm not going to have an excuse for missing the gig now.'

All the way back to Portsmouth I nursed his mobile,

hoping Claire would ring, but she didn't. I was glad that he hadn't allowed me to drive.

Ollie pulled a jacket on and kissed me. 'Are you sure you don't need me to stay with you?'

I laughed. 'Darren will never forgive me if you don't go.'

Ollie pulled a face. There was a shout up the stairwell from Mike.

'Down in a minute.' Picking up a cumbersome amplifier, which he shifted from one position to another, Ollie tried to work out the best way to carry it.

'I don't think we'll be back too late,' he said, then added: 'they're not likely to ask for encores.' As he turned, I noticed a wodge of cotton wool hanging from the pocket of his jeans.

'What's this?' I said, teasing it out.

He grinned. 'Ear plugs. Paul's bringing some red food colouring for blood.'

'Eh?'

'Burst ear drums. Bleeding ears.' He adjusted his grip on the amplifier. 'We thought we'd wind Darren up.'

'Are you sure that's a good idea. He's nervous enough as it is. I almost feel sorry for him.'

'Almost?'

I stuffed the cotton wool back into his pocket and kissed him. 'Nah. He deserves it. See you later.'

It was only after I had closed the door that I realised what solitude really meant. Although the stereo beat out dance music, there was an eerie stillness to the flat that hadn't been there before. If anything happened while they were out I was totally on my own. That thought worried me. I went to the landing to check the fire escape was still unobstructed, then I checked that each window latch was unlocked.

Darren's transit was double parked by the entrance. I watched Mike help Ollie heave the amplifier into the back.

There was a brief conversation between them then both climbed in. They were about to set off when a motorcyclist pulled up alongside and the rider leaned across towards the driver's window to talk to Darren.

I turned away and went to change the music, examining the stack of CDs for something mellow. There was a higgledy-piggledy stash of books on the bottom shelf of the cabinet, coated with a layer of dust. I ran my finger along the spines; cold war thrillers, horror novels or biographies. Nothing worth reading. I thought about the new Dorothy Koomson I'd started on the night of the fire. I should have picked another one up in ASDA when we went shopping.

Lowering the volume on the CD player, I grabbed the phone and curled up with it on the sofa. There had still been no call from Claire. Where was she? I tried the number again but there was no answer. By now the need to talk to someone was driving me crazy. I decided to call Jess, my oldest and best friend. If Paul was going to the gig, maybe she'd be in.

I went in search of Ollie's phone book. I knew he had one as he'd started it as a back up after his mobile was stolen last year. I wished I was that organised. In the circumstances, it wouldn't have made any difference of course, as I'd have lost both.

The small red address book was in his laptop case. I found Paul and Jess' number then dialled.

'Hi Zoë. I've been trying to call you,' she said. 'You'll never guess what.' She didn't give me time to reply. 'Paul's asked me to marry him.'

'Oh.' Preoccupied with my own thoughts, I was rather taken aback. Was I going to regret making this call? I needed to talk yet it looked as if I wasn't going to get a chance.

'Is that it?' she said sulkily. 'Aren't you pleased for me?'

Why did she want to get married when they had been

living together for three years already?

'You're not pregnant are you?'

'No.' Jess was horrified. 'You could try to sound pleased.'

'If that's what you want, I'm happy for you. You know my thoughts on marriage.'

'You don't think it's a good idea.'

'For me, no. But you're not me. If you're happy, that's what counts.'

'I am. Really happy.' She didn't sound it, she sounded angry and that was my fault.

'Well, that's all that matters.' I tried to sound cheerful but my mind had begun to sag. It didn't seem right to spoil her happiness by unburdening myself.

'So when did this happen?' I asked.

'Last night. We went to that new Thai place they were advertising on the radio. Paul managed to get a table through a friend of his dad's. It's really nice in there. Expensive. But well, it was a special occasion. Anyway...'

I stopped listening as she babbled on excitedly, barely pausing for breath.

'What are you doing now?' she said suddenly. 'Paul's gone to that awful gig of Daz's. Why don't you come over and go through some wedding magazines I've bought?'

Great! The sound of a key in the front door startled me. What had they forgotten?

'It's a bit difficult. I haven't got a car at the moment,' I said.

Darren's voice echoed around the stairwell: 'You're coming down the pub after, yeah? We're on about eight.'

'I intend to. I like to support local bands.' A man in figure hugging motorcycle leathers appeared inside the flat.

'Hang on, Jess,' I said.

Half hidden by the sofa, I watched the stranger close the front door. 'Hello.' He scanned the room until his eyes met mine.

'Hi. You're Zoë, right? Thanks for seeing me.'
I stared at him uneasily. 'What are you talking about?'

CHAPTER 11

At a guess, he was in his mid thirties, stocky, with surfer blond hair that fell across his face as he bent to lay his crash helmet on the carpet.

'Who are you?' I demanded.

He came towards me, extending his hand. 'Scott. Scott Dickson. Darren's mate?' His voice rose in question and I stared at him, expecting an explanation. Instead he sighed. 'I take it he didn't tell you I was coming then?'

'No. What do you want?' I said, sounding rude but not caring.

'I was hoping we could have a chat.'

'What about?'

'I understand you've been in a fire. I was hoping you'd tell me what it was like.' Dumb-founded by such a brazen display of sick curiosity, I stared at him.

'Who are you?'

'I'm working on an article about coping with the effects of trauma.' He was making me nervous. He unzipped his jacket as if he planned to stay. Reaching into his inside pocket, he extracted a business card. In large capital letters across the top it stated PRESS. 'I was hoping we could talk about what happened to you.'

Darren was dead. No matter how badly the gig went, if he came back alive, I was going to kill him. Setting me up like this was vindictive and nasty.

'It might help to talk,' Scott suggested, perching on the other end of the sofa.

'It might not.'

He rose and nodded. 'Darren said you might not do it. He didn't think you'd be up for it. I'm sorry, it's my fault, I pushed it.' He zipped up his jacket again. The leather was scuffed to grey along the right elbow as if he had come off his bike. 'Look, if you change your mind...'

'What exactly did Darren say?' I boiled with rage at Darren, unsure which aspect angered me most or how to channel it. How dare he do this to me? How dare he talk about me like this. 'I'm not some pathetic fragile little thing.'

'I can see that.'

I sounded hysterical not strong. Scott Dickson smiled. His teeth were exceptionally white and he seemed to be laughing at me.

'You don't know a damned thing about me.'

He shrugged. 'Journalistic intuition.'

His eyes held mine. They were a vivid penetrating blue, too vibrant to be anyone's natural eye colour. Contact lenses? I tore my gaze away. He was well styled, as if each element of his appearance had been precisely fashioned. Of the three tiny buttons up the front of his tee shirt only the bottom one was done up so that his hairless chest was exposed. Did he wax it? Was there other body hair that he removed? The heat of a blush crept into my cheeks.

'Sorry. I'll go. I didn't know he hadn't told you. That's typical of Daz.' Scott made no effort to get up. 'I'm doing this article because I thought it would help people in similar situations to hear how others have coped.'

He was too sure of himself and I knew he was manipulating me. But he was very attractive and I couldn't help but be drawn to him. I turned my attention to the phone. I still had my hand over the receiver. 'Jess, sorry, someone's come to talk to me. I'm going to have to call you back.' I put the phone down on the sofa where it was still within reach. 'How do you know Darren?' I said.

'From the gym.' I didn't dare ask how I'd come up in the conversation. I could guess that it was probably as a result of this morning, when Darren had stormed out. This was pay back.

'You've got beautiful eyes,' Scott said, still watching me closely.

'Oh please!' If he was trying to relax me he was going about it the wrong way. 'I thought you were here to do an interview, not chat me up.'

'I believe in mixing business with pleasure.' He grinned. 'So, are you going to talk to me then?'

I pushed a strand of hair behind my ear, then cringed as I realised he would probably read something into it. I gazed at him and considered, gave a small nod of assent. Funny that it was a stranger who was interested in how I was coping. Ollie hadn't asked. Perhaps he thought I was doing fine, that I would talk if I wanted to. But it hadn't occurred to me to do so. Ollie was here, involved, but not quite feeling it with me, not quite understanding.

A small cassette recorder emerged from Scott's jacket. He switched it on to check that it was recording. 'You don't mind, do you? It's just for my notes. I'm supposed to be going down the fire service training centre next week to watch a training session. I can't imagine how terrifying a fire must be. I believe the police are saying the fire at your flat was started deliberately. That must make it even worse. It might have been kids. What do you think?'

'I don't know. You hear stuff on the news about some nasty kids around but this was Lee on Solent. If you think

I know something though, you're wrong. You're wasting your time on that score.'

'I'm not trying to work out who did it. That's up to the police.'

'So what are you trying to find out?' I said.

'The details of what happened. How the fire started, who was involved, what it felt like being trapped inside a burning building, how you're doing now. But if you've got any idea about who did it, that's good too. It helps build the story. Put things into perspective.'

'Story! Is that how you see it?' I snapped. 'It's not a story. This is my life we're talking about.'

'Sorry. Technical term. I didn't mean anything derogatory.' My confidant gave a weak smile and lifted an eyebrow. He pulled a notepad and pen from an inside pocket of his jacket, turned to a blank page and dropped it on to the coffee table. I stared into his eyes, still trying to work out if they were contact lenses.

'I keep putting my foot in it, don't I? How about I shut up and you just tell me what happened? Any chance of a coffee?'

I waved a hand towards my foot. 'Only if you make it yourself.'

'Sure. No problem.' He stood up and wandered off to the kitchen. I got up too and went to turn the music off. Scott stood in the doorway and watched me hop back.

'So, what have you done to your foot?'

'Broken it.'

'Is it painful?'

'I'm getting used to it.' I took the CD out and switched off the power. The flat fell silent.

'Can you jot your name down on the pad for me so it's spelt right,' he called out. I picked up the notepad and wrote my name at the top of the uppermost blank sheet.

'Which paper do you write for?' I asked.

'I write for various.'

'You mean you're freelance.' There was a lengthy pause while he searched the cupboards. I wondered if he had heard me, or whether the cupboard searching was so that he didn't have to answer. 'The coffee should be in the cupboard above the kettle.' I said.

'Got it.' He appeared in the doorway. 'I write mainly for the magazine market. Articles. Human interest stuff. It's more satisfying than news reports. But I've had stuff bought by The Echo and The News.'

I felt suitably chastised.

He came in with two steaming mugs. 'Did you want sugar? You don't look like a sugar girl.'

'I'm not.'

'See, journalistic intuition.'

He handed me one of the mugs then picked up the notepad and studied what I had written for a minute. 'Zoë with an umlaut. Was your mother foreign?'

'No. Just inconsiderate. Everyone always forgets the dots. And that's kind of like having it spelt wrong.'

I took a sip of coffee and burnt my mouth. I put the mug down.

'I can't think of anything worse than being in a fire. The heat. The smell,' he said.

I shuddered at the memory.

'Sorry. That was tactless. Can you bear to tell me what it was like?'

He was surprisingly easy to talk to, amiable and empathetic. He didn't interrupt me; just let me talk. And when there were silences he didn't fill them with questions. It was as if he was allowing me to deal with the horror of it and sharing it.

'Are you okay?' he said, once I had finished. I nodded. I had always assumed journalists were crass, callous and insensitive. It came as a surprise to find that Scott didn't appear to be any of these.

'So, how long do you think you'll be staying here?' he

said, clearing away the coffee cups.

'I don't know. Depends what happens about my flat.'

'You didn't want to stay with your parents?'

I explained the situation with my stepfather and he indicated that he understood at some level. I was glad I had agreed to talk.

Scott picked up the business card he had produced earlier. He retrieved a Samsung from a pocket in his leathers and started scrolling through for numbers.

'Don't take this the wrong way but I've got a couple of numbers in case you want to talk to someone professionally.'

'I don't need them,' I said.

He shrugged. 'Do what you like with them. Bin them if you want but I'd rather you had them. You'd better write them down, my handwriting's appalling.'

I jotted down the numbers as he dictated them and looked at the detail of the card again. It was amateurish; lines of text of differing sizes and weights. My expression must have revealed my opinion because he was defensive.

'I know. It's pretty crap, isn't it? But it's all I could manage. I need to get some proper ones done.' He pocketed his mobile and stood up as if he was about to leave.

'I'd better make an appearance at Darren's gig. I promised I'd do a write up for the local bands website. Thanks again for seeing me. I'm sorry you didn't have any warning.' He put out his hand and I shook it. 'It's been interesting meeting you.'

'You too,' I said and meant it. But I still didn't like being set up.

After Scott had gone, I mulled over what had been said. Little of the actual conversation had registered but the overall impression was positive. The self-pity that had consumed me was gone. I didn't have time, or energy, to waste on negative thoughts or unnecessary emotions.

The idea that Darren had got one over on me galled

me, but the laugh was on him because his wind-up hadn't worked. Talking to Scott had helped to clear my head. And, if it helped someone else too, all the better.

I went back to my list making, then flicked on the television to catch the news. I had become too inward focused.

When the local news came on, I found out that Neil Wyatt was dead.

CHAPTER 12

It was a drab Sunday. I stood at the window, staring but not seeing, eager to do something but unsure what. Neil Wyatt's death was playing heavily on my mind. It was a purely selfish response. I could have been in intensive care, suffering for days with my skin burned and tubes keeping me alive. Was he in pain all that time? He was probably dosed up with morphine. I shuddered nonetheless. Why was I so shocked by the news? I had known he probably wouldn't make it.

More than anything I needed fresh air. How far could I go on crutches? Could I manage it to the shops? I'd never considered the distance to Albert Road before; it was simply walking distance.

There were a few basic food items we needed if we were going to eat tonight. If I took Ollie's rucksack I could probably carry them. I closed my eyes and tried to visualise the trip. Suddenly with a jolt I realised that, even though I had a few left at Ollie's flat, I hadn't taken my contraceptive pill for days.

I swallowed hard. 'Stupid. Stupid.'

'What's up,' said Ollie.

'Nothing.' I wasn't about to admit my mistake. How could I have become so careless? It was times like this when I wished I'd gone for an implant instead. Perhaps the chemist would be open and I could get the morning after pill.

'I'm going for a walk,' I said.

'Don't you mean hop?' Ollie had been teasing me all morning.

I rolled my eyes.

'I'll come with you. I could do with some fresh air myself,' he said.

That didn't fit in with my plans. I wanted the freedom to pop into the chemist unchallenged. 'I'll be painfully slow,' I warned.

'I realise that,' he said, helping me on with my coat.

Outside it was more dismal than I'd realised, but after the stuffy confines of the flat the dampness was refreshing, even if it was going to play havoc with my hair. We wandered slowly down the road. The wind, funnelling between the houses, tasted of salt and, as we turned the corner, the full force became apparent. It tugged ruthlessly at my coat, teased out strands of frizzy hair from my ponytail, which whipped my face.

With my dawdling pace, Albert Road felt a long way away. The crutches made a click-click noise on the tarmac like the sound of shears trimming a hedge. Soon I had to stop to gather in air and flex my arms, which felt as if the bones were being scraped free of flesh. The muscles complained at the constant jolt of pressure.

We had to stop several more times before we reached the shops where we bought pasta, jars of sauce, and other staples to keep us going.

Making an excuse, I left Ollie to pay while I nipped to the chemist a few doors along. It was shut.

'Is that everything?' said Ollie coming to join me. 'Did you want something in there?'

'Nothing that can't wait,' I lied. 'I just thought I'd have a look at the make up.' I quickly changed the subject. 'Is there a mobile phone shop round here? I really ought to get a new phone.'

'Who's your contract with? They might replace it free of charge. You should give them a call and find out.'

'That's a really good point.' My brain had clearly turned to mush.

We set off back. Would another day matter? Worry made me slower than ever. I began to appreciate what it must be like for old people who can't walk very well and don't drive. How do they manage to carry shopping? If they have to rely on local shops it must cost them a fortune.

Leaves littered the side of the uneven pavement, making it slippery and treacherous. The effort of exercise had triggered the coughing again. It was getting really tiresome. 'I'm going to have to stop again. Why don't you go on?' I suggested, having spied the small park just down a side street.

'Do you want me to fetch the car?'

'No. We're nearly back now. I'm just going to sit down for a minute.'

Ollie headed home and I went across to the bench. Like the car journey, this had proved more exhausting than I'd anticipated.

The park was little more than a few trees in a triangular fenced area of grass where three roads converge. The bench was wet but I sat down anyway. My whole body ached. A feeling of despondency hung about me and I couldn't shake it off. With a rustle of leaves, a squirrel bounced past. It disappeared up a tree, bounding from limb to limb and dislodging the cinnamon coloured foliage. Sheltered from the wind buffeting the other streets, the trees in the park had retained their canopy longer than those elsewhere.

The sky was beginning to skin over with rain clouds. A few heavy drops began to fall, prompting me to move and head back to the flat. When I got there, I found a large spray of orange and red flowers resting against the wall of the small open porch. From the street they were barely visible but I knew they couldn't have been there long or they would have been stolen. I half expected to see a delivery van driving away but for once there was no traffic in the road.

There was a small white envelope poked in among the flowers and in large black ink the name Zoe written on it. Were they for me? Were they from work? Did they deliver on a Sunday? Who really knew I was here? I opened the envelope but inside there was just a blank piece of card. Strange. There were no florist details anywhere either. I was surprised Ollie hadn't seen them and taken them up. He couldn't have been far in front of me.

Bending, I tried to pick the flowers up and carry them inside. They weren't tied as a bouquet around the stem, instead they were fixed in the middle into oasis so there was nowhere for a handhold. I couldn't manage them so I left them where I'd found them.

In the lounge Darren was cutting his toenails over the TV guide. When he saw me he pulled his socks on and left the room.

'You okay?' Ollie said. 'You've been ages.'

'It took it out of me.' I sank down in the kitchen chair. 'There's a bunch of flowers downstairs with my name on. You don't know anything about it do you.'

He frowned. 'Is that a hint?'

'No. It's just that there was no message, just the name Zoe on them. I take it they weren't there when you got back. You can't nip down and get them, can you?'

'Sure.'

He tossed a bar of chocolate at me. 'Here, energy burst.'

Darren headed out. He called back. 'Oh, your flatmate, Claire rang. The number's on the pad.'

'That's good news,' said Ollie.

I rang Claire immediately. She was just on her way out to dinner with her family so we couldn't really talk, but we arranged to meet up in Lee-on-the-Solent on Tuesday. Envious of her close family, I took a piece of chocolate and sucked it hard.

Ollie went out, leaving the door on the latch. When he came back his hands were empty.

'Where did you say the flowers were?'

'Just outside, by the front door.'

'Sorry, but they're not there now.'

'Maybe they weren't for me. Is there another Zoë in the block?'

'No idea. You know what it's like round here, they've probably been nicked.'

Had Darren taken them? Surely he'd realise we'd suspect him.

'They weren't very nice anyway,' I said, 'bit funereal to be honest.'

'Maybe someone was taking them to the cemetery then.'

'There was no message on the card.'

Ollie shrugged. 'Like I said, they've probably been nicked.'

Monday morning was spent making phone calls, or rather listening to the endless instruction to press one number after another on my keypad until eventually I got through to the wrong department or found myself in a queue. I was glad to abandon it, just after one o'clock, when a uniformed policewoman came to collect me for the photofit.

The consequences of what I was about to do worried me. What if I got the details wrong and they arrested an innocent man as a result? Stories abound of people being falsely imprisoned, of police blunders and the need of a result, any result. My hands were sweating, which made it more awkward than usual using the crutches.

The policewoman led the way into the building, through security doors and down a corridor that was sterile and unwelcoming. Behind closed doors on either side, I could hear the trill of ringing telephones. We entered an open-plan office and stopped at a desk just inside. 'Sorry, all the other rooms are being used. Please have a seat.'

I sat down in one of the two chairs pulled up to the desk and looked around for somewhere to prop the crutches. 'Here. Let me.' The policewoman laid them across an unoccupied desk nearby. 'Would you like a cup of tea or coffee?'

'Thanks. Can I have tea, white, no sugar.'

Instinct told me that concentrating was going to be a struggle. Neil Wyatt was dead. Being in the police station made it more real. Made him more real. Neil Wyatt was a stranger, someone existing on the periphery of my life, but he must have had family and friends, though to my knowledge few came to the flat. How many would turn up at his funeral? Not that I would be there to find out. Should I send flowers? I remembered the flowers that had mysteriously disappeared from the front door. The more I thought about it, the more I felt that they were funeral flowers.

'Please don't look so worried.' DI Green approached, carrying a couple of plastic cups. She placed one in front of me and gave me a smile that I think was meant to reassure. 'White no sugar, right?'

'Thanks. Is this a murder enquiry now?' I said.

'Possibly.' Her tone told me she wasn't going to admit to anything. 'Mr Wyatt's death wasn't unexpected given the severity of his injuries. He was in a very bad way when the fire crew got to him.'

'Is the man I saw a suspect?'

DI Green stirred her coffee ferociously before depositing the plastic paddle in the bin under the desk. 'No. We just want to have a chat with him.'

What did that mean? I didn't get a chance to ask as a

tall balding man appeared.

'Zoë. This is Bob Coleridge. He'll talk you through the procedure.' DI Green escaped to a desk across the room.

Although lacking in hair, Bob Coleridge's face was barely lined, so it was hard to determine his age. He ran through the procedure, then asked about the lighting and proximity of the man I'd seen.

The photofit was more difficult than I had imagined. The environment didn't help. Although I was used to working within the noise of an office, this room and all it entailed intruded on my fragile concentration. Focusing on minute details: the width of the nose, angle of the jaw, the distance between the eyes, seemed very hit and miss. Conjuring the likeness of a man I had encountered for just a few minutes was a struggle but I soon realised that I would have had almost as much trouble creating a precise image of someone that I knew well. It would be difficult enough to summon an accurate image of Ollie. Doing so for a stranger seemed impossible.

'How's it going?' said DI Green, returning to check on our progress.

'It's still not quite right.' I said, rubbing my eyes, which had grown tired from staring intently at the screen for so long. 'I can't see what I'm looking at any more. Can you print it out? Things always look different on paper.'

'Sure.'

I considered the print out, searching the features for a clue. Both Bob Coleridge and DI Green seemed indifferent to the man I'd created and I was beginning to wonder if my recall had failed me.

'You don't know who he is, do you?' I ventured.

'He's not known to me personally, but we'll circulate the picture and see if anyone does know him. You've done really well.'

'No, there's something not quite right.' I stared at the image. 'It's the eyebrows. They're not close enough to the eyes,' I said, finally realising where the problem lay. Bob Coleridge adjusted the image on screen then printed it out again.

I stared at the face before me and nodded. 'I think that's the best I can do. So what happens now? If you find him will I have to do a line up?'

'There's no reason to think that. Like I said before we just want to have a chat with him.'

I'd thought the information I was providing was important. It was disheartening to think it wasn't and the photofit had been a waste of everyone's time. Or were they just saying that? Why were they so secretive?

Like Scott Dickson, I thought suddenly. Had he known that Neil Wyatt was dead when he came to interview me? He wouldn't be much of a journalist if he hadn't. Yet he didn't say anything and he must have realised that I didn't know. Why hadn't he told me? But then journalists weren't known to divulge information. From reputation they are supposed to be conniving hacks, willing to trample on anyone at the opportunity of a story.

My good opinion of him began a nosedive. I tried to think back over our conversation for some clue to his motives, but all I remembered was his empathy, his gentle friendly manner. Was that just his way to get informants to open up? If it was, it had worked perfectly and that made me stupid, gullible and naive. But perhaps I was doing him an injustice and he hadn't known.

'I've got something for you,' said DI Green, retrieving an archive box from the floor. 'It's not much, just a few bits and pieces from your flat, your car keys, a few personal effects, paperwork and such like.'

'Really?' Choked up, I felt ridiculously over-grateful. 'I didn't think there was anything left.'

'Well, it's not much. I'm sorry. It's pure fluke that you've got these bits. You've got our new Scene of Crime lad to thank for that.' DI Green picked up the box. 'If you'd like to follow me out to reception, we'll get some transport sorted to get you home.'

The plastic chairs in reception, although functional, did not appear to have been designed for comfort. There was a row of them across one side of room. I took a seat at the opposite end to a woman who was probably only in her late thirties but had a worn out face. She sat forward in her chair and continually tapped an unlit cigarette against the side of a packet. I avoided eye contact; on crutches, even in a police station, I felt vulnerable.

The box sat on the adjacent chair where DI Green had left it. Afraid of disappointment, I didn't open it.

CHAPTER 13

Considering it was supposed to contain simply a few odds and ends, the box DI Green had given me was surprisingly heavy. The policeman who had brought me home had carried it upstairs but left it against the wall so, on hands and knees, I pushed the box towards the middle of the lounge where there was space to unpack it. Like a child at Christmas, I wanted to rip the box open and find out what was inside but I hesitated, aware that it wasn't likely to contain very much.

The central heating was off and the flat felt cold. I got up to switch it on but couldn't override the presets and get it working. So I kept my coat on. Sitting down on the floor again, I took the plastic boot off. It was really beginning to irritate me. It was so big that I kept knocking it. I didn't want to slow the healing process but I wasn't sure how much longer I could put up with it.

I ripped the parcel tape off the box and with a deep breath opened it up. The contents smelled damp and smoky.

The last thing I expected to find were photograph albums. But there were two, standing on end with their spines up. I realised immediately that one was the keepsake album Mum had compiled for me, and the sight of it made me cry tears of joy. The top edges of each album were water damaged, the protective laminate peeling away like sunburnt skin, but at least they were here.

Carefully, I lifted them out, worried that I would cause more damage. The keepsake album contained photographs and memory items such as medical cards, certificates for swimming and gymnastics, even locks of baby hair.

The first few pages consisted of baby pictures. They were the usual compositions; sat in a high chair, on a rocking horse, lying on a rug in the garden. Unfortunately there were few of Mum and I together because most of the time Mum was behind the camera. The thought made me smile. She was such a terrible photographer. There always seemed to be a bit missing and it was usually the head.

Realising my hands were covered in soot, I went to find some newspaper or an old magazine to put down, and a damp cloth to clean everything before I smeared the carpet black.

On a page on its own there was a large picture of Mum and my stepfather on their wedding day. The cream dress Mum wore displayed her slender figure beautifully, though the detail of the material was bleached out. Beside her I was a skinny child, wearing a sparkly, over-frilled pink dress that I'd mistakenly been allowed to choose.

I turned the page. Their wedding was a happy day. The house had been full of flowers. Aunt Jackie, who died in a car crash just a year later, had plaited blossoms in my hair. The memories were like a paper cut. Choking back tears, I laid the album down and began emptying the rest of the box, wiping each item as I took it out and laid it on the floor. The result was a bric-a-brac collection of bits and pieces. There was logic to what was there though; someone had retrieved things of significance. Did that mean there was other stuff that had survived? The battered metal box that had served as a file for important documents still contained what I needed: my passport, car insurance, MOT certificate, and some of my bank account details. It would make sorting things out easier.

At the sound of the front door opening I sat upright.

'Jesus.' Darren clutched his chest, startled by my sudden appearance over the top of the sofa. 'Do you have to hide?'

'I wasn't. Do you always come home this early?'

'Depends. Anyway I'm not stopping, I've got to cost a job up.' Darren threw the post he was clutching onto the sofa and went into his room, returning a few moments later changed and carrying a laptop case.

'Christ, it's cold in here. I'm surprised you didn't put the heating on.'

'I couldn't get it working.' It was appalling to admit and I cursed the manufacturer for making the thing so complicated.

Darren went to the control panel. 'What the hell have you done to this? Tcht! Women shouldn't be allowed to touch these things.'

'I was trying to advance it.'

'Bugger it completely more like.'

Clenching down with my teeth, I bit back a retort. Being pleasant to Darren was becoming difficult. Suddenly the heating clicked on and Darren flicked the control panel closed.

'I can't have buggered it that badly if you got it working so quickly,' I snapped.

Darren gave a huff and left.

My jewellery box was badly damaged. Water had swelled the wood so that the marquetry had opened up. Several pieces had fallen out altogether but it didn't matter. The box itself was unimportant; it was the contents that I was grateful to have back, even if they were all jumbled together in a heap. The locket, given to me on their wedding day by Mum and my stepfather, was tangled with another necklace into a tight knot and it seemed important to unravel it so I sat there for a long time working it free.

I was still sitting on the floor looking through things when Mike came home from work several hours later. He stared at the clutter spread out across the floor.

'What is all that? Have you been to a car boot sale or something?'

'This is the what they salvaged from my flat. The only stuff,' I added.

'Christ, it's not much, is it?'

'Tell me about it. I'll clear it up in a minute'

He shrugged. 'Whatever.' He flicked the music centre on, selecting a dance track, the thumping beat lancing the silence.

'Was there any post? There was nothing downstairs.'

'On the sofa. Darren brought it up earlier.'

'Christ. That bastard's never at work. I wish I worked for myself.' Mike looked through the mail as if searching for something specific.

'Are you expecting something?'

'My car insurance reminder. There's one here for you.' He threw the rest down in disgust.

The envelope he handed me was diamond flapped like the ones used for greeting cards. I held it for a moment puzzling who, apart from my stepfather, knew that I was staying here. It wasn't my stepfather's handwriting, which is a slanted scrawl that heavily indents not only the page but the two beneath as well.

Slitting open the envelope with my fingernail, I took hold of the card inside but as I removed it flakes of burnt paper fluttered to the carpet. It was a sympathy card, and the bottom and opening edge had been burnt away. What remained was half of a photograph of orange and red funeral flowers, similar to the ones propped against the side of the porch the previous day.

I turned it over then carefully opened it, but there was nothing written inside. 'What the hell..?'

'What is it?'

I showed him. Vanishing wreaths, burnt cards. What was it all about? Add into the mix the fire at the flat and it had to be more than a coincidence. It was beginning to creep me out. Was I being targeted? If so why? And by whom?

'Looks like one of those cards you send when someone dies.'

'Yes, but do I really have to point out the obvious? I'm not dead. And sympathy cards aren't normally burnt like this. Why is it burnt? And there's nothing written inside it.'

'Maybe whoever sent it just didn't know what to say.'

'Maybe. But they'd at least sign it. And why is it burnt? Is it indicative of the fact that there as an arson attack on my flat? If you'd been involved in a fire recently, wouldn't you think there was some significance to it?'

'It could just be someone's idea of a joke.'

I returned the ever-decreasing remnants to the envelope. 'It's nothing to do with you then? One of your practical jokes?'

'Give me some credit.'

'Alright. What about Darren? He could easily have slipped it into the pile of post. After all, he doesn't want me here. He's made that blatantly obvious.' Had he changed tactics? Had he jumped earlier because he was guilty?

'It's not his style. He wouldn't do something like this…'

I cut him off. 'He did set me up with a journalist.'

'He thought he was doing you a favour. He said you'd probably feel better having talked about what happened.'

And I had.

'Look, I know you don't like him but he's all right.'

'It's not that I don't like him. It's just difficult. He makes it very clear he resents me being here.'

'Come on Zoë, don't you think you're over-reacting? Daz is okay.'

Was I over-reacting? Coincidence? It was all a bit weird.

'Hmm. Like I'm going to trust your judgement when it comes to people. Just look at some of your ex-girlfriends. Myself excluded of course.'

Mike laughed. 'I have made a few mistakes, granted.' He put his arm around me and gave me a cuddle then picked up the photograph album.

'Please be careful.'

'I will. God, is that you?' He tilted the page. 'You look like a boy.'

There were more photographs, some with Mum in, taken once my stepfather was on the scene. Every summer we spent a week in Devon so there were a lot of those. The photographs were mainly close ups with out of focus backgrounds. Even without a visual prompt I could recall the detail of the place. It was one of those bays that appear on the map like a bite mark: a small elliptical cove dotted with a row of dark rocks, which had been used to form the foundations for a large concrete breakwater. Inside it was protected sandy beach.

Mike turned the pages of the album.

'It brings all the memories back seeing those,' I said. 'We used to go there every year when I was a kid. Funny, I haven't thought about it for years, but I can see it clearly in my mind as if it was yesterday.'

A narrow path led from one side of the bay across the cliff top to the other side. Alongside, in immaculate grounds, a large white hotel overlooked the beach. I used to wish that we could stay there instead of the caravan park a mile up the road. I could recall hurrying down the path to the slap-slap of flip-flops and the screech of seagulls, desperate to spend every possible moment on the sand.

There was a picture of Mum and I sat on the upturned hull of a rowing boat eating ice creams.

'Is that your Mum? She's gorgeous. How come you got the ugly gene?'

Bringing my elbow back I gave his leg a hard whack.

In the photo, clearly melting quicker than I could eat it, my ice cream was running down my face and arm.

'I wonder what the place is like now,' I said.

'Probably full of arcades and chip shops.'

'There was a chip shop back then, almost opposite the slipway, if I remember it right. I used to drop my sandwiches in the sand in the hope of chips instead. It rarely worked.' Around the corner, past the row of tiny fishermen's cottages, there was a general store cum post office cum gift shop where I bought shells wrapped in cellophane containing sweets in the shape of pebbles.

'We used to go to Spain. Chips are all we ate for weeks. It was great. Though I wasn't so keen on the sunburn,' said Mike.

There was a photo of me and my partially-decapitated stepfather making sandcastles at the edge of the sea. The picture had been taken just at the moment of removing the bucket, and despite the fact that the turrets had crumbled I looked triumphant.

I stared at the image. When the tide receded it exposed a playground of rock pools where, when I was a child, with net and bucket Keith and I hunted for shrimps and crabs. As a child, Keith was my father-friend, always willing to stop whatever he was doing and play with me. We shared a special bond.

'Your stepdad? It looks like you were close once.'

I nodded. In my childhood years Keith had been my Dad and I had loved him. Back then Keith was fun. My biological father had deserted us before I was one, but Keith had always treated me like his own. Which was why it was still so hard to reconcile him with the bastard who had betrayed us, and the fussy pedantic man he had since become.

Getting up, I moved away so I didn't have to look at it any more. I didn't want to think about happy times with my stepfather. 'It was a long time ago,' I said.

CHAPTER 14

It started to drizzle as the taxi reached the motorway and by the time we approached Lee-on-the-Solent it was raining hard. Beyond the promenade the sea and sky had merged, creating a blank grey canvas broken only by the faint silhouetted bulk of a container ship. Across The Solent, the Isle of Wight had been entirely erased by the weather.

The taxi pulled up in the lay-by a couple of doors down from the Blue Bird Café. I paid and clambered out, pelted by shards of icy rain before even getting upright and my arms into the crutches. Adjusting my rucksack, I kept my head down and hurried into the café.

On a weekend, if Ollie hadn't stayed over and we were both around, Claire and I often came to the café for breakfast. It was a vibrant place, frequented by bikers, who spilled out onto the pavement where they hung about in small groups, chatting amiably. Today, on a wet weekday, it was quiet.

Once inside, the familiar territory gave me a boost, and made me believe things could be normal again. The mingled blend of coffee, ketchup and cooking oil billowed out like an old friend in greeting. Then the smell of cooking meat hit me and the memory of burnt flesh made me gasp. For a moment I stood, stunned by the shock of it.

'I was beginning to think you weren't coming.' Claire broke the spell, her voice sharp. She was sitting at a table by the window, the misted glass wiped in a small arc.

'Sorry, the taxi was late.' Negotiating a route between the tightly packed tables, I went to join her. She looked as cross as she sounded. 'It's good to see you,' I said. 'God, it's horrible out there.'

'It's not much better in here. The place feels really grotty on a day like this.' As we embraced she was rigid and lifeless to touch.

'Do you think so?' The café, though small, was clean and warm. I swung the rucksack down then unzipped my coat, contemplating whether taking it off was a good idea or not. The idea of putting it on again wet made me decide against it and I kept it on.

We settled down and I took a napkin from the blue plastic dispenser in the middle of the table and patted my face dry.

'Have you seen the flat?' Claire said.

I recalled the blackened building with revulsion. 'I saw it the morning after the fire. There isn't much left, is there?'

'It's all boarded up and derelict looking now. It doesn't feel as if it was our home at all.'

We were silent for a moment. Drips from my wet hair kept running down my face. I wrung my hair into the napkin and patted my face dry again. I thought about Neil Wyatt. 'We were lucky.'

Claire stared out of the window and didn't answer. 'I see your car's still at the flat.'

'There not much point moving it. It's so frustrating not being able to drive. I hate having to be dependent on everyone.'

'I've only just picked mine up. Mum brought me

down. We had to get a new set of keys from Ford. That's why I saw the flat. Otherwise I wouldn't have gone round there. It's too upsetting.'

I knew what she meant but sometimes you had to face things.

'I can't seem to get the fire out of my head,' Claire said, rubbing the bridge of her nose. 'It's like a DVD on a permanent replay. I keep reliving it. The flames when you opened the hall door. That poor man when they brought him out. Coming here was a bad idea. The place stinks of burnt flesh. It makes me want to throw up.'

'Do you want to go somewhere else?'

Claire shrugged. 'Where else is there to go? Another café? There's no point. It's the smell…'

'Cooked meat? It got me on the way in.'

'I know it's irrational but…' I waited for her to continue but she didn't. 'What do you want? Hot chocolate?' she said suddenly. 'Do you want anything to eat?'

'Please, the boys have never got any food in. But can you sub me? Ollie gave me some money but the taxi was more than I expected. I've just got enough left to get back.' I had my rescued passport in my rucksack and hoped the bank would understand my predicament and help me out, but I couldn't depend on it.

Claire stood up to go and order. 'What do you want?'

'Some chips would be nice. Thanks.'

The café was almost empty. The only customer was an elderly man sat towards the back reading a paper, an empty breakfast plate pushed to one side of his table.

Claire returned with two mugs. Her movements were slow and she seemed to be hunched into herself. As she put the mugs down I studied her. It had only been a few days since the fire but she seemed thinner and, from the dark circles around her eyes, looked as if she wasn't sleeping. 'Are you okay?' I asked.

Claire flopped down in the chair and stared into her

mug as if it were a crystal ball where the future she saw was not a pleasant one. 'Not really. No one understands what it was like.' From the way she said it, it sounded as if she was alone in the trauma of the fire.

'Why would they? They haven't been through it like WE have,' I said caustically. In the few minutes I'd been here Claire's black mood had begun to rub off on me. Meeting up wasn't going to be the help I'd expected.

'I just feel...I don't know...I'm up one minute and down the next,' she continued.

'It's called shock.'

'I know.'

'And it's early days.'

She nodded.

'It'll take time but we've got to move on.'

'I'm not stupid.' The words were snapped, angry. I'd seen Claire wallow in self-pity before and she wasn't pleasant to be around when she was like it. I wanted to tell her to pull herself together, but hoping it would help me too, instead I found myself asking if she wanted to talk about it.

'I've done nothing but talk,' she mumbled. 'It's not doing much good.'

The waitress arrived with a bowl of chips and put them in front of Claire, who promptly shoved them across the table at me. 'Aren't you having anything?' I asked.

Claire screwed up her face as if the idea was offensive. 'I don't really fancy food at the moment.'

'Really?' That wasn't like Claire. I salted the chips and took one but it was too hot and I dropped it back into the bowl. 'Have you seen a counsellor?' I asked, thinking that for Claire it might be a good idea.

With her free hand she played with the salt granules that I had spilt. She pushed them into a pile then dabbed at them with her finger. 'Yes. Now Mummy keeps badgering me about going to see the doctor as well. But he'll only give me tranquillisers again.'

'That seems a bit drastic.'

'It's our family doctor's answer to everything.'

'Can't you ask to see another doctor?'

She shrugged. 'Do you know, I haven't cried since.' Claire continued to play with the salt, picking up some of the grains for a moment before scattering them again.

'Shock comes out differently in everyone,' I suggested. A sudden battering of rain hit the window, making us both jump.

'You seem to be handling it okay.' There was bitterness in her voice. Its immediate effect was to make me want to slap her. How could she sit there and say that? At least she had a family to support her. I didn't.

'Not really. But there's no point wallowing in it. I'm just trying to focus on getting things like banking and somewhere to live sorted, then I can get back to some sort of normality.'

Claire sighed. 'I guess, but it all seems so damned insignificant.'

It might be insignificant to her, but she had doting parents and wasn't living in a flat full of boys. 'It's got to be done.' There was no ketchup on our table so I took some from the adjacent one and squeezed an unhealthy dollop onto the chips. 'It's one of the reasons we're here, isn't it?' Taking a chip I stabbed it at the ketchup.

She shrugged. 'I'm going away for a while.'

'You're going on holiday?' I asked, incredulously. Was it going to be down to me alone to find a new flat for us?

'Not exactly. It's just that I might be in danger if I stay.'

The card and flowers sprang into my mind. 'What do you mean? Have you had stuff sent to you too?'

Claire wasn't listening. She seemed to have gone into her own world. 'It's to do with Daddy. I think that's why the fire was started,' she said.

What was she talking about? What did that have to do

with us? Or what I'd been sent?

Claire played with the salt while she told me about a family in Winchester who had lost their daughter in a road accident, and how the father blamed the council for not putting speed restrictions in the area. 'My dad was on the committee at the time. He's had really nasty threatening letters...' her voice trailed off as with one swift movement, she swept the salt granules off the table. I tried to absorb what she had said.

'That's a long way from torching our flat. Why our place and not your dad's?'

She shrugged. 'He lost his daughter. He said something about my dad knowing what it was like. I saw one of the letters and he sounded a right psychopath.'

'Did you tell the police?' I said, thinking the man was probably grieving rather than a psychopath.

'Of course.'

'And what did they say?'

'That they'd look into it.'

I shook my head, still trying to make sense of it.

'You don't believe me, do you?' Claire said.

'Of course I do. It's just that I always assumed that, if it was deliberate, it had something to do with Neil Wyatt.' Although, I was beginning to wonder about that. Who was the target? A chill ran through me making me shudder.

The remains of my hot chocolate had turned into an unappealing sludge and my appetite for the rest of the chips had gone. I pushed them both away and stood up. 'We ought to go and see the letting agent,' I said.

'But Zoë...' She was about to object so I cut her off. 'I know you want to put it off but we're both here now. I need to get something sorted even if you don't. I don't have the luxury of parents to go home to.'

Claire didn't look very happy but I wasn't about to be talked out of it.

Claire had an umbrella, which she held over us as we made our way from the café to the letting agent's office around the corner. Fortunately the rain had eased, but it hadn't stopped altogether, and the pavements were wet. Within minutes I could feel the dressing on my foot getting soggy.

'Zoë, I don't...' Claire was reluctant to go in but I pushed the estate agent's door open and ushered her inside.

'It's better to get it sorted.'

In a chair near the door, a spotty youth of about eighteen was virtually horizontal, his feet resting on the desk as if he'd been there some time. A music magazine lay open in his lap and an Ipod was tucked into the top pocket of his shirt. He looked at us blankly.

'Is Mr Matthews about?' I said. 'We need to talk to him about our flat.'

Reluctantly he removed the headphones from his ears. 'Wot?'

'Mr Matthews, the letting agent.' The thumping beat of pop music spilled out from the Ipod, which he hadn't turned off.

'Don't know anyone of that name.'

Claire sidled in and hovered like my shadow behind me.

'Tall chap in his late thirties. Glasses,' I insisted.

'Oh him. He left.'

'Well, who's doing Lets now then,' I said impatiently, my gaze drawn to his pimply skin.

'That'll be Ray.'

Adjusting the position of my arms in the crutches, I tried to straighten and make myself more comfortable. 'Can we talk to Ray then?'

'He's not here.'

'Are you being deliberately obstructive?'

'Wot?'

I glanced at Claire for support but didn't get any. 'When are you expecting Ray back?' I said instead, wondering if the man was out for a short while or the whole morning.

The youth shrugged. I dropped into one of the faded chairs by the door. 'We'll wait then,' I said, determined to make this a productive exercise. Claire remained standing.

Half an hour later a man practically fell into the office, shaking an umbrella back onto the pavement. He shuddered and slid the umbrella deftly into a stand by the door.

'Christ, it's pissing it down out there.' He spotted us. 'You waiting for me?'

He was a dour looking middle-aged man with a thick handle-bar moustache like a piece of sculpted black Plasticine: a Nick Park character. He shoved the youth's feet from the table.

'We're waiting for whoever's responsible for lettings,' I said.

'That's me. Raymond Banks. What can I do for you?' He looked at the youth. 'You didn't offer them a coffee, did you?'

The youth looked vacantly back at him. Raymond Banks gave a cluck of his tongue and raised his eyes towards the ceiling. He took his rain mac off and directed us to a large cluttered desk in the corner.

'What happened to Mr Matthews?'

'He left a few months ago.' Raymond Banks had no lips. When he spoke his voice was disembodied. I watched his moustache, not quite believing that there was actually a mouth beneath. 'What sort of property are you looking for?' he said.

'One with a roof,' I suggested, but the irony was lost on him. 'We're already on your books. Our flat burnt down.'

'Ah. Oh.' Raymond Banks slowly stroked his moustache, remoulding it as he reassessed us. 'Yes. I believe it'll be some time before the place is habitable again. You had a lucky escape. I understand the other tenant wasn't as fortunate. Have they got any idea what happened yet? I hear the fire was started deliberately.' Without waiting for an answer, he rose and went to a filing cabinet across the room, and retrieved a file. 'So, what can I do for you today?'

'We'd like to know what happens now?' I said, sitting down in chair in front of his desk.

'How do you mean?' It was clear that this was not going to be an easy meeting.

'Well, we haven't got anywhere to live,' I told him in a tone that implied he must be stupid if he hadn't worked that out for himself.

'Oh. I see. You'd like another flat?'

'Yes,' I said.

'No.'

I span to face Claire. 'What do you mean, no?'

'That's what I've been trying to tell you. I don't want another flat.'

'Do you want a house or a bungalow or something?' I thought she meant somewhere single storied. 'We're not going to be able to afford that.'

'No.' She paused, and her face gave an involuntary twitch. 'I mean I don't want to share. I'm going to live back with my parents.' She looked at me with a pitiful expression and her voice was soft and low like a child admitting a misdemeanour. 'I'm sorry.'

Anger exploded in me. 'Well thanks for telling me.'

'I tried…' Her voice trailed off.

'When?' The implications of renting alone hit me. I couldn't afford a flat by myself. It had been a nightmare trying to find someone to share with before. I didn't relish doing it again.

Raymond Banks looked at us in turn.

'Can you give us a minute?' I said, feeling foolish and angry and abandoned.

The letting agent shrugged and disappeared out to the back of the office. I heard what sounded like a kettle being filled.

'Claire, this is complicated enough without you

making it worse. We need to get something sorted.' I said. 'You'll be fine once the shock's worn off.'

Claire looked sceptical. Blankness crawled into her features. 'I doubt it.'

I felt like sand in the receding tide. What about me? If Claire could see that she was dropping me in it, she clearly didn't care. 'What are you planning to do then?' I snapped.

'I'm not planning anything. I'm just not ready to get another flat.' Her hands became the focus of her attention as if they could help her explain. 'Please don't be like this.'

'How do you want me to be?' I exhaled, controlling my breath in a long slow release as I counted to ten, but my voice was still a hiss. 'You've just told me you're not prepared to share a flat with me anymore. You've just made everything a hundred times worse. How did you think I'd react?'

'I'm sorry. I wish there was something I could do about it, but…'

I glared at her. I didn't know what to do. The letting agent made himself a cup of coffee while Claire and I argued. He came back, looking wary. Despite what he'd said to the youth, he hadn't made us drinks.

'Have you got any one bed or studio properties?' I said through clenched teeth.

Raymond Banks sat down at the other side of his desk and scrolled through details on his computer. 'It doesn't look as if there's anything on the books right now.' He shook his head. 'Well, there is one. In Gosport.' He read off the address.

'That's a pretty rough area isn't it?' murmured Claire.

'Um.' He raised his eyebrows. 'If I'm honest, we're having trouble letting that one.'

'How much is it?' I groaned when he told me the answer. Alone I couldn't even afford the rent on a grotty flat in a horrible area.

'Isn't there anything else?' The desperation I felt had

transferred into my voice.

'Not at the moment. But something may come in.'

The heavy pulse of a tension headache fingered my forehead. My feelings towards Claire were nothing but anger and I had to get away from her. What made it worse was that I'd had such high expectations of a shared experience. What a fool! I should have known how Claire would be. Now I just wanted to get away from her.

'We'd better have our deposit back and any outstanding rent so that I can go somewhere else then,' I said.

'That could take a while. The trouble is the place burnt down.'

'Funny enough, I'm aware of that.' I couldn't stop the sarcasm.

The letting agent picked up a couple of files and moved them to another spot on his desk. 'What I mean is, because the police are involved and there's some question as to how the fire started, the insurance company won't release any funds.' He lifted his hands theatrically.

'That's just stalling tactics. That doesn't affect our deposit.'

'I am afraid it does. Until it's been ascertained who's responsible they won't pay out.'

'But the fire was nothing to do with us.' Recollection of Claire's reasoning about the cause flashed into my mind, and flooded heat to my cheeks.

'That's as may be but until it's proved… It is standard procedure. As per your contract.'

'Which you know damned well we can't check. As it was lost in the fire.'

He raised an eyebrow. 'I'll arrange to send you a copy.'

'Very helpful,' I snapped. 'Where exactly are you going to send it? Seeing as I don't have anywhere to live. Can't you do it now? I'm sure you must be legally obliged to provide us with a copy.'

Raymond Banks didn't look pleased but after a few

moments the printer started whirring and he handed me a couple of sheets of solid text. I shoved them in my rucksack, there was no point trawling through them now.

Claire had taken a back seat as if she wasn't involved. I wanted her to back me up but she said nothing. So much for red heads having a fiery temper.

'So how long will it take?' I asked, seeing myself still camped out at Ollie's flat in six months time.

He shrugged.

'You must have some idea. Is it going to be days? Weeks? Months?'

'I don't know. I can't recall ever having a case like this before.' He pushed a lined A4 pad across the desk. 'I'll contact the insurance company and get some forms. Is there an email address I can send them to?'

I stood, leaning forward on his desk, and wrote down my gmail address. 'However long it takes, I'm going to keep badgering you until I get it,' I told him.

He smiled wanly and glanced at Claire as if for support. 'Clearly you're upset. If you're experiencing financial difficulties my advice is to try Social Services about somewhere to live.'

'Don't patronise me. You know full well there's not a cat in hell's chance of any help from them.'

A tug at my sleeve pulled me upright. 'Let's go. You're not going to get anywhere like this.'

I yanked my arm free. 'I need my money,' I hissed, as she dragged me towards the door.

'You were a bit hard on him,' she said, once we were outside. She was probably right. I hadn't handled it very well. It seemed to me that the letting agent had been almost as obstructive as the youth before him, but that wasn't the real reason for my bad temper. It was Claire.

'Yeah? Well, thanks for your support in there. It looks like it's going to be ages before I see any of that money and you might not need it but I do,' I said.

Claire's face burned. 'I am sorry.'

'Of course you are.' I scanned the properties in the window but they were all way beyond my means. I knew she wasn't sorry. 'Look, if you change your mind, you will let me know, won't you?' I didn't hold out much hope of it and, after what she'd done, I wasn't sure I wanted to live with her. But I needed someone to share with.

A pained look pinched her face. 'I don't think I will. I've kind of been thinking about moving back for a while.'

Now I was really angry. 'You never said.'

'I hadn't decided. This has kind of made up my mind for me.' It was a prime example of Claire's way of looking at life. She never reached out and grabbed things but waited, like a sea anemone glued to a rock, for things to drift to her.

'That's it then,' I said.

She nodded. 'You will keep in touch.'

'Sure.' I knew full well that once she had moved out of our circle of friends we wouldn't. Nevertheless Claire took a pen and paper from her bag for me to write down my contact details. 'How long do you really think you'll be able to live with your mum?'

'She's okay really. Dad keeps her in check. See you then,' she said, hugging me. This time it was me that stood there stiffly.

After we'd parted I wondered what to do next. Everything seemed insurmountable. I felt deflated and betrayed. The road to normality stretched out before me, and every little bump seemed to become a huge hill once I got closer. Exhaustion washed over me. I was a piece of cardboard that been saturated in the rain, which had dried out again leaving me buckled out of shape. Better that than to disintegrate into pulp as Claire had done though.

I turned towards the bank, ready for another fight.

CHAPTER 15

As usual, the heating wasn't on during the day and when I got in the flat was cold. Rather than risk wrecking the programming, and Darren's resentment again, I changed out of my damp clothes and pulled on a couple of Ollie's sweatshirts, one over the top of the other. I took the sodden dressing off my foot, which was wrinkled and cold. It was the final straw, I was ditching the boot. I would manage with trainers. If I loosen the laces I could probably still wear the dressing if I needed to.

The telephone rang and I went to answer it. 'Hello.' I couldn't hear anyone on the other end. 'Hello.'

I put the handset back in the cradle and set about making dinner from the provisions I'd bought. Soon the heat of cooking warmed me and the smell of spices filled the kitchen.

The phone rang again. 'Hello.' There was a crackling sound, as if someone was ringing from a mobile. 'It's a bad line. I can't hear you.' I ended the call and rang 1471 but the number was withheld.

Although it had taken nearly all day, the rest of the trip

to Lee-on-the-Solent had been reasonably successful, and I had come away with money in my purse and my overdraft facility extended. I had checked on my car but, with the high clutch, driving it back wasn't feasible. However, down the side of the passenger seat, I had found my mobile. The battery was flat, and I didn't have a charger for it, but it was the SIM card with all the numbers that was important.

Giving the curry a final stir, I turned the cooker off. With dinner underway, I curled on the sofa, nursing the replacement Dorothy Koomson book I'd bought earlier, and waited for the boys to arrive home. I checked the time. Was it Ollie trying to get hold of me to let me know he was going to be late? I found his number and gave him a call.

'Hi, it's me. You haven't been trying to call the flat, have you?'

'Hi babe. No. Why?'

'The phone keeps ringing. I guess it must be someone with a bad connection. Where are you? I made dinner.'

'I'm at the gym. Actually, you just caught me, I'm about to go on court.'

'You never said.'

Ollie was apologetic. 'I know. I forgot to tell you this morning. I left a message on the answer phone earlier though.'

'I'm a guest here. I'm not going to check that, am I? I'd really feel as if I was intruding if I did.'

'Don't be daft. You live there too now.'

'That's just it – I don't.' Brimming with frustration I was desperate to burn off some energy. 'I could have come with you. God, what I'd do for a run. Not that that's an option.'

'You shouldn't run before you can walk,' Ollie cackled until he realised I wasn't laughing and the hilarity petered out. 'Never mind, you'll be running again soon. But you're right, you could have come to swim. Or even just use the jacuzzi.'

It wasn't the same as running but gentle exercise might have made me feel better, conned my brain into thinking I had used my body. 'I'll have to buy a swimming costume,' I said, thinking that I really couldn't afford to waste money.

'They sell them here. Do you want me to get you one? Size 12, yeah? By the way, how did you get on with Claire?'

'Long story.' What could I tell him in the few moments before he went to play squash? 'She doesn't want to share a flat with me any more.'

'Why? She doesn't think the fire was anything to do with you, does she?'

'No. If anything she thinks it's something to do with her dad.'

'Her dad? Seems unlikely. But you know what she's like, flaky at the best of times. She's self centred.'

'You've never really liked her, have you?'

'It's not that I don't like her. I just find her too self absorbed and one-dimensional. She's actually quite a boring person...' His voice tailed off and I could hear talking in the background. 'Listen, I've got to go. We're on.'

'What time will you be back?'

'About eight.'

With a sigh I put the phone down. He could have suggested that I join him. I could have got a taxi and met him there. By the time I'd organised it, he'd have probably been home, but he could have suggested it nonetheless. I felt lost and in need of diversion. The book wasn't it and, now that I was out of the warmth of the kitchen, I was growing cold. Borrowing a pair of Ollie's socks I pulled them carefully over my own and curled up on the sofa to watch TV.

With them all out, I could watch any of the soaps without ridicule. The television in the lounge is a vast flat screen with surround sound. I switched it on then went to put some rice in the microwave. The others could eat when they got in but I was hungry now.

I stared around at the flat with a feeling of isolation. This was what it would be like living on my own, only there wouldn't be the expectation of someone joining me later. This would be it - just the television for company. Hell! Living alone wasn't going to work for me.

The phone rang, making me jump. I couldn't hear anyone on the other end. With numerous media remote controls I wasn't familiar with, it took a moment to locate the right one and reduce the volume on the TV. Then the microwave began to ping. On the phone there was still silence. I hung up and keyed in 1471 but it was still a withheld number. It probably wouldn't be one that I recognised anyway, not being my flat after all.

The phone kept ringing, stopping as soon as the answer phone cut in. I ignored it and served up my dinner, but it kept on ringing. Eventually I snatched it up.

'I still can't hear you, you moron. Why don't you go away? Your phone's clearly not working.'

'Zoë?'

'Oh.' I put my plate down on the coffee table, knocking the fork onto the carpet in my haste. 'Shit.'

'Is everything okay?'

I recognised my stepfather's voice. 'Sorry. Yes,' I apologised as I headed for the kitchen and a cloth. 'Have you been struggling to get through?'

'Yes. The line's been busy for a while. How are you? Managing to get sorted?' He sounded remarkably cheerful.

'I'm fine.' I picked up the fork and dabbed the carpet with the damp cloth.

'Good. You're a strong girl.'

It was on the tip of my tongue to tell him that I'd had a lot of practice, and to ask him how he knew I was strong when he hadn't been around to see it. But there didn't seem any point in being vicious. Silence stretched out between us.

'Did you ring before?' I said. The carpet was dark with damp. Had I got rid of all the curry? I bent for a closer inspection. The carpet wasn't especially clean anyway, but I didn't want to give Darren ammunition against me.

'Yes. Last weekend. Some chap answered.'

'What about this evening?' I said, scrubbing hard at the floor.

'Is something wrong Zoë?'

'No. It's just that I've had silent phone calls since I got in.'

'Could be a fault on the line, especially with all the rain we had earlier.'

'Maybe.' Rising, I perched on the edge of the sofa. I hadn't considered that.

'Or it could be someone on a mobile. Were you worried they were crank calls then?'

After the other strange things that had happened it had crossed my mind. I tried to rationalise: 'It's probably one of the girls Mike's dumped. He does have a habit of ending his relationships badly.'

'Well, I've only got through this once,' Keith said. 'Is Ollie looking after you all right?'

I folded the cloth in on itself and put it down on the table. 'He's out playing squash. If that's looking after me.'

'Ah. But other than that?'

'I don't need looking after,' I said watching the TV as Eastenders came on.

'I'm not suggesting you do. You're not a child. But I can't help but worry about you. That's what parents do.'

But he wasn't my actual parent. He was a stepfather. Even so, he sounded genuinely concerned. I softened.

'I made a bit of progress today. The bank gave me some cash and extended my overdraft facility.'

'Do you need money? You've only got to ask.'

'That wasn't a hint. I don't want your money.' I thought about the flat deposit I wasn't going to get back for a while. After everything that had happened between us it would be hypocritical to take his money.

'I understand you want to be independent and all that, but these are unusual circumstances. If you get stuck, I hope you'll swallow your pride and come to me.'

'Is that what this is all about? A ploy to win me over?' Was there a subtext here that I'd just picked up on? Was this all some elaborate plan to get me back?

He sighed, but didn't get cross. 'No. It's just a spur of the moment offer.'

On the television two of the characters were having a discussion as they walked through a market. Behind them an elderly woman was buying flowers from one of the stalls. It reminded me of the flowers I'd received.

'You didn't by any chance send me some flowers over the weekend?' It wasn't the kind of thing I would have expected of Keith but I had to ask.

His response was tentative. 'Do you think I should have done?'

'No. It's just that there was a bouquet sent but nothing written on the card to say who'd sent it.'

'Crank calls and anonymous flowers. You're beginning to worry me. You're not in trouble are you?'

'Not that I know of.'

'Are you sure? What with the fire as well.'

'The fire had nothing to do with me,' I said, watching the drama on the television.

'Hmm.' He didn't sound convinced. 'By the way, your portfolio's still here.'

'I'll come and get it as soon as I can drive again. It won't be cluttering up your house too much longer.'

'That wasn't what I meant. Why do you always have to misinterpret everything I say?'

'I don't.'

'Yes, you do. I hope you don't mind but I had a look at it.'

I wasn't sure if I minded or not. I didn't want him criticising me again.

'Is that all stuff you've done?' he said.

'Of course.'

'It's good. Not that I know much about it. Is it a good job?'

'It's okay.'

Another silence lengthened between us as I contemplated going back to work and the logistics it would entail.

'I'm glad you're all right. That's all I wanted to know.' Keith breathed deeply down the phone. 'Look, I know we've had our differences but…well, that was a long time ago now. I let you down. I know that. But this isn't what your mother would have wanted, us bickering and that. Please don't be a stranger, Zoë. I miss you.'

The idea of holding a grudge against him felt suddenly pointless. It came to me in a rush. If the fire had done anything, it had reminded me just how fragile life was. I should be grateful for what I had. Besides, I didn't really have the energy for anger. Despite what had happened in the past, he was the closest thing I had to family.

What could I say to him? 'I'll be in touch,' I said simply. He could interpret that whichever way he chose.

For the next half hour the phone continued to ring. I turned the handset to silent but I could still hear the faint trill of one in another room and the click of the answer phone cutting in and out.

CHAPTER 16

Being at the flat during the day was unsettling and, with everything that I could realistically do now done, I decided I might as well return to work and some semblance of normality.

When I arrived at the office the next day, Nick was standing by the entrance. As usual, instead of putting his coat on so that it was obvious he was creeping out for a cigarette, he was huddled into himself against the cold. Cigarette and mug of coffee in hand, he watched me clamber gracelessly out of the taxi.

'Guy never said you were back today.' The statement was almost an accusation and I had the impression he wasn't pleased to see me. I swung my rucksack onto my shoulder and leaned heavily on the crutches, wondering if I'd made a mistake in coming back so soon. If Nick was like this, what was Guy going to be like?

'He doesn't know. I only decided last night,' I said, noticing the way the sunlight bounced off the pale brick walls of the office. It gave a sense of warm invitation that contrasted harshly with the frostiness Nick emitted. I stood down wind of him, away from the smoke.

'How's it been while I've been off?'

'You mean did we miss you?'

That wasn't what I'd meant. I was referring to the workload. But Nick was vain and that would be what he'd have wanted to know if the roles were reversed.

'Of course you'll have missed me. You'll have had no one to referee between you and Gemma. Has it been all out war?'

He swallowed the last of his drink, and threw the dregs out into the gravel. 'You could say that. I nearly killed her Monday. She sent a file to the printing company without converting the spot colours to CMYK, so the client's logo and all the headlines were missing when it was output. Brainless bint. And don't get me started on the new look.'

'It's an easy enough mistake to make. I imagine it was caught at proofing stage anyway.'

'That's beside the point. She should know better. It's a basic error.' Nick took a drag of his cigarette, lifting his head to blow out the smoke. He looked tired, and was clearly on another downer with Gemma. If he actually allowed her to get on with the job, instead of constantly knocking her confidence, she might make fewer mistakes. But I didn't need an argument. The courtyard clock struck the half hour. I was now very late, which was not a good start on my first day back.

'What sort of mood is Guy in?'

He shrugged, and a shiver of apprehension ran through me. My pulse had already quickened. It wasn't so much what Guy was likely to say. It was more the attitude with which he would deliver the inevitable lecture.

'Marvellous! I suppose I'd better go and face the music.' The heat of the office hit me like a wall as I went in.

'Hey Zoë. Are you okay?'

'I'm fine. Thanks.'

'Sorry to hear about what happened.'

'Good to see you back.'

The attention as I made my way across the office made me feel appreciated. Their concern was touching and I knew most of them wanted me to stop and talk, but I didn't want to make it too obvious I was late.

I swung my rucksack to the floor and sank down in the chair. My desk had been used as a dumping ground. The computer screen was littered with post-it notes. There was a pile of mail, an old creative magazine and a paper swatch, several job bags that I hadn't got around to filing, and a penicillin experiment in a mug that no one had bothered to remove.

Gemma waddled from the stationery cupboard, carrying a box of paper for the laser printer. 'OMG. It's Long John. Ooh Arrr,' she said.

'Ha bloody ha. Says the girl who looks like she's had a pot of paint tipped over her head. It looks good, by the way.'

'Thanks.' Her new magenta hairstyle glowed as it caught the light.

Gemma dumped the box on the desk and grinned. 'Nick said it wasn't very professional, and Guy groaned when he saw it. But then everything I do at the moment pisses him off. I think it brightens up the place. You don't reckon it's a bit too cerise do you?'

'Depends if you're trying to make a statement.'

Gemma rubbed her rounding belly. 'Just thought it would make me feel more normal.'

Nudging my mouse to see if the Mac was on, I said: 'There is nothing normal about cerise coloured hair.'

She grinned. 'What do you think of the colour?'

'I'm not a great lover of pink. It's not my colour.' It wasn't Gemma's either, but I didn't say as much. I clicked onto the email but someone, probably Nick, had been checking it regularly and there were only a few marked as personal. 'Should you be lifting?'

'Stop fussing. I'm pregnant not ill.' Gemma pulled a ream of paper from the box. With a crackle of stiffness, the laminated wrapping ripped and fell away. 'I'm glad you're back. Nick's been a prize prick, and Guy's been in a right arsey mood since you've been off. Reckon he's missed you.'

'Behave.'

'I'm serious.' She filled the printer tray and perched on the edge of the desk, speaking conspiratorially. 'He's definitely got a soft spot for you.'

Seeing Gemma reminded me that I had never managed to get to the chemist, had never taken the morning after pill. It was too late now. I'd been so preoccupied with everything I'd put it out of my head. I just had to hope that it would be okay, after all I'd been taking the pill up to the fire and I was taking it again now.

'I think that baby you're carrying has eaten your brain.'

'You could be right. I went for another scan yesterday. Do you want to see the pictures?' Before I could answer Gemma had delved into her bag and drawn out grainy black and white images of what appeared to be a blob and a few ragged lines. She perched on the edge of the desk to show me.

'Everything's okay isn't it?'

'Yeah, course. It's just that stupid midwife panicking. She keeps nagging me about exercise and proper diet. Honestly, you'd think the lot of them had only just qualified. They don't seem to know a thing about being pregnant. Anyway, what about you? Did you get saved by a hunky fireman?'

'I've no idea. It's all a bit of a blur,' I said, fobbing her off. The whole point of coming back to work was to forget; the last thing I wanted was to discuss it with another set of people.

'Zoë, you're hopeless.'

The email pinged and I glanced back at my computer screen.

<YOU'RE BACK THEN.> The text was large across the entire body of the email. I smiled.

'Looks like someone's pleased to see you back. Have you got an admirer? Perhaps it was Guy. Oh shit, talk of the Gerbil...'

Gemma slipped back to her desk. I turned towards Guy's office. He was standing in the doorway motioning me over. I hadn't even taken my coat off.

'Wish me luck.'

With a glance at the clock on the wall, Guy closed the office door behind me as I shuffled in. 'Hello Zoë. Is this a flying visit or are you back?'

I didn't take the bait about my lateness. 'Um. Back. It's been a difficult time.' I was annoyed that I felt I had to justify my absence when quite frankly I didn't need to. 'I still don't have a permanent address, but I got some of the basic stuff done...'

'Hmmm. Have a seat.'

I stood stiffly upright.

'Do you mind if I don't? Getting up and down's kind of awkward.'

In truth, I didn't want to give him any more of a psychological advantage than I had to. Guy leaned on the back of his leather executive's chair, resting forward with his arms bent in a semblance of casualness as he scrutinised the crutches and my general appearance. He was probably thinking I looked scruffy.

'I understand that, but I have to say I'm a little disappointed in you, Zoë. The least you could have done is kept me informed. I've got a company to run. I need to know what's going on, what staff I've got for projects. Nick's taken over the logo you were working on, which is a shame because I think you'd have done a better job. If I'd known you were coming back today I could have stalled the client a bit.'

So that was why Nick looked so tired and seemed irritated to see me. Wait, was there a compliment in Guy's statement? It was flattering, but in the scheme of things the logo was unimportant. There would be others.

'I'm sorry I had to take time off unexpectedly.' I thought carefully about how to phrase my response. 'But to put this into context: I was nearly killed. Everything I had is gone. So, to be honest, I know it's not what you want to hear, but work has been the furthest thing from my mind.'

Guy drew himself up. Watching me closely, he pulled out his chair and sat down. Very quietly he said: 'Sit down Zoë, you don't look very comfortable like that.' He clasped his hands together, fingertips touching, and peered at me over the top of his glasses. Obediently I pulled out a chair.

'I'm not having a go about you having time off. That was unavoidable.' He looked thoughtful. 'This company operates because of people like you. We're a team working together to come up with solutions for our clients. Without our team members we aren't going to get very far. Are we?' Guy spoke softly. 'Now, you've been off for several days and I didn't know when, or even if, you were coming back.'

What did he mean if I was coming back? Was this a preamble to being sacked? Guy looked straight at me. I didn't want to meet his gaze so looked away, scanning the floor, the desk, filing cabinet; anywhere other than at him. My face burned with guilt. I suppose I should have rung in.

'You haven't kept me informed and I'm not even clear what happened. Talk to me. Despite what everyone thinks, I am not a monster. And if you need more time off you just have to ask. This is an exceptional situation, I realise that. But I do need to know about it. Talk to me.'

Usually he was a cold condescending bully, but today he seemed to be understanding and supportive. Maybe Gemma was right and he had missed me. I shook the thought away, and told him about all that had happened, about the fire, about the police, about trying to sort everything out. 'I still haven't got anywhere permanent to live. I'm staying with my boyfriend and his flat mates at the moment. It's very crowded.'

He nodded. 'I expect it's a relief to be back at work then. It'll probably take a few days for you to get into the swing of things again.' He pushed his glasses further up the bridge of his nose. 'Let me know when you need the time off to go and look for a flat. I dare say we can come to a mutual agreement.'

'Thanks.' What had happened? Had this man had a personality transplant over the time I'd been away? Or had his nicer twin brother moved in instead? 'If the police get someone for the fire I might have to go to court,' I said.

'Well, we'll deal with that when it happens.' Guy picked up a sheaf of papers and drew them towards him. 'Nick's got a couple of things you can help out on.' I was dismissed, but it took a few seconds for it to register. I stood and turned to go, then stopped. As he was being so reasonable I decided to push my luck a bit further.

'Actually there is one more thing. I need to get back on my feet and I could really do with a pay rise.'

Guy peered at me over the top of his glasses. He nodded. 'Let me think about it.'

'Thank you.' Making my way back to my desk, I couldn't help but smile.

'What happened?' asked Gemma. 'I didn't hear any shouting.'

'There wasn't any. He was nice.'

'Guy – nice?' She stopped typing and gave me a quizzical look. 'Guy and nice. There's two words you don't hear in the same sentence. Said he fancied you. If that'd been me he'd have really let rip.' She gave the keys of her keyboard an occasional tap in a half-hearted attempt at pretending to work.

I didn't even bother answering. From the corner of my

eye I caught sight of Guy watching us. 'Suppose I'd better see what Nick wants me to do.'

'Well, it won't be your logo. He's been pushing that through himself. And dumping all the crap on the rest of us.'

'So I heard.' I thought about what Guy had said that I'd do a better job and felt appreciated. 'What are you working on?'

Gemma held up a pile of papers. 'This shit and it's doing my head in. You should see this crap. I've got hardly any pictures and the ones they have supplied are either downloaded from their web site so they're useless, or they've been taken by some David Bailey wannabe. They're nearly all low res. Why can't these plonkers get it into their heads they're no use to print from?'

'You sound just like Nick,' I said, grinning as I went to talk to him.

Gemma called after me. 'That is so not funny.'

Nick looked up as I approached. In contrast to my desk his was immaculate.

'What do you want me to do?' I said.

He picked up a job sheet. 'These ads need artworking. Gemma was supposed to do them but she's so far behind she'll never get round to it. They're due out this afternoon.'

If they were that urgent why wasn't he doing them? I didn't argue though. Nick explained what needed doing and I set to work but it wasn't sufficient to fully occupy me as the style was already set and it was just a matter of following previous versions. A large part of the job was searching the archives, retrieving files and making adjustments. It was mind numbingly tedious so the day dragged.

The Mac pinged with an incoming email. This time the text was so small it was almost impossible to read. I leaned closer.

<DID YOU LIKE THE FLOWERS?>

I stood up and glanced around at my colleagues but

there was no telling if one of them had sent it. I stared at the sender's email address, blaisefiero@gmail.com. I didn't know anyone called blaise, nickname or otherwise. Blaze? As in fire. Fiero? What the hell was this all about? The email had mentioned flowers and the only ones I'd received were that ugly wreath thing that had mysteriously disappeared.

'Gemma, do you know if anyone sent me any flowers when I was off?'

'No. I did suggest it. But Isobel pointed out that, as your flat was gone, we didn't know where to send them or how to find you.'

I stared at the screen. Gemma had a point, and that raised some horrible thoughts. It must be someone in the office to know that I was back; someone who had somehow found out where I was staying. Or someone who knew where I was staying who had somehow found out I had come back to work. Was I being paranoid or was someone stalking me?

I clicked reply. <Who is this?> And hit send.

CHAPTER 17

The rest of my first day back at work was uneventful. I was bored rigid with what I was doing, and irritated that Nick was working on my project, but more than anything I was worried about the implication of the emails. Whoever sent them hadn't responded and nothing else had come through but the more I thought about it, the more unnerved I became. By the time I left work I was twangy.

As she lived in Portsmouth, I'd persuaded Gemma to give me a lift home, but even before we hit the motorway I began to think it was a mistake. Having never been in her car for more than the few minutes it took to nip into Fareham, I hadn't realised how bad her driving was: erratic at best, dangerous at worst. To be fair, the traffic was heavy, but Gemma struggled to concentrate and seemed blissfully unaware of the vehicles around her. When she finally slammed to a halt outside of Ollie's flat I was shaking.

'I'll pick you up at 8.15 tomorrow,' she said brightly.

'Okay.' I said, racking my brain for another way of getting to and from work without paying for it, but failing to come up with an answer. How was I going to cope with weeks of journeys like that? For a long time after her tail lights had disappeared, I stood at the kerb feeling weak. My body had dissolved to jelly, and my limbs refused to work. It seemed as if all signals from my brain had been rerouted and coordination was gone.

It had been an exhausting day. In my own flat I'd have had a hot bath and chilled out in front of something brainless on the television, but in Ollie's flat that wasn't going to happen. I hauled myself up the stairs, squaring myself against another evening with three men but even before I'd taken the key out of the lock and was fully inside, Darren sprang from the darkness like a ghoul. 'You going out?'

'God, you nearly gave me a heart attack. Does it look like it?'

'No, I mean are you going out tonight?' Darren's face was a pattern in Morse: a series of pinched dashes and dots rather than features.

'I haven't even got through the door yet. Why are you so keen to know if I'm going out?' I began to yank my coat off but co-ordination hadn't properly returned and my hands caught in the cuffs.

'It's a lad's night. We don't want girls here.'

'Since when?'

'Since now.'

All the anxiety and anger from the day poured out: 'And what the hell am I supposed to do?' I snapped, trying to hang my coat on the overloaded hooks and failing. I left it lying on the floor.

'Keep out of the way,' Darren said walking off.

Angrily I went into the lounge. Mike and Ollie were sprawled across the sofas watching television, both already nursing cans of lager. How long had they been home?

'Alright babe?'

'What's going on? I've just had a mouthful from Darren about a lad's night.'

'Don't worry about him. You know what he's like,' said Ollie.

'A miserable little git?'

'For God's sake don't let him hear you call him little. You know how sensitive he is about his height. Can you move out of the way? You're blocking the TV.'

I glared at him. He hadn't even asked how my first day back at work had been. 'What's Darren on about?' I demanded.

'He's got PMT,' murmured Mike.

I exhaled angrily. 'Why can't either of you ever give a straight answer?'

'I am. PMT. Pre-match tension,' said Mike.

I should have guessed. On the television a commentator was discussing the previous football match and giving an endless droning prophesy about the outcome of this one.

'Some of the lads are coming round,' Ollie said.

'Oh, that's just perfect!'

'I take it you didn't tell her then?' Mike said to Ollie.

'No. He didn't,' I snapped.

Stretching forward Ollie grabbed a couple of nachos from a half empty bowl on the coffee table. 'You can join us if you like?'

I stared at him. 'Darren made it very clear I wasn't welcome.'

'Oh, don't take any notice of him. You know what he's like.' Ollie took a swig of beer and belched loudly.

'Why do you always say that? It's like you're making excuses for him.'

'Okay, he can be a prat sometimes but he's sound. I'm not going to take sides.'

'Come on,' coaxed Mike, patting the sofa beside him. 'It should be a good match. And it'll be all right as long as you don't ask any dumb questions.'

'Like what's the off-side rule?' I suggested, sitting down next to Ollie.

'Exactly.'

I took a swig from his can, which was nearly empty, and considered my options. It was dark outside. I'd had a tough day. It wasn't practical to hide in Ollie's room all evening, or to wander the streets. Alone I'd only start to brood and worry. And if I was being stalked was I even safe?

Darren came into the room looking cross. 'I was sitting there,' he said.

'What, snuggled up to my boyfriend?'

He glowered at me, making me feel really uncomfortable. Was he blaisefiero? I stood. 'I'm going to get changed,' I said, making it clear that I wasn't moving for his benefit. 'So you can have a cuddle with Ollie.'

Darren pulled a face then sprang into the space I'd vacated. 'Is she going out?' he demanded.

'Christ. Can't you leave it? We can't exclude Zoë,' said Mike as I left the room.

'It's not the same with birds hanging round. You've said so yourself.'

'I know. But Zoë isn't a bird,' defended Mike.

'She isn't one of us. Not unless you've grown a pair of tits as well.'

'Well we can't chuck her out,' said Ollie.

'Why not? It's supposed to be a lad's night. It's always been a lad's night.'

'Don't be such a prick,' said Ollie. 'Zoë stays. Two against one.'

'How long is she going to be here anyway?' Darren's tone was bitter.

Ollie was defensive. 'I don't know.'

I stood against the bedroom wall out of sight, listening, feeling small and hurt. My fingernails had made deep slashes in the palms of my hands.

'Well, is it gonna be days, weeks or what?'

'I said I don't know. She can stay as long as she likes.'

Darren wasn't happy with that. 'It's my name on the lease. I should have a say about it.'

'You just have,' said Ollie. 'I don't know why you're being such a dickhead. I thought you liked Zoë.'

'It doesn't mean I want to live with her. She's always here. You can't fart these days without her being there.'

'For Christ's sake cut her some slack.'

'She's got you right under her thumb.'

'Don't be ridiculous.'

'Actually she has, mate,' said Mike, laughing.

Unwilling to listen to anymore, I silently eased the bedroom door shut. On the top of the chest of drawers were Ollie's wallet and mobile. I snatched up the mobile and scrolled through. Who could I call to come and rescue me? There were a lot of contacts I didn't recognise then I found Jess and Paul's number. I rang it but no one answered. I searched through other numbers but it was no good. I sat on the bed wondering what to do.

From the lounge the volume of voices had increased as other people arrived. Eventually, when the match started, I went to join them. Squeezed on the sofas and surrounding floor, seven men filled the room: Ollie, Mike and Darren, the journalist, Scott, who acknowledged me with a nod and a smile, another man I'd never seen before and wasn't introduced to, one I knew by sight, and Paul.

Darren gave me a disparaging glance. I leaned on the arm of the sofa to talk to Paul. 'Where's Jess this evening then? I tried to call.'

'Out with Neesha,' he murmured, attention fixed on the game. 'They've gone to a gig in Brighton. I can't remember who.'

I looked around for somewhere to sit. The lounge seemed to have shrunk. All of the sofa space was occupied, and limbs stretched across the carpet. Two of the visitors were smoking. I glared at the culprits.

'Who are we playing?' I said, watching to see what

one of the men was going to do with the cigarette stubs.

'Kazakhstan.'

'Where the hell's that?'

'Shh.'

Darren raised his hands and let them fall. 'See, that's why birds shouldn't watch football.' All heads turned towards us. Annoyance flicked across Darren's face.

'Where is it then?' I said. 'I don't think you know either.'

'Course I do,' Darren responded a little too sharply, prompting an outburst of ridicule.

'It's somewhere near India,' Paul informed us matter-of-factly, and the bickering immediately dissolved as the focus of attention shifted.

'How do you know that?' said Ollie.

'They told us earlier if you'd been listening.'

'Ooooh,' Mike and Ollie chorused in high-pitched mocking voices that made them all laugh. After that things settled down. The atmosphere was charged with masculine camaraderie and testosterone. I took a can of lager and flopped down in a beanbag but only a minute or two later the door buzzer rang.

'That's probably the pizza,' said Darren but nobody moved to answer the door. No one wanted to miss the game.

'Get the door, Zoë,' ordered Ollie. It was tempting to tell him to get it himself but I didn't want to create a scene so, with an effort, I hauled myself to my feet.

From the intercom I let the pizza boy into the building. He arrived carrying a large battered red bag from which he withdrew three large boxes and asked for money.

'Who's paying for these?' I called back to the lounge.

There was no response and I stood there awkwardly, breathing in the delicious scent of hot cheese. I shouted back towards the lounge, 'Can someone come and pay the pizza guy.'

Finally it was Scott who came to the door. The pizza

boy shoved the boxes at me while they sorted out payment and I balanced precariously, aware that I couldn't move.

'Here, let me.' With one hand Scott deftly shut the front door on the retreating delivery boy, the other slipped beneath the boxes and his fingers brushed mine.

'Thanks.'

'No problem.' He carried the food through to the lounge where a frenzy of snatching hands, that reminded me of a tank of piranhas, immediately grabbed at the food. I eyed the contents, looking to see what type of pizzas they were.

'Fetch me another beer while you're up, babe.' Ollie spoke too loudly, as he always did when he was getting drunk. His attitude was offhand. I flashed him a look that was supposed to remind him that I was struggling to walk, let alone carry anything. But he was oblivious.

'I'll have another one an' all,' said Paul, leaning forward and staring at the television. 'What's he playing at? The referee's blind.'

'A beer?' said Ollie as if I needed reminding.

'I'm not sure I can carry them.'

My words were drowned out by a sudden burst of cheering. Grudgingly I went to fetch what they wanted. The cans hadn't even made it to the fridge and I wondered why they hadn't been taken into the lounge in the first place. I slammed them down on the loaded coffee table in front of Ollie.

The pizza boxes were already empty. They hadn't left me anything. And where had my can of lager gone? Selfish bastards. With an explosive crack, Ollie opened his can and the contents sprayed everywhere. 'Zoë!'

The depth of his animosity shocked me. Blood rushed to my face, making it glow hotly. A bitter retort curled like a snake in my mouth and only my clenched teeth kept it in. I measured my words.

'You should have been more careful. I told you I'd struggle to carry them,' I spat.

'You sure you didn't do it on purpose?' The accusation was a painful incision. The cruelty of his attitude appalled me. I shrank from the room.

In the kitchen I crumpled as the weight of the day overpowered me. My sugar levels were exhausted but there was nothing in the cupboards. Gremlins had been at my meagre supplies again, though they were not completely gone; the discarded dregs of a tin of tuna remained, but there wasn't enough to make a sandwich.

There was bread at least. It was doughy, white, and tasteless, but it would make tolerable toast. I dropped two square-cut slices into the toaster. I had a sensation of being anaesthetized. If I was a snail I'd have pulled my head in and shut the world out.

'I take it you don't like pizza.' A pair of black motorcycle boots appeared in my line of vision and I looked up to see Scott standing in the doorway.

I wasn't pleased to see him. Already humiliated by Ollie's remarks, I was defensive. 'Actually, you know what, I love pizza. But those greedy bastards haven't left anything. I don't know why I'm so pissed off. They were all meat so I couldn't have eaten them anyway.'

'I'd never have taken you for a veggie.'

'What does a veggie look like then?' I said frostily.

He thought about it for a minute and tilted his head to look at me. 'You know, skinny, hippy, Jesus-sandal-wearers normally.'

'Doesn't that strike you as just a bit prejudiced?'

Scott laughed. 'I'm only joking.'

'Right,' I said. 'Ha ha.' Humour wasn't in my vocabulary just now, so I ducked my head into the cupboard. I found a half filled jar of strawberry jam, but a thick coat of blue mould skinned the surface and grew in patches on the side of the glass. I put the lid back on and binned it.

'So how come you didn't order a veggie pizza?' said Scott.

'I didn't order any of them. Apparently I wasn't supposed to be here,' I said simply, and kept my voice even. 'I didn't know they were planning this. If I had I could have made other arrangements.' Reaching into the fridge I extracted margarine and cheese. 'It's irritating but It is only one evening.'

'Not if we get through to the next round.'

I unwrapped limp plastic cheese. Cheese on toast was proving a miserable compromise, but I couldn't justify the expense of ordering a take away.

Just then there was a chorus of groans from the lounge.

'Is that likely then?'

Scott shrugged. 'Not if tonight's game's anything to go by.' He swung up so that he was sitting on the worktop beside me. For a muscular man he was surprisingly agile.

The toaster creaked. A small grinding noise indicated that the bread was stuck. 'You're missing the game,' I said, finding that the toast wasn't cooked and popping it back in.

'So are you.'

I put the bread back in. 'I'm not a footy fan though.'

'Who says I am?'

'Why did you come then?'

'To see you.'

'Oh, please.' I was too tired for games. I was suddenly very conscious of him; the sheer mass of his parted thighs on the work surface, his large hands caressing the edge of the laminate. It sounded as if he was flirting with me, although there was something about his mannerisms that made me doubt it. He was tall with the muscular attractiveness that makes men arrogant. I tore my gaze away and glanced towards the lounge where Ollie was just about in view, slouched down in the sofa as if he didn't have the strength to remain upright. He looked drunk.

'I think at the moment he's more interested in the football than what you're up to,' said Scott. 'Look, I don't mean to pry or anything…'

I cut him off. 'You're a journalist aren't you. It must be second nature.'

'True.' His smiling response faded. 'I thought Ollie was out of order before.'

I didn't say anything and could feel the wave of heat heading for my cheeks again. Yet even though I agreed, I found myself defending Ollie. 'He's had a drink so he's not himself.'

'And you're all right with that?' He gave me a hard stare. I didn't answer. 'You shouldn't have to put up with it. Especially after what you've been through.' He paused for a moment and seemed to be studying me.

'It's no big deal,' I said.

'It would be for me, if someone treated me like that.'

Embarrassment for opening up the last time we'd met made me self-conscious. To my annoyance I could feel myself on the brink of doing so again.

'How did your article go?' I said, directing the subject away from myself.

'I'm still working on it. I need to follow up on a few things, do some more research.'

'What kind of research?'

'Boring stuff. Look, I really was hoping I'd see you. I understand you're a graphic designer and I was wondering if you'd design me some decent business cards. I know they're crap but I saw your expression when I gave you one. I could really do with something more professional.'

I blushed, embarrassed that my thoughts had been so transparent. 'It's a bit difficult at the moment. I haven't got a computer. Well, I've probably got access to a computer but not the right software.' Relying on Gemma to get me to and from work meant I couldn't even stay on and use my work's Mac. Although I might be able to knock something up in the lunch break, I was reluctant to take it on. With more than enough to sort out, I didn't want to add to the list of tasks.

'I'll pay you of course.'

Did he think I was stalling because of money? Fair play that he wasn't expecting me to do it for nothing. The sooner I got some money up together the sooner I could afford to find a place of my own. Business card artwork wasn't going to provide much towards it though.

'Look, why don't I call you, maybe we could go for a drink and discuss it?' He sprang down from the worktop. 'When there's a match on if you like.' He grinned, then scooped up the plastic cheese and bread and tossed them into the bin.

I was angry. 'Now what am I going to eat?'

'Not that shit.'

'Well there isn't anything else.'

'That's still no reason to eat it.' He took out his mobile. 'I know a decent pizzeria. Not that rubbish we were eating,' he said making the call.

He turned his attention to the person on the phone, and from the way they were chatting it was obvious they knew each other well. He ordered a vegetarian pizza and even persuaded the person to bring a bottle of white wine. I considered the unnecessary expense and tried to make him stop but Scott waved away my protests. 'My treat. If you're offended by it take it off the cost of the business cards.'

I thought about what he'd said and acknowledged that he'd manoeuvred me into doing the design work for him after all.

'It'll be here in forty minutes,' he said, slipping the phone back into his pocket and leaving the room. His departure left me dazed, uncomfortable, yet grateful for the kindness too.

CHAPTER 18

It was late by the time they had all gone and I could finally begin to unwind. By then I was past sleep. Insomnia was becoming a habit.

Ollie slipped into bed beside me. 'Fancy a shag, babe?'

Sex might have helped me relax, but I didn't want him touching me. I was still angry. I thought he was going to try and coax me into it but instead he fell asleep, throwing an arm across me and pinning me to the bed.

In direct line of his beery breath, I inhaled stale air. His hair stank of smoke and the smell worried me. I couldn't shake off the idea that someone had failed to stub a cigarette out properly and the place was going to burst into flames. The thought niggled. The memory of the chain-smoking man was vivid. I had to be sure that every cigarette butt was extinguished before I could sleep. I tried to wriggle free but Ollie held me fast. Angrily, I threw his arm off.

The pizza Scott had ordered for me I'd eaten in the privacy of the bedroom, where I didn't have to share it. It was delicious. The box was still on the chest of drawers, and I caught a faint whiff of cheese as I passed. Moving slowly in the dark, I made my way out into the hall, putting my weight onto my heel instead of using the crutches. An empty beer can clattered against the skirting board. To avoid kicking another, I switched the light on, then wondered why I was bothering about being quiet when they hadn't shown me any consideration earlier.

In the lounge the smell of cigarettes hung thickly. The room was a war zone, no one had made any effort to clear up. A saucer, which had been used as an ashtray, brimmed with pale bent stubs. I scooped it up, emptied it into the sink, dousing the butts with water until they floated. The sodden ash left mucky trails on the stainless steel as the water drained away and cigarette ends clogged the plug hole.

There are usually black bin bags in a drawer in the kitchen. I vaguely thought about collecting up the empty cans, then decided not to. Why should I? Another saucer-ashtray was hidden at the foot of the sofa. I sloshed it down the sink, then got a cloth and wiped ash from the coffee table. That was as far as I was prepared to go. It was their mess, so let them clear it up.

The window rattled in its frame as I pulled it open and cold air blasted in to ventilate the room. The wind had risen, making a tarpaulin on the front of a house across the road slap viciously. Now the lounge curtain did the same. Deeply I inhaled the cold night air. The sky flickered white then returned to black. There was a storm coming. Switching the light off, I eased the flapping curtain back to watch. I should go back to bed, but I was wide-awake.

I retrieved the last of the wine from the bedroom then perched on the windowsill, drinking from the bottle. It had started to rain so I slid the window further down. Like globules of mercury, rain spotted the glass then meandered down the pane. I traced their inevitable path with my finger. What was I doing here?

It wasn't long before my thoughts settled on what had

been bothering me all evening. Ollie's attitude appalled me. He often showed off when he'd been drinking, and maybe I was more sensitive than usual, but he'd never been like that before. It was a side of him I didn't recognise and didn't like. Scott had a point.

Was this what our relationship had become? Had moving in with him made him complacent? Were there other aspects of his personality I hadn't seen before?

It reinforced my fear of living together. Better to know sooner rather than later, I supposed.

Were we together simply out of habit? Damn. Was tonight the beginning of the end? The sudden doubt made me sad. My thoughts moved on to Scott, who had been so considerate and kind, and to Mike who, rather than Ollie, had defended me. Getting up for work in the morning was going to be a struggle, but I had to clarify what I wanted. And whether that included Ollie.

The hypnotic force of the weather kept me glued to the window. The sky was an old black and white movie; flickering and heavy on contrast, one minute dark, the next bright. The storm seemed to echo my conflicting feelings. A sound startled me and I turned. The door of Darren's room was open. Naked, he wandered towards the bathroom. The streetlight, casting an amber gash across the carpet, hit his bare torso with pale light that made him ghostly. He was unaware of me.

'You were vile this evening,' I said loudly.

'Fuck!' He jumped, then span, trying to locate the source of the voice. My shadow was a large hunched shape on the wall near him, something sinister from a Hitchcock movie.

'You scared the shit out of me.'

'Good.' He gaped dozily at me although my face must have been in shadow.

'You might want to cover it,' I suggested. He was stupid with drink and his reactions were protracted. The sudden realisation that he was naked sent his hands launching towards his groin as he tried to hide himself. He moved forwards then sideways so that the sofa shielded him.

'Why do you hate me so much?' I asked.

'I don't hate you.' He moved again, this time trying to avoid the glow of the streetlight, but I wasn't going to let him get away with it and pushed the curtain aside so that the interrogating beam was wider.

'Well, you certainly do a good impression of someone who does.' A streak of lightning momentarily lit the room. The theatrics of the situation appealed to me. I couldn't help but toy with him: the cat and the mouse – no not a mouse, a rat. My turn. Thunder crashed overhead. When it had subsided, I said: 'What were you trying to do earlier, get the others to gang up on me? "I can't even fart without her being there," you said.'

He shifted.

'Well you needn't worry. I don't want to live with you any more than you want to live with me.'

He didn't say anything.

'I'm going to start looking for another flat tomorrow. So you can have your precious bachelor pad back.' I wasn't aware of having made the decision, it just came tumbling out but, having said it, I realised it was right - as long as I could afford it.

The splash of footsteps echoed in the wet street as someone hurried head down through the rain. Opposite, a tree shook violently as a sudden gust battered it.

When I looked back Darren had made his escape. I pulled my sweatshirt closer and rubbed my arms. The chill of sitting by the window was getting to me and soon I'd have to go back to bed simply to get warm.

Ollie prodded me in the ribs. He had been up for an hour, showered, dressed and eaten breakfast, seemingly unaffected by the indulgence of the previous night while I languished in bed, feeling dreadful.

'You're going to be late.'

'I don't care.' I pulled the pillow over my head. Ollie jerked the pillow aside and bent to kiss me. I turned away.

'You're in a right mood this morning.'

'What do you expect?'

'Have I done something?' He threw a tie around his neck and knotted it deftly.

I glared at him. 'You don't remember?'

The bed shifted as he got up. 'Oh God, did I fall asleep during sex?'

'No. You were an absolute bastard with your mates.'

'You know what we're like. We'd had a lot to drink.'

Was that all the apology I was going to get? Did he think his behaviour was justified? 'Well, that's all right then.'

Ollie glanced at his watch. 'We're going to have to talk about this later. I haven't got time now.'

'How do you know I'll be here?' He gave me a look, implying where else was I going to go. Bastard. Little did he know that I'd made my decision to move out.

'I've got to go. You should get up.'

As he left the room, I hurled a pillow at his retreating back. It fell short, landing on the floor at the end of the bed. I sank back, angrier than ever. Despite sitting up half the night thinking, my feelings about Ollie were still unclear. But I knew for certain that we couldn't continue living together like this. On a number of levels it just wasn't working.

My head banged. I shouldn't have drunk so much. I shouldn't have stayed up. I lay there reeling, and then caught sight of the clock. There were less than fifteen minutes to get ready. Wishing I'd got up sooner, I dragged myself towards the bathroom, every movement sending a wave of pain into my skull.

Someone had made a start clearing up but hadn't got very far. The empty pizza boxes and beer cans had moved from lounge to kitchen but hadn't made it to the bin. I took a couple of Paracetamols from the cupboard, poured a glass of water, gulped them down.

The bathroom mirror was milky with steam. Hollow eyes stared out of the mist. I looked as bad as I felt. Dark circles ringed my eyes and my hair needed washing. Only there wasn't time. No, there would have to be time, if I didn't freshen up properly I'd feel crap all day. Hastily I showered then scraped my wet hair back in a ponytail. It would have to do. Dressing in the first things I could find, I dumped eyeliner and mascara into my bag. There wasn't time for breakfast, as somewhere in the street below a horn blared.

'Damn.' From the window I saw that Gemma was waiting, though not for long. Another car came down the road behind her and she was forced to go around the block. It bought me some time. As quickly as my hangover and mobility allowed, I descended the stairs. Before I had reached the bottom the sound of the horn blasted again.

'I'm coming,' I tried to force the front door open over the cascade of post. Bending to push it out of the way, I noticed that the uppermost envelope was addressed to me. I pocketed it and hurried to join Gemma, ignoring the protests of the vehicle we were holding up.

'God, you look knackered,' Gemma said as I opened the car door and clambered in.

'I had a bit too much to drink last night. And I was watching the storm.'

'What storm?' She took my crutches, which I was struggling to find a home for, and, narrowly missing my head, tossed them into the back of the car.

'You must have heard it. It started around two o'clock.'

'I sleep like the dead. In fact, I'm worried this kid'll die of starvation if it tries to get my attention at night.'

'Don't they say you become attuned to your own baby's cry?' I suggested helpfully.

'Maybe. I think I'll just let Mum or my sister do the night shift. They're so keen to take control.' The bitterness in her voice didn't necessitate a response. It was safe to assume that she'd had another row with her family. She cut down several unfamiliar side streets until we emerged onto one of the main roads.

'We're going to be late, but I need to get some petrol,' she said, 'I've been driving on fumes for days. Did you see what Nick's done with that logo you designed?'

I stifled a yawn. 'What do you mean?'

'It's a long way from what you did.'

'Maybe Guy'll give it back to me then. Between you and me, he said yesterday he thought I'd make a better job of it than Nick. Not that I feel creative at the moment. I think I'd welcome some brain dead artwork today.'

'If it's up to Nick, that's what you'll get.'

The garage was busy but a pump near the kiosk was free. Gemma chicaned between other cars to get to it and I flinched, fearing we were about to hit something.

'You do look rough. Why didn't you pull a sickie?' she said, cutting the engine.

'What, after one day back? Anyway I've got to get away from that flat.'

While she was filling the car, I retrieved my make-up and tried to make myself more presentable. A motorcyclist was watching me and it made me self-conscious.

It took Gemma ages to fill the car with fuel. We were going to be very late but I didn't care. I dropped my head back against the headrest and thrust my hands deep into my pockets to warm them. Stiff paper contacted my fingertips, and I dug out the envelope I'd hastily shoved there.

Ripping the flap open with my forefinger, I pulled out what at first appeared to be a greeting card. Orange flames filled the front of the card. Superimposed over it was an image of my flat in Lee-on-the-Solent, boarded up as I'd last seen it. It was horrible, but the inside was worse. Stark words leapt out at me: 'YOU should have died in the fire!' Was I the target after all? Did someone want me dead? Who? A cold feeling swept over me and I swallowed bile, thinking any minute I was going to be sick.

Rapidly blinking, I tried to dispel the image on the card. I squeezed my eyes shut until it hurt. When I opened them again, nothing had changed.

Who would do something like this? My left temple throbbed and my hands were shaking. I tried to rationalise what I was seeing - but couldn't. With our conversation about Nick fresh in my mind, I wondered if this was his handiwork. But why? To scare me away from work so he could take over the job? That was ridiculous. Wasn't it? If it wasn't Nick, then who? You didn't need to be a designer or even an expert with Photoshop to create something like that image.

The driver's door opened and I screamed. Gemma yelped and clasped her chest, dropping whatever she had been carrying.

'What? What's the matter?'

'Sorry. I...' I was breathless.

'You look like you're having a bad trip.' Gemma bent to retrieve her shopping. She threw a number of chocolate bars into my lap before squeezing back in behind the wheel.

'Look at this.' I handed her the card. 'It was on the mat this morning.'

'That's evil. Who do you think sent it?'

'I don't know. I wish I did. I'm a bit freaked.' I searched the envelope for some clue, but there was nothing, just a typed label on the front.

Gemma started the engine and headed out towards the dual carriageway. 'Did you say that was in the post? Only there's no stamp on it. Oh shit. Look at the time. Guy's going give us hell. Well, me anyway.' She was driving fast and wasn't paying attention to the road. 'Bollocks!' she yelled, slamming on the brakes as we approached the static camera. 'Did it flash? God, I can't afford any more points on my licence.'

The car lurched violently as she floored the accelerator immediately we were past.

'You haven't upset anyone have you?' she said.

'Well...' Darren sprang to mind. 'There is one of Ollie's flatmates, but I'd have thought this was beyond it even for him.'

'Are you sure?'

'No. He could easily have left it on the mat on his way out this morning. But I doubt he'd have had the opportunity. He does like technology so he could well have the software to do it.' I breathed deeply, trying to force down the fear that was engulfing me. 'I think I should speak to the police. After all it's not the first thing I've received.'

'Do you want to go to the police station now?' There was an eager note to Gemma's voice at the anticipation of getting off work. I thought about it for a moment, but didn't think I could cope with a police interview. And I needed to take copies of the emails and get my thoughts in order so I didn't sound hysterical.

'No, I'll give them a call later, once this hangover's gone. I've got a number for the detective somewhere,' I said, delving into my bag to check I still had the business card. I glanced up as we swung out into the heavy traffic of the M27, slipping in dangerously between two trucks. I shut my eyes. If Gemma didn't kill us first.

CHAPTER 19

As we were late, and some of the bays had become flooded by the overnight rain, the car park was more restricted than usual. Gemma drove around looking for somewhere to park.

'Do you think we'd get away with using one of the visitor spaces?' she said.

'I don't know. You know how stroppy they are about that.' I didn't care, my mind was still on the card, which was burning a hole in my bag, as if the fire depicted on the paper radiated heat. It was making me sweat.

'Yeah, but everything else is flooded. I'm not talking about the ones up by the office. Oh, sod it, I'm going to risk it and park here. After all, you're on crutches and I'm pregnant. There have got to be some perks to our conditions.'

We made our way up the slope towards the office complex, walking at the side of the road in the absence of a pavement. I turned at the roar of a large vehicle and saw a black Range Rover bearing down on us. It showed no sign of slowing.

I shoved Gemma onto the verge. The grass was

slippery and my foot slid out from under me, forcing me to put weight on the fractured foot. Pain seared through me. I sucked in air.

'Prick!' yelled Gemma, shaking a fist at the retreating vehicle. 'That was close.'

Leaning heavily on the crutches, I breathed deeply and waited for the pain and feeling of sickness to subside.

'You okay?'

'Yeah. You?' I asked. A gull screeched overhead, making me jump. I was skittish. 'I don't think he even saw us. Did you recognise him?'

'No. What a pig. I'm bloody soaked.'

'Me too.' My trousers were muddy and clung unpleasantly to my legs. When I didn't have many clothes, knowing that my one pair of decent trousers would now need washing and drying overnight made me angry. Was everyone against me at the moment? Sod being treated like this. The Range Rover driver was an ignorant pig, but whoever was sending me stuff was malicious. Well, they were going to answer for it. I wouldn't allow them to make me feel like this.

When we got to the office, the Range Rover was squeezed into one of the three visitor bays immediately in front of the entrance and we were forced to manoeuvre by it sideways, which was not easy for either of us.

'Why is it nearly everyone that drives one of these things is an arsehole? Makes you want to get your own back doesn't it?' snapped Gemma. 'Put a deep gouge down the side of his nice shiny paintwork.'

'You wouldn't?'

She shrugged. 'I'd like to,' she said, knocking his wing mirror as we edged past.

It was warm in the office and the sudden heat made me aware of how damp it was outside. Heading straight for my desk, I delved into my bag, dragging out stuff and depositing it in a heap. A lip salve rolled across the table and clattered into the bin. The zipped pocket at the back of the rucksack was where I found DI Green's business card. I stared at it for a moment.

The idea of being the focus of unwanted attention was horrible and made my stomach churn. Whoever it was must really hate me to do something like this. That realisation brought with it a whole new level of fear – if someone hated you what were they capable of?

I picked up the phone and began dialling. Whoever it was had already spent considerable time setting things up. What were they going to do next?

'There you are. Is that useless bint with you?' Nick's voice jerked me out of my concentration and instinctively I banged the phone down, hiding the business card in my palm.

'Guy wants us in a meeting. It's a new client,' said Nick.

'I need to make a call first.' Clicking the spacebar I woke my computer.

'It'll have to wait. Don't look like that. You're late. If you'd got here earlier you could have done it. And made a coffee and touched up your make up.'

'Fuck off.' I began to gather up the spilled contents of my bag. 'I'll be in in a minute,' I said, dialling the police station again.

'No. Now. The client's already here. Where the hell's Gemma?'

'The loos I expect.' I followed Nick's gaze to the arrogant-looking man sitting in Guy's office. He was the driver of the Range Rover. 'Oh great. Is that him?' The telephone connected. I put my hand over the mouthpiece. 'This is private.'

'Hurry up,' Nick hissed. He seemed to see me for the first time. 'You'd better tidy yourself up a bit and all.'

'Hello?' said the voice in my earpiece.

Irritated, I waved Nick away. The client could damned well wait.

'Hello...yes...' I stalled as I waited for Nick to move

out of earshot. 'Can I speak to Detective Inspector Green please?' Suddenly I wondered if I was being rash calling the police. After all, there was no actual threat. But there was an implied one. And it was creepy. It had to stop.

'DI Green's not here at the moment,' the voice on the phone said. 'Can someone else help?'

'It's about the fire at Lee on Solent.'

'One moment.'

I turned my attention to the computer where an unusually large number of emails filled my inbox. Scrolling down the screen, I noticed that a lot were e-newsletters from companies selling fire equipment, fire stations and other fire related stuff. I exhaled slowly, fighting back the fear constricting my throat. My heart was racing. How long had it taken to sign me up to all of these? And what the hell could I expect next?

'DS Smith. How can I help?' a man said.

How was the best way of saying what had happened so that I didn't sound pathetic or neurotic? I introduced myself and briefly explained the circumstances. The officer listened without comment.

'Can you come in to the station?' he said, once I'd finished.

'Not easily. I'm at work, but also on crutches. I can't drive at the moment.'

'Can you get someone to bring you in?'

I thought about asking Gemma but I couldn't expect her to ferry me around all over the place. I wouldn't ask Ollie.

'There isn't anyone.'

'Ah. Hang on.' From the muffled speech, it sounded as if the policeman was talking to someone else in his office. 'Can you gather together any things you've been sent? Someone will pop in to see you. Will you be at work all day? What's the address?'

As I came off the phone afterwards, I felt relieved.

He hadn't exactly been sympathetic but it was as if a weight had lifted, knowing the police knew about it. Then I remembered that there were several recent cases where women had been murdered by their stalker. And the police had been no use at all. I determined not to dwell on that or I'd scare myself stupid.

Across the office Guy was looking irritable. With a flick of his hand he beckoned me and I knew I had to clear my head and get into the meeting.

At that moment Gemma reappeared, so we entered Guy's office together, both looking grubby although Gemma with her short hair didn't look quite so dishevelled. Guy's eyes travelled over me, making me feel that I might as well have been naked. I tried to imagine him in the same compromised position, but it wasn't a pleasant image and did little to ease my discomfort.

'Sorry about the state of us,' Gemma said. 'Some idiot in a Range Rover ran us off the road as we were walking up from the car park.'

The visitor looked blank. It was just as well he hadn't understood; it wasn't the best way of starting a working relationship. Gemma gave him a look that said: 'Yeah, YOU dickhead.' But he didn't notice. He was watching me as I made my way around the table. His gaze reinforced my worries about being stalked. I sat down.

'Right, let's get started,' said Guy who had clearly understood Gemma's comment and didn't want to risk her making further trouble.

Preoccupied, I struggled to concentrate during the meeting and hoped that I wasn't going to be asked to contribute. I needn't have worried, Nick, as always, took over.

Some time later, when we were discussing the finer detail of the project, there was a tentative knock on the door.

'I'm really sorry to interrupt but there's somebody

who needs to see Zoë urgently.' It was a bit cryptic and the receptionist looked nervous at having to disrupt us. Guy shot me an angry glare. I knew what he was thinking – first you were late, now this. With a mumbled apology I got up.

'There are two police officers here to see you,' the receptionist whispered once the door was closed.

'Can you tell them I'll be there in a minute? I need to get something.'

Hot, and flushed with embarrassment, I wondered whether, in hindsight, it would have been better to have made my way to the police station rather than do this in front of my colleagues. I grabbed a plastic sleeve, put the card inside, then printed out several of the e-newsletters and a couple of screen grabs.

DI Green and her colleague, DC Banstead, were studying the marketing material displayed on the walls of the small reception area when I entered.

'Hello Zoë,' said DI Green with a smile. 'Is there somewhere more private we can talk?'

'The large meeting room's free,' the receptionist offered.

I led the two police officers into the room, which although unoccupied, was cluttered with the large cartridges that hold exhibition panels. It explained why we had held our client meeting in Guy's office. Through the glass walls I could see Guy watching and hoped he wasn't going to give me hell later.

'Can you run through what's happened for me?' said DI Green.

I sat down, pushing a couple of note pads towards the middle of the table, out of the way.

'I've been getting odd things sent to me.' I pointed at the card, which was uppermost in the plastic sleeve. DI Green drew some latex gloves from her pocket, pulled them on, and sifted through the evidence.

'Today I got that. And the other day there was a

sympathy card. Only it wasn't just an ordinary sympathy card, it had been burnt all around the edges.'

'Did it say who it was from?'

'No. It was blank inside. Also on Sunday there was a bouquet of flowers propped against the front door. Well, I say bouquet, it looked more like a funeral wreath. It had my name on. But I couldn't carry it up to the flat and when my boyfriend went down for it a few minutes later it had gone.'

DI Green frowned. 'Do you still have the burnt card? It isn't here.'

'It's at my boyfriend's flat. I wondered if it was a sick joke, but now I think there might be more to it. I came to the conclusion that maybe the flowers had been for someone else in the block but when I came back to work there was an email asking if I liked them. I've no idea who it was from. I've had other emails too. In fact, today my inbox is full of junk mail. I've printed some of them out. It's as if someone's subscribed me to lots of e-newsletters. I haven't opened many, but quite a lot seem to be fire related. Presumably there are others that were caught by the spam filter.' My voice had croaked and I swallowed hard. Said like that, it didn't sound much or very threatening, and I wondered what they would make of it.

'When did this start?' asked DI Green.

'At the weekend. I know it's only a couple of days, but it's the nature of the stuff. It's not exactly threatening but it's horrible. That card's the worst. It says I should have died in the fire.'

DI Green lifted the front of the card with her fingertip.

'Do you feel threatened by it?'

There was no point in pretending otherwise. 'How else should I feel? My house burnt down. The man who lived downstairs died. Someone knows where I'm living and has found out my work email.'

DC Banstead was writing in his notebook. He looked

up. 'What about personal email accounts? Have you had anything sent there?' he said.

'I haven't looked.'

'Can you access your personal account from here?' asked DI Green.

'I can log in via the website. Do you want me to go and check?'

'I think you should.'

The inbox of my personal account didn't seem to be clogged with the same quantity of rubbish. 'No. That's okay,' I said coming back into the meeting room.

DI Green nodded. 'Work emails are easy to guess at. It's not so easy to find out personal email addresses.' She started gathering up the contents of the plastic sleeve and putting them back in. 'I don't know what this is about. But at this stage there's no other evidence to suggest you were the target of the arson attack.'

'What does that mean? Is that supposed to make me feel better? Because it doesn't.' I didn't know how to feel. 'This isn't normal.' I argued.

DI Green agreed. 'No. it's not. All I'm saying is that at the moment it's circumstantial. There's no evidence to suggest that whoever started the fire was, and is, targeting you. However, I can assure you we are taking this seriously and we will look into it. We may be able to trace the user's IP address. It depends how clever he is.'

'He?'

'Figure of speech. Nothing more,' DC Banstead said.

DI Green took over again. 'I know we asked you this before, but can you think of anyone who might have a grudge against you? It may be worth thinking about it again. Can I also suggest you compile a list of everyone you know, socially and through work. Even if you don't know their name.'

I must have looked doubtful.

'Statistically most incidents like this don't come

to anything,' said DC Banstead. 'The person doing the stalking usually gets bored when they realise it's not achieving anything.'

I thought about the women who were murdered by their stalkers. Statistically, they were still dead.

'So, do you think it's someone I know?' I asked, as my brain started scanning for possibilities.

DC Banstead shook his head. 'Not necessarily.'

'But more than likely,' DI Green said quickly.

I wasn't sure which was worse - the idea of it being a faceless stranger or someone I knew. At least if I found out who it was, I could try to avoid him.

'I know it's easy for me to say, but try not to worry.' DI Green stood up, drawing the conversation to a close. She handed me a small reference card. 'Those are numbers for victim support if you need to talk. But if anything else happens, or you get anything sent to you, don't hesitate to give me a call.'

I saw them out then stared at the reference card she had given me, unwilling to accept that I was in any way a victim.

CHAPTER 20

The meeting in Guy's office looked to be drawing to a close, which meant, thankfully, I didn't have to go back in. I sat at my desk, toying with the small card the police had given me, and thinking over what they had said. I was not a victim. And I refused to behave like one. I stopped rolling the card around in my hands and looked at it properly. Perhaps later it was worth visiting one or two of the websites listed; there might be better advice than the detectives were giving.

As I bent to pull my rucksack from under my desk, a light-headed feeling swept over me. It was now late morning and I hadn't had anything to eat. Or even drink. I put the card in the pocket of my rucksack, then shoved it back under the desk. It was too early to pop across to the Courtyard Café, but I needed to raise my sugar levels fast. And Gemma had chocolate.

There was no evidence of it on her desk, however. I searched her drawers but found none, and when I looked in the bin I saw why. The greedy cow had eaten it all.

'What have you lost?' Gemma startled me and I nearly fell over.

'You made me jump.'

'That's your guilty conscience. What are you snooping for?'

'I was hoping to beg some of your chocolate. I'm feeling a bit wobbly.'

Gemma looked shifty. 'Ah.'

'Ah,' I repeated and held up the bin. 'I can see you've pigged out. Have you really eaten all that? When?'

'When I popped out of the meeting.'

'I thought you needed the loo.' I reached out to the desk to keep upright as I lowered the bin back to the floor.

Gemma laughed. 'My bladder's not that bad. I went just before the meeting. Sorry. I would have saved you some if I'd known.'

'Hmm. You did say you were going to share. I thought you meant with me not the bump. You do realise that babies can be born obese.'

'No they can't. That's ridiculous. Hang on...' She poked around her desk and located something small and flat. 'Hobnob? '

'Is that the best you can offer?' The biscuit was crumbly and barely covered in the remnants of packaging. It didn't look very appealing, but I was desperate.

Gemma pulled an apologetic face.

'I'll make you a sugary coffee in a minute. But first we're wanted in Guy's office. I think we're about to get a telling off.'

'I was half expecting it. He gave me a filthy look when I was called out of the meeting.' I took a large bite of the biscuit so that it didn't fall to pieces in my hands. It tasted stale and dusty so I swallowed it quickly.

'Were they cops you were talking to?'

'Yes.'

'He can hardly blame you for that.'

'No, but he probably will,' I said, pushing a wedge of gooey biscuit from my back teeth.

'I bet I'm going to get my ears bent for complaining about being soaked by that wanker.'

'You were a bit gobby.'

'Something needed to be said. I wonder how much he earns a year? Wish I could get a job like that. I wouldn't mind swanning round in a fancy car organising design stuff.'

'There are a number of problems with that, mainly that you're not in the least bit organised. Suppose we'd better get in there,' I said, tossing the biscuit wrapper in the bin and standing unsteadily. Gemma groaned.

The door to Guy's office was open but the room was empty. 'Good he's not here. Let's get a drink.' said Gemma.

'Don't go anywhere,' snapped Guy, appearing from the direction of the toilets. 'Close the door.'

I slumped down in the nearest seat even though I hadn't been invited to do so.

'Well,' said Guy. He stood behind his chair and leaned on the back of it. 'I have to say I'm not impressed with either of you. That was an important new client. We've been courting them for months and the minute we get an opportunity of some work you two make us look as if we're not interested.' His voice had raised and he gesticulated wildly. 'You let me down big time. It was disgraceful. How dare you make snide comments at the client. Yes, I understood it, Gemma. Fortunately, I don't think he did.'

'No. I don't suppose he did. We were invisible to him, chauvinistic pig.'

'Don't interrupt me. I'm not interested in your excuses. It's your professionalism inside the office we're discussing.'

'Well, if that idiot hadn't run us down I'd have been a lot more professional towards him. Look at the state of us. He ran us off the road.'

'It's idiots like that who pay your wages. You might want to remember that,' said Guy.

Gemma's jaw clenched but for once she didn't respond.

Guy steepled his hands, as was his habit. He exhaled loudly.

'If you ever do anything like that again there will be consequences.' He turned to me 'What was that all about this morning, Zoë? Why did you leave the meeting?'

I felt as angry as Gemma and could feel the heat of a blush in my cheeks.

'The police wanted to see me. I'm sorry it interrupted the meeting, but I can't be held responsible for the police's timetable.'

'Are you expecting any more impromptu meetings?'

Did he think I could see into the future? 'I can't anticipate what the police are going to do.'

Guy couldn't really argue with that and he clearly didn't like it. His face contorted, the small muscles around his mouth and eyes twitching in a sequence of expressions. He couldn't bear not having the last word.

'Hmm. Well, I'm sure there are things you've got to get on with. But the pair of you need to up your game.'

Dismissed, we went back to our desks, Gemma cursing and complaining en route. She collected up the mugs. 'What did the police say?'

'Sshh. They've taken the card away and say they're taking it seriously.'

'Why don't you want anyone to know? It's hardly going to be any of this lot, is it?' She waved her hand, vaguely indicating the rest of the room.

'Why not? I don't know who sent it, do I? For all I know it could have been someone here.'

Scanning the office, or at least the people that were visible, I noticed that Gemma was doing the same. Had she said something to someone, blabbed about my situation? But I didn't think it was anyone at work. For a start it seemed unlikely that they would know where I was staying. Someone could easily have followed us home yesterday but the timings didn't fit with that: the flowers had arrived on Sunday and I hadn't been back to work then.

'As far as this lot are concerned the police were here about the fire. They don't need to know anything else,' I said.

'Sure if that's what you want. I won't tell. Coffee?'

I hoped she wouldn't say anything. 'Can I have tea? I don't really fancy coffee at the moment.'

Instead of settling down to work I decided to see if there was any information online about how to cope with stalking. Using the addresses on the card the DI had given me, I started a quick search. Within a few moments it became clear that the general advice seemed to be don't ignore it. If you did something early you stood a chance of stopping it but you shouldn't try to talk to the stalker about it, even to tell them to leave you alone. It wasn't very helpful and it was all very well if you knew who was stalking you. I didn't.

Having promised Darren I would start looking for a flat, I thought I'd better do so or I'd be accused of reneging. I trawled through a few estate agent web sites but all of the flats were out of my price range.

'The newsletter you were working on is approved.' Nick had come to stand behind me, making me feel I should make excuses for what I was doing.

'What, no changes?'

'No. But they've decided to get it printed. They've realised it'll have a lot more impact than an email. And they want it for next Tuesday.'

'What's the matter with these people? I'm going to have to redo it. I don't know if the images are even good enough. I'd better ring the printer and see if it's even possible.'

He nodded to the screen. 'You looking for somewhere to live?'

'Do you know anywhere?'

'No. But I can ask around.'

'I was just having a quick look. They're all so expensive. I'll need to find a new flatmate first.'

'I thought you had one. Have you tried that place in

North End? If you register with them they'll match you up with a flatmate.'

It went through my head that I could end up with some weirdo that way. But what choice did I have. 'What are they called?'

'I can't remember. I'll know it when I see it.' He leaned over me and scrolled down the page of estate agents. Finally he clicked on a link. 'This is it.'

I watched him. Was he trying to steer me into using them for some reason? I was really beginning to question everything. I didn't know who I could trust. 'Thank you,' I muttered.

'No problem.' Nick sat down in Gemma's vacant chair and viewed her cuddly-toy-cluttered desk with a look of disgust. 'Where's the newsletter artwork saved? I'll have a look at it if you like.'

I stared at him. Why was he being nice to me?

It was late afternoon, and I didn't want to go back to Ollie's flat. I had to find somewhere else to go. Despite being preoccupied with everything that had happened during the day, I hadn't forgotten what Ollie had done. And I hadn't forgiven him either. I didn't want to see him.

The fire had happened a week ago and I'd made little progress getting straight. In fact, with every day that passed, my situation got worse. Claire was lucky that she had parents to look after her. Why couldn't I have had a family? I didn't have anyone close and it made me feel lonely. I thought about my stepfather. If there was nowhere else, I suppose I'd have to stay with him.

I needed somewhere to go this evening though, and a diversion. But what? Suddenly it came to me. I didn't know Jess' number, but I brought up her email address.

<Hi Jess. How was the concert? Feels like ages since we got together and we haven't had a chance to celebrate your news yet. I was wondering if you fancied doing something this

evening. Going through a few wedding magazines maybe? I know it's short notice but it'd be great to get together. Zoe. p.s. Can you email me your number. Don't have my mobile> It wasn't strictly true as I did have my mobile, it just wasn't usable.

Almost immediately a reply popped into my inbox. Jess is one of those people that use text speak for everything.

<Hi Zoe. concert fab. L8nite tho. Knckd. B gd 2 cu>

<That's great. Can I stay over?> I typed. I'd have to go back to Ollie's flat for a change of clothes. I dreaded having to encounter him. It had been an awful day and I just wanted to run away from it all without more grief. <Can you pick me up? I can't drive at the moment>

<Why?>

<Long story. Can you pick me up from Ollie's?>

It was nearly ten minutes before her email response came through. <Wot time?>

I emailed her back immediately. <Can we make it early? 6.30?>

<No probs. cu L8r>

Afterwards I realised I hadn't really thought it through. I'd solved the problem of where to go tonight but had caused myself other problems: I wouldn't be able to have a lift into work in the morning, I'd have to use a taxi again, and that meant getting cash from somewhere tonight. How much longer would everything be so complicated? If I could drive life would be a whole lot simpler.

There was a raw feeling in the pit of my stomach as I approached Ollie's flat. As I opened the front door, subdued classical music and the scent of cooking met me. My heart sank. It meant Ollie was home. Only he would play that sort of music. The lights were dimmed, and the contrast to the previous evening was marked. Just then Ollie emerged from the kitchen.

'Hi, babe. You're later than I expected. Had a good day?'

I glared at him incredulously. Still no apology then? I considered telling him about my day and the visit from the police just to make him feel bad.

'What do you care?' I snapped instead.

'What's that supposed to mean?'

I headed straight for the bedroom to change, pulled clothes from the drawer, laid them on the bed as I considered what I needed for work and what to wear. I spotted a plastic bag over the back of his drawing board and snatched it up. Inside were a couple of files, which I emptied onto the bed. Then I began stuffing my clothes in.

'You're leaving? But you haven't given me a chance to apologise.'

I stared at him. He thought I was walking out for good! Where did he think I was going? 'I didn't think you thought there was anything to apologise for.' My voice was harsh with anger.

'Of course I realised.' Ollie dropped heavily onto the bed. He grabbed my hands to stop me packing. 'I had things on my mind this morning. A really important budget meeting. It's no excuse for being insensitive, but…'

'How dare you! Insensitive? You were an arsehole last night. If you hadn't got so pissed it might have helped.'

'I know that. It was bloody stupid getting drunk. That's why I was so edgy this morning. I knew it was going to be a tough meeting and I wasn't on top form.' He pulled me down to sit beside him on the bed. 'I really am sorry, I was a shit. I honestly don't remember, but it was unforgivable. I promise it'll never happen again.'

Even though he looked genuinely sorry, it was more of an excuse than an apology. He hadn't got a clue. I spoke slowly. 'Do you know what day it is?'

'Thursday.' His voice was low, little more than a murmur. I thought that was all he was going to say but then he added: 'It's a week since the fire.' He came forward and eased my coat off. 'I wasn't sure you'd want me to make anything of it.'

I stared at the bag I'd been filling. I didn't have much stuff, but it wasn't big enough. Looking at it made me feel like a refugee, totally dependant on other people's kindness. A bag lady. Could this be the end for Ollie and me? Our eyes locked. He looked upset. If I walked out, what then?

'Stay. Please. I've run you a bath. And dinner's on the go. I wanted to pamper you. Show you how special you are.'

That was all very well, but with Mike and Darren around it wouldn't feel that way. 'Where are the others?'

'They're under strict instructions to keep out.' He pushed his arms through my elbows and held me awkwardly to him. I stood there stiffly, feeling torn.

'Did you say you've run a bath?' I went to look, Ollie following like a puppy at my heels.

A warm pocket of steam hung just below the bathroom ceiling, heavy with floral scents.

'Bath oil?'

'I nipped out at lunchtime and got it. I think it's the one you like.'

'You don't work anywhere near the shops.'

He didn't answer.

The mirror had changed to frosted glass and showed only my faint silhouette as I moved in front of it. Perching on the edge of the bath, I bent to feel the water, which was scalding. 'You can be nice to me all you want now. But I'm not going to be treated like that.'

'I know. I promise it won't happen again.'

He looked genuinely sorry but I couldn't forgive him that easily. I wanted to. But I couldn't. 'I'd better phone Jess and tell her I'm not coming over,' I said.

'Sorry. I didn't realise you had plans. I'll call her for you.'

I shut the bathroom door and leaned against it. What was I doing? The bath looked appealing albeit difficult to get in and out of. Time in the bath would give me an opportunity to think. Had Ollie cleaned it before filling it? A couple of tea lights had been placed at one end, one glowing more brightly than the other. I shuddered and blew them out.

I let the cold water run as I undressed, then tentatively stuck a foot in and waited for it to acclimatise to the heat. I got in, my legs pinking to a severe line. It took some time before I could sit down, and I hung half in and half out of the water for a while, my arms taking my weight. By the time I was fully in the bath, it was almost overflowing and a thick blanket of foam slid over the side.

As I lay down I could hear the trickle of water in the overflow pipe. I cleared a path in the bubbles and sank deeper, feeling the heat on my shoulders, then neck, then ears and finally the top of my head. I lay motionless for some time while my brain did acrobatics. In the last week everything had turned upside down, swivelled sideways, twisted and turned again. It was as if my identity had been erased. Nothing of my old life remained. Was it shock or being displaced that was making me so unsure of myself? The water against my skin burned. Was it better to drown than burn?

I thought again about leaving. It entailed so much. Would moving around be better or worse for someone who is being stalked? Are you more or less vulnerable? It would mean the stalker had to keep a constant watch on you to keep up, and then surely there was more chance of them being caught. You could slip out in the middle of the night and they wouldn't know you had gone. That idea wouldn't work if you still had to go to your job each day though. And besides, why should anyone keep moving around? That's essentially running away.

I wondered about the situation here at the flat. Was I safer in a crowd? Or was it one of them? Was I actually at physical risk? The police didn't seem to think so. Or were they trying not to frighten me? So many questions, and I didn't have the answers to any of them.

And laying there thinking was just making me anxious. Even in the bath I felt vulnerable. I washed my hair and got out.

'You weren't in there long,' said Ollie as, clad in a towel, I went to get dressed.

'Too much on my mind. It wasn't relaxing. I'm going to get some clothes on.'

'Hang on. I've got you a present.' Ollie handed me a small ring-sized jewellery box and panic swept over me. He wasn't going to propose again, was he?

'What's up? Oh no. It's not that.' He scooped the box from my hands and opened it, presenting it back to me. My eyes locked onto a pair of stud earrings. 'They're real diamonds. It's a bit frivolous I know, considering you need to replace so much but I wanted to give you something special.'

I swallowed. He expected me to say something and I didn't know what to say. I had been holding my breath. Now I gasped for air.

'I can always take them back if you don't like them.'

'No. They're lovely.'

Ollie laughed mischievously and tried to slip a hand inside the towel. 'What did you think it was?' he teased.

I shifted out of his grasp. I didn't want him touching me. He knew exactly what had gone through my head.

'I don't know what to think any more. My head feels about to explode.'

'I'm not surprised. You've had a lot to deal with. After we've eaten I'll give you a massage.' What would he say about the stalking? I wasn't sure I was going to tell him about it. I was already being treated abnormally. His response would be to smother me. Or to think I was losing the plot. I didn't want to have to deal with either reaction. At the moment I just needed normality and stability.

Tenderly he touched my face. 'Let me take care of you.'

CHAPTER 21

Nearly every Friday night a group of us meet in a lively bar on the corner of Albert Road. It started years ago with those of us who went to college together: Jess, Paul, Mike, Ollie and various others. Since then the group has morphed, some leaving, others arriving, partners changing. Sometimes, afterwards, we go on to a club and really party.

I was looking forward to a night out. The day had been uneventful, so I was less freaked. I had began to wonder if involving the police had scared the stalker off. That seemed to imply that it might be someone at work after all. I shook the thought away, unwilling to think about any of it tonight.

We were late and by the time we arrived the bar was heaving. We stood just inside the entrance, trying to locate our group. 'Looks like they're right at the back,' said Ollie.

About as far from the exit as it was possible to get, I thought, struggling with the urge to abandon the idea and retreat. Outside, a couple of shivering girls had been leaning against the wall, smoking. If a fire started there would be a stampede. I looked up at the ceiling, checking that there were sprinklers installed. Strange, I'd been coming here for years and it had never occurred to me to look before.

Ollie saw my hesitation. 'You okay?'

'It's very crowded.'

'Should be a good atmosphere then.' Was he being positive? Or obtuse? The bar hummed with conversation, and only the thumping beat of the music could be heard.

'It's not going to be easy getting in there on these,' I said, indicating the crutches. I was glad I'd had the sense to put the plastic boot on again tonight, it would protect my foot.

'I'll clear a path.' He started threading his way through the crowd. I braced myself to move further into the room, but my hesitation was a moment too long, and the gap behind him began to close. Forcing my way through the swarm between the bar and booths wasn't easy. I was jostled like a skittle. Ollie looked around and, realising I wasn't in his wake, headed back for me.

'I thought you were behind me.'

'You're moving too fast.'

'Sorry.'

Jess was standing on the seat, waving at us. Everyone seemed so happy to see me. It was lovely to be amongst friends and back to our usual routine. Even though I'd only missed one week, it felt like ages since we'd been together. I was calmer now, and once I'd had a drink, or three, I was sure I'd be okay.

Jess leaned across the table towards me, making it awkward for Alex because she was talking across him. 'You look nice.'

'Thanks.' I was wearing the sparkly top Ollie had bought me, and I looked okay considering it was only cheap.

'So what happened to you last night?' asked Jess.

'Sorry. I had to sort something out.' I glanced around the table, wondering how much they could hear. I didn't want them all knowing Ollie and I were having problems.

'That's very cryptic. Hang on. Alex, can I swap places

with you?' She stood up and clambered across the booth to get to me, apologising as she jostled against him.

'We had a row,' I murmured. 'Ollie was trying to make it up to me.'

She grinned. 'Say no more.'

'It's not always about sex, you know.'

'Isn't it? Anyway what did he do?'

'Don't ask.'

Suddenly she turned serious. 'Why didn't you tell me about the fire?'

You were too preoccupied with your wedding plans, I thought, but didn't say it. I didn't want to hurt her feelings. 'There wasn't really an opportunity,' I said instead.

'Did I go on about the wedding? I did, didn't I?'

'No.' From the look Jess gave me I could tell she knew I was lying. 'A bit,' I admitted.

'You should have told me to shut up.'

Easing out of my coat, I balled it so that I could slip it behind my back.

'You were happy. I didn't want to spoil it.'

'It doesn't make me much of a mate though, does it?'

'It's fine. Just because things are up in the air for me at the moment doesn't mean it has to affect everyone else.' That was an understatement if ever I'd heard one. The fire wasn't the only thing I hadn't told her about.

I looked around for somewhere to put my crutches where they wouldn't be in the way, or stolen.

'Give them here,' said Mike. 'I'll put them over the back by the window.'

'Thanks.' I stared past the reflections in the glass to the street beyond. At least having a window made it feel a little less claustrophobic, even if the window didn't open.

'Oh God.' Recognition sent a shiver running through me. The man who had been at the flat looking for Neil Wyatt was standing in the road with his arm around a petite woman with long dyed blonde hair and heavy make up.

There was another couple with them and they just seemed to be standing there.

I motioned to Ollie until he bent to listen. 'The man who came to my flat is outside. The one the police want to talk to.'

'Where?'

I pointed. 'There. Short greying hair, brown leather jacket.'

'What's up?' said Mike.

Ollie explained.

Mike clambered onto the side of the booth and craned to see. 'Are you sure it's not just someone you recognised from here?'

'I'm sure. Do you think I should ring the police?'

Ollie's face crinkled with scepticism. 'And say what? I imagine the police are over stretched as it is. You know what it's like on a Friday night.'

'I know but...'

The reflections in the window were a bright mirror of the room and I had to focus them out. Beyond them a taxi had pulled up and the man was getting into the back.

'What are you going to say? I saw that man we were talking about getting into a taxi?' said Ollie.

'I don't think it'd go down well. The police turning up here,' said Mike, jumping down again.

'Give me your mobile,' I said, 'Quick.'

'Why?' Nevertheless Ollie dug his phone out. I grabbed it and flicked through to the camera and held it against the glass.

'What are you doing? He's already in the taxi.'

'I know but at least I'll know which cab firm he used.' I cursed myself for not thinking of it sooner and tried to zoom in but the image was shaky. I took a number of shots. 'The police might be able to trace him from where they dropped him off.'

'Good thinking,' said Mike, clearly impressed.

'They might not be going home,' said Ollie, taking

back the phone. 'It's early.'

'He's got to be in his forties. Middle-aged people don't tend to last the distance,' said Mike.

I sat down, pleased with my quick thinking. Tomorrow I would ring the police. In the meantime, I was going to have a good time.

In the next booth, a group of girls who were clearly part of a hen party were drinking heavily and screaming intermittently.

'Nine,' someone yelled, pointing at a bloke at the bar.

'Oh no. Seven.'

'He looks like Harry from One Direction,' said the bride, who was decorated with a veil and L-plates over a pink bodice dress and silk stockings.

'What was that all about?' asked Jess, nodding towards the road.

'Long story.'

I glanced at Ollie and wondered how they would rate him. With his dark hair and sharp features I'd have given him a nine. He caught me looking at him. 'What do you want to drink?' he said.

'The usual, please.' He nodded and fought his way to the bar. I wondered fleetingly how the hell I would stagger home if I got drunk. Maybe alcohol would numb the pain enough to walk. It seemed unlikely. Ollie and Mike could worry about that. If need be they would just have to carry me, I thought, and pushed the problem from my head. Tonight I was going to enjoy myself.

In the morning I wasn't so sure drinking had been a good idea. My skull felt as if it had split, and my senses were fuzzy. And I could easily have put myself in danger. With everything that was going on right now it hadn't been sensible. But it was cathartic. It had been a fun night.

In the lounge Darren was sprawled across an armchair, soundlessly fingering chords on his electric guitar. Thank

God he didn't have it plugged in.

Mike was in the kitchen, thumping the toaster. He glanced up as I entered. 'You look like shit.'

'Thanks. I'd say the same about you, but my eyes aren't quite in focus yet. And actually you don't.' I plopped down in a chair. 'How is it you can get totally plastered and still be so bright the next morning?'

'Years of practice?' Mike up-ended the toaster and deposited two slices of bread and a mountain of crumbs over the work surface. 'Bloody piece of crap.'

'Can you get me a glass of water?' I said pathetically.

'You need a hair of the dog.'

'I'm going to give alcohol a miss for a while.'

'I've heard that one before.' He laughed, and got the water I'd asked for.

I gulped down the first couple of mouthfuls, but the dryness in my mouth persisted. I sank back in the chair, holding the glass. 'How did we get home?'

'Can't you remember?'

'Not really.'

He looked at me hard. 'You don't remember the group sex then?'

It was a horrifying thought, but I didn't believe it for a minute. I caught the twinkle of mischief in his eyes and decided to play along.

'Yeah. It's coming back to me. You were the only one who couldn't get an erection,' I said.

'You cheeky minx. As if.'

I watched him make marmalade sandwiches from the bread he had retrieved from the toaster.

'So what are you up to this weekend?' he said.

'I don't feel like doing much right now. I might go to an art exhibition. At least it'll be quiet.'

'What's on?'

'Some contemporary stuff. Katherine something or other. She's Hampshire based. One of the guys at work recommended it.'

The conversation with Nick filtered to the forefront of my brain, and Gemma's scathing dismissal of contemporary art: 'It's all bullshit,' she'd insisted.

'No, it isn't. It's just that you're too thick to understand it,' spat Nick.

'What's there to understand? Most of it looks as if it's been done at kindergarten.'

Nick had sneered and shook his head, but didn't bother responding.

'When are you going?' asked Mike.

'Tomorrow, probably. Today I've got the lovely job of doing the laundry. If I can cope with the excitement of it.'

'Any chance you could do mine as well.'

'Bugger off.'

'Oh go on. You're bound to be better at it than I am.'

'Why? Because I'm a girl?' I knew he was only teasing.

'Exactly,' he said.

'Well, as much as I'd like to help you out, you're not going to learn if you don't try,' I said. 'Now stop grovelling. There's nothing worse than seeing a man beg. Anyway, I doubt I'll be able to carry mine, let alone yours.'

He sighed. 'It was worth a try. Do you want some toast? Well, bread actually, seeing as the toaster's buggered.'

I got up and refilled the glass, and drank it down. 'No. I'm going to call the police then go back to bed.'

Ollie's phone was still in his jeans pocket. The photographs I'd taken were mostly blurred or over exposed, but the name of the cab firm was clear enough. I rang the police station but DI Green wasn't available so I was put through to another of the team. I went through the usual process of explaining who I was and told him about the man I'd seen. He asked me to send across the image, which I did. And that was it. I went back to bed and didn't get up again until I felt less hungover.

The laundrette had an oppressive soapy warmth. The flat in Lee-on-the-Solent had a washing machine, so I wasn't used to using a laundrette, and I was surprised by the cross-section of customers.

'Is this free?' Ollie asked a young goth girl who was talking into a mobile phone and examining her chipped black nails with minute interest. She was sprawled across the only unused machine. Like a large slug the girl slid across to the next one. She watched as we started loading clothes in.

'What's the betting all her clothes are black,' Ollie whispered.

'I wouldn't use it,' the goth said suddenly. 'It doesn't heat up properly.'

Ollie glared at her and began unloading it again. Why had she waited until he had put most of the clothes in before telling us?

Everywhere there were handwritten notices. Do not overfill the machine. No overalls. No change given. The goth girl was still muttering into her mobile, but once her machine had stopped she unloaded it with her free hand, then indicated that we could use it.

'You were almost right,' I whispered to Ollie, noticing that all of her clothes were red or black.

Ollie stuffed our washing into the machine. I passed him the box of powder. 'So which one of these programmes do you normally use?'

'Just a quick wash normally,' he said. 'I don't know whether it's right or wrong, but it seems to do the trick.' The machine gave a long hiss and started to suck in water. 'Are you sure you don't want me to stay?'

'There's no point. I'd have done it all myself if I could have carried it.'

'I'll see you later then. Give me a call at the flat when you're ready and I'll come and get you.' He handed me his mobile and a bag of change then, glancing at the goth girl added: 'I wouldn't leave it unattended.'

I looked around at the other customers, checking them out. A group of students were congregated by the driers at the back of the shop, playing a game together on their phones. An old man sat reading a paper, and a young woman with two small children who were playing tag hurried to fold up her clean washing.

Despite Ollie's warning I did leave the shop. While the machine was running there was no chance of anyone getting at our clothes, and there was nothing of mine worth stealing. There was a newsagent only a couple of doors down from the laundrette; a pokey shop with narrow isles crammed with everything from newspapers and snacks to Christmas decorations, cards and toys.

I bought a magazine, went back to the laundrette, and sat down on a plastic chair next to a new arrival, a spotty teenager who was head down over a scientific textbook. The beat of music from his headphones thumped to a vicious rhythm that jarred with the therapeutic whirr of the washing machines.

'I thought it was you.'

I looked up to see Scott standing before me. 'Hello,' I said. 'I was miles away.'

'Somewhere nice?'

I held open the pages of the magazine article to reveal the shimmering images of a tropical paradise.

'It looks great, but you'd be bored in a week.'

'I'd be willing to risk it.'

There was suddenly a lot movement around us as a number of machines finished at the same time and people got up to deal with them. A seat almost opposite became free and Scott sat down. He spoke conspiratorially: 'How you doing? Has that inconsiderate boyfriend of yours been treating you any better?'

I laughed. 'He's not normally like that.'

Scott looked sceptical. He was watching a couple of

young women who had just come in together. I closed the magazine and held it on my lap.

'Thanks again for the pizza,' I said, reclaiming his attention. 'It was really kind of you.'

He waved away my gratitude. 'It just seemed so unfair leaving you out like that. You certainly seem a lot chirpier today.'

'I am. That was my first day back at work. I was tired and everything had got on top of me.'

He nodded. 'So everything's settled down then? Even with Daz? I imagine he can be an inconsiderate bastard sometimes. I don't think he does it intentionally.'

This time it was my turn to be sceptical. 'I think he does.' The wash cycle for my own load finished but I had to wait for a drier. I put the wet clothes into a basket to free up the washing machine.

'You can't really blame him when you know his background,' said Scott. 'Did you know he was brought up in care? Don't let on that you know.'

'No.' I thought about what that must have meant. Was that why he was so insular? And territorial? That would explain the almighty chip on his shoulder. 'He wasn't abused was he?'

'Who knows.' Scott's voice was bitter. 'Adults can do a lot of damage to kids.'

'Do you come across a lot of that sort of thing in your job?'

'It's not a subject I like to deal with. Still, can't afford to turn work down.'

The comment reminded me that he was expecting me to put together some business cards for him. 'Do you want to have a chat about your business cards?'

A drier became free, and Scott helped me load the wet clothes in. He held up a pair of my big pants and raised an eyebrow. 'Don't say a word,' I said, and snatched them from him. 'They were an emergency buy. Business cards?'

Scott laughed. 'Sure.'

Although the laundrette was warm, every time the door opened a draught fingered my ankles. Our conversation was punctuated by the sound of washing machines chugging tediously, and the slam of drier doors. Scott and I were still chatting when Ollie came back.

'Wasn't I was supposed to call you,' I said. 'It's not quite dry.'

'I thought I'd head down. It must be nearly done by now.'

Scott stood, offering his seat to Ollie. 'I'd better be off. I'll wait to hear from you.'

Ollie didn't sit down until Scott had gone. 'What did he want?'

'He wants me to do some business cards for him.'

'Haven't you got enough on your plate already?'

'It's only a business card. I didn't know Darren was brought up in care,' I said changing the subject. I felt a sudden empathy with Darren. If my mum had died a couple of years earlier, and without my stepfather on the scene, I could have ended up in care too.

Ollie looked at me puzzled. 'Is that what he said? I don't know where he got it from, but as far as I know it's not true. Daz has got a mum. She's a bit of a slapper, and he doesn't see her, but he's never said anything about being in care.'

'Just because he's got a mum doesn't mean anything.'

'Suppose so. Strange that he should have talked to Scott about it though.'

'I thought they were friends.'

'They are, but I think they only met recently.'

I shrugged. 'I think Scott has a way of wheedling information out of people. He is a journalist after all. Or maybe Darren was winding him up and strung him a line. I wouldn't put it past him.' If it was true though, what were the implications? Did it mean that Darren was damaged and flakier than I'd suspected? Had he learned a way of behaving that had continued into adulthood?

'Did you plan to meet up with Scott?'

'What?' Jerked out of such worrying thoughts I was shocked by the question. 'Why would you think that?'

'You seemed to be cozied up.'

'No we weren't.' I studied him. 'Are you jealous?' The drier stopped and I got up.

We began pulling clothes into one of the plastic baskets again. Ollie didn't answer my question but instead said: 'What do you make of him?'

I picked up a tee shirt, folded it and laid it in the large holdall. What did he want me to say? He was clearly suspicious. 'He's a bit of a charmer. But he's been kind to me.' I didn't mention that I thought he was attractive and personable.

'Hmm. Can't say I like him.'

Definitely jealousy, I thought. What the hell did he think was going on?

CHAPTER 22

Craving solitude and open spaces, in fact anywhere away from the flat, a trip to the art gallery seemed the perfect solution to fill a dull Sunday afternoon. So I wasn't exactly pleased when Mike decided to tag along, until I realised it meant free transport.

'You'd never find this place unless you knew it was here,' observed Mike as we drove down the narrow street.

'I take it you've never been here before either,' I said. 'I think that might be it.'

The gallery wasn't immediately obvious until you were on top of it. Two large glass doors opened in off the street, but from the side the grey sky reflecting onto the glass made them appear as uninviting as thick steel panels.

'Do you want to get out here and I'll find somewhere to park?'

The gallery was a single deep room dissected into bays by moveable partitions. All the surfaces were white: even the wooden planked floor. It reminded me of that psychological question about how you feel being in an all white room and what it says about your perception of death. I wandered around the small entrance area, thinking about it while I waited for Mike.

The place was library quiet, the only noise the murmur of a group of students crowded around a painting at the far end, and the faint chink of crockery from the café on the next floor down. A large arrow pointed to a steep flight of metal stairs that were not exactly disabled-friendly.

'This is all new, isn't it'? asked Mike, joining me just a few minutes later.

'That was quick.'

'I got lucky. Someone pulled out just as I came down the road.' Why did things like that always happen to Mike? He seemed to live a charmed life. I'd have been driving around for ages.

I took the laminated card the woman standing by the counter offered. In contrast to the surroundings, most of the canvases were large, bold and colourful.

'This is shit,' said Mike.

'Sshh. I thought you liked this sort of stuff. You were always going to modern art exhibitions when we were at uni.'

'Only so everyone thought I was intelligent. You can spout total bullshit about this sort of stuff and no one's going to argue with you.'

I laughed. 'You fraud. I never realised that was why you went.'

He grinned. 'You really never worked it out?'

'Sometimes my perceptive blindness frightens me,' I admitted. 'What else have you been lying about?'

He leaned towards me though there was no one around to overhear him. 'I've led everyone to believe I've got a huge dick.'

The heat of a blush rose in my cheeks. I leaned closer to him. 'Well, unless you've had an operation, I know for a fact that's not true.'

He gave me a mock pleading look. 'Don't let on, will you.'

'Why not? Unless you can convince all the girls you sleep with to keep quiet, it's going to get out.'

'Yeah, but they're all besotted by my winning personality so I'm pretty safe.'

I laughed, and moved on to a very simple painting that struck me as engaging. I stood looking at it for a long time, trying to decipher the content.

Mike tilted his head this way and that. 'What do you make of that?'

'A landscape, I think.'

The painting consisted of little more than a block of vivid green with a couple of wispy lines towards the top. There was a roughly outlined black square with a horizontal mark across it at the bottom. I let my imagination run. It could have been a field, with hedges and the shadow of an open gate. I liked the feel of it. There were no confines and even the hedge, if that was what it was, looked patchy and full of holes.

'Yeah. I suppose it could be. What does the blurb say?'

'You read it.'

'I'm not trudging through that lot. It's got line lengths of about three hundred characters.'

'Exactly. Neither am I.' I wondered if the painting would have such poignancy if my circumstances were different. 'Do you think certain types of art are more relevant depending on what's happening around us?'

'Crikey. That's a bit deep.'

I laughed. 'Come on. I know it's Sunday and you've probably switched your brain off, but what do you think?'

'I think a lot of art's crap.'

'You sound like my work colleague. But that doesn't answer my question.' We moved on to the next painting. This one consisted of vertical blocks in shades of purple, brown and black with white and cream areas between. It made me think of a dense pine forest, although I wasn't sure why. 'For example, I find this one a bit creepy,' I said.

'There's nothing particularly sinister about the subject matter, but the contrasts are so extreme that it makes me think there's something nasty hiding there somewhere.'

Mike looked puzzled. 'Really?'

I glanced at the card. 'That's what I mean. Does it seem that way because things in my life are dark right now?'

Mike put his arm around me and gave me a hug. 'You'll get sorted with another flat soon. It's not been long, and there's no hurry to move out.'

I didn't say anything. Mike read the detail on the card.

'Apparently this is about, and I quote, reflecting a fascination and feelings for things remembered, of isolation and the effects of weather on a place.' He stared at the picture. 'Can't have been happy memories then.'

I moved away from the painting. I didn't like it.

'Do you remember that life-drawing teacher we had at uni, the one that used to come down from London? She was always spouting crap like that. She did stuff like this too. Used lots of bold dark lines. I always thought her work was creepy,' said Mike.

'She was pretty creepy! Normal people don't make you go to the morgue for an art class.'

'It wasn't the morgue. It was a hospital.'

'There were feet in jars.'

I shuddered and he laughed. 'Yeah. I remember. Will Ashford puked.'

For a moment I struggled to recall who Will Ashford was.

There was something very striking about the small painting on the end wall of the gallery where the students had been gathered when we came in. The shapes were strongly defined with lines of thick paint that cut into the background colours. The powder blue at the top of the canvas was topped with a wisp of yellow. It could have been sky. It could have been clouds. It could have been distant hills. Or perhaps it was just blobs of colour. Either way it was more peaceful than the previous picture. I sat down on the bench facing it.

'Do you ever wish you'd done a different course?' I asked, thinking that it was a long time since I'd done any drawing or painting.

'All the time. I suppose my approach is more utilitarian than creative. And graphics doesn't pay nearly as much as I thought it would. I think that's why I've ended up doing web design. It's more coding than anything else so it's extremely boring to be honest, but the pay's better.'

'If you were eighteen again would you still go into design?'

'No. I'd do engineering like my dad wanted me to do. It's got to be better paid. What about you?'

'If money was the decider, then I suppose marketing's probably a better option.'

Without being able to stop it, my thoughts drifted to my stepfather. He wasn't an artist himself, but it had been his encouragement that had made me consider design as a career. I began to recall the trips when he'd taken me to visit art exhibitions as a young teenager. Until I was old enough to go on my own, the two of us had travelled throughout the south coast to look at artwork, but the trip to London to see the Renoir exhibition was the most memorable.

We set off early and went up by train, taking with us a flask and some ham sandwiches for breakfast. I remember being surprised that the paintings were so much smaller than I'd anticipated. Afterwards Keith had taken me to Covent Garden for lunch, with promises to bring me to other exhibitions. But we never went, because it wasn't long after that mum got sick the first time. I should have invited Keith to my final show at college, I thought guiltily.

'Is this watercolour?' asked Mike.

'The colours are a bit vibrant for watercolour.'

There were few solid lines in the painting. All the edges were soft and blurred, one colour merging into the next. Flecks of white made me think of dandelion clocks, and the faint smudge of yellow in the background was like a small ray of sunshine.

'I quite like that one.' The woman who'd handed us the cards when we came in was watching us as if she didn't trust us.

All of a sudden I had a need to be creative. Even before the fire I'd got bogged down with working and socialising. And there never seemed to be the time. How had that happened? Keith had always encouraged my creativity. 'It's about time I did some painting again,' I said. Perhaps I was in the process of reinventing myself, a phoenix rising from the ashes. Perhaps it was time to sort things out with Keith once and for all too. When I picked up my portfolio I'd talk to him properly.

'Why the hell do they do it to us?' Gemma grumbled at work the next morning. 'You get a decent job in for once, and they give you no flaming time to do anything with it.'

She was right. We'd been briefed first thing on a new project, and Guy wanted our initial thoughts by lunchtime. Okay, it wasn't finished visuals, but it was still a ridiculous deadline.

'What do you think of this?' Gemma turned her Mac to face me.

I wasn't sure she had understood the brief properly, but telling her so close to the deadline wasn't helpful. 'Have you worked out how you're going to pitch it?'

She shrugged. 'No. But I don't suppose it really matters what I say. It'll be yours or Nick's work that'll get chosen.'

'Not necessarily. You need to think it through. Think about why you've done it like that. You might want to increase the size of the headings. They need to be a bit punchier.'

She didn't look convinced. 'Anything for me?' asked Gemma as the receptionist, who was handing out the post, put a manila jiffy bag on the corner of my desk. The receptionist gave her a bemused glance.

'You weren't honestly expecting something were you?'

'Nobody sends me anything,' complained Gemma.

'It's probably only paper samples,' I said.

'I wouldn't care what it was. I just love getting stuff in the post.'

The receptionist was still close by, sorting out a couple of items to leave for Nick. 'Actually, that didn't come by post,' she said. 'It was on the mat when I came in.'

Gemma picked up the envelope. 'Whatever it is it's pretty solid.'

'If you're that interested open it up. But it won't be anything exciting.'

Gemma didn't need telling twice. She pulled open the flap and slid the contents out.

'A picture,' she said, sounding unimpressed. 'And not a very nice one either.'

I glanced down. It was an ugly, gold, moulded picture frame with a print of a gloomy medieval style painting inside. In the focal point, at the top left corner, was a woman in a white dress. I bent to take a closer look. The woman was tied to a wooden pole in the middle of a bonfire. 'Shit!'

'I don't get it,' said Gemma.

I took the picture from her and turned it over. A label was stuck to the back:

THOUGHT THIS MIGHT BE MORE YOUR THING!

Jeanne d'Arc. Lenepveu.

'Why would anyone think you'd like something like this?' said Gemma.

'I don't think they do,' I said, rereading the label. 'That's not the point of it.' Nick was the one who had told me about the art exhibition. Was this down to him?

'Then what is? Who is she? A witch or something?'

There was nothing else in the envelope. I crouched to

search the floor, wondering if anything had fallen out. But there was nothing. I hadn't really expected there to be.

I looked again at the label. 'Jeanne d'Arc. Not a witch. It's French,' I said. 'Joan of Arc.'

'Who the hell is Joan of Arc?'

'I can't remember the exact details, but I know they burnt her at the stake. Something to do with politics or religion.' I gazed at the face of the woman, feeling an affinity with her. The detail wasn't good, as if the image had been downloaded from the Internet. She wore a detached look that was probably meant to be beatific but looked plain resigned to me.

'Alive?'

I nodded. How had Joan of Arc coped, knowing what was about to happen to her?

'God, that's awful. Can you imagine what that must have been like? Just waiting for the flames to…' She shuddered.

'I've got a fair idea,' I murmured, Googling Joan of Arc.

'Shit, sorry.'

I shook her apology away. 'I'm more concerned that this is something else from him.'

'But why is it more your thing?' asked Gemma.

I tried to work out if there was a connection between Joan of Arc and me apart from fire. 'What's more worrying is the fact that it should happen now. It's got to be his way of telling me he knows I went to an art gallery yesterday.' Had he been there with us in the same room? Apart from Mike there hadn't been anyone I recognised at the gallery. The place hadn't exactly been busy and no one had stood out. There was the woman who worked there who'd been staring at us, but I didn't honestly believe she had anything to do with this. My mind began a tortuous game of rationalisation. I looked up Mike's office on the internet and rang the number.

'Did you send the picture?' I demanded when he I was finally put through to him.

'What picture? Who is this?'

'It's Zoë. I'm talking about the print of Joan of Arc.' Fear had made me loud and I glanced around, aware that I was being watched.

'What are you talking about?'

I lowered my voice. 'The painting by Lenepveu.' I stumbled over the unfamiliar name, unsure how to pronounce it.

'Who?' That one word confirmed what I already knew. I began to backtrack.

'Never mind. You didn't see anyone hanging about the gallery yesterday, did you?'

'Everyone hangs about at galleries. That's the point.'

'Yes but...' frustration made me bolshie. 'Anyone who looked out of place? I don't know.'

'Darling, we're talking about artists, aren't we? They all look odd. What's this about? You sound weird yourself.'

I didn't just sound weird, I sounded psychotic. Guy came to the doorway of his office and shouted: 'Ten minutes people.'

'Shit. Never mind. I've got to go.' I slammed the phone down. Time was up, and I was nowhere near ready. I rubbed my eyes with my fingertips in a desperate but ineffectual attempt at massaging away the tension. Was this down to Nick?

I tried to focus on work but it was impossible. How was I going to pitch my idea with the painting occupying every inch of brain space? Pitching to Guy was always a daunting and demoralising task. Trying to get across the potential for developing a concept often felt like an interrogation. Even the most impressive idea could be destroyed in a minute if it was presented incorrectly, or inarticulately. And this time my brain was tuned to another channel. I should have been scribbling a few notes, but the bottom line was that I didn't care. I was worried, and the more I thought about it the more afraid I felt.

Ten minutes later I gathered up my papers and, like cattle to the abattoir, we went into the meeting room.

'So. What have we got?' said Guy, once we were all assembled. 'Nick. Do you want to kick off?'

Guy did not join us at the table. Instead he stood in the doorway, blocking the exit as if afraid one of us was going to try and make a run for it.

'The way I see it, it's about facets,' Nick said. 'The multiple layers of management. The people the company deals with and the image it wants to present.' Nick always did a much better job of selling his work than Gemma or me. 'The imagery I've used is abstract, a combination of angular planes to represent industry and softer curves or faces representing the core of any company - its people, staff, customers etc...'

What Nick was saying sounded good, it sounded well thought out. It was a load of bullshit. But when it came down to it that was what it was all about at Stanton, Summer and Cox. The ability to come up with something brilliant was unnecessary, being able to bullshit with proficiency utterly vital. Nick was fantastic at it. The language he was using was familiar though, and I realised he'd borrowed some of the phrases from the art gallery literature. He'd obviously gone then.

I tuned out and played with my pen. My brain kept whirling round, toying with the facts of everything that had happened, everything that had been sent to me, and why it was happening. What would DI Green make of the picture? It was becoming increasingly obvious that if I was going to have to keep running to the police station, I was going to need my own transport.

Guy paced the room. 'Comments anyone?'

With a shock I realised it was time to give my opinion. Nodding, I made it seem as if I agreed with whatever Guy had said, even though I hadn't heard much of it. I thought that, despite the bullshit, what Nick had come up with was predictable and dull. I wanted to tell him so but knew I didn't have the resources to argue. It was a pity. I would have liked to wipe away his smug expression.

'Okay Gemma. Let's have yours next.'

Gemma's presentation was short. However, her design, although clumsy, had potential – just not for this particular project, and Guy didn't spend long discussing it.

'And Zoë. What have you got for me?'

I rummaged through the pile of printouts. They weren't particularly good but I'd been working on autopilot. 'I um, focussed on the modern aspect of the company too. Although I felt trying to show too many aspects was over-complicating it.' I fed off of what I had heard Nick say and tried to turn it to my own advantage.

'I'm not sold on the colour choice,' said Guy.

'I wanted something on-trend.'

'You seem to have a thing about green, though,' he said. 'It's not an environmental company.'

Anger flushed through me. 'What colour do you recommend?'

'You're the designer.'

Yes, I thought. And you're a marketing man with no creativity. So don't criticise.

'You need to simplify it or it won't reduce very well,' said Nick.

'It's a rough concept,' I pointed out. 'Of course it needs work.'

Nick put his hands up defensively.

'Okay. Any more feedback? No? Right, you all know what you need to do to put this to bed. I want your finished visuals on my desk by 11.00 tomorrow morning. It's the full package.' He could see from our expressions that we weren't happy with the deadline. 'I know, it's tight. And if it means staying on this evening, so be it. But I want good quality well presented visuals. And that means you too Gemma.'

'Bastard,' she murmured when we were barely out of earshot.

'At least he didn't rip it to shreds.'

'Well, if he thinks I'm staying on he's wrong. I've got an antenatal class tonight.'

'Are you going to get this done in time?' Nick stood over me with his arms folded like a Guy clone.

'I'll have to,' I said crossly. 'It's a ridiculous time scale.'

'Yeah, well, we came into the running late. They're a blue chip company so Guy's bound to want to pull out all the stops.'

'That's all very well. But we're hardly likely to win the account if what we come up with is mediocre.'

'We're just going to have to make sure it's not then.' He picked up a couple of my print outs. The way he was poking around irritated me.

'Did you want something? Or are you looking for inspiration?'

'Just thinking.'

'Well, go and think somewhere else. I need to get this finished before close of play. Until I can get my car back I don't have the luxury of staying on. I'm reliant on Gemma.'

'How long until you can drive again?' he said.

My car keys had been in my bag since they were returned to me. I wasn't totally convinced I was ready to drive yet, but I was fed up with being dependant and, with everything that was going on, awkward too.

'I think I can drive now. But my car's in Lee on Solent and I haven't had a chance to pick it up yet.'

He gave me an uncertain look. 'But you're on crutches,' he said.

It was on the tip of my tongue to remark how observant he was. Instead I just said: 'You don't use the same parts of your feet.'

'Suppose. Is there a bank in Lee? If you really think

you can drive I could drop you down there and go to the bank at the same time. It would save struggling to park in Fareham.'

I considered. If it hurt too much I could always leave the car in the office car park. If I could drive okay I'd have my freedom, and that was kind of exciting. 'Alright. Thanks.'

After he'd gone I wondered why he was suddenly being helpful.

CHAPTER 23

As we reached his car, I wondered again if Nick was responsible for everything I'd been sent. There were Jekyll and Hyde elements of his personality that worried me. But what was his motive?

The drive to Lee-on-the-Solent was the ideal opportunity to quiz him. I got into the passenger seat, removing a phone charger to sit down.

'Chuck that over the back,' he said. 'It's only an old one. I need to get rid of it.' I glanced down at it, sure that the connector was a similar size to the one my phone used.

'In that case, can I borrow it? I think it might fit my phone.'

'Sure. Have it.' I stowed the cable in my bag, thinking that if the charger did fit I'd have a working phone again, and that was even more positive than getting the car. It felt odd not having contact with people.

Traffic was heavy for lunchtime, and it was dangerous getting onto the roundabout. Not wanting to distract him, I kept silent until we reached the dual carriageway. 'I take it from the influence on your design stuff you went to the gallery this weekend,' I said as we turned onto the road to Lee-on-the-Solent.

'Yeah. It was good. You should have gone.'

Did that mean he didn't know I had? In which case, the picture wouldn't have come from him. Or was it a bluff? I met the condescending tone with one of my own. 'Why do you assume I didn't? Don't forget there's a speed camera down here.'

'You didn't mention it.' Nick's focus was on keeping his speed down. 'There were some interesting pieces of work, weren't there?'

'Is modern art what you like then?' I said, remembering why Mike used to go to exhibitions.

'Not especially. I've got pretty wide tastes.'

'What do you think of medieval painting?' I said.

He gave me what seemed to be a quizzical look. 'That's a hell of a leap from the stuff at the exhibition.'

'You said you have wide tastes. I just wondered if they extended that far.'

'I can't say it's really my thing,' he admitted, which was an interesting choice of phrase. 'We covered it in history of art but not in any great depth.' I let the conversation slip onto ground where he was more comfortable. So for a while it was about work, and more specifically Nick's philosophy on what the company should be doing to expand. I let him give his lecture while I analysed what he had said. Either Nick was a damned good actor, or he had no knowledge of the things sent to me.

'You need to turn right here,' I said when we got to Lee-on-the-Solent.

Nick turned abruptly and I didn't need to tell him where to stop. 'Jesus,' he said, pulling up in front of the burnt out building.

'Not a pretty sight, is it?' I stared across at the boarded-up shell. It still sent goose bumps rippling over me. For a moment I was back on the landing, cowering by the open front door, with the sound and smell of the fire all around me. Would the memory ever lessen?

'Can you wait? I want to make sure the car'll start.' In truth, I needed to see if I could actually drive it, but I didn't tell him that.

A damp smell from being shut up hung about the inside of the vehicle. I hauled my crutches into the back and clambered into the driver's seat. I worked the pedals, pushing down hard. If it had been a sharp spear of pain I would have abandoned the idea, but the dull ache was bearable. Miraculously the car started first time.

The passenger door opened and Nick crouched to look in. 'Okay?' He began riffling through the CDs on the passenger seat.

'I think it's all right,' I said, stroking the wheel. Having the car back would make me more independent. It also made a difference having things that were wholly mine and not bought for me or borrowed.

Nick put the CDs down. 'I'll go to the bank and see you back at work then.'

'Thanks for the lift.' With a thud the door shut.

I let the engine continue to warm, using the time to check the fuel level and poke around in the glove compartment. There were all sorts of surprises in the car. I had a rummage around, finding odds and ends, a tub of lip-gloss, a pair of running trainers and a woolly hat in the back. I turned the heating to max. When I looked up Nick's car was gone and it hit me that I was on my own. If someone had been watching when I went to the gallery they could be watching now. Why hadn't that occurred to me before? I'd been so caught up in the idea of having the car back I'd failed to recognise the implications. I slammed the central locking on. Then I laughed at the irony of it. Everywhere I'd gone, I went around unlocking things. Now I was doing the opposite.

I wanted to drive straight to the police station and

give the picture to DI Green, but Guy would kill me if the project wasn't finished on time. And although unpleasant, there wasn't actually a threat in the picture, only an implied one. A few hours wouldn't make any difference, I decided and, putting the car into gear, I set off.

It was a bright day and the roads were busier than I'd have liked. I drove cautiously. Instead of heading back to the office the way we had come I took a detour, turning right, then right again, braking early at each junction. Having to use the pedals hurt more than I'd anticipated but it wasn't intolerable. I headed for the seafront. I missed living in Lee-on-the-Solent: running along the beach, seeing the sea every day, which always had a soothing effect on me.

Pulling over, I let the engine idle while I stared out at the choppy water. The car was stuffy and I opened the window a few inches. Cold air rushed in. With my face against the glass, I breathed in the calming salt air. All of the fear and anger began to disperse as I sat there using yoga techniques to concentrate my breathing.

After a while, I flicked the CD player on and, calmer than I had felt all day, pulled out into the traffic and headed back towards the office. Concentrating on driving, I wasn't immediately aware of the music that was playing. It was a while before the heavy rock screamed lyrics struck me: *Fire! Fire! Build the funeral pyre higher.*

I swerved, realising I'd strayed onto the wrong side of the road. I flicked forward to the next track: *Burn, Baby Burn. You set my love on fire.* It sounded like the same rubbish rock band. A wave of coldness passed through me. This wasn't a CD I recognised. I skipped to the next track, listening intently. This time it was one I recognised, Light my Fire, by the Doors. I swung into a lay-by, slamming the car to a halt. A spear of pain shot through my foot at the sudden force. With a yank, I ratcheted the hand brake on.

I ejected the CD, impatient at the sluggish way it slid out. It wasn't a commercial recording. And it wasn't mine.

I also knew that no one had lent it to me. Someone must have put it together specially and that someone had been in my car.

The hedge alongside the car was winter thin and dotted with rosehips. Through the undergrowth the new housing development half a mile away was just visible. There were no other vehicles in the small lay-by but the stream of passing traffic was steady. As each vehicle sped by, the car rocked violently. I felt exposed.

When had someone put it in the car? How had they got in? Had it been there for a while - or had Nick put it there? The hairs on the back of my neck stood erect. Could Nick have slipped the CD in when I wasn't looking? I tried to rerun the sequence of events. I almost wanted to believe it was Nick. At least then I'd know who I was dealing with.

A knock on the window scared me. Nick mouthed through the glass. 'Are you okay?'

I started winding the window down then, realising it was a stupid move, stopped. My heart was racing. I stared at him, trying to read his expression for clues of guilt.

'Is driving a problem? Or have you broken down?'

'Neither.' I said, thinking quickly. 'I just needed to adjust the seat position. I'm all right. I'll see you back at the office.'

'I can follow you back if you like. I was looking out for you in case you had a problem.'

'Thanks. I'm not going back to the office yet though.'

'What about the project?'

'I didn't say I wasn't coming back. I just need to do something first.'

Nick's eyebrows shot up. 'It's your funeral.'

In my rear view mirror I watched him get back into his car. Stopping in the lay-by had been a mistake. I should have driven somewhere where there were people around. Pulling away, I followed Nick to the end of the road before turning off and heading for the police station.

There were double yellow lines immediately outside

the building so I was forced to park a little way up the road. It had occurred to me on the way that the CD might not be the only thing someone had left in my car. Nervously I began a meticulous search, inspecting every nook and cranny, lifting mats and lowering sun visors but there was nothing out of the ordinary. I put the CD into the envelope with the picture, locked the car, and went into the police station.

Unless the fire escape is left open, there is no way of slipping into work unnoticed. In the winter, of course, it was shut so I had to use the main entrance. I didn't feel like going back at all.

As I walked towards the entrance I tried to think of an excuse for being so long, but I couldn't think of one and my foot hurt like hell. The police hadn't said much, just taken the items and said they would look into it, which did little to reassure me.

I scanned the office. My entire body was on high alert. Initially I thought my luck was in and Guy was out, but as I slipped into my chair I saw him leaning against the dividing screen of one of the marketing girls across from where I sat. I leaned my crutches against the edge of the desk and began to take my coat off. Guy came straight over. 'My office, now.'

Clenching my teeth, I followed. If he started shouting at me, I was either going to cry or explode. And the idea of both appalled me.

'Where the hell have you been? How do you expect to make the deadline if you don't spend any time at your desk?' he barked. I bit down on the fury coursing through me. My hands were shaking. I balled them into fists to try and make them stop. Even my body wasn't behaving normally. 'Well?' Guy prompted, dragging my attention back to the room.

'I went to fetch my car,' I said. 'So that I can stay on

tonight.'

'And it took all this time? Where the hell was it, Brighton?'

'Lee on Solent.'

'So why have you been gone a couple of hours?'

I studied his desk, fixating on his ornate silver fountain pen. It was so pretentious. Why couldn't he use a biro like everyone else? There was a risk that the conversation could disintegrate into a slanging match, ending with me telling him to stick his job. And that would be a disaster. Should I admit what it was really all about? In some ways it would make it easier, but in the long run would it really help? I'd have it hanging over me all the time I worked here.

'Zoë! Are you even listening? What's the matter with you?'

And besides, Guy couldn't do anything about what was happening. Would he even believe me? If he did I might get his pity, and that was worse than his anger.

Guy stared at me. 'What's going on? You're clearly upset.'

I didn't answer.

'I'm beginning to think perhaps you came back too soon. You're preoccupied much of the time.' He paused. 'You're no use if you're only half here. I suggest you take some more time off. I think you need to get yourself together. Talk to someone, get some counselling, because you clearly aren't coping.'

God, he knew how to put the knife in. I had nothing and he wanted to take away my income. 'I can't afford to take time off. I need the money,' I said.

'It's more important that you get yourself together, for your sake and the company's. Otherwise you'll make yourself ill. I'll have a word. Arrange for you to be off on full pay. Okay?' Guy glanced at the clock.

I nodded.

'Think about what I've said. Talk to someone. Get this

project finished before you go, but I'm not expecting to see you in for the rest of the week.'

Was it obvious to everyone that something was wrong? Did all my work colleagues think I was falling apart?

As I worked I considered what Guy had said. I decided to talk to Ollie. He'd soon tell me if he thought I was going mad and he hadn't said anything so far.

At just before four o'clock the phone on my desk rang. 'I've got Ollie on the line for you,' the receptionist said.

'Thanks.' The phone clicked as the call was put through. 'Hi, Ollie.'

'Hi, Babe. Thought I'd better let you know I'm not going to be back tonight. In fact, I might have to stay down here for a few days. We've got problems on site. Bit annoying, as I didn't bring any clothes with me.'

Before I could stop him, he proceeded to relate the details. Shut up, I thought, and sank forward with my head in my hands. It was like being in a vortex: everything whirling around me.

'Zoë? You still there?'

'Yes.' Resentment made me sharp.

'I know you're probably not happy about me leaving you in the flat with Daz but it can't be helped.'

'I know. Ollie, there's…'

He cut me off. 'Hang on…' There were muffled sounds at the other end of the line. 'Sorry, I'm going to have to go. I've got the surveyor on the phone again. I'll give you a call tomorrow.'

I sat with the phone in my hands. So much for talking about it. It certainly wasn't going to be with Ollie.

CHAPTER 24

It was half past eight and the office had all but emptied. That wasn't late by usual standards but in the build-up to Christmas no one wanted to stay longer than they had to. For hours I had been mulling over what Guy had said about talking to someone, but none of my friends was the type to actually listen. And none could give me advice on how to cope with stalking. I considered calling one of the victim support numbers the police had given me, but the idea of speaking to a stranger made me decide against it. I needed to talk to someone who understood me and knew I wasn't neurotic. Then it came to me that a few years ago my cousin Nathan's wife had done some training as a counsellor.

I saved my final files and sent them across to Guy's email. Nick was still working steadily at his computer. Outside it was black. The idea of venturing into the car park alone scared me, but I was eager to get to Nathan's.

'You done?' Nick said without turning round.

'Yes.' I stood behind him, wanting to ask him to walk me to the car.

'See you then,' he said irritably. 'I suppose I'm going

to be doing everything now.'

'If you've got a problem with it take it up with Guy. He's the one insisted I take the time off.'

By the front door I hovered, eager to go, yet afraid to, and angry at my fear. There was no one about. Damn. Then after a couple of minutes a woman from the adjacent office walked by. I hurried after her. It wasn't easy keeping up; she wasn't walking particularly fast, but she was moving quicker than I could. I glanced into the darkness. Was someone out there?

The woman reached her car, which was closer to the offices than mine, so I was forced to carry on alone. Sweating heavily, I clambered in and slammed the central locking on. I threw the crutches into the passenger side, and started the engine. I sat there shaking, then span around in my seat as it occurred to me that there could be someone hiding in the back of the car. If they had got in once they could do it again. Smacking at the space of the back foot wells with my fist, I contacted nothing. I wanted to make sure no one had been in my car, but it wasn't wise to stay in the dimly lit car park alone. It was terrifying how quickly someone had turned me into a gibbering wreck.

I'm not sure how I arrived at Nathan's house. On autopilot, I crawled up the M3. I didn't have a number for Nathan to be able to call ahead and it occurred to me that they might be out, but with a small child the chances were probably slim.

The house blazed with light. Upstairs the curtains weren't drawn. Downstairs light seeped through the gaps between the lounge blinds in warm horizontal stripes. Through the front door it was transformed into a patchwork of pale colour by the frosted glass.

I rang the bell and a voice called: 'I'll be there in a minute.'

With a rattle, the door opened and a face appeared in the gap above the chain.

'Hi, Melanie.'

She took a moment to register who was standing in front of her. 'Zoë?' The door shut and the chain was removed. 'What are you doing here?' There was something about her manner that inferred she wasn't pleased to see me.

I hoped she wasn't about to send me away. 'Have I come at a bad time?'

'No. I was about to put Harrison in the bath, that's all.' As I stepped over the threshold she nodded towards my crutches. 'What on earth happened to you?'

'Long story.'

There was a squeaky holler from the top of the stairs and I could see Harrison, face pressed against the bars of the stair gate.

'Can you manage the stairs? If not, make yourself at home and I'll be down in a while. Help yourself to coffee.'

'I'll come up.' I was too wired to wait.

'I don't suppose you remember Zoë, do you Harry?' Melanie said when I reached the top of the stairs. Harrison frowned and blinked at me. He nodded vehemently but he couldn't have remembered.

'You were just a baby when I last saw you,' I told him, feeling resentful of the little boy for distracting his mother. 'You're not now though, are you?'

'Tell me about it. That's the second pair of shoes in four months.' Melanie glanced at her watch. She'd lost weight since I'd seen her last and she looked tired. 'Come on rascal, let's get you in the bath before the water gets cold.'

Harrison offered me a bright plastic train with a blue chimney and red wheels. 'Is this for me? Oh, you want it back now do you?' He stood there for a few moments examining it while Melanie tried to undress him. The overpowering scent of fruity bubble bath filled the room.

'Harrison! Stand still.'

'Don't won barf.'

'You've got to have a bath. Plonk yourself down, Zoë.' She nodded towards the toilet seat. 'What brings you here?'

'Like I said, it's a long story.' I sat down on the toilet lid and fidgeted. I was all geared up to talk and it was frustrating to hold my tongue while she fussed over her son. I was appalled at myself for thinking that way. 'What time's Nathan home?' I asked, aware that the more time that passed the less chance we'd get to talk.

Melanie pulled a pinched face. 'He won't be. We split up.'

'Oh. I'm sorry. I thought you two were sound.' It was a stupid thing to say, and I regretted it as soon as I'd said it.

She shrugged and stroked Harrison's hair. 'So did I. But it seems Nathan got bored with family life. It was "too restricting".' She spat the last few words out. 'I thought he wanted kids. But I don't think he knows what he wants.'

'I'm sorry.' My thoughts drifted to my own relationship. Ollie said he wanted the whole thing, but when it came to it did he really?

Melanie tested the water and added more cold. 'How are you managing?' I said, not envying her the task of looking after a small child on her own. 'It can't be easy.'

Melanie shrugged. 'I've got to stay positive for Harry's sake.' She picked up her son and lifted him in. The bath was littered with plastic boats, a couple of pirates and a worn purple cow. There seemed to be stuff everywhere. 'Besides I haven't got the energy to be angry and bitter,' she said. Harrison began emptying the bath of his toys, throwing them over the side or handing them to one or other of us. 'Harry, stop showing off.'

She talked about the separation for a while and I realised she was grateful for the opportunity to pour out her problems. I leaned back against the cistern. Everyone around me was wrapped up in a crisis of their own.

'Anyway, listen to me babbling on. You can tell I don't get out much these days. What happened to you?'

'Ow!' Harrison pushed Melanie's hand away as she

tried to shampoo his hair.

'It's got to be done,' she snapped.

Harrison complained loudly.

'I jumped from a window.' Gratefully I poured out the whole sorry story. 'The police say it was arson,' I concluded. 'And now, just to top things off, someone's stalking me.'

'What do you mean? Harrison, sit down. I said, sit down.'

'Someone's sending me things. I think they're trying to freak me out.' I told her about all that had happened.

'So everything's got a fire theme?' She gave me a sympathetic look. 'And there's me ranting about my domestic situation when you've got all hell breaking lose in your life. Have you got any idea who's doing it?'

'No. That's what makes it so bad. It could be anyone. That's why I came to see you. I didn't know who to talk to and I knew you'd done some counselling.'

Melanie poured some baby soap into her palm. 'From what I've read about stalking, it's usually someone you know.'

'I read that too.'

'What have the police said?'

'They warned me to take care and that was about it. I wish I knew what they were doing about all of it.'

Harrison flinched as Melanie rubbed soap over him. She looked thoughtful. 'The trouble is, if you're not careful in these situations you end up becoming a recluse, afraid of your own shadow. And then the bastard's won.' She mouthed the word bastard.

'So how do I cope with it?'

Melanie sat back on her heels. 'I don't know, is the honest truth. I guess I'd always make sure I was never alone.' She must have realised the implications of this in relation to her own situation because she shuddered and resumed cleaning Harrison. 'I'd try and carry on as normal. I'd probably try and show him that what he was doing was pathetic and wasn't significant to me. If you do find out who it is, don't get into any kind of conversation with him about it. It's asking for trouble. I don't know whether that's good advice or bad. It's just what I'd do.'

'I've been trying to carry on as normal. But it's beginning to get to me. Even my boss has picked up on the fact that something's not right.'

The phone rang but she didn't get up until the answer machine cut in and Nathan practically shouted: 'Oh for Christ sake Mel, pick up. I know you're there. I just wanted to talk about…'

'Look after Harry will you.' Melanie raced downstairs. 'Of course I'm here. Where else would I be? I'll have you know I'm in the middle of giving YOUR son a bath…No of course I haven't left him in there on his own… Actually I've got someone with me so I'll have to call you back. No. It's not a man. But it wouldn't be any of your damned business if it was.' The phone was slammed down and, as she came back upstairs, I could hear her mumbled curses. 'Sometimes that man really drives me mad,' she said, squatting beside the bath again and filling a plastic jug to rinse the soap off Harrison. She stopped suddenly, jug raised. 'What about hiring a private investigator?'

'What made you think of that?'

'Ex-husbands. Not that he's ex quite yet. It's what women like me do in American movies when their husbands abandon them.'

'Have you considered it then?'

'No. Though there have been times when I'd have liked to know exactly what Nathan was doing while I was stuck in of an evening.'

'It would probably be too expensive,' I said, 'I don't have the money.'

'Alright then, let's use some lateral thinking. Who else investigates and digs up facts?'

I thought for a moment. 'Archaeologists?'

Mel groaned. 'Fraud investigators?'

'I don't know any.'

'Who else?'

Harrison stood up and, like a chunky fountain cherub, peed into the water. Then he splashed heartily, thumping the water with both hands and soaking us. 'Harry! Sorry about that.' Melanie grabbed the soap and started scrubbing her son's legs again. 'How about a researcher of some sort,' she suggested. 'For TV or something.'

'A journalist!' A ripple of excitement ran through me. 'They've got an uncanny knack of digging up things that other people want to stay hidden.' Why didn't I think of that before?

'I take it you know a journalist then?' She stood up and reached for the child. Harry moved to sit on the plug and prevent her pulling it out.

'Sort of.' I smiled. It felt as if I had suddenly been given some hope. 'He might have contacts within the police. It's worth asking. Mel, you're a genius. I knew coming to see you was a good idea.'

'Glad I could help. Do you fancy stopping over tonight?'

'Is it a good idea?'

'Why not? Or do you think you're in danger.'

'I don't know what to think.'

'From what you've told me, he does things that are unobserved, which strikes me as cowardly. Have you eaten? No? Let's get this little man to bed then and grab something. I'd really appreciate some adult company.'

It was a pity Mel's house only had two bedrooms, otherwise I could have suggested moving in permanently. As she put Harrison to bed, I turned my attention to working out how I could do the artwork for Scott. Now I wasn't at work it was going to be a problem, but I needed it as leverage.

Early the next day, with a plan of action in mind, I headed back towards Portsmouth. Taking a cross-country route to avoid the motorway rush hour traffic proved a bad idea; everyone else was doing the same and the going was slow. Driving was painful so I kept to the straighter A roads as it hurt less. I was on a mission: hoping to make it to Jess' before she left for work, but I was running late.

With the charger Nick had given me I'd managed to get my phone working overnight so now I had all my contacts again. It had been too early to call Jess when I left Mel's, and a text would have been long-winded and inappropriate. I stopped in a car park on Portsdown Hill to call her. I speed dialled the number and sat in the car with the engine running, listening to the ring tone and looking out over the Portsmouth coastline with its network of pulsing veins. A fine mist hung over the sea, partly obscuring Portchester Castle so that it looked as if it was floating.

'Zoë? What's up?' said Jess when the call connected.

'Why do you assume something's wrong?'

'Well you don't normally call me at this time of the morning.'

She had a point. 'True. I was wondering if I could come round and use your Mac.'

'Sure. But I won't get home till seven tonight. I've got a yoga class.'

'I meant this morning,' I said. 'I was hoping to come round now.'

'I've got to go to work.'

'I know. I was hoping I could stay on just for half an hour. I really need to get something done. And I don't have access to another computer.'

'Why the urgency? Aren't you going to work then?'

'I've got a few days off. My boss doesn't think I'm coping,' I said, sounding bitter. I was unwilling to go into detail. 'It's all a bit of a mess to be honest. That's why I need to use the computer.'

'Sounds ominous. I've got to leave in fifteen minutes. Can you get here in that time? Oh, hang on. It's not connected up. We gave the spare room a lick of paint at the weekend and I haven't got round to putting it back together yet.'

'I can do that.'

There was a pause. 'Don't take this the wrong way but I'd rather not. I know where everything plugs in. Does it have to be a Mac? Can't you go to the library or something?'

'I doubt they'd have the software.'

'Fair enough. Well I can't do it now. My boss'll kill me if I'm late again. Come round tonight. I'll have it connected up for you. Look, I've got to go. Come round at seven.'

And with that she was gone, leaving me frustrated. I'd left Mel's earlier than I needed to. I'd had it all worked out. Do the artwork. Call Scott. Persuade him to do some digging. Listen to what he'd found out. Move on. If I didn't get the first part done the rest was way off. I wanted productivity. Instead, I was at a loss how to even fill my day.

My stomach rumbled. In my urgency to leave I'd refused breakfast and there was probably still no food in Ollie's flat. Several vehicles were parked towards the entrance of the car park where there was a tea wagon. I drove over to it and went to join the group of men huddled around the front where the heat of the hot plate cut through the chill morning. I bought a mug of coffee and a fried egg roll, then texted Ollie to let him know I had my phone back. Then I sat in the car scrolling through the numerous text messages that filled my inbox, but there was so much spam I just hit 'delete all'.

Mel's advice about carrying on as normal rang in my ears, and it occurred to me how to use my time. For the next forty minutes I searched through estate agent websites on my phone. I rang the one Nick had mentioned, told them I was looking for a flatmate and arranged to see a couple of the cheapest properties, then drove back to Ollie's flat for a quick change of clothes.

CHAPTER 25

The first flat was in a run down, purpose-built block. The idea of looking at flats had seemed fine in principle, but now that I was here I wasn't so sure. Being somewhere I didn't know with someone unfamiliar worried me. Thankfully it was a woman I was meeting.

'Zoë Graham?'

'Yes.'

The estate agent's tart red lips parted in a smile that exposed crooked nicotine-stained teeth. From the smell, she had just put a cigarette out. I shuddered. 'My name is Nadia,' she said in a thick Eastern European accent. 'We go in?'

Slowly I followed her clipping heels along the communal hall. She was a heavily made up woman of indeterminate age and her suit hung off her as if she had borrowed someone else's clothes.

Three doors led off the corridor. Nadia headed for the closest. She stood back to allow me to enter first. I hesitated, then told myself not to be so stupid.

The room was a reasonably sized lounge, but it was

like being marooned in a murky lake; an expanse of dirty night blue carpet crept towards pale green walls on three sides, a kitchen area on the other.

A musty smell hung about the place. 'How long has it been empty?' I asked.

'I no sure. A couple of weeks I think.'

'You'd think the landlord would give the place a clean. It's not exactly selling it.' And the fact that he hadn't probably indicated that he was a bad landlord.

Nadia started running through the details. 'Two bedrooms... kitchen area with refrigerator, electric cooker... quite near shops... garage in block around back...'

Switching off, I tried to look past the decor and current feel of the place and imagine what it would look like once it was clean, aired and painted. At least it was on the ground floor.

'Lovely compact kitchen,' the estate agent enthused insincerely.

Compact meaning miniscule. The kitchen area was just one wall of pale old-fashioned brown units with a metre of curling lino in front of it. The estate agent followed me as if she thought I was going to steal something, though there was nothing to steal. I opened a few of the cupboards. Except for a couple of screws and a dirty cleaning cloth they were empty. A fine layer of dust coated everything. We were at the back of the building overlooking the car park where the concrete glittered with shards of green glass.

My mobile rang. It was Ollie. Typical that he should call now. When he learned that I was looking for a place alone he was going to be hurt. I wasn't in a hurry to tell him. 'Hello.'

'Zoë? Where the hell were you last night? The boys said you didn't come home.' Ollie's anger fuelled my feelings of guilt.

'Since when I did become accountable to you?' I went into one of the bedrooms and pushed the door shut.

'I was worried about you.'

'Trying to control me, more like.'

'As if I'd try. I was just worried. I had no way of knowing where you were. I even thought about ringing the police.'

'You didn't though, did you?'

'No of course I didn't.' He was silent for a moment. 'What's wrong with you? You're mega touchy. It feels like I can't do anything right.'

'Yeah? I know how that feels. I've got enough to worry about without you giving me grief.'

'I'm not giving you grief. I was worried. Oh, what's the point! I know you're all right, that's all that matters.' The line went dead.

'Bastard.' That was precisely why I needed my own space.

I went back to join Nadia who was watching two young women with pushchairs arguing in the street. 'Well?' she said, not turning. A couple of toddlers kicked at the door of a car but the two women ignored them.

'What's the neighbourhood like?' I asked with little hope of her contradicting my suspicions.

Nadia shrugged. 'Is cheaper area.'

Cheap meaning dodgy? Like an omen, dead flies littered the windowsill; stiff bent legs pointing accusingly towards a dirty white ceiling. I'd had enough of danger. 'Is that why it's not been taken? Only it seems unusual in this current climate. Actually, you know, this isn't what I'm looking for,' I admitted.

Nadia sighed and we headed out. 'If you not like this one I know you not like other flat,' she said.

'I ought to look at it. I need to know what's available.'

'Your budget too tight. Even with sharer.'

The second property was close to where Jess lived. Like so many of the houses in this part of town, the building had been divided into two flats, one up one down. The flat Claire and I had shared had once been a semi-detached house but as flats it had decent sized rooms. The one I was about to view was part of a terrace and therefore much smaller. The street was narrow; the houses opposite close, stepped back from the road by tiny buffer gardens mostly tarmaced or paved. Even though it was half way through the day the road was choc-a-block with cars and it was impossible to park anywhere near the house. In the evening it would be worse still. I told myself not to be too quick to judge.

Nadia patiently perched on the low wall waiting for me. The front door of number 145 opened into a tiny square of hall. To the left was a white door, thick with runs of paint. In front of us were carpeted stairs. I left my crutches propped at the bottom and hauled myself up by the handrail. My sense of smell seemed to be over sensitive. The reek of cats was pungent, and my immediate response was one of disgust even though the place looked clean.

At the top of the stairs there were two further paint-dribbled doors. I waited a couple of steps down while the estate agent fiddled with the keys.

'You need to jiggle it.' The voice came from behind me. An immense woman with an enormous fluffy cat tucked under her arm filled the small hall below.

'Ms. Jackson. I not know there would be anyone in.' The estate agent rattled the door with what seemed like increasing urgency.

'Do you want me to come up?'

I eyed the area at the top of the stairs, wondering how that was even possible.

'No. I get in in a minute,' Nadia assured her. The tarnished handle was just above the lock and there was barely room to twist the key back and forth. Finally I heard the click of the lock springing open. To our confusion the door neither opened inward nor outward.

'It slides,' the voice from the bottom of the stairs shouted.

On rickety runners, with a sound like a train moving off, the door slid along the wall. I went in. 'Is that legal?' I said, examining the door from the inside and thinking of its dubious fire resistance.

'Probably no. I get someone to have word. This flat only one bedroom.'

I took in the lounge. It was surprisingly bright with a large window at the front and net curtains. The primrose walls had recently been painted and the curtains with large yellow flowers made the room seem fresh and clean. Only the worn brown carpet let it down. The furniture was in good condition and the place had a homely feel. I began to wonder whether I could consider living in the flat despite the problems of parking and the woman downstairs. In the corner there was a television and a trumpet. Everywhere there were stacks of books.

I wandered through to the bedroom, equally as well furnished and decorated. The fat ginger cat followed me in and curled up on the bed. At the sound of heavy breathing I turned and found the woman behind me in the doorway, puffing and panting from climbing the stairs. Close up she looked much younger. The smell of her was strong, a combination of body odour, unwashed clothes and Ibuleve.

'Who's living here at the moment?' I asked.

'My sister.' The woman wheezed in breath. 'But she's buying her own place.'

'It's a nice flat. Nice and fresh,' I said.

She scowled. 'She likes bright colours.'

I wandered over to the window and looked out at the untidy concreted yard below.

'Who does the yard belong to?'

'The garden's mine. I've got patio doors out to it.' Strangely she was proud of the miserable square of neglected space. I couldn't think why.

'Pity. So how much of this comes with the flat.' I waved my hand around indicating the furniture.

She shook her head. 'This is all my sister's stuff.' My face must have fallen because she added: 'Oh I'll sort out some curtains and stuff.'

I smiled bleakly. 'That should be a fire door. Does it lock properly?'

She became defensive. 'It's not been a problem in the past. I've got a key anyway.'

From that one comment, I got the impression that the flat would never be completely mine. At some point I would come home to catch this woman straining the springs on my sofa, watching my television, or rooting through my things.

'Better have a look at the kitchen then,' I said, wondering where it was.

'There isn't a kitchen as such,' she said. 'There's a couple of burners in the lounge.' She took me back into the lounge and lifted the top of what I had mistaken for a cupboard and showed me an antiquated two-plate hob. I eyed it with dismay but smiled.

'Oh well. I see there's an Indian down the road.'

The estate agent hid behind a sheaf of papers and gazed out of the window. Where was the bathroom? Stepping back out onto the landing I pushed open the other door. It was a small bathroom with a window high up and a suite of putrid avocado disguised under an array of huge washing. I stepped out of the room again.

'Is it a shared bathroom?' I enquired.

'Yes. And I expect whoever moves in to keep it up together,' the woman informed me.

Instead of you, or should that be in spite of you? I thought. 'I think I've seen all I need to,' I said, heading down the stairs in a bid for freedom.

'You can't move in for a couple of weeks,' the woman bellowed after me. 'My sister won't have completed.'

'That's not a problem.' I assured her. Did the deluded woman think I was impressed? I waited outside, breathing in large lungfuls of air, which set me coughing. The estate agent seemed to take forever.

'I say you not like,' she said. 'I think maybe she a bit mad.'

'Hmm. That door can't be safe. If there was fire you wouldn't stand a chance.'

'I get someone to write her a line.' She sighed. 'I take it you not interested?'

'No.' I thought about how much easier it would be for me to just rent a flat with Ollie rather than put myself through all this. But that would be using him. And besides, if we carried on arguing we wouldn't even be together in a few weeks. I thought about when Claire and I had taken on the lease before. It had been a gradual process and we had sorted it out together. Maybe in time she would change her mind about sharing again. But I needed to get somewhere sorted soon.

I sank down on the wall, springing up again at the twitch of curtains from inside the house. I suddenly felt a bit queasy, with a dull ache in my groin as if my period was due. No wonder I felt so emotional. 'Is there anything else I can look at?' I said, thinking that I'd better find a chemist and buy some supplies. In fact, if I was going to eat, I'd better do a grocery shop too.

'Not at moment. Keeping check internet. You find all property there. Give me call if anything of interest,' she said, handing me a business card.

I'd bought the ingredients to make some cupcakes as a way of keeping occupied rather than sit around brooding, and also of saying thank you to the boys. It had even occurred to me to buy a tin to cook them in.

I was still angry with Ollie and was glad that he was away so that at least I had some space. I creamed together the margarine and sugar, guessing the quantities when I discovered there were no scales. What Ollie had said made sense but I still felt as if I was being kept tabs on. I beat the eggs into the mix. The buzzer for the building front door startled me.

'Who is it?' I snapped into the intercom.

'Parcel for Flat 4.'

'Okay. I'll let you in.'

I buzzed the front door open and went out onto the landing to wait for him but I couldn't hear anyone moving around. I called out but no one answered so I went to get my key. When I got downstairs the package was propped against the door frame. The parcel was addressed to me. It was the kind of brown corrugated card I would have expected to contain a book, DVD, or CD but I hadn't ordered one and that made me suspect it was something from the stalker. I tucked it under my arm and made my slow journey back upstairs.

Once in the kitchen I cautiously pulled open the seal. If it was despatched from a distributor it was unlikely to be of use to forensics, but there might be a billing address of who had ordered it. Nestled between the layers of cardboard were two DVD's: Ladder49 and below it Towering Inferno. I groaned. Talk about predictable. Rather than being spooked, I was furious that I'd been forced to go up and down the stairs unnecessarily. The persistent harassment, I realised, was beginning to have less effect. I folded the cardboard once more and went back to my baking.

My mobile beeped with an incoming text. It was from Ollie. 'Sorry. Wasn't checkg up n u. Jst wrried. Luv u. Mayb bck tmrrw.'

Great. I'd have preferred a bit of distance right now. The house phone started ringing and I immediately assumed it was Ollie again, this time wanting to talk. I didn't want to. I was aware that I was being irrational. One minute I wanted him here, the next I didn't. I wanted to talk to him and then I didn't. I let the answer phone cut in.

'Hello. This is a message for Zoë. It's Scott Parker. I just wondered if you'd managed to do anything about my business cards. Sorry. I'm not trying to hassle you but I've got a couple of important meetings lined up next week and

I could really do with something more professional than what I've got. Can you...'

I picked up the call and cut him off. 'Hi.'

'Zoë? I was going to leave you a message. How come you're not at work?'

'I've got a few days off.' How was the best way of asking for his help? I couldn't just come straight out with. Or could I?

'You are coping okay?' Scott sounded cautious.

'Of course.' I wasn't about to admit differently. 'It's all pretty tedious but I'm getting there.' I quickly changed the subject. 'Look, I'm sorry I haven't been in touch but I should have something for you tomorrow.'

'That'd be great. I didn't mean to hassle you.'

'It's okay. It's just been awkward trying to get the opportunity to use the right software. Anyway I've arranged to borrow a friend's computer this evening, so I'll have the proofs for you tomorrow. Maybe we could meet up and I can talk you through them.' I kept my fingers crossed that he didn't suggest emailing them instead.

There was a pause. 'I've got a meeting in the morning and a deadline in the afternoon. But I can do lunchtime if that suits you. I could pop round about one o'clock.'

'Fine. Actually, can we meet somewhere else?'

'Don't you trust yourself with me?'

Heat flushed my cheeks and I was grateful he couldn't see me. 'I've got a few chores to run,' I improvised.

'Let's meet at Pepe's café on Albert Road then. Do you know it? They have great chocolate cake. And you strike me as a chocolate cake kind of girl.'

I laughed.

'Have you got a mobile number in case I get delayed,' he asked. I told him the number and he rang off. I sat there for a few minutes, smiling like an idiot. Now I was making progress. And when I eventually found out who was tormenting me he was going to pay for it.

CHAPTER 26

The radiator in Jess' hall rattled out welcoming heat as I stepped in from the cold night. Soft oriental music flowed from the lounge, and above it came the sound of female voices, carrying like scratches on an old recording. Jess hadn't mentioned that she would have company, but it didn't matter; I'd be out of their way.

Jess gave me a hug. As she released me I saw that it was Vicky and Neesha in the lounge. They waved.

'I thought we could make a party of it,' said Jess, stepping back.

I felt manipulated. How could she be so damned insensitive? 'Jess it's…'

Vicky bounded into the hall. 'What do you want to drink?'

'Nothing, thanks.'

Unperturbed Vicky persisted. 'You can't party without a drink.'

I wanted to tell her that I wasn't here to party. Instead I said: 'I can't drink, I'm driving.'

'Really…' Vicky looked surprised. She glanced

towards my crutches.

Neesha was holding back as usual. The subtle scent of massage oil clung to her. 'Hi,' she said quietly. 'We're having an evening of pampering. I've brought a load of nail stuff and trial face packs from the salon.'

How was I going to get out of this? 'Can I have a word, Jess?' I said, heading towards the kitchen.

'Are you okay, Zoë? You seem really twangy,' said Jess as I closed the door behind her. 'I thought you were when you phoned earlier. That's why I asked the girls round. I thought you could do with chilling out in some female company. It can't be much fun in the flat with those boys. I'm sorry if I got it wrong.'

Her words made me feel guilty. 'You didn't. It's just that all I can think about right now is using the computer.'

'Why?'

She was one of my oldest friends but I didn't want to confide in her. Jess never actually quite listens. 'It's a stepping stone towards getting back to normal,' I said simply.

'I don't understand.'

'Sorry. I'm not trying to be cryptic. It's just complicated. It's one of the few things I can do and it's important. It won't take long. I promise,' I said, 'Quarter of an hour, tops.'

'I'll switch it all on for you. But then we party, yeah?'

'Okay.' I followed her back along the hall and up the stairs. The bedroom was set up with the computer by the window. The smell of fresh paint lingered and the room was cold as if the radiator hadn't been turned on again. I shut the blinds and sat down at the desk while the computer booted up.

'Give me a shout if you need anything,' said Jess as the desktop finished loading. 'In fact, why don't you stay over like you were going to the other day? You said you're not working. If I know you, you've probably already been out flat hunting and trying to get everything sorted, haven't you? You're allowed to give yourself a break.'

'Maybe.'

In fact, it took about half an hour to produce three layouts in various styles, print them out and burn the file to disc. I could have done it quicker but there was little content, and I wanted to give Scott something impressive so that he felt obliged to help me. I sat back feeling satisfied. I put the disc and print outs in my bag, then went to use the loo so I didn't have to come upstairs again. Now that the card was done the idea of a party seemed like just the tonic I needed.

There was giggling from the lounge. Coming down stairs, I saw that my crutches were being used by my friends. I stood on the lowest step watching them.

'Mind the coffee table!' screeched Jess.

'Come on Neesh, let me have a go.'

'You had a go.'

Silently I crept forward and as Neesha lunged precariously across the room. I bellowed: 'What do you think you're doing?'

Neesha, caught off balance, fell over, banging her shin on the coffee table. 'You scared the life out of me!'

'It's not that you're pissed then?' said Vicky.

'I've only had one glass of wine,' said Neesha, sheepishly handing over the crutches. I leaned on them, grateful for the support. The room had been darkened, the light now emanating from two side lamps. The scent of lavender made my nostrils twitch. When I realised it was evaporating from a burner I stared at the naked flame.

'Oh, sorry.' Jess scrambled to her knees. 'Let me get rid of it. We never thought.'

'Sorry,' said Neesha, 'I always use burners to create ambience.'

'I...leave it. It smells nice and I've got to get over these things.'

'You sure?'

I nodded. 'Yeah. Do I get a drink then?' I said, changing

the subject, and deciding that I'd stay over as suggested.

'How about we play the drinking game, Neesh?' taunted Vicky.

'Oh God,' muttered Jess, pouring a glass of wine. 'I had a hangover for three days last time we played that.'

'Me too.' I refused the glass Jess was trying to hand me, unwilling to risk spilling it if I wasn't sat down first. 'No matter how many times I threw up, it just didn't seem to help,' I said.

'Lightweights. You're almost as bad as Neesha.' Vicky jabbed a thumb at her. 'At least you didn't go to sleep in a corner, like some, though.'

Neesha's eyes narrowed. 'You know I don't drink much alcohol. Anyway, who fell over next door's wall when she was leaving?'

'That was the cat's fault. He tripped me up.'

The two girls sounded as if they were about to launch into a playful argument.

'Do you want the sofa, Zoë?' asked Neesha as I tried to get down onto the floor. The sofa is a tired piece of faded red furniture, which is horribly uncomfortable.

'No thanks. I don't fancy a spring up my bum.'

'Oi,' said Jess.

Neesha laughed. 'She's got a point.'

Vicky cackled uncontrollably. 'Yeah, up her bum if she sits on that.'

'Tcht!'

I accepted the glass of wine, which was strong and fruity. Whorls of light glinted from the surface. 'This is nice.'

'It's only cheap plonk from the Co-op.'

Vicky joined me on the floor. 'Talking of things up your bum. Did anyone see that sex program the other night?'

'What sex program?' asked Jess.

'I forget what it was called. It was on on Monday quite late.'

The CD faded off as the album came to an end and Jess got up.

'They had three couples,' explained Vicky, 'and they filmed them having sex. I tell you they had cameras everywhere; in every room and from just about every angle too. There was even one in the shower.'

Byron slinked in, rubbing his head against anyone who happened to be in his way. He ambled around the room, exploring. I stroked his head, and with a purr of satisfaction he arched his back with pleasure and settled down on my lap.

Jess took a CD from its jewel case. 'Normal couples?'

Vicky laughed and flicked her dark hair back over her shoulder. 'Hardly. Normal couples don't sign up for that sort of thing.'

'They weren't porn stars, were they?' said Neesha.

'No way. You wouldn't pay to watch these people. They were gross.' Vicky tilted her head. 'The really funny bit was that afterwards they had a discussion about how good or bad they each thought it was.'

'That's a bit insensitive,' said Jess.

'Funny though.'

Jess shuddered and put a CD in. 'I can't imagine what it must be like to have the cameras watching you like that.' Her face was puckered, lips drawn in as if she'd eaten something sour. She shuddered and sat back down.

'Why? Isn't Paul much good in bed?'

Neesha looked horrified. 'Vicky!'

'Jess knows I'm only teasing. Anyway, what about you?'

'What about me? As I don't have a boyfriend it's irrelevant, isn't it?'

'Not really. What if you did?'

'No. It's disgusting.'

The idea hit me with a gasp. Cameras! It sent an appalling thought spiralling through my mind. What if the flat was bugged? If someone was watching me, what extent had they gone to? Or was I being paranoid, overreacting to every idea that presented itself? With webcam it was probably easy to spy on someone. I shuddered. It was an utterly creepy idea. When I got back to the flat I was going to search the place.

'Are you okay, Zoë?' said Jess.

'Yeah, you're keeping very quiet.' Vicky looked interested. 'Do you fancy it, Zoë?'

I stared at her and saw her shift uncomfortably as she realised something was up. 'I can't think of anything worse than being watched all the time,' I said. 'Especially with something intimate.'

I took a sip of wine, swirling the liquid around my glass, a visual end to my response. The cat shifted in my lap. I put my glass down and moved him so that his claws weren't scratching.

'I agree,' said Neesha. 'What kind of person does that? Someone who invites the cameras in like that must be weird.'

'I thought you were secretly up for it,' teased Vicky.

'Stop it,' Jess reprimanded. 'Can you really imagine any of us taking part in something like that? What if your friends, or worse your family, saw it?'

'I hope my parents don't watch programs like that,' Neesha said. 'Urgh.'

I don't have to worry about that, I thought, and reached for the glass again, but it was gone. 'Which is my drink?' I asked.

'That one,' said Jess, pointing to a now half empty glass Vicky held.

'I thought this was mine,' said Vicky.

'That's why she can't hold her drink,' said Jess. 'Because she not only drinks her own but everyone else's as well.'

'Er, sorry.' Vicky handed back my wine and refilled it. 'That is so not fair.'

'But true,' said Jess.

I held up the glass. It was thick like a camera lens. Now it was in my head, I couldn't shake off the idea of being spied on. Were there cameras in the flat? Darren was an electrician. He probably had the skills. He certainly had the opportunity to have set something up. But why would he?

'I've brought some new face pack samples I thought we could try, if you want to?' Neesha got up to fetch her vanity case, which she'd left on the floor by the door.

'Bring another bottle in while you're up, Neesh,' said Jess.

'Do I look like the hired help?'

'Yes,' said Vicky and Jess in unison. As we unpacked the cosmetics the conversation moved on.

Neesha smoothed cleanser over my face with a cotton wool pad while Jess opened another bottle of wine. I sat with my head against the sofa, my mind full of cameras. Neesha murmured so the others wouldn't hear. 'Zoë, your skin's getting bad.'

'I know. It's because I'm eating crap food and I'm totally stressed.'

'Well, hopefully tonight will help then,' she said. 'You should drink more water.' The face mask smelt sweet, and my skin tingled as it began to dry. My nose itched.

'Right. I'm just going to wash my hands and then I'll start on everyone's nails.' With an efficiency I'd never seen in Neesha before, she bustled out of the room, then a few moments later started laying out bottles and files. 'Who's first?'

'Me,' said Vicky, 'I don't think you'll make a very good job soon.'

'What do you mean?'

'I mean, after another glass of wine you'll be painting our knuckles.'

I sat listening to the banter while my face mask set.

'I'd better get the chilli on,' said Jess. 'I hope everyone's okay with veggie chilli.'

Even though I was the only vegetarian everyone seemed content with it. I was touched by the effort Jess had made on my behalf. Shoving the cat off my lap, I staggered to my feet. The wine had gone straight to my head. I followed Jess out to the kitchen. Even with the crutches I was unsteady on my feet. 'Thanks for thinking about a veggie chilli,' I mumbled, trying not to crack the face mask.

'You haven't tried it yet.'

'True.'

Jess punched me on the arm. 'I figured you probably hadn't eaten properly since you'd moved in with the boys.'

'You're not wrong.' I appreciated Jess's thoughtfulness at getting the girls together. Even Vicky's brashness was a relief; at least she wasn't tiptoeing around me. I gave Jess a hug. 'Thanks for organising this. I wasn't too impressed when I arrived to find them here, but actually you were right, this was just what I needed.'

'That's what friends are for. Actually, and by all means say no if you don't want our cast offs, but there's a bag of clothes in the lounge. We all had a poke through our wardrobes. It's not crap, I promise.'

I went back into the lounge. 'Thanks for the clothes,' I said. 'Jess has just told me.' I smiled, feeling the layer on my skin pull tight then crack.

'No probs. If you don't want any of it give it back,' said Neesha. 'I won't be offended. Do you want to sit down so I can take that off before Jess ends up with it in her carpet? Or you end up with it in your dinner.'

Obediently I sat. Jess came into the room looking puzzled. 'Did anyone drop these?' She held up a box of matches. 'They're not mine, but I've found them on the mat by the front door.'

'Do you think someone posted them through the letterbox?' suggested Vicky. 'It's probably kids.'

'At least it wasn't dog shit,' said Neesha.

I stared at the matchbox. Coldness crept over me. If it was from him that meant he'd followed me here. Neesha began wiping off the face mask and recounting details of the racist attacks in Southampton when she was a kid. But I wasn't listening. Suddenly I was sober and my brain was somersaulting. Everything I did, everywhere I went, was spoilt now.

'It's not kids.' My voice was louder than I'd intended. I'd interrupted Neesha's flow and now there was an expectant hush.

Jess gave me a funny look as if she was analysing me. 'Well who else would it be?'

'Someone's stalking me,' I said. 'This isn't the first thing that's turned up.'

'Seriously?' Vicky leaned forward conspiratorially. 'Who is it, an admirer? Cool.'

'No, not cool. It's sick,' I snapped. 'Everything he's sent has had a fire theme. And when you've recently been in a fire that's not funny.'

'A stalker's not like having an admirer, Vicky,' Jess chipped in. She looked worried, and had wrung her hair into a tight spiral, which sprang loose the minute she let it go.

'Fire theme? What do you mean?' asked Neesha.

'I don't want to talk about it. Someone is sending me things, that's all.'

'You can't leave it at that,' said Vicky.

'She said she doesn't want to discuss it,' said Neesha. Vicky poured herself another glass of wine.

'Talk about a cliff hanger.'

'Shut up, Vicky.'

'I can smell burning.' I sprang to my feet and pain shot through my foot.

'The chilli!' Jess bolted from the room.

I should have kept my mouth shut. It all sounded melodramatic. Earlier when the DVDs had arrived it hadn't bothered me. But knowing that someone must have followed me here was freaking me out.

Vicky was defensive. 'Don't tell me you're not curious to know what's happened.'

'No,' said Neesha, but I knew it wasn't true. She looked worried. 'Do you think you're in danger Zoë?'

'I don't know.'

'You know, it wouldn't be a bad idea to try and pre-empt him,' said Neesha. 'It is a him, isn't it?'

I shrugged. I hadn't considered that it could be a woman, but there was no reason why it couldn't be. But who? One of my friends here?

Jess reappeared with a couple of plates of food. 'Er, the chilli's done.'

'Done or buggered up?' clarified Vicky.

Jess handed me a plate. 'Well, I think it's still edible - just.'

'Yum!'

'You should write it all down,' suggested Neesha. 'Keep a journal of everything that happens. There might be a pattern. And if there is, you might be able to work out who it is and what he's likely to do next.'

I prodded the food around my plate. I wasn't hungry and it was dotted with bits of chewy blackened lumps. 'When I tried to recall it all for the police it got confusing. The detail,' I said.

'You went to the police?' said Vicky.

'Of course I did. This all started with my flat burning down.'

'Maybe we could help,' said Jess. I looked at her dubiously as she settled back on the floor with her food. 'If you talked us through each event. We might be able to extract the facts for you.'

'That's a good idea,' said Vicky, clearly eager to find out the details. She wasn't going to let it go.

'And thinking about it, you could also ask the people who have been there at the time to write it down too,' suggested Neesha. 'That's what the police do isn't it, get different witness perspectives.'

After we'd eaten Jess fetched a notepad and biro. 'Let's start at the beginning,' she suggested.

'It's rather hazy.'

'Alright. Let's do it in reverse then. Why don't we start with tonight? Vicky, can you make some notes?'

For the next hour we went through what had happened, only stopping when Paul arrived home. 'We'd better get going, Vic,' said Neesha, digging out her mobile. 'I didn't realise it was so late. I'll phone for a taxi.'

'Blimey, is that the time?' Vicky shoved the notebook towards me and scrambled unsteadily to her feet. 'I'd better have a wee first.'

I gave both girls a hug. 'I really appreciate tonight.'

Perched on the sofa, I looked over page after page of Vicky's bold round writing. Once I'd read it over a few times I might be able to make some sense of it. Vicky came thundering down the stairs, almost tumbling down. She tugged on her coat. 'Bye Zoë,' she called out.

Vicky's handwriting had deteriorated as the evening had worn on. There were a couple of paragraphs I couldn't decipher. I could still hear them talking in the hall so I went to join them and ask what it said.

Vicky's words brought me to a standstill. 'Didn't either of you pick up on the fact that there's never anyone around when these things happen? I mean, take tonight. Zoë could have put the matches there herself.'

'Why would she?' said Neesha.

'I don't know, attention seeking maybe. It's all just a bit convenient.'

'I don't believe that,' said Jess, but there was uncertainty in her voice.

'She has had a horrible shock with the fire,' said Neesha.

'Are you suggesting she's having a breakdown?' asked Jess.

'I don't know,' said Neesha. 'But she's not the Zoë we know. Is she?'

'You bitches!' I wanted to shrink away but I was too angry. 'I thought you were trying to help me.'

'Zoë!' Jess reached out a hand towards me but I knocked it away. 'We were just....'

'Just what? Accusing me of all sorts by the sound of it. I thought you were my friends.'

'You've got to admit it's odd,' defended Vicky.

I turned, grabbed my belongings. 'Where are you going?' Jess barred my way but ushered the others out.

'Home.'

'Don't be stupid,' said Jess. 'If you want to go home I'll get Paul to drive you.'

'I'll get a taxi.'

'No you won't. Think about the implications of that. We don't really think you're doing this to yourself. You know how tactless Vicky is. She was just raising a point. He's singling you out and raising doubts. Now come and sit down. I thought you were staying over.'

'I don't want to.'

'Stay there then. I'll get Paul to run you home. He's probably not in bed yet.' Jess went upstairs. I didn't want Paul to take me home. I didn't want to be beholden. I hated them all. How could they think that of me?

Despite leaving alone, and the fact that I'd been drinking, I grabbed my bag and coat, and left. As I drove away, Neesha and Vicky banged on the car to try and stop me.

I was strung out and angry. How could my friends think like that? Did they really believe it was possible that I was doing this to myself? Did they really think I was some kind of wacko? I was stressed sure. But I wasn't mad.

I'm not sure how I got back to Ollie's flat. I must have been on autopilot. I stood in the lounge, guiltily thinking about it. The journey was a blur.

Looking around the lounge my thoughts were filled with cameras. I went to make a coffee and sober up. On the table there was one cupcake left. I ate it greedily. While I waited for the kettle to boil, I thought about the implications of cameras. There was only one person capable of installing stuff like that - Darren. He'd kept out of my way for days, but what if that was because he had another way of keeping tabs on me. Grabbing a chair, I clambered onto it and ran my hands along the top of the units, but the only thing I found was a thick layer of dust. I had no idea what I was looking for anyway. Cameras were so small these days they could be hidden in anything. I remembered seeing one on the TV recently that was hidden in a phone charger. And that led my thoughts to Nick.

God, it was frustrating not knowing who was doing it and therefore how I should respond.

'What's going on? What's all the noise about?' said Mike, appearing in the doorway in his dressing gown.

I climbed carefully down from the chair. 'Nothing,' I snapped, picking up items from the worktop and examining each in turn.

Mike shivered and yawned. 'Well, what are you doing then?'

I didn't answer. 'Do you want one?' The kettle had boiled so I made a coffee.

'No thanks.'

'Does Darren fit surveillance cameras and IT as well as electrical stuff?' I said bluntly.

'Random.' He shrugged. 'Zoë, have you taken something?'

'What?'

'Drugs.'

'When have you ever known me to touch stuff like that?'

'It's just you seem wired.'

I took my coffee into the lounge, suddenly aware

that alcohol had dulled the pain in my foot and I could walk more easily without crutches. I scanned the room, wondering where to start. The media centre seemed an obvious place to hide something. I looked at each item, examining it.

'What are you looking for? It's obvious you're looking for something.'

'Not sure.'

'And what was that about yesterday? Something about a painting.'

'Oh, it was a mix up.'

'You sounded really stressed. Zoë, you are all right aren't you?'

'Yeah.' For a moment Mike stood there watching me, as if he didn't believe me, then yawning he turned and went back to his room.

I searched the lounge from top to bottom but an hour and a half later I'd not found anything.

I sat on the bed in Ollie's room, thinking. What about this room? Urgh. He'd have watched us having sex. I began the search process again but there was nothing that looked like a camera. However, on the top of a pile of receipts I found one for the DVDs I'd received. The top had been torn off but they'd been bought online just a few days beforehand. I stared at it. It couldn't be Ollie behind it – could it? Or had it been planted?

CHAPTER 27

In the cold light of morning I knew I should not have driven. From the hangover I nursed, I must have been well over the limit, and I was grateful that the short journey had been uneventful. At least, I hoped so. In truth, I couldn't remember the drive, just the white anger. Guilt washed over me.

In the kitchen by the kettle, a scrap of paper in Mike's handwriting read: Jess rang. Said sorry.

So she should be. I found the painkillers and swallowed a couple to take the edge off my banging head.

In the hours leading up to the meeting with Scott I was fidgety. Like a caged animal, I paced the empty flat, trying to make sense of Ollie's involvement and how I should move forward. I'd been awake for ages in the night. The more I thought about it, the more likely it seemed that someone had planted the invoice. Or was I being naïve, unwilling to accept the obvious?

I got out the notebook and read what I could decipher of Vicky's writing. Her words reverberated around my head again, filling me with renewed anger. It was the tone more than what she'd said that got to me. How could they suggest that I was doing this to myself? I thought again of what they'd said about it being a woman. Was it the kind of thing a woman would do? Who? Someone from the office? I rubbed my temple. It felt as if my brain was going to explode.

'What can I do for you, Zoë?' DI Green asked bluntly as she sat down at the table opposite me.

'You can stop whoever's doing this. 'I pushed the matches and DVDs towards her. DI Green glanced down at the wrapped items.

'What are they?'

'More stuff someone's left or sent me.'

DI Green was wearing one of the suits I'd seen in ASDA. It was a grey pinstripe with large buttons and didn't seem classy enough for the job. Then I realised that if she was running around chasing villains it would probably be ruined soon anyway.

'Tell me about them,' she said, adjusting her wrist watch to subtly check the time. I gave her a hard stare, trying to weigh up her attitude towards me. Was she losing patience with me?

I took the notebook from my bag. 'The DVDs were delivered yesterday. And those were shoved through my friend's door while I was there last night. It's all in here.' I pointed to the notebook. 'My friend wrote it down. Every incident. As far as I can remember them.'

DI Green took the notebook and studied the cover. 'What made you write it down?'

'My friends said it might help. It might show a pattern or something.'

'Has it?'

I shrugged, feeling like an idiot. 'Not that I can see. But then I'm not trained to analyse this stuff.'

DI Green opened the notebook and started reading, her eyes running swiftly across the page and back again. I was surprised how easily she could decipher Vicky's scrawl.

One of her eyebrows twitched upwards, questioning like a sneer. I had a feeling she thought I was obsessive and neurotic. All I cared about was that she took it seriously.

'Has this got something to do with what happened to Neil Wyatt?' I blurted. 'I know you said before you didn't think so, but…'

DI Green looked up but said nothing.

'Who was Neil Wyatt? Was he a drug dealer or something? It must have been something like that, otherwise he wouldn't have had his flat torched.'

'What makes you say that?' DI Green's face was impossible to read but her posture was stiff and I knew I was on the right track.

Why couldn't she give me a straight answer? 'I don't know. But normal people don't get attacked, do they? Not unless they've done something to someone.'

'That's not true. You haven't done something to upset someone, have you?'

'Well, no.'

'But you seem to have attracted someone's attention.'

I stared at the stain on the table surface. Didn't she believe me either? She seemed keen to be rid of me.

'Do you think this,' I stabbed at the items on the table, 'is anything to do with the fire at my flat?'

DI Green glanced at her watch again. 'We're trying to find out. I'm sorry, Zoë. The problem is, there isn't really a lot to go on.'

I poked the notebook. 'I know you think I'm obsessive, but I'm struggling to make sense of it.'

It was difficult to read the smile she gave me. I couldn't work out if it was sympathetic or patronising. I had a feeling it was the latter. 'No one thinks you're obsessive,' she said.

'No? I can see it in your face.' Tears threatened, the result of tiredness and frustration. 'I'm getting really scared,' I admitted. 'It's doing my head in and I just want it to stop.'

'I know. And I'm sorry. The police take matters of

stalking very seriously. But the nature of the crime means we often don't have much in the way of leads.' DI Green flicked through the notebook again. 'Can I keep this?'

Now that I'd recorded it all I didn't think I wanted to part with it. I hadn't analysed it yet and there could be clues in there. 'Can you copy it?'

'Okay.' She got up to go.

'I just want this over,' I said.

'I know. The trouble is, unless this person makes himself known to you, we haven't got a lot to go on. I'll send these to forensics but it'll take a while. We may be lucky and get a fingerprint, but unless this person is on the police records his prints won't be much use.'

'Well that's just brilliant!'

DI Green looked at the table and said quietly: 'A piece of advice, Zoë. I know you're anxious at the moment but watch how much you have to drink. You can be over the limit the morning after.'

I felt the blood drain from my face. How did she know? I knew I looked rough. Were my eyes bloodshot? Or my tongue still purple? DI Green didn't say anything else. With a knowing look she strode from the room and I was left staring guiltily at the table, wondering if she was about to come back with a breathalyser test.

I waited nervously but when the door opened again it was the desk sergeant who handed back my notebook and let me out. Half expecting to be pounced on the minute I started the engine, I scanned the road for signs of police activity, then drove away as fast as I legally could.

I hadn't told them about the receipt I'd found. I wasn't sure why but I was worried about implicating Ollie when I didn't believe it could possibly be him.

The bright lights of the café made it an oasis on such a dull day. I pulled up just along the road, squeezing into a space that was, I realised too late, barely big enough and took some shunting to get into. My offside wing was sticking out into the road slightly and I had to hope no one hit it.

After struggling to park, I was a few minutes late, but Scott wasn't there. I hoped I hadn't missed him. I felt a ridiculous sense of guilt meeting up with him, as if there was something clandestine about it. I found a spot in a comfy chair, away from the draught of the door but not too far back, so that Scott could see me as he came in. The artwork sat in a manila envelope on the arm of the chair. I pulled my coat and scarf off and sat down, checking my phone to ensure he hadn't called to cancel.

I still felt agitated and glanced around the café. The place had a feeling of decadent laziness that was very appealing. Tinsel had been strung across the front of the counter and over the top of bright abstract paintings that hung on the walls. I stared at the decorations and wondered where I'd be spending Christmas this year. It was a depressing thought.

I read through the menu, but I knew what I wanted. I'd seen the chocolate cake as I came in. I did a brief reckoning of the calorie count then thought to hell with it. The door opened and Scott entered, removing his crash helmet as he strode towards me. He grinned.

'Hi,' he said, sitting. 'Have you ordered?'

'Not yet.'

He waved the waitress over. 'I'll have an espresso. What about you?'

'A latte.' My eyes drifted to the cakes peeking out from behind the tinsel in the glass counter. 'And some chocolate fudge cake please.'

Scott raised an eyebrow. 'I knew you were a chocolate cake girl.'

'Show me a girl that doesn't like chocolate cake.'

Scott's face was full of humour and he laughed. 'Fair enough.'

'This is nice. I haven't been here before.'

'I like it. Sorry I can't stay long. I'm really up against

it with a deadline and I've been waiting on stuff to get on with it. Well you must know what it's like.'

'Yeah. We're always working to ridiculous deadlines. Clients are the bane of our lives.'

'Are you okay? You look... I don't know.'

'Hungover?' I suggested.

'I was going to say hassled.'

'I'm all right. I've just come from the police station that's all. They're useless.'

'What were you doing at the police station?'

'Trying to find out what's going on. To get an update on the fire.' After what had happened with the girls, I wasn't in a hurry to tell anyone else about it.

'And?'

'And nothing.'

An attractive waitress wandered lethargically around the room, halfheartedly wiping at tables and clearing away crockery. I could see Scott watching her appreciatively.

I pulled the envelope onto the table and took the printouts from it, eager to get business out of the way. 'Business cards,' I said. 'I've given you three options. Mostly typographic.' I turned the sheets towards him as if I was doing a presentation at work. 'I forgot to ask how it was going to be printed. Or rather how many you wanted as that'll determine how it's printed.'

He seemed to be studying me rather than the visuals, which was off-putting so I kept talking. 'The cheapest way these days is in full colour with a matt laminate both sides. The colours aren't right on these. Home printers never seem to render colour very accurately.'

His eyes had drifted to the visual. I moved the front sheet to the back, bringing the next image forward. The coffee arrived and I had to move things out of the way so that it fitted on the table. I spilt my coffee. 'Blast!'

'Are you sure you're okay? You seem jumpy.'

I tried to smile as I took a forkful of cake. 'I think my

sugar levels are a bit low.'

'Are you diabetic then?'

'No. It's more a psychological need than a physical one.' I sucked rich cream filling from my teeth. 'This is scrummy.'

Scott watched me over his coffee cup as I explained about the next visual.

'Have I got chocolate on my nose or something?' My mobile rang. I fished it from my bag and when I saw that it was Ollie calling threw it back in again.

'Someone you don't want to talk to?'

'Something like that.'

Scott laid his empty cup on the table. 'What's he done?'

'He?'

'I take it it was Ollie?'

I stared at him. 'Sometimes you're scarily perceptive.'

He gave a small laugh then drew my attention back to the visuals. 'I like this one.'

'Yes, it's cleaner than the other one. It just depends whether you want to go modern or classic with the fonts.'

He shrugged. 'What do you think?'

I turned the page over. 'I prefer this one myself.'

'Blimey. I didn't expect you to go to this much trouble.'

'Force of habit.'

'They're all great.'

'Thanks. Why don't you take them all away, check the spellings and phone numbers and that.' As I spoke it dawned on me that I was going to find it a problem making those changes if I didn't resolve things with Jess.

He nodded. 'Thanks. Look, sorry it's such a rush but I'd better go.'

I pushed thoughts of his cards away. I'd got it into my head that I had to win him round with the visuals and I hadn't been able to deviate from that even though the ideal opportunity had presented itself earlier in our conversation. If he was off I had to ask for what I wanted now.

'Have you heard anything about the case? The fire at my flat I mean?' I ventured. 'I mean, in your job there must be ways of hearing about stuff.'

'Like what?'

It wasn't the answer I was hoping for. 'I don't know. I just thought…in your line of work you might hear things. Have contacts in the police or something.'

Scott looked quizzical. 'You think I can get inside information from the police?'

'I don't know. But the police aren't telling me anything.'

'Maybe there's nothing to tell.'

'There must be. That fire was started deliberately. The police must have some idea who's responsible.'

He glanced at his watch. 'Leave it with me and I'll see what I can do. Is that why you're so strung out? Are you worried for your safety?'

I didn't know how to answer and tried to laugh it off. 'No. The police don't think it's got anything to do with me.'

Scott stood and dropped a ten-pound note onto the table and picked up the envelope. 'I'll see what I can do. I'll call you.'

For a while after he had gone I sat there, feeling disappointed and wondering if he would actually come up with anything. The waitress took the money and cleared away the empty cups.

I reran our conversation in my head. Scott hadn't promised me anything. All he'd said was that he would look into it, but would he actually do so? I'd put all my energy into building up to this meeting, now abruptly it was over and I was at a loss what to do next.

Scott was perceptive. He must have picked up on my need to know but did he realise how impatient I was for answers.

CHAPTER 28

The local radio station was playing back-to-back Christmas songs. The holidays seemed remote but I turned the stereo up, tuned my thoughts out, and sang along.

I began to wonder if my stalker had got bored. Over time the gifts that he'd sent had got tamer, as if he'd run out of ideas, and the last few days had passed without incident. As each day went by, I relaxed a little more.

Ollie's room was a mess. It had been on my mind to tidy up for a while but the hints and comments he kept making annoyed me so I hadn't felt inclined to do it. I could understand why he was getting frustrated; my belongings were everywhere. A bag of clean washing was still where I'd left it days ago. I'd been living out of it ever since, and the contents were spilling onto the floor. There seemed little point trying to find a home for it. There wasn't really anywhere to put things. Besides, it felt too permanent; as if I was accepting that I was stuck at the flat indefinitely. Today I thought I'd tackle it. I went through the clean washing, refolding garments then stacking them into two unstable piles on top of his chest of drawers. At least it wasn't on the floor any more.

Ollie appeared in the doorway holding a towel. 'Here.'

'I'm not going to the laundrette today.' I laid a tee shirt face down on the bed and began refolding it.

'Eh? Oh. That's not why I was giving it to you. We're going down the gym.'

'We? You mean you and Darren?'

Unravelling the towel, Ollie revealed a black piece of cloth, which he waved at me. 'And you. I popped in earlier and got you a swimming costume. And I've booked a massage for you.'

'Seriously?'

Ollie grinned. 'I thought it might help you unwind. You've been so stressed. I've arranged to have a game of squash with Darren myself.'

I reached up and kissed him on the cheek. 'That's really sweet.'

As if he'd heard us, Darren appeared in the doorway, tapping his watch. 'We need to get going mate. She ready?'

'She?' I said indignantly. 'I've only just been told about it so no, she isn't.'

Darren gave a cluck of the tongue and, mumbling about being late, wandered off.

'Why didn't you give me some notice?' I demanded.

'You were finally tidying up. I wasn't going to stop you 'til I needed to.'

'Oi! Well I need to get some bits together before we go, and I'd like to try this cossie on rather than look a muppet in the changing rooms. Did you keep the receipt?'

'Somewhere.' He began digging through his pockets.

'I'll get my stuff together,' I said, making a mental list: make up remover, mascara, shampoo etc. 'Can I borrow your goggles?'

Darren was leaning against the wall of the hall looking cross, and as Ollie joined him I saw the exchange of glances.

'Why don't you go ahead?' I suggested. 'It's probably a good idea anyway. I can come back when I'm ready then.'

Ollie nodded. 'Okay. I'll tell them you're on your way. The massage is booked for quarter to.'

'Great.'

It was as well they hadn't waited. It took nearly fifteen minutes for me to get ready and that didn't include the long journey down the stairs. I'd never have lived it down.

The gym was busy. Through the glass partition I could see all the equipment and was envious that I couldn't do a proper work out. I wriggled my toes. My foot was feeling better, although I still couldn't put any weight on it without pain. Hopefully it was a good sign for swimming though. I signed in as I'd done on previous occasions when Ollie had brought me here. The girl on reception looked at my crutches doubtfully.

'My boyfriend's just told me he booked a massage and a swim for me,' I said. 'The massage is booked for quarter to, but I can't really go in the pool afterwards. Is there any chance of swapping it round?'

'I'll ask. What's your name?' She picked up the phone. 'They can put it back half an hour.'

'Okay. Thank you.' I headed for the changing room, high on the smell of chlorine.

The pool isn't large or deep, but it was an opportunity to do some exercise, which was the main thing. It was busier than I'd have liked, with a couple of families drifting from side to side on rubber rings. I laid my crutches down where they wouldn't be in the way and eased into the water. It was colder than I'd expected. Keeping to one side, I swam up and down, irritated by the constant stopping when people got in the way. I kept my feet still and ploughed through the water mainly using my arms. The muscles were working hard and it felt great. I counted the lengths.

I clung to the edge of the pool, catching my breath. It felt good to exercise. After a few moments I carried on, swimming up and down, being careful when I turned and pushed off again.

Soon I got fed up having to stop and swim round people, and my eyes stung where Ollie's goggles didn't fit too well. I got out, grabbed my crutches, and went over to the jacuzzi.

A middle-aged man with a huge protruding belly watched me intently, making me self-conscious. I stared at him, wondering what form of exercise he'd done. Beside him two girls were gossiping about one of their friends. From the lack of distance between the man and girls I surmised he was probably their father. There was another man in the jacuzzi. I'd only seen the back of his head and when I got closer I realised it was Scott. He was stretched back with his eyes closed.

'Hello, Scott,' I said, cautiously clambering in and feeling inelegant and self conscious. He opened his eyes as I sat down in the space opposite him.

'Hello. How's it going? You haven't been using the gym, have you?'

'I wish. No, just the pool. I've done about thirty lengths.'

'Impressive.'

'Hardly. It's a small pool.'

'And it must be irritating with all the kids, I imagine,' he said, nodding towards the pool. While his head was turned I checked him out. His torso rippled with muscles, and was hairless as I'd suspected. Too bare. He definitely waxed. I tore my gaze away and hoped that the heat of the jacuzzi hid my blush.

The water was hot after the pool and the bubbles luxurious. I sank further into it, feeling the pounding of jets across my lower back. I wriggled my foot into a jet coming up from the bottom and felt it massaging my toes.

'Are you here on your own?' asked Scott. His damp hair was dark and smoothed back, away from his chiselled face. Was it the light or was that fake tan? My own skin looked pale in comparison.

'No. Darren and Ollie are playing squash.'

The pot-bellied man was listening in, and watching although he was trying to make it look as if he wasn't. The girls had finished bitching about their friend and had moved on to one of the boy bands.

'Maybe we can all go for a drink after then,' said Scott. 'Do you know when they had the court booked for?'

'Half past, I think.'

'They should be done soon then.'

'Probably. I won't be able to make it though. I've got a massage. If you see the guys can you let them know I altered the time and I'll catch up with them back at the flat.'

'How are you getting home?'

'We came separately. I drove my car.'

Scott looked thoughtful. 'How is your foot? It can't be too bad if you're swimming.'

'It's okay as long as I don't put weight on it.'

The pot-bellied man stood up, adjusted his too-tight trunks and climbed out. The two girls sniggered. From the comments that followed it was apparent they weren't with him after all. I moved to the space the man had vacated which was closer to Scott.

'Did you find out anything?'

'Not yet. I'm meeting up with my contact tomorrow, so hopefully I'll have some news for you then. I'll give you a call. He did hint at some stuff, but they're waiting on some forensics. So, what kind of massage are you having?'

'I never thought to ask. Ollie booked it.'

'It's probably an aromatherapy one.'

'I wouldn't know. I've never had one before. The only massages I've had have been for sports injuries. You sound very knowledgeable.'

'Not really. I tend to steer clear of that sort of thing. I always seem to end up with butch women that pound the hell out of me.'

I laughed. 'I'm hoping this is going to be a bit more relaxing than that.'

Scott checked the clock on the end wall. 'I'm going to get out. I'll see if I can catch up with the others. Enjoy your massage.'

The treatment room was no bigger than a cupboard. There were no windows and it would have been claustrophobic if it hadn't been so sparse and light. The walls were cream. The carpet was cream, and there were navy and cream towels positioned carefully on the massage table. The thick scent of almond oil and lavender filled the air as the masseur stepped aside to let me enter. Soothing instrumental music played softly in the background, and a tiny water feature bubbled in the corner.

'Hello. My name is Suzie. I'll be doing your treatments today.' The masseur was Asian and spoke with an accent.

I put my bag and coat down on the floor and stood there awkwardly. 'This room very small. Can we put your bag in one of lockers outside?' she suggested.

'Er yes. Course.'

She opened the door and indicated a row of narrow lockers in the corridor. Very few were being used so I had my pick. I chose the nearest one, locked my bag and coat inside and took out the key.

'I need ask you a few questions about your health and skin care.' She picked up a clipboard and pen. 'Okay,' she said, once we had finished, 'would you like massage or facial first?'

'It's just a massage.'

'No, reception told me facial been added.'

I quite fancied a facial but I couldn't afford unnecessary expense if she'd got it wrong. 'Are you sure you've got the right person?'

'Yes. All here and paid for.'

'Okay, if you say so.' It seemed unlikely but I didn't

want to argue. 'Massage first, please.'

'Certainly. You get undressed and lie face down on bed. I'll be back in moment.'

I did as instructed and lay on the bed, staring at the floor through a small uncomfortable hole. I pulled one of the towels up across my lower half. The towel felt warm and comforting. The masseur was back about five minutes later and began working on my back. I listened to the gentle music and felt the stress of the last few weeks ebb away under her touch.

'You are very tense,' she said.

'Sorry.'

'No need to apologise. That what massage for.'

Her hands glided over my oiled skin, kneading out the knots in my shoulders and neck, making me struggle not to moan with pleasure. My skin felt warm where she had been working and chilled where she hadn't. Once she had finished the massage, I lay on my back wrapped in a warm towel. Then, with eyes closed, I listened as at each stage she told me what she was doing, cleansing my face, using steam and a face pack. While she got on with it I let my mind wander.

Afterwards I felt more relaxed than I had been for weeks. I went to my locker and retrieved my bag and coat. The door was dented along the lock edge as if it had been wrenched open at some stage. Funny, I hadn't noticed that before. I headed back to my car, thankful to Ollie for arranging such an enjoyable couple of hours.

My keys were not in my bag. I tried my coat pocket. Nothing. I emptied the contents of my bag onto the tarmac but my keys were not inside. Had someone stolen them from my locker? It had certainly been damaged and I hadn't noticed it when I first used it. Or was I just being paranoid? I turned to go and ask at reception if anyone had handed them in, and then I saw them. They were lieing on the tarmac by the back wheel, just underneath the car. I must have dropped them.

With relief I got into the car, but it was short lived. Immediately I realised that someone had been in it again. The seat was too far back, as if someone else had driven it. And when I looked in the mirror it was askew, tilted as if for someone of a different height. I had a look around the car but nothing seemed out of place. It was odd and just as unnerving as if I'd found something. What was it about? Had my keys been stolen? Should I drive? What if someone had done some damage, cut the brakes for example? I didn't know what to do, but I couldn't sit in the car park indefinitely. I decided to risk driving and get Ollie to take a look for me.

There was a commotion on the stairs when I got back to Ollie's flat. Darren was ranting and chucking bin bags onto the landing. 'I want you out,' he yelled at me.

'What's going on?' I stared at him, wondering what was wrong. I'd never seen him so angry.

Darren sneered into my face. 'Don't try the innocent act.'

'What the hell's got into you?' The clothes I'd folded earlier were spilling out of the bin bag onto the grubby carpet. 'This is my stuff.'

'No shit, Sherlock!'

'Why are you being like this?'

Ollie appeared looking strained.

'What's this about?' I glared at him, demanding an answer but he didn't say a word. He stood back, watching us, as if he wanted no part of it.

'Ollie. Tell me what this freak is on about?'

Ollie wouldn't meet my eyes. 'You drove straight at him,' he murmured.

'What?'

Darren hovered over me. 'Don't pretend you don't know what we're talking about.'

I ignored him. 'I haven't got a clue what you're referring to,' I snapped at Ollie.

'It was your car,' Darren said. 'I saw the number plate and that dog thing on the parcel shelf.'

'You're not serious. Why would I try and run you over?'

'You tell me. Maybe you're trying to get me out of my own flat?'

Angry at the accusation, and even angrier that Ollie was doing nothing to defend me, I shouted back: 'It's hardly a reason to try and kill you. Though at the moment I admit it does have a lot of appeal.' I turned to Ollie who was standing with arms folded.

'Are you buying this shit?'

He spoke quietly. 'I was there.'

I glared at him, shocked by what I was hearing. 'You don't honestly believe this crap? If someone ran Darren over then it wasn't me. I expect there are plenty of people he's pissed off.' Someone had driven my car though, and they were clearly trying to put the blame on me. 'Couldn't you see it wasn't me through the windscreen?'

'The sun was behind the car. And it was low, I couldn't see into the car. It was only once it got past I realised it was you.'

'It wasn't me.'

Ollie didn't believe me. 'You've been acting pretty weird lately,' he said.

At that moment I wondered if I should have told him exactly what I was going through. 'You don't know the half of it!'

Darren gave a derisory sneer and I decided I wasn't going to tell Ollie with Darren listening.

'I haven't had the opportunity,' I said, realising nothing I said was going to make any difference. 'I was swimming, then in the spa.'

'Bullshit. We looked for you. You weren't in the pool after your massage.'

'I swapped it round. There's no point having a massage

and then washing it all off in the pool. I saw your mate Scott. He'll tell you.'

Darren shook his head. 'You're such a liar.' His next comment was directed at Ollie. 'I'm sure she's got a thing for Scott, probably having it off with him'

I slapped him. 'How dare you, you vicious stirring bastard!'

'At least I didn't try and run you over,' he said touching his face where my hand had contacted. My fingers stung.

'No. But I bet you're responsible for everything that's been happening to me.'

'Are you accusing me of starting the fire?'

'I never mentioned the fire.'

'I think it might be best if you went,' said Ollie. 'Give everyone a chance to calm down.'

Darren wasn't about to be contained. 'I ain't gonna calm down. That bitch tried to run me over. I still think we should call the police.'

'You do that,' I shouted. 'Get them to take your fingerprints while you're at it.'

Ollie stepped forward. 'Just go, Zoë. Please.' The door shut in my face.

'Why are you doing this? It wasn't me.' I whacked the door with one of my crutches, leaving a dirty mark in the paintwork. 'Oh, screw you.'

What the hell had just happened? Why hadn't Ollie stood up for me? I gathered up my things then wondered how I was going to get them down the stairs. I scooped up any stray clothes, then tying a knot in the bin bags, launched them and let gravity carry them down. Struggling along the street with one of the heavy bags, I was glad I'd managed to get a parking space quite close. I shoved the bin bag into the back of the car and saw that on the passenger seat there was a glossy red gift box secured with a wide cream ribbon tied in a bow. Someone had been in my car again.

Leaning in I picked the box up. My immediate

thoughts were of slinky underwear, it was that kind of box, but it was too heavy. I laid the package on the bonnet of the car, tugged at the ribbon and lifted the lid. The box was filled with pink tissue paper. I eased it out of the way, opening it out, then stumbled backwards.

A face stared at me. A pale dead eye, the eyelashes still intact though congealed in the fatty flesh of the face, or rather half a face – a burnt face that looked up from amongst the tissue. I vomited. It took several moments to steady myself. When I could finally look again, I saw that the ghastly face had probably been a pig once but the nose area was missing and what was left appeared remarkably human. I looked up, expecting to see one of the boys walking towards me and to find that it was all some elaborate unfunny joke.

Reaching for my phone I speed dialled Ollie but it went straight to voicemail. 'If this is your idea of a joke you need help,' I shouted. 'Where the hell did you get that thing? And how did you get into my car? Or is this that bastard Darren setting me up... Oh - what's the point!' I cut the call, shoved the lid back on the box so that I didn't have to look at it any more and threw it onto the pavement. Then I went back towards the flat for the other bag of clothes, laying where it had landed when I'd thrown it. I picked it up and headed for the car again.

'Zoë.' Ollie came panting to join me. I glared at him. 'I'm sorry,' he said. He snatched the bag from me and we walked back towards the car.

'Sorry for what? Accusing me of all sorts? Or sorry for that thing in my car?'

'What thing?'

'The head. That gruesome head. On the pavement.'

'What am I supposed to be looking at?' he said.

'It was there.' I looked around, expecting to find the box and bow in the gutter or over a wall. But they were gone. 'A red box. About this big,' I said, indicating with my hands. Ollie gave me a sympathetic look, pulling in his bottom lip as if preventing himself from saying what I knew he was thinking.

'What was in this box?' he said. This 'imaginary' box - that was what he was really saying. My mind would never have conjured such a grizzly image.

'A vile charred pigs head. It was made to look human.' I indicated the splatter of vomit. 'It made me throw up.' From his expression, I could see that Ollie didn't believe me. A slither of pink tissue, nestling against the back tyre, caught my eye. 'There,' I said, 'that's the paper that it was packed in.' Even as I spoke I realised a small piece of paper didn't prove anything. Not to Ollie anyway. To me however, it confirmed my sanity.

I got into the car, anger burning through me, my mind flipping through possibilities. Had he just run down the stairs? Or had he come down via the fire escape? He could have got from the back of the building by slipping along the side of it. And he could have sneaked down the row of parked vehicles to my car then back to the front door, dumping the box somewhere en route? It was quite possible. I could move quite fast on the crutches now but he'd have had the time. Or had Darren been part of it?

I got out of the car and made my way along the route I guessed he'd taken, Ollie following.

'What are you doing?'

I peered over walls and scanned gardens. Nothing. 'Did you cook this up between you?' I said, moving on to the next property and bending to look under the adjacent car. I could see nothing but a crisp packet and cigarette butts.

'Do you know how irrational you sound?'

'Oh, I'm aware, all right.' I rose. 'This isn't achieving anything, is it? I don't believe you and you won't believe it wasn't me driving, even though I didn't have the opportunity, and there is plenty of proof that I had a swim, then went for the massage and facial.'

'You had a facial as well? I didn't think you wanted to spend any money.'

I gaped at him in disbelief. 'They said...' This was all linked wasn't it, the facial was so that I was out of the way. It was a deliberate attempt to make it look as if I was losing the plot. Ollie started to say something but whatever it was I didn't want to hear it. I walked back to my car, got in and shut the door. I had to get away, to disappear for a while. I had to make it stop. I had to feel safe.

CHAPTER 29

I thought about going to the police but DI Green hadn't been very sympathetic last time, and as I had no evidence there was little point. The only thing it would achieve would be to make me look deluded. I was wired, and drove around aimlessly. Was this down to Ollie? Had he and Darren concocted it together. I almost wanted to believe it, so that I knew who I was dealing with. Everything seemed to point that way, but something deep inside me refused to accept it. Either way Ollie had betrayed me and I didn't trust him any more.

My priority was to get away. But where? I was back to that again. I had no family except Keith, and now I'd fallen out with my closest friends I really was stuck. I wondered if Claire's parents would take me in but I doubted I'd even be able find their house again. It was pointless trying. They were hardly going to offer a home to a stranger.

Spotting a newsagent, I pulled over. The smell of vomit hung about me; as if I'd got some on my clothes, though I didn't think I had. My mouth felt rancid so I nipped in, quickly bought a bottle of water and a packet of mints and hurried back to the car, afraid that something else could have been planted while I'd been in the shop. Thankfully this time the car was still locked and I couldn't find anything obvious. I scanned the street, wondering if I'd been followed. I couldn't see anyone, but that didn't mean there wasn't someone watching. God, I'd got paranoid.

Taking a large mouthful of water, I sloshed it around my mouth then spat it into the gutter. Then I got back into the car and locked the doors. For a while I sat there drinking, and frantically wondering what to do. Then, suddenly it came to me – Mel! I got my phone out and rang her.

'Hello!' Mel sounded cross.

'Hi Mel, it's Zoë.'

'I'll have to call you back. My 'darling' ex is here and I'm just about to skewer him with a bread knife.'

I knew exactly where she was coming from but I didn't get a chance to answer because she'd already gone. For nearly an hour I waited but Mel never rang back. It went through my head that she might have gone through with her threat, or been killed herself. But I reasoned that just because things were surreal for me didn't mean they were equally surreal for anyone else. She'd probably just forgotten, but that didn't help me. I tried her number again, but she didn't pick up.

The only solution was the one I'd been refusing to acknowledge. Even the thought of Keith made my hackles rise. I had a good excuse to visit because I still hadn't collected my portfolio. He had also said if there was anything he could do to help I just had to ask. Dropping my head to the steering wheel, I knew I had no choice. I was about to ring him but thought better of it. I'd just turn up. That way I could assess how things were without committing, and if in the meantime Mel rang back I could leave. A horrible thought occurred to me. If there was any chance I was in danger I could be putting Mel and her child in danger too. And I wouldn't do that. Mel's wasn't an option after all.

As I drove away I checked the road for signs of someone following. At each turn I watched the road behind but I didn't think there was anyone keeping up with me. Did that mean I was going to be safe, or had the stalker anticipated where I was going? Either way, I wasn't going to take unnecessary risks.

When I rang the doorbell at Keith's house there was no response. I thumped the door in frustration. It was as if everything was conspiring against me. Despondently, I went back to the car and waited. And waited. The grey sky darkened to a denser shade, tinged with fluorescence as the streetlights kicked in. Where was he? Occasionally the curtains of the neighbouring house twitched. Two hours went by and there was still no sign of him. Was he at his fancy woman's house? Was he out for the evening, or worse, the night? I was cold, hungry and thirsty, the water long gone. I wondered if the curtain-twitcher next door was Mrs Bennett, if she still lived there and still had a key. I went to find out.

The front door opened and I was examined from the narrow gap above the chain. 'Mrs Bennett? It's Zoë. I used to live next door.'

'Was that you in the car all this time?'

'Yes.'

'I was about to telephone the police.'

'Sorry. I didn't mean to frighten you. I was hoping to see…Dad.' The word stuck in my throat but I wasn't sure how Mrs Bennett would react if I referred to him as Keith. 'I don't suppose you happen to know where he is?'

'Actually he's away for the weekend, dear. He's not back until tomorrow.'

In that moment my world collapsed. I didn't know what to do next.

'Are you all right? I wish you'd knocked earlier, sitting in the cold so long. Why don't you come in and warm up? You look frozen. And I'd rather not heat the street.' Mrs

Bennett stood back, holding the collar of a small yapping terrier. She let the dog go to close the front door and put the chain on again. The terrier jumped up at me, yapping furiously. 'Stop it Rachel. Be nice to our guest.' The scruffy terrier circled me, eyeing my crutches suspiciously. She bared her teeth and growled. 'Rachel, no. She gets a bit excited with new people. But her bark's worse than her bite. I don't mean literally. She won't bite you. So, what have you done to yourself?'

Following her into the warm lounge, I told her how I'd hurt my foot. I expected to see Mr Bennett in his armchair by the fire but the chair was empty. The stack of newspapers that had been alongside it throughout my childhood was also gone. Mrs Bennett must have noticed where my gaze had fallen. 'Ted passed away nearly three years ago.'

'I'm sorry. I didn't know.'

She shrugged. 'It was very sudden. A heart-attack. Best way to go, in my book. Better than...' She clapped her hand to her mouth. 'Oh Lord, I'm sorry, dear.'

'No. You're right,' I acknowledged.

She nodded. 'Warm yourself, child.'

The room was cosy. A large gas fire in a tiled surround belted out orange heat. I shivered as the sudden change in temperature made me realise how cold I'd become. 'Would you like a hot drink?' Mrs Bennett said.

'That would be lovely. Can I have tea, milk, no sugar please?'

Standing by the fire, with my hands held down towards the heat, my fingers began to sting. The lounge hadn't changed much since I'd been here last. The same swirly-patterned carpet was a little threadbare in front of the seating, but had worn well. The papered walls were beginning to peel and the paintwork had yellowed with age. The chink of crockery from the kitchen was so loud I thought perhaps Mrs Bennett had dropped something.

'Do you want me to give you a hand?' I called.

'No. You stay there and get warm.' Moments later she shuffled in with a tray, the dog trotting at her heels. The teapot, cups, and side plate filled with digestive biscuits were all of matching china. I couldn't help thinking Mrs Bennett didn't get many visitors and was giving me the V.I.P. treatment.

She was an elderly woman whose grown up sons hadn't visited much when I'd been living next door. Somehow I couldn't imagine that things had improved. 'Is that your son?' I indicated a photograph of a smiling family group on the mantelpiece.

'Yes. Do you remember Shaun? He's married now with a couple of babies. Ever so busy.' She picked up the photograph and brought it over to me. Shaun was no longer the gorgeous man I'd had a crush on when I was a teenager. The years had taken most of his hair and he now looked very like Mr Bennett had done.

'That's his wife, Kerry, and Oliver and Sophie. Gary, my oldest, is living in New Zealand with a Maori girl with some unpronounceable name.' I didn't ask how long it had been since she'd seen any of them. She sank into her chair and poured the tea. 'Did I see you here before?'

'It's possible. I stayed over the night I hurt my foot.' I took the cup she offered and held it gingerly. It looked too delicate to actually use.

'Your Dad was telling me about the fire at your flat. You have been in the wars.'

'I got off lightly. The man downstairs died.'

'Dreadful.' She started tutting.

'I've been crashing at a friend's flat, but I was hoping Dad could help me out for a couple of days until I can get something else sorted.'

'Oh, dear. I suppose you could stay here. I'll have to dig the spare blankets out and give them an air.'

'Thank you, that's really kind. And no offence, but I'd really like to be in my old home. I don't suppose you've still got a spare key?'

I could see her considering. 'I don't know whether I should,' she said. 'You and Keith haven't exactly been friendly all these years.'

'I know. But you saw me here before.'

'I suppose. It was a shame you two fell out. Everyone needs family. I know he misses you.'

I chewed my lip and bit back a vicious retort. 'We had a difference of opinion.'

'About Yvonne. I know.'

'Yvonne?'

'The woman from his work. Keith told me about it.'

'I suppose he had to if he was going to bring her to the house.'

'He never brought her back to my knowledge. No. It was much later. He told me that the two of you had fought. He was devastated. Not only had he lost your mum, but through his own stupidity he'd lost you too.'

'He betrayed Mum.'

'Oh, I'm not condoning what he did. He was an idiot and he knows it. He's had to live with the consequences every day since. You've both lost out. So it's good to find you're back in contact again.'

I didn't tell her the level of that contact was virtually non-existent, but she seemed to sense something was amiss. I took a sip of my tea.

'You have managed to patch things up, haven't you?'

I spoke carefully, aware that if I said the wrong thing she might not give me the key. 'We've made a start. It's a slow process. Some things aren't easily forgiven.'

She nodded. 'I think Keith's more aware of that than most. He hasn't forgiven himself. Even though your mother forgave him.'

'She knew?'

Mrs Bennett put down her cup. 'Of course she knew. But your Mum wasn't one to hold a grudge. She understood it was his way of coping. Yvonne was a diversion, a comfort so he didn't have to think about what was really happening.'

'I expected to see that woman living here. I thought he was going to be the sort of man that marries less than a year after their wife's death. As if they can't live alone.'

Mrs Bennett patted my hand. 'Don't be too critical. When someone's ill for a long time you do a lot of grieving before they pass on. Oh look, it's started sleeting. Are you warmed up? I'll fetch that key for you before the path gets too slippery. The last thing you need is to have another fall.'

'Thank you.'

My footprints left slushy grey marks on the drive, back and forth from the car. I put the two bin bags down on the path and unlocked the front door. The house was silent apart from the click of the radiators heating or cooling. 'Hello,' I called. No one answered. I dropped one bag on the hall floor and reached for the other. The place felt familiarly reassuring. Perhaps being here again so recently made it feel comfortable. I wasn't sure whether it was better or worse without my stepfather. I craved both company and solitude.

Through the wall I could hear the muffled but reassuring sound of Mrs Bennett's television, otherwise it was oppressively quiet. I felt very alone. I put the bag down, shut and locked the door, then went around the house drawing curtains, and checking the doors and windows. Upstairs I found that the bed in my old room was already made up with clean sheets. It was as if Dad had anticipated my return. I sat down on it and considered what Mrs Bennett had said.

If only Mum was here. I went into my parents' room and stared at the collage of photos. Mrs Bennett's words were haunting me, running over again and again in my head. I hadn't known. I hadn't understood, hadn't wanted to understand, if I was honest. Perhaps I had been too harsh. I didn't know Mum knew all about his affair. How could she have forgiven him? And yet at this moment I could appreciate the need of a warm hug. I reached out and touched the main photo of Mum. If she could forgive him, maybe...

I went in search of something to eat, and found a packet of microwavable risotto. I shoved it in and grabbed a handful of fruit from the bowl. For company I put the television on, and with my dinner on a tray, curled up on the sofa. Unwilling to dwell on what had happened at the flat, instead I remembered happier times when I was a child.

CHAPTER 30

A billboard outside the church entrance gate advertised the forthcoming Christmas services. As I walked down the path the breathy sound of a pipe organ started up, drowning out the murmur of cars on the main road across the valley. A few old people, shuffling towards the church doorway, cast me a look that said, aren't you coming in? It was the wrong time to go to the churchyard but I'd lost track of the days. And it hadn't occurred to me that there would be a service on. I just wanted to visit Mum's grave. Guiltily I averted my gaze and wandered past.

Much of the main graveyard was unkempt. Ancient, decrepit tombstones leaned precariously, a line of ivy-clad dominos ready to collapse. The modern cremation plots were sited in the last available area, towards the back of the churchyard. The memorial stones were all of uniform size and equally spaced, as if someone had been out here with a ruler. I realised with some horror that it had been much longer than I'd thought since I'd visited. In that time there had been a number of changes. Mum's grave wasn't where I expected: many others had been added, and whereas it had previously sat in a carpet of turf, now it was surrounded by a layer of cat-litter gravel.

'Hello Mum. I'm sorry, it's been a while.'

Mum's stone was more towards the centre now. It was black marble with gold lettering that declared her name, the dates of when she was born and died, and the message 'Much Loved'. Wording that said nothing about my Mum, how I missed her, and her struggle to live.

I picked up the remnants of a decaying posy from the vase behind Mum's stone and moved it out of the way. The chrysanthemums were limp and downcast, carnations brown and crinkled. So, my stepfather had been here, bringing her flowers to appease his guilt. No, that wasn't fair. At least he'd come. I hadn't. And my own flowers were a poor selection, purchased from a roadside stall on the way. I should have taken a detour and gone to a supermarket. But it was just a memorial stone. She wasn't here. So why was I visiting now?

Reassurance and comfort, the empty air around me seemed to say. I could have thought about Mum anywhere. I wasn't any closer to her here. 'There's a service going on in the church. I got some filthy looks because I didn't go in. I'll bet it's cold in that church. It's pretty cold out here. The wind's quite strong. But the sky's clear.' The sound of the church organ ceased, suddenly making me aware that I was thinking aloud.

When I was a child the sky was always blue, or at least, that was how it seemed. Slowly the memories crept in. Mum, Keith and I were happy. I wondered why Keith and Mum hadn't had children together. He was nearly ten years older than her, but they were young enough when they got together to have had more children. So why hadn't they? Keith clearly loved children. I could have done with some family right now. I tried to conjure an image of Mum, laughing and happy, but my mind had a habit of providing a grimmer picture, the fragile woman she became.

'I wish you were here, Mum. I'm in trouble. And I'm scared.' Once again my mind had slipped back onto what had happened the afternoon before. Despite thinking about it time and again, I still couldn't make any sense of it. 'Someone's stalking me. And I've no idea why or what they hope to gain from it.'

Had someone really tried to run Darren over? He couldn't have made it up if Ollie had witnessed it. Or were they in it together? If so, what were they trying to achieve? To make me think I was going crazy? Was I? Had I done it but had no recollection? It was enough to make my brain burst.

If Mike had been around, he might have stood up for me. Typical that now I needed him, he was up north on a techie training course. Or was he?

I sank down on the bench a little further along, feeling nauseous. I tried to think about it from a different angle. What if someone had tried to run Darren down? That put Darren and Ollie out of the frame for stalking me. But who could it be? Scott had been at the gym. He might have had the opportunity. But what possible motive could he have? Darren and Ollie said they hadn't seen him. Had I imagined him being there? I was seriously beginning to question my sanity.

Nick came to mind. I hadn't considered him for a while, but just because he was out of sight didn't mean it wasn't him. And what about the girls I knew? There was no reason to think that the stalker was a man. What if it was none of them and someone completely unknown to me?

I'd been down this route before, but what if it was someone linked to the fire? Maybe they thought I knew something and were trying to wreck my credibility. I got my phone out to ring Scott. There were a couple of missed calls from him and several from Ollie. I'd switched it to silent and forgotten to put the volume up again.

'Hi. I thought you were avoiding me,' were Scott's first words when he answered.

I pulled the zipper of my coat higher. 'Why would I

do that?'

'I don't know. Because of Darren.'

'Guilty by association, you mean? No, I forgot to take the phone off silent. Did you find something out then?'

'I heard what happened with Darren - well his version anyway.'

'It's utter crap.' A squeal of brakes startled me. I looked up to see a cyclist freewheeling along the path, heading for the housing estate on the other side of the churchyard.

'Are you okay? He said you tried to kill him?'

I sighed. 'I know. And I would like to now. But I didn't.' I watched a robin land on a tombstone. It stopped and looked at me as if interested in the conversation.

'You don't sound particularly bothered by it,' said Scott.

'I'm not. I've not got anything to prove.' I played it down, hoping I didn't betray myself. Mum's memorial stone was marked with dried spots of rain. Distractedly, I wiped it over with a tissue, but it would take more than a meagre effort with a rapidly disintegrating three ply to polish the marble. I changed the subject. 'So have you found out anything?'

'Maybe. I've got a copy of some paperwork here.'

'From the police?'

'I haven't had a chance to read it through yet. I thought you might want to swing by and read it for yourself. I've got an assignment to do or I'd come to you.'

'You're working on a Sunday?'

'There's no working week when you work for yourself, especially in this business. Look, it's up to you, but I'm tied up tomorrow and Tuesday so the earliest I can see you other than today is going to be Wednesday or Thursday.'

I thought about the implications of finding out. Perhaps once I knew what the police were thinking, things would start to fall into place.

'Okay,' I said, rummaging in my rucksack for a pen and paper. 'What's the address?'

I went back to Keith's house to pick up my car. When I got there his Renault was parked on the drive. Because of what Mrs Bennett had said, I hadn't expected to see him until later, and hadn't prepared what I was going to say to him. I took a deep breath and went into the house. Keith was standing almost directly behind the door, still wearing his coat as if he'd just got in.

'Zoë?' he said, clutching a carton of milk to his chest. 'You scared the living daylights out of me.'

'Sorry.' I shut the front door behind me. 'I stayed here last night. You did say...'

'Of course. It was lucky you still had a key.'

'I didn't. I borrowed this one from Mrs Bennett. I don't think she was very happy about letting me have it but I talked her into it.'

'I bet she was surprised to see you. I am.'

'Something like that.' I stood there awkwardly still holding the milk I too had bought on the way back.

'Shall we have a cup of tea?' he said. 'Seeing as we've got so much milk.'

'Okay. But I'm going out again soon,' I said.

'Oh.' He sounded disappointed.

'Would you mind if I stayed here for a while?'

'No, of course not. You're always welcome.'

'Thanks.' I decided that honesty was the best policy. 'I hope that offer's genuine because it's not working out living at Ollie's.'

'I rather gathered there was problem between you. He left a message on the answer phone. I'd just listened to it when you came in.'

'What did he say?'

'He just wanted to know if you were staying here and that you were all right.' I followed Keith into the kitchen. 'It's a shame,' he said, filling the kettle. 'He seems like a nice young man.' How do parents always manage to make that statement sound like something bad?

'I'm surprised he even bothered to call after what happened.' Keith turned towards me but didn't push me to explain and I didn't. I still couldn't fathom what had happed, let alone articulate it. 'I went to Mum's memorial stone,' I said instead. As if sensing I needed to talk, Keith didn't comment. He took two mugs from the cupboard. 'It's changed. When did they put that awful gravel in?'

He smiled. 'It looks like cat-litter doesn't it?'

I laughed. 'That's exactly what I thought.' The kettle boiled and he turned away to deal with it. I decided to try and talk to him about the source of our fall out. 'Mrs Bennett was telling me about when Mum died,' I said. 'About Yvonne. She said Mum knew. I didn't realise. I didn't…understand.'

Keith stopped what he was doing and for a moment remained motionless.

'I'm not having a go,' I said.

He turned to face me, looking sad. When he spoke his voice was soft. 'You were struggling with your own grief.' He looked down at the spoon in his hands. 'I was weak. I couldn't cope. I saw my own Mother go the same way. Not cancer. She had a stroke, but she lingered on. And I… couldn't deal with it. I'm not proud of what I did, Zoë. I know I was weak. I just wish I'd supported you better. But I can't turn back the clock. I only wish I could.'

I nodded. 'I wish she was still here.'

'So do I, love. So do I.'

'Did you know I went in search of my biological father after she died?'

'I'm not surprised. I remember you asking lots of questions about him. But I couldn't tell you anything.'

'I thought you were just being obstructive.'

'No. I didn't know much. I just remember your Mum telling me things. He didn't sound very pleasant. So, did you find him?'

'Yes. And he wasn't. He was running a dive of a pub in Portswood. I went there with my friend from college and he spent the first twenty minutes chatting us up. He was very charming. Until I told him who I was and he changed just like that.' I clicked my fingers. 'Did you know he'd done it again? He's abandoned another women after Mum.

'I'm sorry, love.'

For a while we sat and talked, making the first tentative steps towards reconciliation. As a result it was much later than I'd intended when I went to Scott's. Although he'd given me directions, it wasn't an area I knew, so before I left I borrowed Dad's laptop and Googled the address.

Following the directions, I finally turned onto an unmade road. The internet had shown it as narrow but I hadn't imagined it to be so narrow - and so pot holed. Had I got it wrong? I was beginning to think I'd have to find somewhere to turn around when, as I rounded a shallow corner, I spotted a gate pillar with a name on it. Standing back from the lane was a large brick house. The name didn't match the one Scott had given me, but at least it proved there were houses down here so I carried on, hoping I didn't meet anything coming the other way.

After a few minutes I came to large ornate metal gates that sagged on their hinges. One was shut, one open, allowing just enough room to drive through. On either side, the low wall was swamped in a vast hedge. From the lane it was impossible to see much of the house and if it hadn't been for the motorbike parked by the front door I would have thought it was the wrong place.

The branches of a nearby tree brushed the roof of the car with a clatter, initially making me fear I'd hit one of the gates as I drove through. In the rear view mirror, I saw the culprit was a cankerous silver birch with tired limbs it seemed incapable of supporting.

As I drove up the cracked and patchy tarmac I saw that the house was large, though neither grand nor imposing. It stood in a vast garden of neglected flowerbeds and looked almost derelict. To the far side, tucked back so that they didn't intrude on the look of the house were garages and outbuildings.

The place was a weird choice for someone like Scott. I didn't know him well, but I would have imagined him living in a flat like Ollie's, or an immaculate, spacious waterfront apartment; a sparsely furnished chrome and unimaginative white-paint-everywhere place. Not a large rural family home. Perhaps this was his parents' place but it hardly looked lived in.

I parked by the front door and got out, strangely excited that I was going to put together pieces of the puzzle that would lead to understanding. I stood for a moment listening to the silence. The flap of a bird and soft mooing of cattle were all I could hear. It was so tranquil.

The bell was a tarnished brass button that looked original. I rang it and somewhere deep inside the building a bell chimed. Closer now, I saw that the house had a split personality. An upper window frame was gleaming white as if it had recently been painted while the rest of the house had paintwork that was yellowed and peeling. Wouldn't it have made more sense to strip all the windows, undercoat them in one go and then top coat them? It would have saved cleaning brushes all the time. I'd have started with the front door so that at least I could see my handiwork every time I came in, but the front door hadn't seen a lick of paint for years.

When no one answered, I rang the bell again, leaned across a flowerbed to peer in at the window, but on the other side of the pane the curtains were drawn.

'Hello, Zoë.'

I jumped, and stepped back on a plant, snapping it off. 'Shit. Hi. Sorry.'

He shrugged indifferently as I stamped soil off my shoe.

'I'd given up on you.' He sounded irritated.

'Sorry. Something cropped up. Is it a bad time?' I didn't want to interrupt if he was still working, but I wasn't prepared to go away empty handed.

'No. It's just that I was expecting you earlier.'

He ushered me inside and indicated to carry on down the hall, which was wide and looked as if it too had recently been decorated in cream and white. A neutral beige carpet led up the stairs.

'Is this your place? What made you choose it? It's a bit out of the way.'

'Yeah, nobody bothers me here.' We entered a kitchen that was old-fashioned and disjointed but clean and sparsely tidy, the work surfaces devoid of the usual clutter that always seems to accumulate. As a result the kitchen looked impersonal and unused.

'Drink?'

'Thanks. Tea would be great.'

'I was thinking something a bit stronger.' He gently shook a bottle of vodka he'd taken from one of the cupboards. 'Or I've got gin and tonic if you'd prefer?'

'I think I'll stick to tea if it's okay with you. I'm driving.'

'Not for a while, though.'

I shook my head. 'Better not. The police are hot on it at the moment. You know what they're like at this time of year.'

He flicked the kettle on then poured himself a large tumbler of vodka and took a swig of it, eyeing me over the rim of the glass. He looked tired. There were bags under his eyes and where yesterday his skin had looked tanned, it now had the grey cast of partly dried concrete.

'Look, if I've come at a bad time I can grab the stuff and go. I don't want to hold you up.'

He rubbed his hands across his face. 'I've been working late. It's been a frustrating project, not quite going to plan. But I'm there now.'

'I can sympathise. Your industry's probably worse than mine for deadlines.'

The kettle boiled. 'Can you get the tea bags?' he said. 'They're in that cupboard behind you. By the sink. Top shelf.'

Turning away I reached up to the top shelf, painfully standing on tip-toe to grasp them. The window was spotted with the residue of dried rain. The garden beyond was mostly laid to lawn but with well-established shrubbery at the borders. A child's rope swing hung from a naked beech tree, swaying gently as if pushed by some unseen hand. Standing closer and taller, I now saw that there was a battered summerhouse and in front of it a swimming pool, dry except for the puddle of rainwater.

'Wow. You have a pool. Do you use it?'

'The pump's broken,' he said.

'Oh. I suppose it'll be expensive to fix.' I handed him the box of tea bags. He pulled one out and dropped it in the mug.

'It's old. They probably don't even make the bits anymore.'

Even on a dreary winter afternoon I could imagine how the late afternoon sunshine might cast a golden spotlight on the water in the height of summer. At that time of year it must be beautiful and timeless. 'What a pity! You could have some great parties.'

He handed me the mug and stood back sipping his own drink. The tea was milky and didn't feel that hot so I took a large gulp.

'So how long have you had this place?'

'A while.'

'You must have got on the property ladder young then. I can't ever see me being able to afford a studio flat let alone something like this.'

'No. I had a legacy. Anyway you don't need to worry about that now.' He sounded smug, nasty. What did he mean? My brain seemed to have dropped to half speed or less. Scott started talking fast about property and finances. I glazed over while he talked, sipping my tea and nodding, but not actually listening. I felt suddenly tired and dizzy. Then my legs gave way and I blacked out.

CHAPTER 31

The world was upside down as I was carried over Scott's shoulder. I felt sick as everything span around me. Time and movement spiralled together out of control. What was happening? I had a sense that I was in danger, but I was powerless to stop it. Strong arms held me while my own limbs didn't seem to want to work. Then I blacked out again.

When I came to a horrible musty smell was overpowering my senses. As my focus improved I saw dirty crumpled carpet in my limited line of vision, while the rest of the room was askew. I tried to get up but I could barely shift position. I lay there helplessly for a long time, getting my strength back.

Then behind me someone moved. Black motorcycle boots came into view.

'What happened?' I said, my words sounding slurred and not quite right.

'Haven't you worked it out?' He gave me that smile I was so used to but then it turned sour.

'I don't...' I felt out of it.

'I added a little something to your tea.'

'Vodka?'

'Not alcohol.' He grinned.

'What…'

'Ah. I can see you've worked it out.' He leaned down and hauled me into a sitting position, making my head throb so that I wanted to vomit. I could hardly hold myself upright.

'You drugged me!'

'Well done. Though for a bright girl you can be incredibly stupid sometimes.'

We were in a decaying room that was out of time. Swirling manic wallpaper in the kind of design that would make you mad was peeling from the walls. There were dark patches where pictures must have once been.

'What are you planning to do?'

He shrugged. 'At the moment I'm just enjoying watching you not in control.'

'I don't understand.'

'You will.' There was the slightest of twitches at the corner of his right eye, like a tick. How could I have been so blind that I hadn't seen what he was really like? Out of everyone, he was the one I was sure I could trust. He was the one that was intuitive and sympathetic. Now I knew that wasn't so. He wasn't intuitive - he just knew what was going on. If he'd put so much effort into doing all this what the hell did he have planned now? Could I move? Make a run for it? I tried to stand but I was still weak. I needed to think.

'Where are we?'

'The lounge.'

It was hardly that. Years ago it might have been. But now there wasn't any furniture. 'Don't you believe in comfort then? Why did you bring me here?'

'Well, I couldn't leave you lying on the kitchen floor.'

'That's not what I meant.'

He didn't answer. Instead he kicked at the edge of the carpet sending up a cloud of dust like a thick layer of ash. What was happening here? The decayed state of the room?

His weird attitude? I tried to see if I could get up.

'Stay where you are.'

I carried on nonetheless, reaching out towards the wall to steady myself. Slowly I managed to stand. Where were my crutches? Turning to look for them made me giddy. I stood still and closed my eyes. Where was this room? If it was at the front of the house, could I get to the front door? It was worth a try.

'Sit down.'

He grabbed my arm. 'Why can't you bloody do as you're told?'

'I just want to go home.'

'And where's that exactly? No one wants you any more,' he said.

'You're wrong. I thought you had some information for me. Or was that a lie?'

Something in his eyes changed. Anger radiated from him as he shoved me back to the floor. His eyes flickered over me, like acid on my skin. Was he going to rape me? Was that what this was about? Why this dreadful room?

'Me. Me. Me. That's all it is with you. You think you're something special. You think everything in life revolves around you.' Spittle hit my cheek as he spoke. 'You think you're invincible. Well, you're gonna find out you're not.'

How could I have trusted him? 'No one's invincible.'

'No,' he said, 'they're not.' There was a long pause then he said. 'Yeah, I know who started the fire. But it won't help you.' He turned and in three strides left the room, swinging the door shut behind him. Weakly I went after him but the door was locked. I yanked at the handle, banged hard on the wood.

'Let me out. Let me out.'

I leaned against the door, my ear flat to the wood, listening for sounds of him coming back. But he didn't. There was no sound of movement at all. I yanked the door handle, hoping I'd got it wrong and the door was just stiff. Could I kick one of the panels in? Not with a fractured foot.

There was nothing in the room at all, nothing to help me get out. I sank back against the door, feeling spent. My breathing was hard and ragged as I sucked in the dusty air. I was trapped. What if something happened? If there was a fire...

A car started up. I went to the window, pulled the curtain back, and saw my car being driven round to where the garages were - where it would presumably be out of sight from the lane.

Twisting the handle I shoved hard, pushing with every ounce of strength, but the window was stuck. It was old fashioned; the panes long and narrow, and made of metal not wood but not double-glazed. I glanced around, wondering what I could use to smash the glass. In a cascade of dust, I pulled one of the curtains down, bundled it up and, wrapping it around my arm, used my elbow to smash the pane. The shattering seemed loud. I waited, expecting the door to fly open again. When it didn't I knocked out the rest of the pieces. I climbed onto the sill, but it was no good. The gap was too narrow. I'd guessed that it would be but I'd had to try. No matter how many different positions I got into I couldn't squeeze through. I dropped back to the floor, defeated. Now what? I'd slashed my jeans and the edge of the torn fabric was growing scarlet.

A sound caught my attention. It was dusk and the hedge of trees along the perimeter formed a dense high barrier, an ominous black prison wall that cast the garden into shadow as the light faded. In the darkness I could just make out someone watching me. He moved forwards out of the shadows. 'You didn't honestly think I'd leave you in there if I thought you'd be able to get out that easily.' He laughed and turned away. 'Never mind.'

'Let me out.' I screamed. Then an idea took hold, and I shouted with all my might through the broken pane. 'Help me. Help me. I'm trapped. Help me.'

'There's no one to hear you,' he laughed. 'Don't you remember how isolated this place is?'

I did but that didn't stop me yelling. There could be a dog walker out there for all I knew. Despite the laughter, Scott sounded slightly worried.

'Help me. Help.' I carried on shouting until my throat got sore.

He was back outside a while later with several pieces of wood. I saw immediately what he intended to do, and sure enough he placed one piece of wood across the broken pane but he hadn't thought it through. The frame was metal and there was nothing to hammer nails to.

'Why are you doing this?' I demanded. 'Why don't you just let me go? I won't tell anyone.'

Scott didn't respond. He was deep in thought as if trying to work out how he was going to solve the problem.

I tried to distract him. 'Scott, please. This isn't like you.'

He looked at me with a gaze of pure hatred. 'You don't know anything about me.'

'So tell me. What's this about?'

'Ah!' he said suddenly, and disappeared again. When he came back he had a drill and several pieces of timber. He put down a lantern on the windowsill and began making holes in the bits of wood.

'Why are you doing this?'

Scott held a piece of timber up to the wall beside the window frame and began drilling through the holes into the wall. When he'd finished he looked at me and said: 'You wanted to know who started the fire didn't you?' His tone was conversational as if we were in the middle of a discussion. 'You always assumed it was linked to what's been happening to you.' He sniggered. 'It isn't.' He pushed rawl plugs into the holes he'd made and tapped them in with a hammer.

'When are you going to let me go?' I asked again.

Scott put the drill down. 'I thought you wanted to know about this. That was why you came here, wasn't it?'

'I don't care anymore. I want to leave.'

'That's crap. Of course you want to know.' He picked up the drill again. 'The bloke who started the fire is called Barry Hammond.' I didn't recognise the name. Scott smirked. 'You don't know him. He's a builder from Pompey. Your neighbour probably didn't know him either, but he knew his wife. Intimately.' He paused while he positioned the drill. 'Seems the bastard was giving her one and the old man didn't like it. Especially when she said she wanted a divorce and intended to take half of what he owned. Which by all accounts is quite a lot.'

I tried to absorb the information. It didn't make any sense.

Scott began drilling again. He stood back. 'But that's not the bit you want to know, is it?' His tone was smug. 'You want to know who's been leaving stuff in your car and sending you emails and watching you.'

For once I was one step ahead of him. 'I've already worked that out.'

'Clever girl.' He let the drill run, the burr of it grating the air. He flicked a switch on it and the noise changed to a deeper sound equally abrasive. He began making holes in the ends of the timber.

'I just don't understand why,' I said.

'Because you think you're strong. I wanted to see how much pressure it would take to make you crack. But no matter how bad things got you just wouldn't. Well sooner or later you will.'

What did he mean by that? 'Why me?'

He shrugged. 'You were in the fire. You should have been vulnerable.'

'You've been following me since the fire?'

'I saw you there. But I didn't know where you'd gone. It a stroke of luck that your boyfriend goes to the same gym as me. Saved me a lot of work. All I had to do was get friendly with Darren and I had my way in.'

It was hard to reconcile Scott with the psychopath before me. I couldn't take it in.

'Aren't you going to gob off again?' he said.

'What's the point? You're clearly mad.'

Scott picked up the piece of timber and held it across the window, turned it around as if it was upside down then wound some screws into it. 'Oh surely you've got something on your mind? Aren't you going to ask me what I'm going to do to you? That's what you want to know, isn't it.' He laughed and positioned the wood at the wall again, this time screwing it home with the drill. 'You like excitement, don't you? Is this exciting enough? It's giving me a hard on.'

Instinctively I stepped back from the window. Scott made a licking movement towards the end of the drill bit then laughed. Was he going to rape me? I thought about things I'd heard about rape being about submission and power. And this was clearly about power. 'Don't flatter yourself darlin' this isn't about sex. I can get that anywhere with my looks.' He moved to the other side of the window and began drilling again, working faster this time.

'What do you want?'

His face appeared in front of me, distorted by the grime of the glass. He jabbed at his forehead. 'I want what's in there. By the time I've finished with you, you'll have cracked.'

Our eyes locked. 'What have I done to deserve this?'

He didn't answer but moved away from the window and shifted one of the large pieces of board he'd brought out originally. He swung it up to the sill and let it rest there while he put a couple of pieces of timber in place.

'Has it not occurred to you that I'll be missed?' I said, feeling increasingly claustrophobic and desperate.

'You've been acting so weird lately everyone's going

to think you took off somewhere.'

He was right. It was frightening. He had been working up to this. And here, in this isolated house, anything could happen. He could kill me and bury me in the garden. And who would know? There could be bodies out there already for all I knew. This room, with the boarding he was screwing in place, was like a coffin that he was sealing me into. I shuddered.

'You planned for this all along,' I said, trying to keep him talking.

'No. It's developed over time.'

'How did you know I'd fall for it?'

He laughed. 'I've been watching you. Analysing how you tick.'

'Following me?' No wonder I'd been so creeped out. 'Is that how you knew which was my car? How did you get into it the first time?'

'It's not difficult to break into a car if you know what to do. You went to it the day you met up with your flatmate but I could have guessed which one was yours anyway. It's not exactly rocket science. I mean girls tend to drive certain cars, plus it didn't move for days on end and you had running shoes in the back. So, pretty obvious really.'

He sounded so smug. His voice had become muffled though and I realised that mine would be too. If I shouted now how would anyone hear or make out what I was saying?

'You should be flattered,' he said. 'There aren't many people that would go to so much trouble. Most people just stick to letters and phone calls. But that's a bit boring, don't you think? My stuff was more creative.'

The relentless sound of the drill and his complacent tone were annoying me. It was now almost pitch black. 'Am I supposed to be grateful?'

'Flattered at least.'

'You're a psychopath. Mentally deranged.'

He lifted another piece of wood in place and suddenly it was dark. It took several moments for my eyes to adjust.

'And I'm in control,' he said.

'Don't do this,' I screamed as he screwed the last piece in place.

CHAPTER 32

The light didn't work. I pressed the switch on and off, on and off, but nothing. There might not have been a bulb in the pendant. I hadn't noticed. I sank to my haunches beside the door. The idea of getting down on the carpet again made my skin itch, but sooner or later I'd have to. The room was cold. Either the temperature was dropping or I was cooling after the adrenalin rush. I hugged myself and a fingernail snagged on my fleece. I bit the jagged edge away. The room gave me the creeps, but at least in the dark I couldn't see the manic wallpaper. Why was it like this? I half expected to see a ghost come walking through the wall. The thought scared me. The darkness was like a curse, making me more jittery and nervous as time passed. For a while I stayed by the door, waiting to see if Scott would return and if I could make a run for it when he did. But the hours slipped slowly past and there was no sign of him.

Occasionally, I thought I heard the sound of movement in the hall or the creak of stairs. Several times I heard the faint but unmistakable ring tone of my mobile. Someone was trying to get hold of me and that gave me hope. For a long time I thought about that. Was it my dad? He'd be expecting me back. But he didn't have my number. Was Ollie trying to get hold of me? After what had happened it seemed unlikely. I'd kept him at a distance, not telling him what was going on. Why? Because deep down, I suspected he was involved. If I'd told him everything, would I be in this predicament now? Eventually my mobile stopped ringing. I wondered if whoever it was had given up or the phone had been switched off.

The area by the door was too dark to bear so, despite the cold, I went over to the window and perched on the sill. All I could see between the slats was a small glimmer of moonlight through the trees, but it was enough. Everything else was blackness. When I got too tired to stay upright I sank down onto the filthy carpet beside the window. What had I done to deserve this? Why me? What was he intending to do? I was thirsty and hungry and strung out. I tried to think of a way of escaping. But in the dark it was impossible to see anything.

Then suddenly the moon disappeared behind the trees and it was utterly black. Without light, there was no point sitting in a draught so I moved towards the back of the room. My jumper wasn't adequate. I shook out the curtain to dislodge any shards of glass, coughing at the sudden stirring of dust. I wrapped the filthy fabric around me. It was cold and I found it impossible to sleep. I curled into the corner.

Through the small sliver between the slats I watched it get light. I felt wretched. The trees whispered in the wind, making a sound like tissue paper being screwed up. And there was bird song, irritatingly cheerful. Later I could hear Scott in the hall and kitchen. 'Scott! Hey, what about something to drink?' I banged on the door.

There were footsteps in the hall and I thought he was going to come in but then there was a thud like the front door closing and the sound of his motorbike starting up. I went to the window and shouted but he didn't even glance in my direction, simply rode off. What if he never came back?

The sound of the engine faded. I checked my watch. It was ten o'clock. How long would he be gone? If I was going to escape, now was my chance. I tried the door, yanking it hard and relentlessly as frustration took hold. I stepped back a few paces and ran at the door. It didn't budge and I hurt my shoulder. I examined the lock. It looked new, and wasn't fitted straight. I kept yanking at it, wondering if I could snap it off. It might not have been fitted well but it was fitted securely. How did they do it in the movies?

Running my fingers around the edge of the carpet I yanked it free. It gave little resistance, virtually disintegrating under my touch. As I'd suspected underneath were newspapers. Pulling a couple of pieces free, I fed them under the door by the handle then rolled up another piece and poked it into the keyhole. With my ear to the door, I listened for the small bump as the key hit the floor. The paper bent in a zigzag. Angrily I yanked it out, straightened it and tried again.

I thumped the door and immediately regretted it. Again I tried to retrieve the key. After numerous attempts I knew it wasn't going to work. The key should have fallen onto the paper then I could have pulled the paper back under the door and unlocked it from the inside. Why did things never happen like that in real life?

I yanked the paper back into the room and rubbed my inky hands down my jeans. There was no point letting Scott know what I'd been doing. At the very least he'd be unbearably smug at my failure. I sank down by the fireplace wondering what to do next. How wide was the chimney? Was it possible to climb it? I crawled into the small hearth and, lying on my back, looked up. The flu was narrow and bent at a severe angle. It was not a way out.

Near the door the carpet was bunched into a fan where

I'd pulled it back. It disintegrated more every time I touched it. I pulled it further away from the wall, wondering whether there was a cellar of some kind. The ancient floorboards had been up several times by the looks of the damaged edges. I found the widest gap and stuck my finger in and tried to work it free but it was firmly nailed down. Despite an inch-by-inch search, none of the floorboards would work loose.

All I could do was stand at the window and yell for help. I knew it was unlikely anyone would hear, but it was my only chance.

It was mid afternoon when the motorbike returned. I recognised its throaty roar as it came up the lane. Hurriedly I pulled the carpet back in place.

'Water!' I yelled as a shadow passed across the narrow gaps in the wooden panels across the windows. My mouth was parched and my tongue felt large and rough, my voice was hoarse from all the shouting. The shadow passed away. I rapped on the window. 'Water?' But it was late evening when I heard to rattle of a key and the door finally swung open. I sprang to my feet and moved towards it.

'Here.' Scott threw me a small bottle of water and placed a plate of sandwiches on the floor. I gulped the water down then stopped, as it occurred to me that he might have drugged it. Then I realised I'd broken the seal on the cap to get into it. Hungrily I grabbed a sandwich. I don't normally like Marmite but I gobbled it down, grateful that I'd held some of the water back and could rinse away the taste.

'You're like a stray dog snatching scraps from a rubbish bin,' Scott observed. I didn't care. The food jogged a thought. I reran our conversation in the kitchen, as far as I could remember it. The detail was elusive but there was something about his manner when I'd talked about the house. Why was it like this? Maybe it wasn't even his. In that case, maybe the owners would come back and find me. But Scott was too meticulous to risk that. No, there was more to it. It was as if this house was an extension of Scott and his split personality.

'Why did you buy this house?'

Scott stared at me, then walked out without answering. After a while the motorbike started up again and he left. I couldn't see my watch, but it was late when he returned.

The next day followed the same pattern. And the next. Scott wouldn't talk to me. I tried to make conversation but he wasn't having any of it. For something to do I read the papers from under the carpet and found out about current affairs in the late 1970s. It was a limited distraction.

My thoughts ran in a cycle around ways to escape, what I could have done differently, and the sudden additional realisation that I was probably pregnant.

It had occurred to me when I was peeing in the corner of the room that I was very late and constantly feeling nauseous. A baby was something to take my mind off the situation. The thought would normally have filled me with horror, now it was a distraction. If I survived, what kind of a future could I give it? Where did Ollie come into the equation? My experience of families with my biological father and Keith always led to betrayal. Ollie was immature and he'd already shown that, when things got rough, he wouldn't be there for me.

Suddenly Scott hurried into the room. He tossed me a bottle of water. I pulled the cap off and started drinking. As I did so he grabbed me and pulled me to him, pushing the bottle out as his hand closed across my mouth. Holding me tightly, he walked me back towards the door and held me there. Silent.

The doorbell chimed and I realised what was happening. Someone was here. I tried to bite his fingers but he had them tight against my tongue, making me want to gag. I tried to scream. The sound that came out was barely audible. Who was out there? Would they find my car? I had to try everything. I bit down with all my strength on Scott's fingers. He murmured as if it had hurt but his hold didn't slacken.

A shadow passed by the window and I felt him tense. He'd taken to putting his motorbike round the side of the house, presumably in the garage or one of the outbuildings, as if he was afraid someone would come looking. I had to try everything. Biting, wriggling, kicking, stamping, elbowing him in the ribs. But he was too big and too strong. It seemed as if we were standing there for ages. I heard voices but couldn't make out what was said. Hoisting me off my feet, he carried me over to the window then let me go. Through the sliver between the slats I could just see the lane and the red glow of tail lights. Then the car was gone.

Someone was looking for me. Would they come back? I had to believe they would. As I turned around the force of his hand sent me stumbling back against the window. He left me then and didn't come back until the following evening.

When he did, I tried to get him talking. Scott glared at me. 'I thought you'd have cracked by now,' he snapped. 'The others did.'

'Others?'

'You didn't think you were the only one.' He laughed. 'You really are self-centred.'

'I suppose I shouldn't be surprised. After all, you've got it all so well thought out.'

'Thank you.'

'It wasn't a compliment. You're practiced, not clever.'

'Not as stupid as you, though.' He tapped the side of his head. 'I know psychology. I've been inside your head. I know how you tick. You still think one of your so-called friends will rescue you.'

'Someone came looking for me. They'll find out what you've done.'

'Perhaps,' he sounded doubtful. 'By then it'll be too late for you though. Anyway no one's going to suspect me.

I mean I'm one of your friends.'

'You're no friend of mine.'

He laughed. 'I'm hurt. Anyway it doesn't matter what you think. Everyone else thinks we're friends that's all that counts.'

'I can't imagine you've got any friends,' I taunted. 'That's why you've bought a secluded run down heap. It suits your personality.' The sting from his slap across my face made me reel backwards.

'You don't know what you're talking about.'

I held my face. 'I'd say I've touched a nerve. I'd say you know a lot about psychology because you've spent so much time with shrinks.'

He glared at me. 'Don't think you know me. You haven't got a clue.'

'You're screwed up. I know that.' I knew I shouldn't be winding him up, but I couldn't stop myself. 'What was it, boarding school? I'd guess that's where you went.' I watched his face but his expression didn't change. It was blank and cold. I glanced towards the door, calculating whether I could get past him and escape. 'Not the school then. Must be the parents. Oh, my God. This house. It makes sense now. It was your parents' place! A horrible isolated house to bring up a child in.'

He blinked. 'We're not that unalike you and me. Where are all your friends, eh? Ollie thinks you're not answering his calls because you're in a strop with him. He's given up trying now.'

'I don't believe you.'

'It's the truth. I've seen him, talked to him. It would look suspicious if I disappeared as well. I've been to the gym as usual. We had a chat about you. I said you were probably off somewhere feeling sorry for yourself. Quite accurate really, wouldn't you say?'

I turned away. 'You won't get away with it.'

His voice was soft and close to my ear. 'Yeah, I will. I

always do. And no one will be any the wiser. So keep your fucking amateur psychology to yourself.'

Who was it that had come looking? Ollie? Dad? The police?

'You said there were others. What...?' Was it sensible to ask about them? Did I want to know what had happened? Would he tell me the truth anyway?

'What happened to the others?' he said. 'They're not dead, if that's what you're asking. But they are having... treatment.'

What did that mean? I didn't dare pursue it. 'How long are you intending to keep me here?' I said.

He leaned back against the wall, a self-satisfied expression on his face. 'Depends how long it takes. It's up to you.'

'What are you expecting? Why are you doing this? And why this mausoleum? This place has got something to do with it, I know it has.'

'It's just a house.'

Who was he trying to convince? 'It's more than that. Did something happen here? What did your parents do to you?'

Something snapped in him. 'I'll tell you what they fucking did. They ignored me, then they left me. Left me to the mercy of that cruel bitch. My Grandmother.' He ground the words out, loaded with hatred.

I thought of saying something but didn't know what to say and he carried on. 'They were always leaving me with her, only she was a vicious cow. They were so wrapped up in each other. I was invisible. The kid. My name's Scott, for fuck's sake, but my Mother never used it. And then she killed them and I was stuck with the bitch for good.'

It was a sad story, but he was pathetic. And he called me self-centred! I gazed at the open door, wishing he was just a bit further away from it. For a moment he was still and quiet. 'Who killed them? What happened?' I probed, keeping him talking.

'There was a car accident on the way back from one of their parties. My mother was driving.' He spoke with utter venom. 'And she was pissed...' My focus was on the door rather than what he was saying. I took a step closer then made a run for it, into the hall and a few steps towards the front door. He grabbed my hair, pulled me to a halt. I screamed with pain, reached up to loosen his grip.

'Stupid bitch,' he yelled, yanking me round. 'You think it'd be that easy.' He marched me back towards my cell. 'Where the hell did you think you'd get to?' Propelled across the room, I landed in a heap by the fireplace. 'You'll pay for that. You won't hold out for ever. And things are going to get a whole lot worse for you now.' He slammed and locked the door.

What had I done? What would he do? I tried to make sense of all that he'd said. Had he really kidnapped women before? Had there been others here? The room had seemed undisturbed. What did he mean about them having treatment? The article he was writing was about coping, if he was actually writing anything. Was I his research? Was that how he chose his victims? Was it always about making women feel weak and powerless? Was this because of the women in his childhood? Because they were cruel, or domineering, or were simply indifferent to him? It was only a guess, but it made sense. What the hell was he capable of?

CHAPTER 33

My nose twitched. I could smell smoke. 'Fire!' It was faint, but unmistakable. Shit, not again!

Was that what Scott meant about other girls having treatment? Burns? My senses were on full alert, sniffing and listening. It was definitely smoke. And it was wafting in under the door. I blasted the door with my fists as panic seared through me. 'Let me out. There's a fire.'

I stopped. Listened. I could hear the unmistakable crack and pop of burning. The sound seemed to be getting louder, enveloping me, as if it was in the room. I span, terrified, hysterical. I yanked the door handle, pulling, desperate. 'Fire!'

Where was Scott? He had to let me out. What if he didn't? Coughing, I staggered backwards, scanned the room, picked up the curtain I'd been using as a blanket and stuffed it against the door. Now what? I collided with the wall and realised I'd been moving backwards. Crackle, crackle. It almost seemed as if the fire was louder further into the room.

My ears were banging with the pounding of my pulse.

I leapt towards the window, elbowed more glass out. The panes shattered loudly. I tried to kick out the wooden shuttering Scott had installed, but it wouldn't budge.

'Help! Fire!' I yelled. Where was he? Had he started the fire deliberately? Was he responsible for the one at the flat too? Was that story he fed me about Neil Wyatt a pack of lies?

Crackle, crackle. There was a sound of something shifting. I sank to the floor terrified, sick at the realisation that there was nothing I could do. Nothing happened. It could have been my imagination, but the noise seemed louder in the middle of the room. Was it overhead? Was the ceiling about to fall in on me? I reached up to feel for heat near the ceiling, but it wasn't hot. Where was the safest place to be? The fireplace was pretty solid. Or was I better off by the window? Nowhere was safe in a fire, but I couldn't give up.

Crackle, crackle. The sound of something shifting again. The smell of smoke was less acrid than it had been at the flat. It was more like wood smoke. Did that mean the floorboards were burning? Crackle, crackle. It was almost hypnotic, it was so repetitious. The sound went on. Time stopped. But nothing else happened. My stomach muscles ached with clenching.

I got up, went cautiously to the door, and bracing myself, pulled the curtain free. Smoke began wafting in again, but not much. I sniffed. It didn't smell like the fire at the flat. Perhaps there was less man-made stuff in this old house. I thought again that it didn't sound as loud as it did in the middle of the room.

I went to stand underneath the light pendant and listened. Crackle, crackle, followed by the sound of something shifting. It was as if I was listening to a recording. What if this wasn't a real fire? What if it was some twisted mind game? It was a big if.

Sweat ran down my back in a slow unpleasant trickle,

tracing my spine. Bundling the curtain into a ball, I stood on it, and stretched up. A couple of inches shorter and I'd never have reached but I could just scrape my fingers along the ceiling. I scanned the area around the light pendant.

It took a while to find in the dim light, but eventually I spotted what looked like patching to the artex. Stretching as high as I could I scraped my nails along the filler and revealed a thin black wire. I gave it a tug and bits of plaster flaked off, revealing a small speaker disc. I yanked it free and the sound diminished. I stared at it in disbelief, hysterical laughter bubbling up inside of me. He'd planned my imprisonment meticulously.

I went to the window and breathed in fresh air, sat on the floor trying to work out how I felt. I let my head drop to my knees. The adrenaline was ebbing away fast, leaving me spent. If he'd thought far enough ahead to install speakers what else did he have planned? I thought about my response to the fire? I'd panicked, but even before I'd realised about the sound reason had taken over. So there was a good chance I was getting over my fear. Did he really think I was that gullible that I'd fall for it?

I didn't hear the door open. 'Did you think I was going to leave you to die? I knew you'd crack eventually. It's just a case of pushing the right buttons.'

His boots were in my line of vision but I kept my head down. He gave me a shake and grabbed my hair, pulling my face up so that he could see me. I wrenched his hand free and rose to face him, laughing, on the edge of hysteria.

'Did you really think I'd fall for it? It sounded nothing like a real fire. It smelt nothing like a real fire. You're the one who's cracking up.'

Anger raged through me but I realised that I was strong. All these weeks I'd been afraid of fire, checking windows and doors everywhere I'd been. But now that it had happened I hadn't been as afraid as I'd thought I would be. I'd tapped into survival mode. I wasn't about to give in.

Scott looked stunned. He lashed out. I ducked and his hand smashed into the wall. I took the opportunity, kicked him hard between the legs. Groaning, he folded. I ran for the door, dashed outside, this time yanking it shut and turning the key. On the floor there was a small pile of burnt paper and twigs that he'd used to create the smoke. I stepped over it.

Where was my car? I ran to the kitchen but my bag was gone. I flung open a few cupboard doors. Nothing. I couldn't afford to stay there too long looking for my car keys. I could hear him lumbering about then there was a thump as he must have launched himself at the door. He was a lot bigger and heavier than me so he might be able to smash his way out. I grabbed his mobile phone, which was lying on the worktop, and fled.

I ran and ran, putting as much distance as I could between us. The lane was uneven and I couldn't see where the ruts were so I kept stumbling. There were puddles too, frozen and treacherous. I glanced at the phone and dialled 999.

'Emergency Services. Which service do...'

'My name's Zoë Graham. Help me. I was kidnapped. I've just escaped but he's after me.' It was difficult to talk and run.

Trees and hedges lined the lane on both sides, making the rutted surface treacherous with dark shadows. I was glad I had trainers on and that my foot was holding up. Spears of pain shot through it with every step but I wasn't about to stop.

Scott's voice echoed into the night. 'You won't get away, you bitch.'

'Please! He's got out. He's going to kill me.' My breath came in a gasp, a white mist in front of my face. The cold seeped through my clothes and made the sweat unpleasant.

'Okay Zoë. Do you know where you are?'

I gave her the address and pushed on, biting back the pain and running as fast as I could. 'His name's Scott Parker. He's been keeping me in an,' I gasped in air, 'old house down a narrow lane.'

The sound of a motorbike starting up broke the silence. How far was the main road? Were there houses nearby? Panting out the details of where I thought I was, I sped on. 'It's an old house. I'm in the lane at the moment. Hang on there's another house here.'

Set back in the trees was a large building but metal gates barred my way in and there didn't seem to be any lights on or signs of life.

'There's no one home,' I gasped in air. I had to get my breathing under control or I was done for.

'Is there anywhere else you can get help?'

'It's the middle of the countryside.' I was aware that I'd slowed down and I needed to speed up or find somewhere to hide. 'I'm going to have to hide. I can't outrun him.' I searched one side of the lane then the other but there was nowhere to go. The lane was fenced on both sides. Brambles tugged at my clothes. I snatched myself free and fell back into the road. The small white dot of a headlight was approaching.

'Okay Zoë, someone is coming out to you. Is there anything you can see that we can use as a landmark?'

'I don't know. It's so dark.' I panted and I had a stitch. I hadn't eaten properly for days and was weak. 'I can't see anything but hedges and trees. I'm at the road now. There's no one about.'

I ran down the middle of the road a few yards. Spotting a five bar gate, I flung myself over it and ran along the side of the hedge where I couldn't be seen.

'No. There aren't any other houses. There's a pylon a couple of fields over.' I concentrated on my breathing, which was loud and ragged. 'I'm in a field opposite the end of the lane.'

A couple of rabbits darted away into the hedgerow. The long grass at the edge of the field sparkled with frost. It made a soft crunch as I moved. White mist hugged the ground where it curved towards a row of skeleton trees in a dip at the bottom of the slope. I began to shiver.

'Anything else?'

'I can't see.' Everything was made of shades of grey. My heart thumped out of control. My ears tingled with straining to catch every tiny sound. It was a clear night and the stars shone brightly. The moon was high and small. 'He's the other side of the hedge.' The bike went past but after a few seconds returned. I rose to a half crouch, began edging further down the field. My foot skidded on something soft.

'I think he kn…'

The phone beeped. I pressed the menu button and the screen lit up. No signal. Fuck! It was probably because I'd gone down into the dip. I should have realised.

The bike was idling, then it stopped. The glint of his helmet was the first thing I saw as he leaned over the gate. I redialled the police but there was still no signal. Scott disappeared again and I thought he'd decided I wasn't in here but then he reappeared, clambering over the gate, his helmet removed.

'There's nowhere to go you daft bitch. I know these fields. I grew up here remember.'

I slipped the phone into my jeans pocket. A cow gave a gentle moo. I glanced around at the darkness, trying to work out where to go, hoping to God that the police were on their way. It had been a mistake to come into the field but where else could I go? I edged further down the slope.

'I can see you.' Scott strode towards me.

I kept moving. 'You don't have to do this. Just let me go.' My voice echoed around the valley like the screech of a banshee.

'I can't do that.'

Now what was I going to do? I glanced around for something to use to protect myself. I was tight in against a holly bush, which scratched and snagged at my clothes. I grabbed a bough and snapped it off.

'Get away from me,' I yelled as he approached.

Scott glared at me. 'Where did you think you'd get to?'

'Leave me alone.'

'It's too late for that.'

'No it's not.' I took a step backwards, waving the holly bough in front of me. What did he mean by too late? Too late for what? What was he going to do with me? He wasn't going to win. He couldn't. 'The police are on the way.'

He laughed and made a grab for the holly. 'That's bullshit.'

I swung at him, catching him full in the face with the branch. His hands flew up to protect himself but he recovered quickly and lunged again. I dodged backwards but he caught hold of my fleece. I slashed out again but he was too close and I couldn't swing the bough wide enough. He grabbed my hair, jerked it painfully, forcing me to fold.

'See, I always win.' His hand came down across my face, striking my jaw. Pain scorched my face and down my neck. He plucked the holly from my grasp, tossed it into the hedge. Then, suddenly the pain shifted as, like a sack of potatoes, he hauled me over his shoulder and marched back to the gate. I punched the small of his back and yelled. But he didn't seem bothered either that I'd hurt him or that someone could hear me.

As we reached the gate, the phone in my pocket rang. Scott took it from me, gave it a cursory glance then threw it into the hedge.

'That'll be the police. If you let me go, it'll give you time to get away.'

'Don't be stupid.'

He wasn't listening but I wasn't about to give up.

'You could be miles away in no time. You could get a ferry. You could be in France in a few hours.'

'Huh!' He sprang the gate open. 'I'm not going anywhere.'

He didn't bother about the bike but forced me forward

up the lane. With my hair wound painfully around his hand I had no choice but to move. It hurt beyond belief to walk and I kept stumbling, which meant his grasp on my head felt as if all my hair was being pulled out.

All the way up the lane I tried to work out what to do, tried to talk to him, persuade him to let me go. But he'd switched off. I kept talking nonetheless trying to distract him from whatever he was planning next. Were the police on their way? How would they find me? I strained to listen, hoping for the sound of a siren but I couldn't hear anything.

We reached his house. The front door stood wide open. The lights blazed but not in welcome. I thought he was going to push me back inside but he didn't. As we passed I saw why, the lounge door had been demolished. It hung at a strange angle with sharp splinters of wood sticking out into the hall.

Scott forced me on towards the back of the house. 'Where are you taking me?'

'You'll see.' He sounded smug, as if he was beginning to enjoy himself. An outside light came on as we approached. I hadn't seen this part of the property before and held so tightly I couldn't see very much now. There were a couple of old style garage doors and at the far end a single door, probably leading to a workshop.

Presumably my car was hidden here. Was there any chance of getting to it and driving off. It seemed doubtful.

We headed for the small door. Scott opened it and reached inside. He pulled out a coil of rope, one end lashed in a loop like a tow rope.

He snatched my sleeve up, looped rope around my wrist and reached for the other hand. I pushed my shoulder across to try and prevent him but it was no use. He tied my hands together. The rope cut into my skin but it was a relief to have him release my hair and be upright. My back and shoulders hurt from stooping so long.

I glanced round and my gaze stopped in the garden where

someone had built a two metre bonfire pyre. Bonfire night was past. Had Scott built it especially as part of his plan?

'You've spoil the surprise now,' he said, following my gaze. 'How's that for a real fire?'

I swallowed hard. Did he mean...? I couldn't finish the thought. I stood tethered like an animal that had been stunned by a tranquilliser dart. A sound shook me out of it and I realised he'd reached into the garage and taken out a green fuel can. 'No!'

'Oh yes.'

'Please.'

'You've done this to yourself.' Shadows played across his face making him look as macabre as he sounded.

'How? What did I do?' My voice had diminished to a pathetic whisper. 'Tell me what I've done and I'll put it right.'

'Too late.' The words were sharp. Finite.

Was this another mind game? I didn't believe that it was.

'At least tell me why.' I tried to stall him but I knew he wouldn't hold out forever.

'So bloody self-absorbed! Just like her.'

'Who?'

He pulled me over to the bonfire. I thought about what Gemma had said about Joan of Arc waiting for the flames to consume her. I was going to be sick.

'She was the only family I had left,' Scott spat, showering me with spittle. 'I'd lost both my parents. She'd lost her son. I needed her. But she didn't want to know. Cruel cold bitch.'

I didn't understand. 'Who?'

'My bitch of a grandmother.'

'But I'm not her.'

He pulled me closer, his breath warm against my neck. 'No. But you're like her.' He shoved me away. 'Scheming self-centred witch. Well, if you won't break you'll pay.'

In horror, I watched him slosh petrol at the bonfire. I looked away and tried not to breathe it in.

'You're wrong. I haven't done anything to you. We're not all the same.' I moved away from him. 'I'm nothing like your grandmother.'

He wasn't listening. He was liberally slopping petrol around and laughing again. It was as if he wasn't here any more; as if he'd slipped into some other twisted surreal world where no one couldn't touch him. He brought the can towards me, clearly intent on dowsing me in fuel. I kicked it and petrol splashed back at him. Dark spots of it marked the legs of his jeans, but if he noticed he showed no sign of it.

'Being preoccupied with something isn't the same as being self-centred,' I shouted, trying to figure out if I could get out of this mess. If a chance arose I had to be ready, but ready for what? I couldn't pre-empt him. I had to stop him lighting a match. 'I'm just trying to get my life back to some sort of normal existence. Nothing more,' I said.

Oblivious, he carried on dowsing the pyre, pulling me after him as he went around it. I glanced around, searching for something I could grab and use to hurt him.

'I should have put a stake in the middle,' he mumbled, tossing the petrol can aside. 'Tied you to it like in that picture.' Instead he gave me a shove towards the bonfire, letting go of the rope. He reached into his pocket and took out a match box. It was going to happen. He took a match from the box, grinned at me and struck it.

Instinct took over. I threw myself sideways away from the fire. Whoosh. Exploding, everything went up in a flash. I scrambled to my feet and ran.

Behind me the roar of flames was a wall of noise. Suddenly I realised the hem of my jeans was on fire. With my hands tied I couldn't just reach down. I had to stop. I whacked at my leg to beat it out. Across the other side of the fire, tentacles of flame stretched out across the grass. Scott was in the middle of it and he was on fire. He let out a blood-curdling scream but I didn't stop. I ran.

I hit a thick wall of trees and headed right, following the hedge until my legs wouldn't work any more and I fell forward coughing, too weak to stay upright. At the foot of the hedge I curled into the darkness and hid until I could recover enough strength to run on. I could still see the image of Scott on fire, a blazing cross against the screen of my mind. Even with the image imprinted there, I didn't believe he wouldn't come after me again. I was on high alert, listening hard as I concentrated on working my hands free of the rope. The palms felt raw where I'd beat at my jeans.

It seemed like a long time later when blue lights in the lane caught my attention. I shielded my eyes against the glare of headlamps as a car pulled onto the property. It was a patrol car. Two policemen got out.

'Zoë?' One of the policeman shouted and headed towards the back of the house where the fire was, the other went inside. There was a shout and the officer inside came running out again and headed for his colleague. One of them ran back to the patrol car and grabbed a first aid kit.

Unsteadily I stood and tried to walk forwards. As if he realised I was on the point of collapse the policeman ran over. 'Are you Zoë?

I nodded and the policeman spoke into a radio at his shoulder as he helped me to the car.

'Are you hurt?' The policeman shook out a space blanket and wrapped it around me. It was like soft tin foil and reminded me of the half marathons I'd run.

'I think my leg and hands might be burnt... Is he...'

The policeman shrugged and didn't say anything. I pulled the blanket up around my shoulders but it didn't stop the shivering. Words ran through my head like a mantra. It's over. I made it. I survived.

CHAPTER 34

The hospital was busier than it had been last time. As the paramedics unloaded me from the ambulance I caught a glimpse of a group of drunks, larking about around the entrance, laughing and taunting one another. We wound our way down corridors to the cubicles: the same lino, the same squeaks as someone walked across it, the same walls, same fabric curtains all down the ward.

DI Green was there when I arrived, hovering by the nurses' station, sipping from a plastic cup. The policeman who'd come in the ambulance with me went over to her as I was taken into a cubicle. Once settled, and after I'd been examined, the burns dealt with and I was connected to a drip for rehydration, DI Green came in.

I'd never seen her in anything other than a suit. She looked different in jeans and a bright red jumper that was strangely too garish for the hospital ward. It made me think of fresh blood.

'Hello, Zoë. We've been very worried about you.'

'I didn't think you were bothered about what happened to me.'

DI Green put her handbag down on the chair beside the bed. 'That's not true. You know it isn't.'

'All I know is no one believed me and then that nutter held me captive.'

The policeman enclosed us in curtains, then stationed himself at the edge of the cubicle.

'Am I still in danger?' I said, nodding to him.

'Not from Scott Parker. He's down the hall in intensive care.'

'Serves him right. Talk about déjà vu. Is he going to make it?'

'He'll be badly scarred and probably crippled if he does.'

'That bastard kept me locked up. He tried to kill me.' I spoke through gritted teeth and it sounded bitter.

'I know. And you're angry. I wish there was something else we could have done, but there wasn't. There simply wasn't any evidence.' There was a long pause. 'Speaking of evidence, I'm afraid we'll need to document your injuries. Are you okay with that.'

I nodded.

'A specially trained officer will photograph your face and any other injuries, and take trace from under your fingernails and from your feet. And we'll need your clothes. Okay?'

'Whatever it takes.'

'I'll get it organised. Your boyfriend and his flatmates were worried about you. And your stepfather. Did you know they lodged a missing person report?'

'Really?'

'I don't know how many times that boyfriend of yours has called me for news. He's on his way in, by the way. Along with your stepfather.'

Emotion got the better of me and I choked up. I remembered the way my mobile had rung repeatedly on that first day. When had they realised something was wrong? Were they thinking and worrying about me all the time I was away?

'I thought they'd think I'd taken off somewhere,' I admitted.

'They might have done at first. It was your stepfather who insisted something was wrong. He rang your boyfriend when you didn't come home.'

Tears welled.

'They ought to stop this drip.' I said. 'I'm leaking.'

DI Green gave a small laugh and handed me a tissue.

'You're exhausted. You've been through a hell of an ordeal.'

I dabbed at my eyes. 'Everyone thought I was making it up.' I screwed the tissue into a tight ball and clamped it in my fist. 'I thought he was my friend.' I sank back against the pillows and closed my eyes.

'I know. And I know it's probably difficult to talk about it, but I'm going to need a statement.'

With a swish the curtain swung back and a doctor appeared. 'How are you feeling?' He looked at my chart then began adjusting the drip.

'Tired.'

He smiled. 'I'm not surprised. You've nasty bruising on your face but apart from that you seem to have got away with it again. I think you should try and keep away from fires for a while.'

'Is that supposed to be funny?' I said.

'No. Sorry. I think we'll keep up the fluids. You're pretty dehydrated and I think we should have another look at this foot.'

He removed my sock. He lifted my foot and touched it gently, but still I winced.

'Hmm. I think we'll x-ray that again to make sure it's setting okay.'

'I think I'm pregnant,' I blurted.

DI Green looked worried. 'He didn't rape you?'

'No. I'm just late.'

'We can do a test,' the doctor said. 'I'll get things organised, then we can get you down to x-ray.'

'He gave me drugs to knock me out. Do you think they'll harm my baby?'

'One thing at a time. We'll cross that bridge when we come to it.'

'Are you hungry?' said DI Green. 'Shall I get you a sandwich? What would you like?'

'Is there any chance of something other than a sandwich? I don't mean to be ungrateful, but that's all I've had for days.'

'Nothing heavy tonight,' said the doctor, 'something light.'

DI Green picked up her handbag and took some money out. She turned to the policeman. 'Pop down to the canteen and get something hot and light for Zoë.'

'No meat please. I'm a vegetarian.'

The policeman disappeared.

'How about that statement before he gets back.'

I nodded wearily. My gaze fell on the curtain and I saw that there was a thread hanging where it must have snagged on something. I told her all that happened. She sat quietly, taking notes while I spoke, only interjecting with a question when I came to a halt.

'I think Scott started the fire at the flat,' I concluded. 'I just don't understand why.'

'He didn't start the fire at your flat,' said DI Green. 'We've got someone in custody for that.'

'Then he wasn't lying? He told me it was some guy…' I couldn't remember the name, and trailed off.

'Barry Hammond. I don't think you know him. From what we've found out it was nothing to do with you, or Scott Parker come to that.'

'Why did he do it?'

'Barry Hammond or Scott Parker?'

I meant Scott Parker, but said: 'Both.'

'I don't know about Scott. He's not in a state to talk right now. But Barry Hammond's target was your housemate, Neil Wyatt. Allegedly, Mr Wyatt was having an affair with his wife. She threatened to leave and take her husband for all he was worth.'

'So he killed him?'

'Something like that. I can't go into detail about the case but he claims he only intended to scare Neil Wyatt.'

'By setting our house on fire? What about Claire and me? We lived there too.'

DI Green shrugged and shook her head. 'Sometimes people can be very blinkered about things. It won't stick. Barry Hammond may try to claim it was manslaughter but it's likely he'll go down for murder. As for Scott Parker, we ran a check on him but he's never been in trouble with the police. Although, there is some family history on file. And I think he's had psychiatric problems.'

'You can say that again.' A trolley rumbled past the cubicle. I thought about what Scott had said about his parents. 'Did his parents abuse him?'

'Not that I'm aware of. His parents died when he was very young.'

'I know. Not much of a reason for madness though, is it?'

There was movement and voices in the next cubicle. Someone was complaining loudly.

'Who knows how it affected him?' said DI Green. 'He may have unresolved issues from that time.'

'He blamed his Mum for their deaths,' I said, catching snippets of the conversation next door about a nail gun injury. 'He said she was a drink driver and they were both killed in a car crash.'

She sighed. 'That might be what he's convinced himself but it's not what happened. It's quite a sad story really. His mother was badly injured in a car accident. It left her crippled and in a lot of pain. Scott's father gave her a fatal overdose.'

'A mercy killing, or he murdered her?'

'They're viewed the same in the eyes of the law. We'll never know for sure because his father committed suicide immediately after. I think Scott might have been the one to find them. His father left a note saying that he didn't have anything to live for.'

A chill ran through me and I swallowed. 'Not even for his son? That's terrible. Christ, he said his parents were totally wrapped up in each other. He also said his grandmother was cruel.'

'It can't have been easy for her having to bring up a child when she was in her sixties, especially one with psychiatric problems. It may be that he never got over it.'

I sank back against the pillows, trying to absorb it all. She put a hand on my arm. 'You're safe now and he can't hurt you any more, remember that.'

She pulled back the curtain. 'Looks like you've got some visitors.'

Ollie stood for a moment in the gap as if he didn't believe it was me in the cubicle. Then he rushed over and hugged me tight.

'Shit, Zoë, I've been going out of my head.'

Over his shoulder I could see Darren hesitate as if afraid of the reception he'd get, but it was Ollie I was mad at. I let him hold me but I couldn't forgive him. 'Did they tell you what happened?' I said.

Tears welled in Ollie's eyes. 'Yeah, some of it. Are you okay? He didn't hurt you? I'm so sorry about what happened. That I didn't believe you when you came back from the massage.'

'I'm sorry too,' said Darren. 'Scott seemed like a decent bloke.'

'It's not your fault. None of us knew he was a psychopathic bastard. He came across as charming and friendly. I thought he was helping me.'

The policeman arrived with a tray of food. 'Vegetable soup okay for you? I got you a coke as well. Sugar boost you know.'

'Thank you. That's really kind.' He nodded and left.

'I never liked Scott,' said Ollie.

'That's crap,' snapped Darren. 'You thought he was okay until you thought he was making a move on Zoë.'

'Stop it,' I said. 'If you're going to argue, go somewhere else and do it.'

Darren looked awkward. 'Do you want a coffee?' he said to no one in particular. Neither of us did but he wandered off in the direction of the coffee machine anyway.

'Don't be too hard on Darren,' said Ollie. 'It was his idea to file a missing person report. Not that it made much bloody difference.'

'You don't know that. Someone came to the house looking for me.'

'That was me and your dad. Your dad's on his way in. He was the one that was convinced something had happened to you. And he kept on calling the cops.'

'At least the police listened when I rang them. If you hadn't filed that report they might not have taken it seriously.'

'We did it through that policewoman that was here just now. She seems all right, for a copper.'

'Yeah. She is,' I said, tucking into the soup, the first proper meal I'd had in a week.

They kept me in the hospital overnight, but by late the next morning I was discharged. Before I left I insisted on looking in on Scott. He had just come out of theatre and was unconscious. He seemed to be bandaged from head to foot. It was a horrible sight and didn't give me any feeling of satisfaction that he'd reaped the reward of his actions, but it was reassuring to know that I was safe from him.

Even if he survived he would be badly scarred, and the nurse said he might lose his legs.

Dad took me back to his house, Ollie following in his car. It was raining and the house felt cold.

'Shall I put the fire on?' Dad asked. 'It'll warm the room quicker than the heating. Will you be okay with it?'

'Yes.'

'I'll put the kettle on.'

The gas fire murmured with luxurious heat. Behind its glass cover it was no threat. I sat on the floor beside it, shivering.

'We need to talk,' I said to Ollie and thought about what I wanted to say.

'You're pregnant aren't you?' he said, watching me closely. 'I found the testing kit. I was thinking we could look at flats of our own. Not right now obviously, but later and maybe…'

I cut him off. 'I didn't get a chance to use the pregnancy kit.'

'I know but… well, when you went off I thought you were trying to get your head round it or something.'

'I didn't go off. You threw me out. Anyway, the point is I'm not pregnant. It was probably just stress that made me late.' Ollie looked disappointed. I got up and sat beside him on the sofa. 'I know you like the idea of a baby. And the idea of the little wifey,' I said. 'But I'm not going to be pressured into it. All the time Scott held me captive I was convinced I was pregnant. I wanted to survive and have the baby. When the doctor told me yesterday at the hospital that I wasn't pregnant I was disappointed, really disappointed. But I'm not ready for kids yet. And I don't want to fall into the same trap my mum did with my biological dad.'

I could smell the familiar musky shower gel on his skin and wanted to reach out and touch him.

'I know you think you want us to move in together, but quite honestly you still want to be one of the lads. The time I spent with you at your flat proved that. When I really needed you, you weren't there for me. I know Scott set it up to isolate me and make the people around me believe I was mad. But you didn't trust me. And you should have done. Unconditionally. What happens next time?'

Ollie looked stunned. It was clearly the last thing he was expecting.

'Are you dumping me? I love you.'

'I love you too, but I don't trust you. Neither of us is ready for commitment. You need to stay with your mates and do the stuff you lads like to do. I need to get my life back. I want - need - to start again, wipe away everything that's happened. And that's going to take time.'

Ollie started to argue, but just then Dad came in with a couple of mugs. 'I'm going to live here with my Dad,' I said, looking to Dad for confirmation. 'If that's okay?'

He looked surprised, then smiled. 'I'd like that, love.'

'It'll be a horrible commute,' said Ollie.

'I know. But that doesn't matter.' I smiled back at Dad. 'This is my home. And it's where I want to be right now.'

Printed in Poland
by Amazon Fulfillment
Poland Sp. z o.o., Wrocław